THE
ALOHA SPIRIT

THE
ALOHA SPIRIT

A NOVEL

BY

LINDA ULLESEIT

SHE WRITES PRESS

Published 2020
Printed in the United States of America
ISBN: 978-1-63152-723-4 pbk
ISBN: 978-1-63152-724-1 ebk
Library of Congress Control Number: 2020902196

For information, address:
She Writes Press
1569 Solano Ave #546
Berkeley, CA 94707

She Writes Press is a division of SparkPoint Studio, LLC.

Book design by Stacey Aaronson

Dedicated to

Carmen Dolores James Medeiros Rodrigues

Hawai'i State Law: 5-7.5 *"Aloha* Spirit." (a) "Aloha Spirit" is the coordination of mind and heart within each person. It brings each person to the self. Each person must think and emote good feelings to others. In the contemplation and presence of the life force, "Aloha," the following *unuhi laula loa* (free translation) may be used:

"Akahai," meaning kindness, to be expressed with tenderness;

"Lokahi," meaning unity, to be expressed with harmony;

"·Olu'olu," meaning agreeable, to be expressed with pleasantness;

"Ha'aha'a," meaning humility, to be expressed with modesty;

"Ahonui," meaning patience, to be expressed with perseverance.

These are traits of character that express the charm, warmth, and sincerity of Hawaii's people. It was the working philosophy of Native Hawaiians and was presented as a gift to the people of Hawaii.

"Aloha" is more than a word of greeting or farewell or a salutation.

"Aloha" means mutual regard and affection and extends warmth in caring with no obligation in return.

"Aloha" is the essence of relationships in which each person is important to every other person for collective existence.

"Aloha" means to hear what is not said, to see what cannot be seen, and to know the unknowable.

(b) In exercising their power on behalf of the people and in fulfillment of their responsibilities, obligations, and service to the people, the legislature, governor, lieutenant governor, executive officers of each department, the chief justice, associate justices, and judges of the appellate, circuit, and district courts may contemplate and reside with the life force and give consideration to the "Aloha Spirit." [L 1986, c 202, §1]

PART ONE

1922-1931

‘

ONE

Honolulu 1922

Dolores's father deemed her useless when she was seven. Neither he nor her older brother, Pablo, ever said that, but every detail of their leaving told her so. Papa had tried to explain the Hawaiian custom of *hānai* to her. All she understood was the giving away, leaving her to live with a family not her own.

Papa had completed his work contract on Kaua'i, but instead of returning to Spain, the place of his birth, Papa had come to Honolulu. Five years later, he decided to go to the mainland to look for work and take Pablo with him. In California there would be no one to look after Dolores, so Papa found a Hawaiian family to hānai his only daughter. Her father said Pablo was smart and strong, so even at nine years old he could work as a floor sweeper or fruit picker.

If she were two years older, like Pablo, she might have gone with them. If Mama had lived long enough to teach her to sew or cook, she might have gone, too. Then again, if Mama had lived, they would all still be at the plantation on Kaua'i, and Dolores would have another brother or a sister.

Her father carried the cardboard suitcase that held Dolores's clothes: a couple of dresses and some underthings. Clouds of dust turned her pale legs gray like an *awa* fish. The air on O'ahu smelled of citrusy plumeria. At home on Kaua'i, on the plantation in Makaweli, the dust was familiar and red, the air scented with sweet pīkake flowers. She looked up at Papa and tugged his hand. "Can't we go home?"

Pablo snickered, but Papa said nothing. "Dolores, quit acting like a baby. Papa's explained all this to you a million times." Pablo believed himself two years smarter, but nine was not grown up. She stuck her tongue out at him. He laughed, and she blushed, embarrassed to have proven his point so quickly.

Wisps of dark hair stuck out beneath the brim of Papa's straw fedora. He squeezed Dolores's hand. "I worked with Kanoa for years on Kaua'i, remember? His wife will take care of you, and she has other children for you to play with."

Dolores nodded because she had no say in the matter. The coconut palms swayed in the late summer breeze. Plantation cottages crowded the road, which was bordered by thick, tough grass. Taro patches gave way to fields of sugarcane in the distance. The plantation owners used every available inch for their money crops. Workers huddled together where they could. They walked past Portuguese Camp with its beehive *forno*. Dolores's stomach growled when she smelled the *pao duce*—Portuguese sweet bread—and the sugary fried dough *malasadas*. Diamond Head towered over everything, but it wasn't as big as Kaua'i's Na Pali cliffs.

They approached a tin-roofed green plantation house, raised off the ground to discourage termites. Fruit-laden banana trees arced overhead, and a brilliant pink bougainvillea climbed the *lana'i*. Scrawny ti plants lined the tin-roofed carport that jutted out from the house on its near side. A rusty truck sat there like it hadn't moved since before Papa was born.

Dolores tightened her grip on Papa's hand, not caring that Pablo called her a baby. Her eyes fastened on a large Hawaiian woman seated on the lana'i. A red hibiscus blossom quivered in the dark waves of hair that fell across her shoulders and down her front. White teeth gleamed in a dark face. Her smile and a graceful wave of her hand greeted them. Yards and yards of fabric, white hibiscus flowers on a blue background, billowed around her.

A piercing howl broke the tension. Dolores recoiled from the wild native boy who screamed as he careened around the corner of the house. Another yelling boy followed, leaped onto the lana'i, and dodged the wicker chairs. He knocked against the cane table, causing a statue of the Hawaiian god Kāne to rock as if alive.

On the lana'i, the Hawaiian woman's booming laugh greeted Dolores's family and sent the children scurrying.

"*Aloha*. You must be Noelani," Papa said. He pushed the brim of his hat back and scratched his forehead as he did when he was nervous.

"Aloha," Noelani said. "*E komo mai, keiki.* Welcome, children."

"Paul isn't staying," Papa said. "Just Dolores."

Paul? Not Pablo? Dolores dropped her eyes to the floor, suddenly shy. Her renamed brother shuffled his feet. She darted a glance at him, but he wouldn't look back. His Americanized name must be something her brother and father had discussed without her, no doubt while they talked about leaving her with a bunch of strangers. She snuck a look at Noelani. How could Dolores convince Papa not to leave her with this stranger?

"Paul?" Noelani asked as she looked at Papa.

"Yes, on the mainland they'll call me Paul, and he will be Paul Junior." He straightened his shoulders.

Noelani nodded. "Welcome to my 'ohana, Dolores. It be big family, blood and hānai, ya?" She grinned as if making a joke.

Dolores smiled, her brain working harder than it ever had in first grade. Family meant Papa and Pablo—Paul—not a strange woman with a bunch of children.

They followed Noelani into the house. The Hawaiian woman moved with an incongruous grace. Her great bulk flowed as if one with its environment. The sway of hands and hips mimicked the motion of breeze and ocean waves. Once inside, Dolores slipped off her shoes and placed them by the door. She glared at her brother until he did, too. The Hawaiians believed wearing shoes in the house brought bad luck, and she'd need all the luck she could get.

Two windows, open to catch the breeze, flanked the doorway. A fan with enormous leaf-shaped blades spun lazily above her. It wafted a soft breeze over a massive rattan couch that dominated one side of the room. Lurid floral patterns decorated the cushions shaped for large Hawaiian bodies. A watercolor painting of a palm tree-lined beach hung on the wall. Through an arched doorway, three steps led down to the kitchen. Noelani flowed in that direction and reached into the open shelving for plates. She tapped first to scatter any cockroaches.

"*Pūpū*, ya?" she said over her shoulder as she wiped a plate with a dishcloth.

Papa, Paul, and Dolores stood in the center of the main room. Dolores flipped her skirt to stir air around her thighs. Papa frowned.

Noelani brought a platter of food bites—shrimp and chicken and fish. She also set on the table a koa wood bowl full of *poi*. Dolores tried not to turn up her nose at the purple paste. Only native Hawaiians could enjoy it.

"You sit," Noelani insisted. She pulled Dolores's arm and dragged her into a large rattan chair. The girl sank into it until her feet dangled above the floor. Papa and Paul perched on the edge of the couch. Noelani stood by Dolores, hand on the random curls that covered the girl's head.

"I must say, this feels odd," Papa began.

"Mo betta' you leave her with someone who knows you, ya? Kanoa and I, we take good care," Noelani said.

Dolores twisted away from Noelani and studied the roughened skin of the woman's palm, her arms the color of Kona coffee. She smelled of frangipani and rich dark soil.

A slim boy a little older than Paul, clad only in short pants, came into the room and helped himself to the poi. He scooped it into his mouth with two fingers.

"Kaipo, this be Dolores. She stay with us, ya?"

His dark eyes glared at Dolores with no hint of welcome. "Where she gonna sleep?" His tone was as hostile as his eyes.

"Be nice," his mother scolded lightly. She eyed Dolores's suitcase. "This all your things?"

Dolores nodded. She liked to think she had memories of her own mother, who'd died when she was two, but in reality, they were other people's memories told so often she had taken them as her own. Pablo said that Papa had actually laughed when Mama was alive. Her mother must have loved clothes. Papa had left her closet alone, and Dolores played among her dresses. Dresses now sold for two passages to California.

A tiny girl with large dark eyes and tangled hair sneaked into the room and took Kaipo's hand. "Leia, this is our new sister," he said. His words dripped scorn.

Leia's gaze bored into her from eyes as deep as the sea, and Dolores's stomach churned. Leia belonged in this place. Dolores belonged nowhere. "No need a new sister," Leia said.

"Show Dolores where she sleep, ya?" Noelani told the children.

Papa handed Dolores the cardboard suitcase and nodded toward Kaipo. Dolores struggled out of the chair. Could she ask Kaipo to help her? He didn't want her there, so maybe he would suggest her father take her with him. But she couldn't find the courage.

Kaipo indicated Dolores should follow Leia as the younger girl ran ahead. Dolores felt his eyes on her back as they walked through the small common room. She peeked past a drapery topped with bamboo rings into the room on the left. It was a jumble of boyishness—clothes, bedding, hats, sticks, and rocks littered the room. Kaipo waved her toward the room on the right, holding its drape aside. An open window caught the trade winds that fluttered thin white cotton curtains. Two big beds left very little room to walk around. The heads of both beds were against the wall to prevent demons reaching in the window to cut off sleepers' heads. The foot of the bed faced the opposite wall, not the doorway. That way a night marcher couldn't drag children out while they slept. Dolores took a deep calm breath. At least her new room would be safe.

"So, you don't want me here," she whispered to Kaipo.

He made an unintelligible noise that meant, "That's obvious."

"Convince Papa to take me with him," Dolores blurted, "and you'll never have to see me again."

"Mama would just hānai another daughter we don't want. You stay." Kaipo smirked.

Dolores gave him a look of disgust and entered the girls' room. Leia perched cross-legged on a pineapple pattern quilt, a pillow on her lap, and stared at Dolores. Two other small girls curled next to each other. An older teenage girl occupied the only other bed in the room. She lay on top of a white-and-pale-pink quilt reading a magazine.

Kaipo nodded to the older girl. He kept his eyes on her while he said to Dolores, "Sleeping arrangements are for you girls to work out."

Dolores must have looked dubious.

"Not good enough?" he sneered.

The teenaged girl looked up. "*Pau. E komo mai.*" The sharp order to stop was for Kaipo, and the welcome addressed to Dolores.

Kaipo slipped out without a response. The girl on the bed

didn't look Hawaiian like Kaipo or Leia, even though her skin was sun-darkened and her hair black. With a sigh, she laid down her magazine—*Paradise of the Pacific*—and sat up. "I'm Maria, Noelani's oldest hānai daughter. You must be Dolores."

Maria? Not Hawaiian then. Maybe Portuguese or Spanish? "*Si*," Dolores told her.

Maria's mouth turned up into a grim smile. "Yes, I'm Spanish like you, but I don't remember my parents. You can come with me to Mass on Sundays."

"*Gracias*, Maria," Dolores said, relieved that she would have the familiar comfort of the Catholic Church.

Leia rolled her eyes. The younger ones giggled. Maria quelled them with a glare.

Noelani hadn't been kidding when she said she had a large family. "You're the oldest, Maria?"

"Of those that hang around here, yes. Kanoa takes the two older hānai boys with him to the cane fields every day. The little boys beg coins from the tourists on the ships. The tourists love their smiles."

Dolores put her suitcase on the scuffed wood plank floor, unsure what to do next. She wanted to run back into the main room and cling to Papa, but she didn't want Maria to think she was a baby like the other girls. Soft footsteps in the hallway saved her.

"Ah, here you are, Dolores. This is nice." Papa smiled at the room full of girls. "You've always wanted sisters, haven't you?"

"Yes, Papa," she answered, too relieved to see him to make a fuss over his words.

Maria laughed. "Well, now she has four sisters and five brothers! I hope she's handy with the laundry!"

Noelani answered, "She be big help *bumbye*."

Papa looked at his daughter, and his eyes softened. "Be a good girl, *niña*."

"Si, Papa." Dolores's eyes tried to tell him everything she

couldn't say in a house full of strangers. *I love you. Will you visit? Will you send for me?*

He turned to Noelani. "She'll go to church regularly? You'll feed her well and make sure her clothes are clean for school? Can you make sure she writes to me?" Suddenly Papa seemed anxious. Dolores's stomach twisted.

"Pau, Paul," Noelani told him. "Is *orait*, ya?"

Papa took a deep breath and rubbed his neck. "Yes, Noelani, it will be all right. I will write to her." His promise sounded weak, an afterthought. He settled his hat on his head once more. "It's time to leave. Our ship will board soon."

Paul hovered in the doorway. "See ya, Sis." His effort to be casual failed miserably since tears were swimming in his eyes.

Dolores looked away. She blinked to stall her own tears.

Papa leaned over to kiss Dolores on the top of her head and whispered, "Remember, be good. *Familia es todo.*"

Family is everything. Her father's favorite saying. Dolores clenched her teeth so she wouldn't sob and beg to go.

Noelani walked Papa and Paul to the door. Dolores trailed after them.

"Aloha, then," Papa said. "*Mahalo.*"

Dolores stood at the open front window and watched her father, with her brother a smaller replica—her entire family—walk along the roadway to catch the streetcar to Honolulu Harbor. Neither looked back.

"Orait, Dolores, they be gone," Noelani said. Her laughing face transformed into one chiseled from cooled lava. "You clean the girls' room, ya?"

A shiver of fear ran down Dolores's spine.

❦ TWO

Laundry Day 1922

The next morning, Maria woke Dolores by climbing over her to get out of bed. Dolores had allowed the teenager as much space as possible by scrunching up on the edge of the mattress. Dolores sat up and rubbed her eyes. In the predawn of what promised to be a warm day, she could barely see the three youngest girls, curled around each other like puppies, beginning to stir in the other bed.

"Time to get up, Dolores. The laundry won't do itself." Maria pulled on the same dress she'd worn yesterday.

Dolores crossed herself and muttered, "In the name of the Father, the Son, and the Holy Spirit." Maria glanced at her, and Dolores continued her morning prayer silently. *God protect Papa and Pablo—no, Paul—in a strange place. Amen.*

She stretched and stepped out of bed onto the bare wooden floor, slipped into her own dress, and followed Maria to the house's single bathroom. Kaipo hunched over the pedestal sink, legs spread and elbows angled to claim it for his own. Dolores recognized the two wild boys from the day before. Polunu and Makaha went to her school. They were not children Papa had allowed her to play with.

"Move, move, move," said Polunu, the youngest and roundest of the boys, as he shoved his way to the sink. He stood on tiptoe and pumped water into the sink basin.

Makaha climbed on the edge of the claw-footed porcelain tub and balanced with his arms raised high. "I am Kāne! Bow to me!"

"Nonsense," Maria scolded. Her tone left no doubt that Makaha was a boy, not a Hawaiian god. Tall enough to look over the boys' heads, she combed her hair and ignored them. Makaha brushed his teeth and spat over the top of Kaipo's arms into the sink.

Dolores longed for the peace and quiet of home with her father and brother. She didn't even have time to wash her face before Maria pulled her along to the kitchen.

Slatted walls in the kitchen allowed a breeze to stir the air and let out some of the heat from the black iron stove where Noelani was frying thick slices of Portuguese sausage. "You sit," she commanded, waving at the girls with her tongs.

Maria pointed to a straight-backed cane chair at the massive koa wood table in the center of the room. Dolores sat. Kanoa nodded at her over the top of the *Honolulu Bulletin* and sipped a cup of Kona coffee. Scars and fresh red scratches from sharp cane leaves covered the weathered brown skin of his arms.

Maria reached inside a screened wooden pie safe to fetch a bowl of fruit—bananas and mangoes and papaya—and set it on the table. Two older teenage boys tossed pieces of silverware on the table and brought pitchers of guava juice and papaya juice from the ice box.

"You no spill dat!" Noelani warned with another wave of the tongs. Polunu and Makaha burst in like a gust of wind and bumped into Noelani. Her thick strong arms separated the boys. "You wanna eat, you act betta'." Clattering plates and pots, she produced a mountain of coconut pancakes, rice, Portuguese sausage, and poi.

The older boys took their seats at the table and scooped rice and sausage and poi onto their plates with the pancakes.

Dolores had seen them last night when they'd returned home with Kanoa, all of them covered with sweat and dirt, smelling of burnt cane. The boys had rubbed their sore backs and nodded to her before they cleaned up and dropped into bed. One was Koa and one was Nui, but Dolores wasn't sure which was which.

The five younger children clambered onto chairs and began to eat. Dolores peered closer at the girls. Kali was the youngest and smallest, maybe two. She guessed the other two to be about four. "What are your names?" she asked.

"Leia," Polunu said. He pointed. "And that's Meli. Say hello, babies."

The girls wrinkled their noses at him but smiled at Dolores.

Polunu and Makaha were closest to her own age, maybe seven or eight. "Stop smacking your food," Kanoa told them. He didn't look up from his newspaper.

Leia rolled her eyes at Meli and Kali who giggled at her joke.

"Guava or papaya?" Maria asked the girls. They squealed and giggled. Maria poured them pink guava juice and turned to the boys. "Boys? Guava juice?" They ignored her, and she handed the pitcher to Dolores. Dolores poured herself some guava juice and tried to remember everyone's name at the table.

This morning Koa and Nui looked more like young Hawaiian gods than overworked sugarcane laborers. The one Dolores thought was Nui had a smile that flashed against his brown face like a stripe of white waterfall against the darker *pali*. Even in the few hours she'd known him, it was clear he loved poking fun at life. Maria sliced a mango and offered it to Koa. Nui laughed and made a dramatic sweep of his arm to snatch the fruit for himself. Everyone ignored him.

Noelani didn't eat with them. After she bustled from stove to table, she sat at a small Singer sewing machine in the corner of the kitchen. It whirred away as if possessed and spit out lengths of perfectly hemmed Chinese silk. "Eat up, Dolores," she said. "Laundry when the family fed, ya?"

Dolores wondered why only Noelani spoke pidgin. Everyone in the islands had a few words of Portuguese, Spanish, Hawaiian, and Japanese, but almost everyone knew English. Maybe Dolores could ask Maria later.

Nui speared a pancake. He dumped it on Dolores's plate with a spoonful of rice. "Must eat to keep up your energy."

Dolores smiled and clasped her hands in her lap. Head down, she said grace to herself. "Bless us, O Lord, and these Thy gifts, which we are about to receive from Thy bounty, through Christ our Lord. Amen." Leia rolled her eyes. Dolores ignored her and put a bite of heaven in her mouth, savoring the coconut pancake and sweet *liliko'i* syrup. Breakfasts with Papa and Paul had been much quieter. The food was better here, and more plentiful. Dolores wondered if this was a happy family—mother, father, lots of kids, lots of noise, lots of food. It felt strange.

Leia crawled into her father's lap and picked up a piece of papaya off his plate. Kanoa put down the paper and kissed the top of her head. He winked at Dolores and smiled. Kali and Meli could barely see over the table. Maria helped them get some pancakes and fruit and then ignored them. Polunu was almost hidden behind his heaping plate, and Makaha's eyes gleamed with mischief. The boys ate with their fingers and kicked each other under the table.

"What are you doing today, Kaipo?" his father asked.

"Surfing lessons to the *malihini* on Waikiki," he answered, his mouth full of rice. He turned to Maria. "The *Maui* is due in port soon. Some of the Hawaiian lei ladies at the Moana Hotel are looking for help."

Maria glanced at Noelani and then back to Kaipo. "Tell them I'll come down tomorrow."

The sugar mill whistle blew, calling the workers to the

fields. Kanoa, Nui, and Koa left through the kitchen door, crossed the lanaʻi, and set off through the taro fields to the waiting cane.

As soon as the men left, Noelani looked up from her sewing machine. "Awake and fed, time fo' work. You go already," she said, and waved them all toward the back door. "Makaha! No leave the chopsticks like that! You no want the bad luck!"

Makaha hurried to his bowl of rice where he had left the chopsticks sticking straight up. He moved the chopsticks to the table, scattering sticky rice as he did so. Then he ran to shove Polunu as they thundered into the boys' room. The little girls scampered to play in the yard. Dolores followed Maria out the same door Kanoa had taken. As they passed the door to the boys' room, Dolores could see sheets flapping like sails and hear thumping as the boys threw things around. She looked at Maria, puzzled.

"They're cleaning."

Cleaning? It looked more like playing to Dolores.

Four overflowing baskets of laundry waited for the girls. Two big metal tubs and a modern washing machine filled one end of the lanaʻi. A battered wicker chair sat in the corner. A few steps across the tiny yard, a glass-paneled door led to what must be Kanoa and Noelani's bedroom. It shared a wall with the other bedrooms but had no door to the inside of the house. She learned later that Kanoa had built it when his wife added more and more hānai children to their family.

Maria arranged herself on the chair in imitation of Noelani.

"Get started, Dolores," she said with a wave of her hand to shoo the younger girl into action.

Dolores stared at her and then peered at the laundry. It was a big household, but the baskets held more laundry than even what Noelani, Kanoa, and ten children could generate.

"Well?" Maria's tone grew impatient.

"I've never done laundry by myself," she admitted. "I can learn."

"What chores *have* you done?"

"Making my bed and putting the clean dishes in the cupboard. I never broke a single one." Dolores stood straighter. Maybe she wasn't perfect, but she had something to be proud of. "And I finished my first year of school."

"What a spoiled *haole*!" she sneered. "Makaha helps with the dishes, and Polunu sweeps the house and lanaʻi. Everyone has a task. Pay attention and I'll turn you into a proper *kanaka*!"

Dolores doubted learning to do laundry would make her a proper Hawaiian, but this would be her chore, so she paid attention as Maria called out instructions like a queen from her throne.

"Take the white clothes out of that soak tub, wring them out, and put them in the machine." Maria pulled out a folded magazine. When she opened it, Dolores saw it was the *Paradise of the Pacific* Maria had been reading the day before.

"Why are you reading that tourist thing?"

"I make money selling leis to the malihini," Maria answered. "I have to know how the islands are being advertised to tourists. If they expect demure native girls, I can do that. If they expect a friendly aloha, I can do that, too. Give them what they expect, and the tip is bigger." She settled back to read.

No tourist had ever visited the plantation camps where Dolores had lived. More things she didn't know. She turned back to the laundry.

Clouds of white fabric floated in the lukewarm soak water. She picked up one corner, surprised by its weight. She recognized a bedsheet and squeezed. By the time she had worked her way to the other end of the sheet, sweat slicked her forehead. She wrestled the sheet into the machine and didn't let it drag on the floor. Proud of her accomplishment, Dolores turned to Maria for further instructions.

Noelani burst through the door. "Wot? First load no pau? You girls talk story?"

Maria jumped off the chair, tucked her *Paradise of the Pacific* under the cushion, and hurried to turn the fill valve on the washer. "Dolores started with the sheet. It took lots of wringing." She motioned to the box of Borax, and Dolores handed it to her.

Once the circular bin of the washing machine filled with water, it began to rotate. Maria poured in the soap, focused on the task and not Noelani. Suds foamed up.

Maria slammed the lid shut. "The lid keeps in the heat, so the clothes wash better."

Noelani's eyes narrowed. "Dolores no do laundry?"

"She's not familiar with this kind of machine, that's all," Maria said.

Surprised at her defense, Dolores said nothing. Noelani glared at each of them in turn then went back into the house. The door crashed shut behind her.

"Thank you," Dolores told Maria.

"You never want to seem lazy to Noelani. Never," Maria warned.

"What happens?" Dolores asked. She thought of her father, who already had no use for her and had given her away.

"Noelani works constantly. She sews dresses for the girls in Iwilei, does ironing and laundry for the army, and even sells some cooking to the camp stores. She has no time for lazy children."

Dolores shook her head, taking it all in. However hard she drove them, it seemed Noelani drove herself harder. Papa worked hard, too. No family had room for a useless child. She blinked her eyes to keep the welling tears inside. "I'm not lazy. And I'm not useless," she said, clamping her lips together. "She can't give me away."

Maria gave her an odd look, started to say something,

stopped, then began again. "You can love someone and not love what they do."

Dolores thought of her father, very much loved, and his leaving. She blinked hard as tears threatened.

"Come on," Maria said, "let's put the boys' shorts in to soak and wring out the next load."

Working together, they had two more sheets ready to go into the washer when the first was done. They pulled it out into a basket, and the others went in. Maria showed her how to rinse the sheet in a tub of clean water. Dolores's hands reddened from the soap and puffed from the water. Her arms ached up to her ears, but she refused to give up.

Once rinsed, the dripping sheet needed to be wrung out again. Maria demonstrated how to use the wringer, and Dolores flushed with embarrassment that she'd tried to do it by hand the first time. The crank and rollers were certainly more efficient, but her shoulders ached.

"How many loads must we do?" Dolores asked. She eyed the stack of laundry.

"Two more loads of sheets, two of dresser scarves, pillow-cases, towels—that sort of thing, and three of colored dresses and shirts."

Dolores groaned and Maria laughed. They laughed as they washed and wrung out laundry, rinsed and wrung again. Finally, they hung everything on a line in the yard to dry. At the end of the day, Dolores felt as if she could flap in the breeze like the laundry. But she and Maria had smiled and laughed. That took the sting out of her aches.

It wouldn't last, of course.

At dinner, Noelani frowned at them. "You *wahine* pretty slow wit the laundry today, ya? Dolores never make beds in the wahine room."

"I'm sorry, Noelani," Dolores said. "We'll be faster next week." Maria had never told her she needed to do the beds.

Besides, laundry had been well underway by the time Kali and Meli rolled out of bed.

"Next *week*?" Noelani turned to Maria.

Maria's smile dimmed. "Noelani's taken on some new laundry customers. You'll be in charge of laundry every day in addition to making both beds in our room."

"Every day?" All the warmth that remained from the afternoon's laughter slowly drained from her.

"And I won't be here to help." Maria's eyes fastened on her plate of *kālua* pork. "Quite a few passenger ships are due over the next few days, and I can make good money putting leis together at the hotel."

A stone settled in Dolores's heart. Tomorrow she would do it all over again. Alone. "Every day."

"So you work faster, ya?" Noelani told her. "On Sunday you go church."

"May I be excused?"

Noelani nodded at her.

Dolores fled before her tears fell. She would not let them see her cry. Locking herself in the bathroom, she sobbed in self-pity, in frustration, and in anger.

FROM the back lanaʻi Dolores couldn't see the stranger who came to Noelani's door on Saturday, but his booming voice carried clearly.

"You're doing me a great favor, Noelani," he said.

Dolores listened hard for Noelani's response while she forced her arms to shove dirty laundry into the machine.

"Bachelor no do laundry, ya? Hawaiian girls best fo' laundry, ya?"

"You got that right!" He laughed like a tourist trying to impress a native with how friendly he was.

Dolores shook her head as she ran another shirt through the wringer. Hawaiian girls? Would this man pay if he knew a young Spanish girl was doing his laundry? After she hung the clean shirt, the last of load number two, she returned to the basket and picked up the next dirty garment—one of the boys' underwear. She spotted a thick brown smear and almost dropped it. Retching in disgust, Dolores carried it with thumb and forefinger to the soaking tub. Chunks of brown fell out, but she didn't smell what she expected to. Upon closer inspection, the smear was mud. Disgust turned to anger. What had she done to the younger boys to merit a prank like this? The mud required more effort to clean. Dolores scrubbed the stain with enough ferocity to wipe noses off faces.

Just as the brown streak disappeared, Noelani appeared. Dolores saw nothing but the hem of her *muʻumuʻu* under a huge stack of clothes. "New customer," she said. The pile of clothes muffled her voice. "Good fabrics, ya? *Mālama pono*— Be careful!"

Dolores glared as she took the clothes. She knew Noelani couldn't see her. But the sixth sense of the Hawaiian woman's ancestors kicked in.

"Is *pilikia*, Dolores? You have problem? You wanna live like *aliʻi*? Ha! You not royalty. I need honest day's *hana* from you. No *faddah* spoil you now."

Dolores didn't respond, but then Noelani didn't wait around for her words either. Honest day's work. No problem. Her whole life was warm water—soak water, wash water, rinse water—and her hands already looked like puffy pink sausages. Where was Papa at this moment? And Paul? Had they found jobs yet? *Please, Lord, give me the strength to do this.* Dolores gritted her teeth, pushed away pitiful thoughts, and wrung the next towel with feverish intensity. When she learned to do laundry well, she would be useful to Papa. And he'd come back for her.

☙ THREE

Our Lady of Peace

On Sunday morning, Dolores struggled into her dress. She winced as she stretched her aching arms to tie the sash at her back. Maria's polka-dotted blue dress hung loosely on her body. The dropped waist gave way to a pleated skirt that swirled when she turned. It had been a fine dress once, but it drooped from over-washing. Still, it was nicer than Dolores's once-white dress. Noelani, pleased with the extra lei money from the past week, had given Maria a few extra coins of her own; this pleased Maria, who hummed as she brushed her hair. Dolores fingered her own coins, hidden deep in her pocket. Noelani had inspected Dolores's work and grudgingly approved. It was more like an allowance than a salary, but it was the first money she'd earned herself. If Papa couldn't come to her, Dolores would save enough to go to him. No matter how long it took. Imagine Papa's pride when she paid her own passage and arrived with useful skills!

Maria placed a felt hat, trimmed in yellow ribbon, on her head. She checked the mirror and tilted the brim on one side as if she were on her way to see a boyfriend. Dolores dropped her eyes to the floor, uncomfortable, having never seen such behavior while getting ready for church.

Maria turned toward her and frowned. "Don't you have a hat?"

Papa had sold Dolores' hat, and most of her meager wardrobe, for his passage to the mainland. Papa hadn't remembered she'd need a hat for church. "No," she admitted. It might take her weeks to save for a hat, and years to save ship's fare.

Maria went to the closet and returned with an old straw hat, its pink ribbon streamers faded by time and sun. She clapped it on the younger girl's head, and Dolores whispered her gratitude. "Let's go," Maria said. "We don't want to be late."

They left Noelani's house and walked down the dirt road. Dolores pretended she was escaping. She would become the famous Spanish laundress of Honolulu, with her own business. It would be easy to save for passage to California. Imagine Papa and Paul's surprise! Even in her imagination, though, the picture faded of a happy family embracing her at the end of the journey. It seemed impossible.

The sun stung her neck and arms, but a nice breeze softened the heat. Palms and banana trees lined the road, and puffy white clouds rolled by overhead. More than half the houses had cars in their carports. Dolores recognized the clusters of plantation cottages they passed by the flowers and foliage in their yards. The Puerto Ricans had coffee and pigeon peas, and the Chinese had *lychee*. The Portuguese grew grapes along wooden fences, and the Filipinos had the *malunggay*. Hawaiians, like Noelani and Kanoa, didn't have their own camp but lived among the others identified by lucky ti plants to protect against *obake*. Dolores shook her head, unwilling to think about ghosts on her way to church.

As soon as they could, the girls caught the streetcar to Beretania Street. Dolores dug deep into her pocket and found a nickel to pay her own fare. Maria chose a seat, and Dolores slid in next to her. The streetcar lurched forward, bell clanging.

"I haven't seen you at Our Lady before," Maria said.

"I used to go to the early Mass with my father and brother."

"Don't tell Noelani there's an earlier Mass. She'll make us go to that one and start our chores earlier."

Dolores groaned. "Chores? On Sunday? What happened to a day of rest?"

"Dust and dirt have no respect for God. Noelani isn't Catholic. She believes we find aloha in hard work, and aloha is her concept of holiness."

"She must think I'm a saint," Dolores muttered. Maria laughed.

They chatted like old friends as the streetcar left the Oʻahu Sugar Plantation camps. With Diamond Head at their backs, the car rattled down its tracks toward downtown Honolulu and Our Lady of Peace, the oldest Catholic church in the islands. Dolores wondered if she would feel embraced or abandoned in the familiar church—she'd never been there without Papa and Paul.

They left the streetcar at the corner near downtown and walked the short block to the church. Dolores's spirits lifted as she sighted the church's concrete bell tower. They walked through the main doors on the long side of the building and arrived behind rows of pews that mirrored similar rows across the center aisle of the church. The polished wooden pews sat under the floor of the balcony. If she stepped into the center of the church, the soaring curves of the ceiling would lift her soul to heaven. She took a few steps in that direction, already anticipating the comfort of Jesus on the cross above the altar, but Maria tugged at her arm.

"This way," she hissed. Dolores followed her to the far end of the church.

The seat Maria chose was so far from the altar they might as well have been on the beach. From here the priest was an ant. The joy of Mass dulled by distance. In front of Dolores, a fussy child cried as soon as the first prayers began.

A soldier sat in front of Maria and turned to smile. Maria giggled. Giggled. In church. Dolores stared at him with eyes wide. His army uniform made him look serious and important, his blond hair slicked back shiny smooth. Blond hair was odd on the island—even haoles seemed to have brown. The soldier's hat lay beside him on the pew, as if distancing him from the baby. Dolores gave him a sympathetic smile. He smiled back, big and warm, and Maria pinched her.

"Stop flirting, Dolores!" she whispered. Her smile focused on him and twisted around her words.

Her words astonished Dolores. She couldn't imagine why she would flirt—she had no interest in boys. They were dirty and noisy. The boys at Noelani's showed that, the younger ones always muddy and the older ones always arguing. Maria smiled and batted her eyelashes. She lowered her head and looked at him sideways from under her hat brim. Maria's giggles and smiles made Dolores realize why the older girl had chosen this pew. She sat here every week, and it had nothing to do with Mass.

During the next hour, the distractions were louder than the priest. Dolores missed the low rumble of Papa's murmured prayers. She tried to find the soothing spirit that reassured her Mama was watching, but she failed. Dolores gave up on squinting to see the priest and watched Maria make a fool of herself.

When the service ended, the two girls left the sanctuary. Maria looked for the soldier. "Isn't he really old?" Dolores asked, a little sharply.

Maria laughed. "Maybe for a seven-year-old, but not for me. I'm seventeen, after all. Peter is a member of the army band. He's very handsome, and he's nice."

Maria pulled her arm, maneuvered them toward the man; then she acted surprised he was there. Dolores shook her head in consternation.

"Peter, let me introduce my younger hānai sister," Maria said. She leaned close as if the crowd were pushing her toward him. "This is Dolores." Maria put her arm around Dolores as if she were her sister. Dolores smiled at him.

"Hello, Dolores," Peter said kindly. "Where did you come from?"

"Pleased to meet you, Peter. I'm living with Maria's family until my father returns for me from the mainland." She said the words aloud for the first time. She hoped Peter couldn't hear the longing in them. Papa would return for her. She knew it in her heart, even if her brain sometimes doubted.

"Pleased to meet you, too, little miss," he said with a grin.

Maria's hand clenched Dolores's shoulder until she winced. "Dolores, have you ever had an ice cream soda at Benson-Smith's?"

Of course not. She shook her head and clasped her lips tight to keep in the sharp words.

"Come on along, then," Peter said.

It had been much too early for ice cream after the Mass Dolores attended with Papa. Papa had deprived her and Paul of a special memory. She shook her head. Papa never had the money for ice cream. Nonetheless, it would have been a nice treat and a wonderful family memory.

Maria stepped up next to Peter, and Dolores walked on her other side. Many of the parishioners from Our Lady of Peace were strolling in the same direction. Others veered off toward Chinatown or headed back up the hill to Punch Bowl. The three of them walked *makai*, toward the ocean. Above and behind the Fort Street shops, Dolores could see the swaying coconut palms that lined Kalakaua Avenue as it snaked along Waikiki Beach past the tourists who were breakfasting at the Moana Hotel.

The clerk at Benson-Smith's cash register smiled as they entered. Dolores scanned the floor-to-ceiling shelves that

contained all manner of candy, perfume, and toiletries. A soda
fountain ran the length of the store. Soda jerks in white uniforms with white caps stood behind a gleaming stainless-steel
counter whose stools already contained a cross section of
Honolulu's population. Two large native men spooned ice
cream sundaes into their mouths and laughed at a joke told in
Hawaiian. At the other end of the counter, a Chinese couple
with their small son sipped root beer floats. The couple sat
straight as surfboards and looked much too rigid and ceremo-
nious to be in this place. Their son had probably begged for
the treat this morning.

Peter selected a stool midway down the counter, and
Maria sat next to him. Dolores scrambled up next to Maria,
who dug Noelani's coins from her pocket.

Peter saw her with the coins and said, "Oh, no, let me pay
for all of us to celebrate Dolores's first visit to Benson-
Smith."

Maria giggled, hid her mouth with her hands, and gasped
her thanks. Dolores looked directly at Peter. "Mahalo," she
told him.

"Are you from the islands?" he asked.

"I was born on Kaua'i, but we moved here when I was
young."

"Like she isn't young now?" Maria said, patting Dolores's
head as she might a puppy.

Dolores sipped her ice cream soda in silent delight.

"Dolores, do your parents go to the earlier Mass? Why
don't you attend with your mother while your father is on the
mainland?" Peter asked.

Dolores looked at Maria in confusion. She'd introduced
Dolores as her hānai sister. Didn't Peter know what that
meant? "My mother died when I was a baby. My father left
me to go to the mainland to find work." She tried to keep her
voice even, but a traitorous quaver snuck in at the end.

"I'm sorry for asking. I should have realized." He looked at Maria and grimaced.

"It's all right," Maria told him. "I'm sure her first ice cream soda makes up for it."

They laughed and sipped their drinks, but Dolores didn't share their amusement. An ice cream soda could never replace her father.

When all three glasses were empty, Peter stood up. "I'd better take my leave, ladies. Dolores, I enjoyed meeting you. Maybe you'll join us next week, too?"

"I'd like that," she assured him. Looking at Peter made her smile.

"We need to go, too," Maria said. "Keep aloha in your heart, Peter." She stood up and brushed off her skirt.

They followed Peter out of the store. He waved good-bye and walked back up Fort Street toward the church. Across the street, Culman's curio shop remained closed like all the Fort Street shops on Sunday. Dolores would have liked to buy a picture postcard there to send to Papa. Maybe Noelani would allow her time to do that during the week if she worked hard.

The girls caught the streetcar and headed back down Beretania toward Diamond Head. Dolores sat back and re-laxed, full of ice cream and holiness. Outside the streetcar, Honolulu lazed in the spectacular Sunday sun. A white bird sang from a clump of bamboo, and colorful parakeets flew among the treetops. People in summer dresses and suits walked along the street. No one hurried. Maria, too, seemed content to sit quietly.

Back at Noelani's, the whirl of activity engulfed them as she prepared a gargantuan feast. Dolores mashed taro roots with a stone pestle to make enough poi for the entire United States Navy. At least with laundry, both arms hurt evenly, she thought as she shook out her poor right arm. Maria shredded the kālua pork, and the little girls attempted to set the table. It surprised Dolores when the door opened and large Hawaiian men and women filled the room. They called greetings in pidgin, Hawaiian, and English and put piled-high plates of food on the table. Everyone talked at once.

"How many people are coming?" Dolores asked Maria.

"Sunday dinners are a big thing," she said.

"Aren't the twelve of us enough?"

Noelani heard them. "Everyone be ʻohana," she said. "It nevah hard work when it for ʻohana."

Dolores disagreed. Everything near Noelani was hard work. And everyone was a stranger.

"What wrong, haole?"

She never could hide what she was thinking.

"People no be perfect," Noelani admonished her with a fierce scowl. "They make the mistakes and have spats, but ʻohana embrace them. It be aloha spirit, muse of the islands. The work of our hands is offering, ya?" She waved a hand off into the distance as if she were performing.

Dolores shook her head, too tired to deal with this raw new family. She spent her weekdays drowned in laundry; now her Sundays would be drowned in poi. Dolores couldn't feel any aloha spirit. "If you say so." The words came out snippy, even to her ears, and she cringed. Noelani's eyes darkened, and her lips clenched into a line, but she said nothing.

When the extra people began to leave in ones and twos, Dolores turned her back on the sink full of dishes. "I'll be outside," she said. Maria, her arms sudsy to the elbows, shook her head. Noelani, with the dishcloth in her hands for drying, clenched her lips again. Dolores turned away before they could see the tears welling in her own eyes. She was so tired, so sore and tired. It wasn't possible for her to work one more minute. In the yard, a group of young men stood and talked. All the women sat on the lanaʻi and talked story. For some reason, they didn't have to work themselves to death like Noelani. Dolores leaned against the lanaʻi pole and absently twisted the bougainvillea until the brilliant pink flower came off in her hand. As the bustle in the kitchen ebbed, Dolores collapsed on the lanaʻi steps.

Kaipo came to find her. "You need to learn to be part of us," he said. He stood above her and leaned against the lanaʻi pole she'd held up earlier.

"What do you mean?" Dolores didn't even look up at him.

His neutral tone sharpened. "When you give Mama attitude, she takes it out on all of us. She ordered Kali and Meli to bed early."

Dolores couldn't help it. She snorted a laugh before she could stifle it. "How did Leia escape their fate?"

Kaipo's eyes darkened. "Those little girls did nothing to you, yet your behavior got them punished."

"I did nothing."

"You made Mama angry with your scowls, and you embarrassed her in front of ʻohana when you refused to do your chores. She always responds by punishing everyone. That's not fair."

"Nothing's fair." It seemed odd for him to warn her about getting the hānai children punished. He and Leia could do no wrong in Noelani's eyes. How fair was that?

"Your life will be miserable if you continue," Kaipo said. "Mama will punish you, the keiki will hate you, and the rest of us will ignore you. Mama's Hawaiian roots are the most important thing to her. The food, the music, the ʻohana—it's all part of a way of life that is being swallowed by haole sugar planters. She works hard to hold on."

"What about Kanoa? Does he feel the same?" she asked.

Kaipo hesitated. "The *lunas* in the fields beat down the men who work for someone else's wealth."

"Not too enjoyable," she said, meaning to convey empathy.

He bristled. "Let me give you some advice. If you want

any chance to enjoy your life, you won't alienate all of us." He didn't wait for her response and slammed the screen as he went into the house.

Still confused about the seriousness of her transgression, Dolores turned away and looked makai, toward the unseen sea, out over the street, over the houses and foliage of the plantation camps. Across that sea, the man who'd always treated her well was trying to start a new life. She must not think of him anymore. She must focus on her own new life.

Standing, Dolores brushed her skirt with her hands and headed to bed. The little girls were already asleep, dried tears on Meli's face. Dolores felt a pang of guilt that something she had done might have caused those tears. As she parted the mosquito netting and eased her aching body into bed, Maria lifted her head off the pillow. "This was a long day, going from church to family dinner. Tomorrow, though, you have school."

"You don't?"

She shook her head. "Noelani doesn't believe in high school. I stopped going when I was in sixth grade. A lot of island kids do."

That meant Dolores had five more years of daily reprieve. Five more years to learn something that would make her useful to someone other than Noelani. To Papa. She would work hard to feel the aloha spirit until she could make a better way for herself.

FOUR

School 1922

olores returned to Waikiki Elementary School feeling like a very different girl than the one who had completed first grade there. As she walked to school with Makaha and Polunu, she tried to lag behind, to distance herself from them, but Makaha seemed to know what she was doing. "Come on, little sis, catch up," he said, waiting for her with a wicked grin.

Polunu pulled from his pocket a grubby piece of sugar cane, about four inches long and almost an inch in diameter. He waved it in the air as if herding her with it. When she scowled at him, he gnawed on the cane, sucking sweet juice from the pulp before spitting it on the ground.

As they neared the playground, Dolores spotted her friends, Rose and Kimiko. Rose had a new dress, stiffly starched, and a matching ribbon in her straight brown hair. Kimiko always reminded Dolores of a doll because she was so dainty. They waited for Dolores as usual. Now the world felt normal. She would spend schooldays with her friends just like she always had. She waved to them with her whole arm. Polunu and Makaha drifted away to find their own friends, or trouble, whichever came first.

"Where were you all summer, Dolores?" Rose asked as she approached. Without waiting for an answer, she continued,

"We went to the zoo in Kapiʻolani Park. They have a new monkey!"

"Really?" squealed Kimiko. "The old one was nasty. He threw things at the people."

"Have you been to the zoo yet?" Rose asked.

The words washed over Dolores as if foreign, from a strange world she no longer knew. She shook her head, overcome with emotion. Her life had changed so much, so very much. If her friends invited her to the zoo today after school, even if Noelani allowed it, Dolores knew she'd be so exhausted she wouldn't be able to enjoy it.

"Dolores? You all right?" Kimiko said.

She opened her mouth to reassure her friends, but before she could speak, a shout drew the attention of every student within range. Makaha stood on a bench. "Just wanted everyone to know Dolores is now my sister! Welcome to my ʻohana, Dolores!" He laughed. Polunu and his friends laughed along with Makaha as they always did.

Dread shrouded Dolores as she watched horror spread over Rose and Kimiko's faces. She swallowed hard and tried not to curse in her head at the boys.

"Dolores?" Rose was already recoiling but gave Dolores one last opportunity. Kimiko tuned away.

"I'm living with their family now," Dolores admitted in a whisper.

"But why?" Kimiko asked.

Dolores didn't know what to say. Because her father had left her? She shook her head and tried to laugh. It sounded like she was being strangled.

Rose said, "Those two are trouble. My parents will never let me come visit you there."

She backed away as she spoke and turned to join Kimiko. They walked to the farthest corner of the yard and looked over their shoulders at Dolores every few feet.

Dolores stood alone on a playground filled with chattering children. Noelani believed working hard would give her the aloha spirit, the feeling of love for all, but when Rose and Kimiko left Dolores alone, no chores could have cheered her.

As a second grader, Dolores sat in the second row. Students in the first row had no desk at all, so the younger *na hāumana* sat there. Dolores's own writing surface jutted out from the back of the first row's bench. She ran her hands across the surface. It gave her a small thrill, at odds with the hurt inflicted by her so-called friends. Polunu sat at the far end of her row, but Makaha sat behind her. Chalkboards lined the walls of the schoolroom on all sides. Above them, open windows invited even scant breezes inside. The back wall contained pictures from Honolulu's history—outrigger canoes, men in full native dress, thatched huts, women gathered under banyan trees.

The teacher sat at a large koa wood desk in the front of the room. Scratched and chipped and scarred, it must have been among the first ever made in Hawai'i. The haole teacher's eyeglasses hung on a chain around her neck when they weren't perched on her sharp nose. Her fuzzy brown hair stayed tightly wound in a bun.

Dolores's forty or so classmates included both first and second graders, most of them Japanese. Makaha should have been in the third-grade room, but the teacher had held him back. The girls wore white long-sleeved dresses, some prim and plain, some with ruffles at the hem, but all of lightweight cotton. The boys wore white shirts and coats. They, at least, were allowed short pants. None of them wore shoes. From the front of the room, the teacher glared at the students as they struggled to sew straight seams with precise stitches.

Makaha kept up a staccato beat against the back of her bench with his feet. Rose and Kimiko rolled their eyes. It was such a superior gesture, an I'm-better-than-you attitude combined with a can-you-believe-this incredulity. Dolores wanted to scold them. Instead, she turned around and hissed, "Stop kicking me!"

He stuck out his tongue. Dolores turned back with an exasperated sigh, but not before the teacher's eyes caught her.

"Dolores? Is your piecework done?"

Of course it wasn't done. If it had been, Dolores would have raised her hand for the teacher to frown over her efforts. "No, ma'am." Dolores found it hard to hold a needle with sweaty hands. Sewing would never give her a valuable enough skill to join Papa in California. Neither would learning to read or do sums. School was nothing but a break from chores, and she'd rather just sleep in.

"I'm on my second piece, ma'am," Makaha said in the sweetest voice she'd ever heard him use. It took every effort of will for Dolores not to roll her eyes like Rose and Kimiko had.

The other girls stitched straight seams and embroidered fancy vines and flowers that made the teacher smile. Dolores didn't know what powers in Honolulu had decided seven-year-old boys could learn to sew, but reality didn't lie. Polunu fidgeted while he hemmed, and everything was puckered and sticky with cane juice. Makaha's grubby hands dirtied the fabric, and Dolores imagined the teacher bringing all the laundry to Noelani.

"Students, put your sewing away, please." The room rustled as the students passed their piecework to the end of the row. The student at the end got up to put it all away on a shelf. "Take out your pencils and copy this. Use your best penmanship!" The teacher passed out passages of text.

Dolores's tired eyes blurred as she tried to read the words she had to copy. Sighing, she set the paper on her desk. She decided to write a letter to her father. He must have arrived in San Francisco by now, but not enough time had passed for a letter to make its way back to her. Noelani would never allow Dolores enough time at home to write. Maybe she wouldn't even give her paper or a pencil! She'd write the letter now and save it until she had his address.

Dear Papa,

She scribed the letters, being careful to stay on the lines. She wanted to make sure he could read it.

I am fine, working hard.

Frowning, she erased the last two words.

I am fine. I have lots to do and lots to eat.

She must make him think she was happy, but not too happy or he might never come back for her!

Dolores looked up at the teacher. She sat at her desk, working on something to torture them with later. The other students were copying the page of text the teacher had passed out. Dolores continued her letter, but she sometimes looked at the paper she was supposed to copy, pretending she was doing exactly that.

I miss you and Pablo very much.

No, it was Paul now. How did you spell Paul? She flexed fingers, sore from wrestling laundry.

Have you found a job and a place to live? I can hardly wait to join you.

Dolores snuck another glance at the teacher. She was scanning the room to find someone who wasn't working. Dolores pretended to peer at the text.

I can make beds now and do laundry by myself. Soon I will learn to cook and sew.

The final bell rang, and Dolores shoved the paper in her pocket. She left the room in a hurry so the teacher wouldn't notice she hadn't handed in the assignment.

Rose and Kimiko waited for Dolores, who smiled and greeted them as if all was forgiven. Neither of her friends smiled. Rose said, "So do you *like* living with those boys?"

"It's temporary," Dolores said. "Only until my father sends for me from the mainland."

"You'll travel on a ship all by yourself?" Rose was skeptical.

"Or he'll come to get me."

"Dolores, what have you done to your hands?" Kimiko asked.

Dolores shoved her reddened hands in her pockets. "I'm helping with the laundry for a big family. That's all."

"Oh, so you've become a servant." Kimiko's knowing tone made Rose laugh.

Dolores turned and ran from the school in a most unladylike way, ran from Rose and Kimiko, and from Polunu and Makaha. She tried not to care what Rose and Kimiko thought of her. She only wanted to be free of her self-styled brothers. The palm trees lining the road waved their fronds to urge her on. She ran until the neighborhood flowers blurred to an orangey pink. The boys sensed a challenge and sped after her, slapping their feet in the dirt to raise great clouds of dust. Instead of passing her, they ran circles around her and hollered loud enough to wake the goddess Pele on the highest volcano.

At Noelani's, which she refused to call home, the usual chaos greeted her. Polunu and Makaha dropped their books in the dirt and shouted at each other as they ran to the back yard. Noelani was singing a Hawaiian song accompanied by the clashing of pots and pans in the kitchen. Dolores sighed as the relative freedom of the morning evaporated. A strange haole man sat in the main room with his hat in his hand.

"Keiki you back, ya? *Wikiwiki*, you work," Noelani called to her as she brought in a tray of pūpū to set before the visitor.

Dolores nodded at the man and hurried to her room to change into her working dress. As it turned out, the new customer ran a small hotel for the tourists who were beginning to overrun Honolulu. He would bring the hotel linen to Noelani once a week on Monday. That meant Dolores would have fifteen sets of sheets and towels to wash after school every Monday. Her shoulders slumped as Noelani explained this to her.

"Stand up straight! You rather live on handouts on the mainland? You know it take your Papa some time to find work. Ha! What *kine* haole you? He work harder dan you, so hard he have no time think of you, safe on the island with big Hawaiian 'ohana fo' look after you."

"A Hawaiian family to look after me? More like work me to death!" Dolores straightened her shoulders and gritted her teeth.

"Watch your tongue, keiki." Noelani glared at her and left, shaking her head as if she couldn't believe Dolores's ingratitude.

The pile of dirty laundry towered higher than her head.

FOR the rest of the week, Dolores sat quietly in class because she was too tired to talk. While she had done well in math the year before, now she scored low on assignments because Noelani's laundry triumphed over homework. Rose and Kimiko continued to ignore her because she could no longer go with them on excursions to Kapi'olani Park after school. Day followed day, and Dolores plodded through with no enthusiasm. Chores, school, chores, bed, repeat. School, at least, gave her body a chance to recover from its labors.

She continued adding to the letter to Papa, but no letter arrived from him. It was hard to add perky, upbeat tidbits without revealing to him how miserable she was.

One breezy Sunday morning, Maria frowned at Dolores

as they climbed aboard the streetcar to head back to Noelani's after Mass. "Dolores, are you all right? You were falling asleep in Mass."

All right? Dolores didn't even know how to answer. She had fallen asleep during math twice this week. She couldn't remember the last time she'd jumped rope with Kimiko at recess. When she closed her eyes, she saw stacks of dirty sheets that seemed to grow as she worked instead of getting smaller, and she hadn't received a letter from Papa or Paul.

"Are you all right?" Maria repeated.

"I guess," Dolores said, shrugging her shoulders.

"You look tired," Maria said. She put her arm around the younger girl. "Love those around you. The aloha spirit will keep you strong even if you don't love what people do."

For a moment, Dolores lost herself in the illusion that she had a sister who cared for her. Then she noticed a new addition to Maria's left hand.

"What's that?"

Maria's smile glowed as bright as the diamond on her finger. "Peter and I are engaged."

"Congratulations! But when. . . ?" Dolores thought about the morning. When had Peter proposed? She'd been with them.

"At Benson-Smith's. When you excused yourself to use the bathroom. I thought you and he had conspired!"

Dolores laughed. "Just a lucky coincidence. I know you and Peter will be very happy. He's a wonderful man."

"He is, isn't he? Peter's bought a dairy farm out by Maunalua Bay. He'll still be in the army but come home at night. I'm sure his saxophone will encourage the cows to give the best milk on Oʻahu!" Her eyes glowed with plans.

She chattered on about the dairy as realization settled over Dolores. Maria would leave Noelani's. Her only friend and ally—except for an occasional encouraging word from Nui—would be gone.

Maria hugged her. "I wish I had the power to spirit you away from there."

Curse her transparent face. "I do, too." Dolores tried for a light tone and failed. Maria kept her arm around Dolores until they had to leave the streetcar.

"Keep aloha in your heart," she told Dolores again.

Dolores nodded. She couldn't keep aloha, though, until she found it. Aloha required family, and she had no family right now.

The riotous flowers that scrambled over Noelani's house projected a peaceful beauty at odds with what Dolores knew waited for them inside. Or maybe sooner. Noelani sat in her chair on the lanaʻi, her thick dark hair twisted into a rope down her ample chest. "Come on, girls, wikiwiki," she said, waving them toward her. "You too long getting home today."

Dolores trudged up the three steps to the lanaʻi, not hurrying as Noelani had asked. Should she stay for Maria's announcement or let Maria deal with Noelani alone?

Noelani held out an envelope. "Letter from California for you."

Dolores's eyes fastened on the envelope, hope filling her heart. All thoughts of Maria and Peter vanished. She took the envelope and turned it between her hands, not looking at it, her fingertips trailing across the envelope, feeling every wrinkle. She wanted to read Papa's words more than she wanted to breathe, but she must do so in private.

Noelani leaned her bulky body toward Dolores, her rope of hair swinging free. She examined the girl critically. Dolores lifted her chin and met the woman's gaze. She refused to suffer when she had done nothing wrong. The big Hawaiian woman's dark eyes softened. "Go read your letter, keiki. All else will wait."

This show of aloha shocked Dolores. Somewhere deep inside, Noelani cared for her. Dolores didn't question it. Kicking off her shoes as she entered the house, Dolores considered where to read her letter, as she heard Maria say, "Noelani, I have something to tell you."

Too many bodies lived in this small house, allowing no privacy. Dolores hurried straight through to the back porch, ignoring the baskets of dirty laundry that awaited her. Sliding her feet into a pair of flip flops, she ran into the yard. Coarse grass covered the tiny space behind the house. She pushed her way behind a huge bird of paradise, tucking herself between it and the large rough trunk of a palm tree. Peering between the orange and purple flowers on the long stalks, Dolores made sure she was alone.

A letter from Papa. The first to arrive in the two months since he had left. To Dolores, those two months had been years of torture. To him, they'd probably flown by. This letter would tell her about his job and Paul's job and their house, and when they wanted her to join them. This letter would be full of how much he missed her and how incomplete his life was without her. Dolores smoothed her hand across the envelope, tracing her name with a finger. Not able to stand it any longer, she ripped the letter open.

Dear Dolores,

I hope this letter finds you well.

She smiled to see that Papa had carefully printed the words so she'd be able to read them. She tracked the words with her finger as she mouthed them to herself.

A shrill undulating scream pierced her calm. Dolores clutched the letter and spied on Kaipo as he chased Makaha in circles around the yard. *Please, Lord, take them away*, Dolores prayed.

"Whatcha got there, little sis?" Kaipo's hands separated the bird of paradise flower stalks.

"Nothing." Dolores tried to crumple the precious letter so she could hide it in her hand, but the movement alerted him. "A letter? Who would write to *you*? Maybe it's a love note from a snotty brat at school? I could take care of him for you. I could pound his tiny arms and legs to a pulp." He punched a fist into his left hand to demonstrate.

Dolores sat still, praying he would leave, closing her eyes for extra concentration.

"*Hiki nō.* All right. I'll let you read your precious letter. Don't care, anyway." He whistled as he went in search of someone smaller than himself to terrorize.

She smoothed out Papa's letter and resumed reading.

Your brother Paul and I are living in a tiny place in Mountain View, California. We have been working at small jobs to pay the rent. In the spring, we should have plenty of work in the fruit orchards, but winter is a difficult time for farmers to hire anyone new. It is a great relief to know that you are safe and well cared for at Kanoa's house. Are you behaving yourself? Paul and I will miss you this Christmas, but we will pray for you.

Love,
Papa

A hundred thoughts crashed into her head. He wasn't planning to write again before Christmas. He didn't want her to join him. He believed she was well cared for and safe. He would pray for her instead of making her a present like he usually did. As a good Catholic girl, Dolores should appreciate that. She did.

A traitorous tear dropped onto the letter.

No, she wouldn't cry. Dolores wiped her eyes with the back of her hand, crumpling Papa's letter in the other. Papa had given up on her being useful to him. Ironic, since every day she learned useful tasks. In the short time since he had left, Dolores had learned to do more laundry than he and Paul could generate. She helped Noelani in the kitchen with Hawaiian, Portuguese, and Japanese food. Maria spent so much time at the hotels making leis for tourists that Dolores cleaned the house almost alone. She'd be doing even more of it now that Maria was getting married. Dolores's thoughts tumbled around the people of Noelani's house, focusing on how best to maintain the peace to get through each day. She must make her own way. Somehow, she must find her own way free of Noelani. In the meantime, she'd finish her letter to Papa and make it clear she wanted to come to California sooner rather than later.

She tucked Papa's letter into her pocket and walked over to the lana'i. Laundry awaited her. From the front of the house, Dolores heard Noelani exclaim with surprise and congratulate Maria. Dolores picked up a shirt and tossed it into the rinse water.

FIVE

Spring 1923

One Saturday in late spring, morning sun lit the kitchen, more light than heat at that hour. Birds sang from their perches high in the still palm trees. Kanoa sat at the kitchen table, hidden behind the *Honolulu Bulletin* as usual, a fork appearing now and again to spear his breakfast of sausage and eggs. Noelani brought a platter of bacon and sat next to her husband. The rest of the family surrounded the table.

Maria glowed, as she'd done all winter. Noelani ignored Maria's imminent departure to a life of wedded bliss with Peter. No doubt she was looking for another girl to hānai.

Breakfast continued in the usual jarring manner as children grabbed food and talked over each other.

Conversations broke into generational groups, which left Dolores with either Maria or Polunu and Makaha. She spent plenty of time with Makaha and Polunu at school, and Maria was in the habit of talking to the older brothers, so Dolores usually chose to eat without speaking. Today, though, she had other plans. With a deep breath to gather her courage, she said, "Noelani, I finished most of today's work yesterday."

"You been workin' hard, Dolores," she agreed, but sounded wary.

Maria nodded encouragement.

"I got up early to finish the rest this morning." Noelani waited. "Maria and Peter are going to the beach and have invited me. May I have the rest of the day off?"

A snort of laughter erupted from Kaipo. Dolores refused to look in his direction. Nui smiled at her. Makaha's feet drummed against the table leg. Maria smiled her encouragement. No one else reacted to her bold request.

"Day off?" Noelani's eyes widened, her voice incredulous.

Dolores sat up straighter. "I've worked every day since I came here, including Sundays after church, doing my chores after school instead of studying, and I never complain."

Noelani just stared. A heavy silence fell over the table.

"You won't be losing income since I won't be leaving any laundry undone. I'll make the beds before I leave. We're going to Hanauma Bay. Peter will pick us both up and have us home before dark," Dolores said. She looked at Noelani and refused to break eye contact.

Noelani had already approved Maria's day with her beau. She turned to Maria. "Dis be true, ya?"

Maria nodded.

"'A'ole pilikia. No problem. I approve." Kanoa went back to his newspaper as if his word settled matters. Not sure, Dolores waited for Noelani to speak.

"Nevvah saw keiki so maha'oi," Noelani muttered. "You take big advantage, Dolores."

Dolores's heart sang. She didn't care if Noelani thought she was rude. She was going to the beach with Maria and Peter!

"Don't think you be goin' to the beach every day now," Noelani said.

Kanoa lowered the paper long enough to wink at Dolores, taking the sting out of Noelani's scolding.

"Get your things," Maria said with a wide smile.

It didn't matter that she'd only had a few bites of breakfast. Dolores hurried, as if being chased by the fiery goddess Pele herself, to gather the towel and bathing suit that Maria had lent her. When they left the house, Dolores urged Maria down the street a few houses so they'd be out of range if anyone should remember a task for her to do. The sun warmed Dolores's skin, but it couldn't shine brighter than her smile.

Soon Peter pulled up, driving a battered black farm truck. Maria waved and climbed into the front seat. "Oh, I'm so glad you could get away, Dolores!" Peter called. "Climb in!"

Dolores squeezed into the front seat. Maria giggled as she pressed closer to Peter, who looked more relaxed without his uniform. Dolores spotted bundles of food, towels, folded-up beach chairs, and an umbrella in the back of the truck.

"Beach Express at your ladies' service," Peter intoned. They laughed at him.

"Why aren't we going to Waikiki?" Dolores asked him, "It's closer."

"Too many tourists," Peter said. "They're taking over the beach! At Hanauma we'll be among locals."

Dolores settled back to enjoy the ride. It didn't matter where they went as long as they made a day of it. Peter told them of his little brother's antics, and they all laughed as they bounced along the dirt roads to Hanauma, east of Honolulu near the Koko Head Crater.

Peter parked just off the road and unloaded the truck. They carried everything down the steep rock-lined path to the sand. Swimmers dotted the lagoons, and bathing beauties re-clined on the sand. In the turquoise shallows, a couple of boys played with a large beach ball. Peter shoved the umbrella pole into the sand while Maria unfolded the wooden beach chairs and brushed off the striped canvas.

Maria held up a towel and Dolores changed into the bor-rowed tank swimsuit. Peter then held the towel for Maria, pretending to peek at her and laughing at Dolores's blush. Peter was already wearing his swim trunks and just had to remove his shirt before racing into the surf.

Most of the people Dolores saw were teenagers. Conscious of being younger, Dolores tried to stand up straight and not embarrass Maria. Peter teased both of them. Dolores never felt inadequate or too young when she was with them.

Maria and Dolores waded into the shallows. Warm water kissed Dolores's ankles, and the glorious sun embraced her body. Peter ran by them and dove into the breaking waves. He came up and shook the saltwater from his eyes. "Come on in, sissies!" He grabbed Maria's hand, ignored her squeals, and dragged her into the water. When she was thoroughly dunked, he came for Dolores.

"No, no! Don't get my hair wet!" She tried to run back to the beach, but it was no use.

He laughed as he dunked her next to Maria. "You can't come to the beach and not go in the water, ladies!"

Maria's hair hung in drowned strands. Dolores's looked the same. They laughed and splashed Peter until he begged for mercy. Down the beach, a group of teenage boys yelled back and forth as they bodysurfed.

"The Medeiros boys," Peter said, his tone rich with disapproval. "They're wild."

Dolores thought it looked like they were having fun.

MUCH later, tired and sunburned, they shook sand out of their towels and loaded the truck. The sky flared orange and purple and red, throwing the palm trees into silhouette as the sun set over the ocean. The beauty of O'ahu spilled aloha from her heart. Feeling happier than she had since her father's letter that fall, Dolores imagined natives in their canoes paddling mail to the mainland. In January, unprecedented rain had drenched Honolulu. Dolores had tried to believe the rain impeded the mail, but she knew better. She had received a short note from him in late February, dashed off as if something to check off a list, thanking her for her letter and saying he was glad she was happy. In her response to him, Dolores asked about whether Paul was attending school and repeated her request to join them even though she was beginning to believe her life now was here in Honolulu. She'd get through the worst days by thinking about the best ones.

Peter pulled up in front of Noelani's house. Dolores thanked him and hopped out of the truck, leaving the engaged couple to say their good-byes in private. Inside, Kanoa sat in his cane chair near the radio. Wild noises from the boys' room identified their location. Leia was in the kitchen doing dishes. Noelani's sewing machine whirred as she shouted instructions to her youngest daughter.

"Did you have fun, Dolores?" Kanoa asked.

"Yes, sir, I did. Thank you for letting me go."

"That leftover kālua pork smells amazing," Maria said, coming inside with shining eyes. "If we clean up, can we eat now?"

Noelani nodded. "Work in the mornin'," she reminded the girls. Her tone seemed gentler than usual, but maybe it was Dolores's relaxed mood. Noelani hummed a Hawaiian melody as she sewed. "Kine nice have 'ohana home," she said. Dolores smiled, but Noelani had already turned back to the machine.

The happiness from the day at the beach didn't last long. Dolores was up to her elbows in laundry before the next day's sun could warm Hanauma's sand. At least Maria helped her today.

Dolores said, "The beach was so lovely. Time to get back to work, though." She grimaced. "Hard work builds aloha." Her mimicry echoed Noelani.

"You know," Maria said, "Noelani may be hard on you, but she never turns away anyone who needs 'ohana. Everyone is welcome in her home. That's the aloha spirit."

"More welcome if they can do laundry," Dolores said in a snippy tone, but guilt made her stomach clench. Maria was right. She had food, a place to sleep, and everything she needed. Only a spoiled girl wanted more, and Dolores had never been spoiled.

"Noelani comes from a big old Hawaiian family and wanted many children," said Maria. "Four of her babies died. I don't think she can have any more. That's why she adopts so many. Remember you can love someone yet not love everything they do or say."

"Oh," Dolores said, guilt reducing the word to the tiniest breath.

"That doesn't mean you have to cower before her, though," Maria said sternly. "Stick up for yourself, or she'll always order you around. To achieve aloha, you need to love yourself first. Feeling sorry for yourself doesn't help."

Stung, Dolores gave the shirt she was scrubbing extra attention. When Maria didn't say any more, she peeked at her friend. Maria waited. "I'm not feeling sorry for myself!" Dolores said. "Just thinking about what you said."

Even after Maria's lecture, it took Dolores a few days to muster the courage to ask about going to Maria's wedding. "Will I be allowed to attend, Noelani?"

The big Hawaiian woman's eyes narrowed. "Pretty cheeky you ask me dis."

Dolores remembered Maria's words and kept her chin up.

"You deserve free time, ya? I never get free time. Make a body lazy."

"I'm not lazy."

Noelani shook her head back and forth, but her eyes lit up. "Weddings important part of young wahine's life. All friends be dere. You go have good time. Laundry, she will wait, ya? We all have de big *lūʻau* after."

Dolores refused to let her jaw drop open. Everyone would go? When Noelani hurried out of the room on an errand, Dolores turned to Kaipo, who had heard the whole exchange. "Who was that woman?" she joked.

"You've made your place," he said. "Passed a test, so to speak. You work hard and Mama appreciates that. Don't expect special favors every day though. The work does have to get done."

Still dumbfounded, Dolores headed to the laundry tubs on the back lanaʻi where she immersed herself in soap, water, and fabric. Had Noelani been getting nicer, or was it just that Dolores knew her job now?

Dolores expected the day of Maria's wedding to be special, but the sun rose as usual. There were no extra bird songs or blooming flowers. It was an ordinary day. It didn't matter. She knew it would always be special in Maria and Peter's hearts. The priest celebrated Mass at Our Lady of Peace with the usual people in attendance. Afterward, as the parishioners trickled out, Peter and Maria made their way to the altar.

Peter and Maria stood before the priest, lost in each other's eyes, as he performed a simple service. God would bless this union, he told them, but Dolores knew God had blessed her friends some time ago.

She rode the streetcar with the newlyweds back to Noelani's for a lūʻau feast. Dolores remembered how shocked she had been by the number of people who attended Noelani's Sunday dinners. That number paled compared to the wedding celebration. An *ukulele* played, and the musician sang a Hawaiian song whose melody flowed around them like the tide.

In the kitchen, Noelani prepared poi, rice, *poke*, *lomi*, and *saimin*. "This dish be like Hawaiʻi," Noelani told Dolores, pointing to the saimin. "It be all mixed up—Chinee noodles and Japanee broth and Portugee sausage. Cabbage from Koreans."

"What do the Hawaiians add?" Dolores asked.

"Eggs!" Noelani laughed.

Dolores had never seen such a light in the older woman's eye. This was what she lived for, a celebration of life with all the people she held dear. Dolores took the big bowl of saimin out of Noelani's hands and put it on the table that was already groaning with food. She said, "Go. It's your daughter's wedding."

Noelani grasped Dolores in her work-roughened hands and squeezed. As Noelani untied her apron and hurried into the yard, though, Dolores saw her wipe her eyes.

Dolores joined the crowd in the yard to watch Kali, Meli, and Leia perform a hula dance in grass skirts and leis. They moved their feet gracefully, skirts rustling as they moved their hips. Dolores had to admit they were adorable. Kaipo led Polunu and Makaha in a tribal dance to a pounding drumbeat. The younger boys needed more practice, but they stamped their feet with youthful enthusiasm. When Koa and Nui unlayered the banana leaves and hauled the kālua pig out of the *imu*, the underground oven, steam curled into the air with a scent to make stomachs growl. Hundreds of guests, most of them Hawaiian, filed past the laden tables both inside and outside. They settled wherever they could sit or lean and dug into plates piled high with good food.

At the end of a long and joyous celebration, Maria and Peter left by carriage for three days at the Moana Hotel on Waikiki. Dolores knew Maria would pretend to be a tourist and let others do the work.

The next day Dolores picked up her work at Noelani's with the lightest heart she'd had since their day at Hanauma. If she expected any long-lasting changes in her relationship with her hānai mother, though, she was soon corrected. Toppled stacks of dirty sheets and stained towels hid her usual laundry baskets. The family's piles of grass-stained short pants, food-stained shirts, and who-knows-what-stained underthings towered over the baskets.

"Have you taken on the laundry for the entire Moana Hotel?" Dolores asked, visualizing sheets and towels showing up from Maria and Peter's honeymoon room.

"None of the smart lip," Noelani said. "You take day off and you make up for it, ya?"

Dolores stayed out of school that day to catch up with the laundry.

One day that week, Meli came onto the lanaʻi. Dolores smiled, pushed a stray auburn curl out of her eyes, and bent to pick up another wet shirt. Without a word, Meli held out a letter, dark eyes wide. "Mahalo, sweetheart," Dolores said. Meli smiled and ran back into the house, the screen door slamming behind her.

Dolores turned the letter over. Postmarked California. This letter might be the summons that rescued her from drudgery. It might not. Dolores's corner of the world consisted of the two metal laundry tubs, the washing machine, and the wicker chair in the laundry corner of the screened lanaʻi. The misshapen seat of the chair molded itself to her as she sat. She tore open the envelope and unfolded the letter.

Dear Dolores,

I am becoming quite the prune farmer! I work at a small orchard in Sunnyvale owned by Granville Savage. Isn't that a curious name? He came by wagon train from Canada when he was just a boy. Now he sells prunes to the California Prune and Apricot Growers, more commonly known as Sunsweet. Much better name, right? They sell

all manner of prune goods—canned, dried, juice—they
even sell apricot pit oil. Sunsweet is a cooperative of small
orchardists like the one I work for. Your brother works
pitting apricots. We are staying at a small place in
Mountain View. California is a beautiful place, sunny and
warm most of the year. Its beaches aren't as nice as
Hawai'i, but it does have flowers and palm trees. I think
we can be happy here.

Love,
Your Papa

Dolores wondered if his "we" would ever include her.
When the laundry was finished, she borrowed a pen and blank
paper from Kanoa to write an immediate answer.

Aloha mai e Papa,

Prunes are disgusting although I do like apricots. My
favorite, of course, is pineapple. Honolulu becomes more
popular with tourists every day. Maria sells leis to them,
and the older boys teach surfing. I help around the house
and go to school. I read well, sew, and do laundry now.
Recently I attended Maria and Peter's wedding.

Me ka aloha,
Dolores

If he wouldn't ask about her, and instead went on about
his life that didn't include her, then she could do the same.
On her way to school, she stopped at the plantation store to
get a two-cent stamp and put her letter in the mailbox. Dolores realized with a start that she no longer pined for Papa
and Paul. She could be happy in a real family, even if it
wasn't hers. It wasn't hard work she detested, it was the

stern Hawaiian woman who stubbornly clung to her pidgin, who had somehow convinced Papa to leave, who created her own family by destroying other families.

Luna 1924

On January 15, 1924, Dolores turned nine years old. Her father had deemed Paul to be useful at that age. She compared herself to her memories of her brother and was satisfied. It had been eighteen months since Papa left. She no longer hoped for him to call her to California. If she didn't care, no one could break her heart again.

Dolores often pictured the day she would walk away from Noelani's with all her belongings in her old suitcase, walk away forever of her own volition and head for a future she controlled. That future still wasn't clear, but it included family and home. She might live with Noelani now, but it wasn't a family, no matter how hard Noelani tried to pretend it was.

One morning at breakfast, Noelani turned from the kitchen sink to face Dolores. Her dark braid fell down the left side of her head and garnished at the top with a plumeria flower. She always wore flowers above her left ear because that told people she was married. To Dolores she said, "You be helping in the kitchen today."

Dolores's fork froze halfway to her mouth. "What about the laundry?"

"When we done making the dinner, you show Leia the laundry."

Dolores's mouth dropped open, and her eyes shot to Leia,

who looked equally shocked, her eyes wide and white against her dark skin. Leia was six now, and Dolores had started doing laundry at seven. She shook her head.

"Whassa matter, keiki? You no like?"

"No, no, that's fine." Dolores set her fork on her plate and cleared her dishes to the sink. Makaha washed the kitchen dishes, and Polunu cleared the counter to prepare the evening meal. Then they muttered something about homework and escaped to their room.

Noelani took a chicken out of the ice box and set it on the counter. "We make chicken. Soy, pineapple, ginger on top, ya?"

Dolores nodded. Noelani showed her how to chop up the chicken. Dolores got a bowl from the cupboard and put the chicken in it while Noelani gathered more ingredients. Together they made a sauce of ginger, garlic, onion, paprika, and vinegar. "Smells 'ono, Noelani," Dolores said with a smile.

Noelani mixed the sauce to cover the chicken. "Delicious, ya." She told Dolores how to make another sauce of soy sauce, pineapple, and brown sugar. "You make now, ya? Put on top after he cooking."

Dolores mixed the sauce and put it in the fridge with the chicken. She would pull it all out when it was time to make dinner.

"Now the laundry." Noelani shooed Dolores out of the kitchen onto the back lana'i. Leia sat curled up on the wicker chair, looking nervous.

"Ready to learn about laundry?" Dolores asked. Leia rolled her eyes. Dolores muttered to herself, "This is going to be a long day."

She didn't make Leia start with a sheet like Maria had done to her. Instead, they started with an easy load of shirts. To Leia's credit, she didn't complain until after the first rinse.

"Now we have to move them into the washer itself," Dolores said.

"But they're so heavy. So wet." Leia's tone was not quite a whine but going that direction fast.

Remembering her own learning process, Dolores said, "Look, it wasn't my idea to teach you. I was a year older than you when I started, and it was hard then."

Leia rolled her eyes. "I'm better than that."

Dolores refrained from slapping her, but just barely. She carried out the rest of the instruction brusquely, with no apology for the heat of the water or the heaviness of the wet clothes. Leia was puffing heavily from exertion by the time they were through with the first load. Dolores smiled. She'd toughen up this spoiled little girl in no time.

They'd finished four loads when Noelani came to the door. "Enough for today. Dolores, I need you in the kitchen."

"Mama, Dolores was mean." And to Dolores's astonishment tears appeared on the little girl's face. Dolores's eyes darted to Noelani. She knew the older woman had never accepted such weakness from Dolores at that age, nor from the boys either.

"You'll learn more tomorrow. Go rest before dinner," Noelani told her daughter. It wasn't a nurturing tone, but she didn't snap at Leia either. Noelani had always favored her own children.

Leia scampered off to her room faster than Dolores had seen her move all morning. Dolores shook her head and returned to the kitchen to cook the chicken and help Noelani prepare the rest of the meal—rice, sweet bread, and a big bowl of Hawaiian coleslaw with cabbage, pineapple, and onion.

Leia dragged herself to the dinner table with a very unhappy face. Dolores remembered how sore her muscles had been on her first laundry day. But then she remembered her first day had been a full day, not just four loads. And the second day she'd been all by herself.

Kaipo looked tired, too, since he'd started in the cane

fields with Kanoa, Nui, and Koa. Kanoa read the paper, Noelani sewed, and the two littlest girls ate silently. They were now in charge of making the beds in both rooms. While Noelani's machine whirred in the background, the girls peeked at the boys from lowered eyes. Makaha, at ten, was in the awkward age between the innocent play of childhood and the hard work of the men in the cane field. Polunu poked Makaha with a sugar cane from his pocket.

"Leia worked hard today, Noelani," Dolores said. "It might be better if she had help tomorrow. Anyone else want to learn?"

Noelani looked up from the sewing machine. "You boys all help with laundry tomorrow, ya?" She turned to Dolores. "It okay if you not finish, Dolores," Noelani said. "You wear dem out, ya?"

Dolores smiled. "I can do that."

As dinner broke up, and the family went their separate ways, Dolores heard Leia whisper to her brothers, "You work hard. Dolores is mean."

At school the next day, Dolores never saw Makaha, Polunu, or Leia. They avoided her with a skill she hadn't known they possessed, and she enjoyed it. For the first time in over a year, she jumped rope with Rose and Kimiko at recess and went back into the classroom with a big smile.

After they returned to Noelani's, Dolores went to the back porch. She stood with one hand on her hip and the other on the washing machine as the two boys came out the screen door. For the first time since she'd arrived, she had the upper hand. Leia was the youngest by three years. Her long dark hair hung in neat braids tied with bows. Dolores couldn't imagine a little girl keeping those bows tied all day, but Leia managed. The boys were only a year apart in age but the same height. Makaha appeared taller because he was so slim and wiry. Polunu would grow up to be a massive Hawaiian man like the ones who played drums at the weekly lūʻau. All three had dark hair and dark eyes with coffee-colored skin that made Dolores's arms look like the white sand on the Big Island's Hapuna beach. They all looked timid, even afraid. Dolores couldn't help the gleeful surge of power that shot through her.

"Bedsheets." She pointed to the stack of dirty laundry. "We didn't do them yesterday, so we have to do them today." She picked up a corner and waited while Makaha, Polunu, and Leia found the other corners. With the bedsheet gathered up between them, they moved it to the rinse water. Dolores remembered Maria letting her wring the sheet out by hand. She half wished she had time to make these three do that. Instead, she showed them the wringer and let Makaha wrestle with the crank.

"Don't just stand and watch him do it," Dolores warned the others. "You have to sort those two baskets and get another sheet ready."

It was a warm afternoon for February. The ever-present trade winds had stilled, and the palm fronds drooped on the trees. Birds sang from hidden shady places in the yard's foliage. Nothing moved that didn't have to. Makaha, Polunu, Leia, and Dolores sweated until they were as wet as the sheets before they went through the wringer.

Makaha stopped the crank at one point and stretched. He reached his arms to the sky and arched his back. Dolores waited for him to finish. "Back to work," she said.

Dolores prodded each of them until they finished the laundry. By that time the sky had turned red and orange from the setting sun. Orange light splashed on the children and made them look as if they were on fire. Makaha's shoulders slumped, and Polunu bent at the waist, hands on his knees, trying to catch his breath. Leia stood next to Dolores and said, "You think you're sore today? Ha! Wait until tomorrow!" Although Leia tried to hide it, Dolores could see fatigued muscles tremble in the girl's arms.

When they all gathered around the dinner table that evening, the usual chatter was gone. Kanoa disappeared behind his paper. Kaipo, Nui, and Koa ate without their usual banter, their hands and arms reddened with sugar cane cuts. Makaha's and Polunu's eyes were half closed. They swayed in their seats and woke up for a moment to eat a bite. Then they drifted off again. Leia wasn't much better. Meli and Kali stared wide-eyed at everyone.

Noelani broke the silence when she brought out a chocolate *haupia* pie. "You all work hard today, ya?"

Dolores's mouth watered as she put a bite of pie in her mouth. Chocolate and coconut heaven.

"Dolores is one strict luna," Makaha said.

Kanoa's paper rustled as he lowered it. "Luna is no joking matter, Makaha. Many very strict men oversee our work in the fields. Cruel men, even. Our Dolores is not a luna."

"Could've fooled me," Makaha said, but so low Kanoa couldn't hear.

ON Easter Sunday in April, parishioners decked the church with strands of plumeria and gardenia and hibiscus. The celebration of the Savior's resurrection lightened Dolores's heart and gave her hope. She vowed to talk to Maria on the ride home about an idea she'd been considering more seriously since she first imagined it.

Dolores regaled Maria and Peter with tales of her three helpers and mentioned learning to cook. She looked at the glow of happiness that surrounded Maria. A new Easter hat and dress made her look even brighter. "Spring is a time of new beginnings," Dolores said, parroting words from the morning's sermon. "I long for a new beginning every day."

"I'm sorry, sweetheart. Wish there was something I could do," Maria said.

The door opened. No more time to plan how to say it. Dolores said, "Maybe you could let me live with you." The words dropped like rocks. The silence that followed them seemed even louder. Dolores's stomach twisted.

"That's a wonderful idea, but I don't think we can manage it just yet." Maria shot a glance at Peter, who looked out the window and seemed lost in his own thoughts. "We're struggling to pay our way and get started. I'll talk to Peter, though, all right?"

Dolores nodded but was silent for the rest of the ride.

Over the next few hours, the heat from the kitchen beaded Dolores's brow and seared future plans from her mind. Dolores crossed herself and cut another onion. Noelani banged through the screen door and collapsed into her chair at the big table. She looked grim, her hair dark with sweat against her face. Dolores put the onions into the pot with shaky arms. "You look tired," she ventured.

"You tired too if you be me." Noelani leaned forward so Dolores could get a better view of the steel in her eyes. "Kanoa hurt his back, ya? His work all pau." Her hands lifted to the sky in a gesture of disgust. "He sit listen to the music, and I work hard to look for the new customers. *Moloā kāne!*"

Dolores frowned. An injury didn't make Kanoa lazy. Her brain whirled with possibilities. If she moved out, Noelani would have one less mouth to feed.

That afternoon's lū'au was more sedate than usual. Softer music played, and it seemed like fewer 'ohana had come. Most of the men would have heard about Kanoa's injury. Were they staying away to make the load easier? Dolores served poi and poke, teriyaki chicken and pineapple rice. She took the empty platters back into the kitchen, rinsed them, and filled them again.

At night, Dolores fell into bed and dreamed of a life with Maria and Peter. She'd never been to the dairy and imagined the house and buildings and cows. At school, she daydreamed of working at the dairy, laughing with Maria, cooking, and cleaning.

After school, she arrived at Noelani's as smiling and happy as if Maria had already agreed. Her three helpers were waiting on the back lanaʻi with fearful expressions on their faces. That gave Dolores pause. She didn't want them to be afraid of her. Maria hadn't been friendly at first, but Dolores had never been afraid of her. She wanted to work with the other children, not lord it over them. "So which basket should we do first today? Leia, why don't you pick?" Leia, startled, pointed at a basket of brightly colored clothes. "Good choice," said Dolores with a smile. "Let's get to work. Shall we sing to pass the time?"

The four of them worked together. Leia sang softly. Peace spread over Dolores. It was pleasant when everyone had a task they completed without complaint. Then Polunu's sugar cane fell out of his pocket into the washing machine. He dove in after it and his belly knocked the laundry onto the floor.

"*Pupule!* Crazy porker!" Makaha held his arm with his other hand. "You wrenched my shoulder!"

"My sugar cane," Polunu began.

"Now is not the time," Dolores said. "We have to redo this entire load. Before we do so, we have to get mangled sugar cane out of the rollers!"

Leia rolled her eyes.

"We have no time for that, missy!" Dolores snapped.

Leia stepped up to help her, eyes wide.

Dolores wondered if they would behave differently if they were doing something they loved. She retreated into dreams of life with Maria and Peter.

❦ SEVEN

Summer 1924

One Sunday late in August, Maria seemed preoccupied during Mass. When they settled themselves on the streetcar for the ride home, Dolores said, "What's wrong, Maria?" Peter grinned like Polunu holding a fresh stick of sugar cane. "What?" Dolores asked. "Tell me."

"I'm going to have a baby," Maria said with an incredulous voice as if saying it out loud was still too new.

"A baby? Oh, Maria, that's wonderful!" Dolores felt her eyes widen and her heart quicken. She reached out her arms and hugged her friend tight.

"Do you want a boy or a girl?" Dolores asked.

"Boy," Peter said.

"As long as it's healthy," Maria said, but Dolores knew she wanted to give Peter what he wanted.

"You'll be a great mom." Dolores's brain spun into action. She knew Maria helped Peter run the dairy. Maybe she would need help with the baby. Before she could stop herself, Dolores blurted, "You'll need help at first. Maybe now I could come live with you? And help?" She wanted this so much her knees trembled. But how forward of her to just ask outright.

Peter frowned, but Maria said gently, "We love you, Dolores." She gripped Dolores's hand as she looked up at Peter with arched eyebrows as if pleading with him to say yes.

For the longest moment in the history of the world, the

streetcar was silent. From the corner of her eye, Dolores could see the sunshine and palm trees that lined the road. They flashed by as if they marked a faster time than Dolores could perceive. The promise of a better life hung just out of grasp, so close her heart yearned to snatch it.

"We won't be able to pay you," Peter said slowly.

Maria turned to Dolores. Her eyes were shining. "But you'll share everything we have. You're my sister, after all."

"Are you serious?" Dolores couldn't believe it had been so easy. She would be free of Noelani and her endless laundry.

"We can't bring you right away," Peter said. "How about end of September? Maria will be quite far along by then and might appreciate the help."

"Might? I get breathless now if I do too much!"

"Then don't do too much," Dolores said, smiling at her friend. The vision sparkled in her head. She would feel the satisfaction of walking out. Only one short month. "September, then. Thank you so much! You don't know how much this means to me."

Maria hugged her close. "Yes, we do. Keep aloha in your heart until then."

They reached Dolores's stop before she could gather words to respond. She hugged both of them good-bye.

"*A hui kaua.* Until we meet again," Peter said with a smile.

Dolores smiled back, her heart full. Numbly she got off the streetcar and walked to Noelani's house that had never been home. She stood for a moment on the front walk. The flowers carpeted the house as they did at all times of the year. Today Noelani's huge wicker chair sat empty. Dolores felt nothing.

Inside, Kanoa sat listening to slack key guitar on the wireless. Dolores thought she recognized Sonny Cunha's "Honolulu Hula Girl." Since there was no harm in being friendly, she said, "Sonny Cunha?"

"Very good. His guitar *no ka 'oi.*" His voice was straining to be kind, unusual for Kanoa.

"The best," Dolores echoed. She didn't hear Noelani in the kitchen. "Where's Noelani?"

"Shopping?" he guessed with no interest.

Dolores peered at him, noticing how awkwardly he was sitting in his chair. "Does your back hurt, Kanoa?"

He nodded. "No more working cane for me until it heals." His voice held so much dejection that Dolores wanted to pat his arm.

At a loss for more words, she headed to the girls' room. Deep under the bed she now shared with Leia, dust covered her old suitcase. The boys hadn't swept as they should have. She pulled it out and used a sheet corner to wipe off the dirt. One month until she would be free of this family. She muttered a prayer under her breath: "Please, Lord, allow Noelani to let me go. Amen." She knew it would be hard for Noelani to let the laundry income dwindle, since Kanoa couldn't work.

"Whatcha doin'?" Leia asked.

Dolores stayed on her knees and pushed the suitcase back under the bed. She turned to see Leia in the doorway. Leia was hanging on to the door jamb with one hand and leaning so her long dark braids swung free like two thick ropes. She seemed so much older than when Dolores had first met her. Big dark eyes regarded her with curiosity. Dolores didn't want to lie to her, but she would not be the first one to hear of her plans. In fact, there was no need to tell anyone anything. Not yet. "Nothing."

She shrugged, bored. "Hiki nō." She bounced onto the bed, captured one of the braids in her hands, and fussed with the yellow bow tied to the end.

For two weeks, Dolores supervised Leia, Makaha, and Polunu doing the laundry while she cooked. Noelani sewed for hours at a time, making up for Kanoa's lack of work. The

Iwilei girls she sewed for had spread the word, and new orders were coming in. Late into the night, Dolores could hear the whir of the machine. Kanoa's back still pained him, but he refused to see a doctor. "No money for that," he said.

Despite Noelani's efforts, the family didn't make as much money as they had before Kanoa's injury. One afternoon at the end of September, when Dolores came in from the back lanaʻi to start dinner, Noelani was sitting motionless at her sewing machine, staring off into space. A beautiful silky fabric of green and gold rippled over the sewing machine table and Noelani's lap.

"Noelani?" Dolores said.

She turned to look at Dolores. "Just tired." She tried to smile. "Time for dinner already? My, the time she fly." Her words were light but worry etched deep lines near her eyes and her tone was flat.

Maybe this was the time to tell her about Maria and Peter. Dolores took a bowl of chicken pieces out of the refrigerator and pushed errant strands of hair out of her face. "I might be able to help."

"ʻAe? Yes?"

"Maria and Peter have offered me a job." Best to make it sound like improved employment rather than preferred family.

"How much kālā you bring home? It betta' make up for the laundry you not be doing."

"ʻAʻole kālā. No money." Dolores told her, hoping the Hawaiian negative would soothe her. "They want me to live with them and work for room and board."

Noelani rocked back in the chair and tossed her chin to the sky. Her hands rested on her belly as she guffawed. "Oh, dat be good! Such an innocent keiki! Why would you leave here and go somewhere else where you have to work hard?"

Dolores kept quiet. It wasn't the hard work she wanted to leave, but she couldn't say that to Noelani.

She shook her head and got to her feet. "You say yes, ya?"
Dolores nodded. "When you go?"

"Next week."

"You crazy little haole, Dolores," Noelani said and bent over her sewing.

The news spread quickly. By the time everyone gathered for dinner, the older boys were staring at Dolores, their expressions ranging from Nui's curiosity to Kaipo's hostility. Kanoa's *Honolulu Bulletin* lay unopened next to his plate. He and Noelani looked at each other, then at Dolores, then back at each other. Part of Dolores wished she could immerse herself in the simpler world of the boys, who pinched and kicked and poked under the table among giggles and grunts.

"Nui, could you please pass the *laiki?*" Dolores asked.

The bowl of rice made its way around the table. She spooned some onto her plate. Normally the table buzzed with conversation. Now even the younger children noticed and fell silent.

Noelani spoke. "Dolores leaves next week."

Her words seemed to give the others permission to discuss her life. Like a floodgate bursting open, the questions rushed toward her.

"Where are you going?"

"Who's going to do the laundry?"

"Is she going to California?"

"Why now, Dolores?"

Dolores didn't know who to answer or what to say. Kanoa answered, "Dolores has taken a position in the Gabler household."

Kaipo and Koa looked at each other, confused. Nui turned toward her. "Maria and Peter?"

She appreciated that he looked at her instead of checking each answer with Noelani. "Their first child will be born later this year, and they've asked me to come live with them and help out."

Nui smiled encouragement, but Kaipo choked on his food. "She needs help with one pregnancy? Crybaby haole!"

Nui's smile disappeared and he turned on Kaipo. "Pau, Kaipo. You've sniped at Dolores for too long. Leave her to enjoy her last week with us in peace."

Silence fell over the table. Dolores wasn't sure if she liked this uncertain calm or not. It was too unusual. When her plate was empty, she escaped the table and went to the back porch. The sky lit up with impending night, producing another stunning Honolulu sunset. Dolores heard someone coming and tensed until she realized it was Nui.

"I know how it is with you," he said. Dolores waited. "You are young and deserve to be happy. Can you be happy with Maria and Peter?"

"'Ae, I can. They're good to me. At first the work will be lighter." Dolores smiled. "It'll be like a vacation. Once the baby is born, it'll be busier. Not just baby work, either. I'll help with the dairy and in the house. I'll be part of the family."

"You're family here," Nui said. Dolores didn't respond. "You work hard. I'm sure you will be an asset."

Dolores beamed at his words. For the first time, she felt pride in the new muscles her work had produced. She *would* be an asset. Confidence flooded her. "Mahalo, Nui. I will miss you the most."

"The most?" He snorted. "You mean the only!"

They laughed together. To her surprise, he wrapped her in a warm hug. "*Pōmaika'i*, little sister."

"Mahalo," Dolores whispered as she savored his good luck wishes.

He patted her head like a big brother would, and then went back into the house.

On Saturday morning, Dolores smiled as she pulled her

packed suitcase out from under the bed. Kali and Meli slept in a tumble, strands of their dark hair snaking across each other. Leia was already up. Dolores dressed quickly and headed for the kitchen with her suitcase.

Noelani and Kanoa sat at the table. The house was quiet, so Makaha and Polunu must have gone out to plan some mischief. Nui, Kaipo, and Koa were absent. Dolores set her suitcase by the door and ignored the fluttering in her stomach.

"Aloha, keiki. Have some breakfast," Kanoa said.

"Aloha, good morning. How is your back?"

He grimaced and gave her a so-so hand gesture.

Noelani said nothing but pushed plates of food toward Dolores. The normal breakfast of bacon, rice, poi, and eggs was there, but she'd also made Portuguese sausage and coconut pancakes. Liliko'i syrup, made from passion fruit, and pineapple orange juice, completed the offerings.

The gesture touched Dolores. Noelani had made an effort to prepare a special breakfast. Dolores smiled and heaped Portuguese sausage and pancakes on her plate, dousing it all with the sweet liliko'i syrup. "Mahalo, Noelani. This is 'ono." It *was* delicious.

Kanoa smiled at her use of the Hawaiian words. "Stay another year and we'll have you speaking Hawaiian like a kanaka."

"Pau, ku'uipo. Dolores made her decision, ya?" Noelani said.

Dolores stared at her plate so her shock wouldn't show. She'd never heard Noelani call her husband "sweetheart" before.

"'Ae, I know," he said. "I'll help with the laundry today."

"'A'ole!" Dolores protested. "Leia and the boys have been doing it all summer. They'll be fine."

An awkward silence fell, and Dolores ate quickly. Noelani returned to the kitchen to do the dishes, and Kanoa disappeared behind the *Honolulu Bulletin*. He was looking at the job postings, maybe hoping for some work he could do until his back healed enough for him to return to the cane fields. Dolores had seen injured men before. If they couldn't work, they had to leave the plantation house. Where would Kanoa go with his large ʻohana? Maybe it would be enough that Kui, Noa, and Kaipo worked in the fields.

She left the table and perched on the edge of a large rattan chair near her suitcase. Peter would be here soon. Outside the palm trees swayed in the plumeria-scented breeze. Behind her, Noelani bustled in the kitchen without her usual humming. Kanoa stayed at the table for another cup of Kona coffee.

When Peter pulled up in front, it was Dolores's moment. She savored it, watching him get out of the truck. In her head, she imagined herself calling good-bye as she flounced out the door. Instead, Noelani came over to her.

"You do good work, Dolores. Maria lucky have you. The younger girls look up to you. They will miss you, ya?"

"Umm, hiki nō," Dolores said. She stood and pushed past Noelani. Peter had almost reached the door.

"Pōmaikaʻi!" Kanoa called. He raised his coffee cup.

"Mahalo," Dolores said, thanking him for the surprising good luck wishes.

She picked up her suitcase and opened the front door. Peter was waiting halfway down the walk. Dolores frowned. She wanted to walk the whole way to the street as she'd always imagined. She looked back at Noelani. The large woman stood alone in the center of the room. Lazy fan blades rotated above her. Her shoulders slumped, and the look on her face was bereft. Dolores hesitated, one hand on the door, shocked. Noelani had always been full of booming laughter. Now she shrank in on herself. Dolores swallowed and pursed her lips. It didn't matter. She was leaving, and Noelani would find someone else to do the work.

Kanoa crossed the room and put his arm around his wife.

"Aloha," he said with a smile. He, at least, seemed happy for Dolores.

"Aloha," Noelani echoed.

"Mahalo," Dolores told them as pulled the screen door shut with a bang. Then Peter was there, taking her suitcase, and her heart flew free.

"Ready, Dolores?" he asked.

"Oh, yes." Dolores climbed into the truck. She never looked back, only forward to her future. She had anticipated this leaving, picturing it as glorious revenge against her papa, against Noelani, even against Kaipo.

❦ EIGHT

Maunalua 1924

She'd never been alone in the truck with Peter before. Shyness captured her tongue.

"Glad to be leaving?" Peter asked as he started the engine. Dolores just nodded. She tucked an errant brown curl behind her ear and bit the inside of her lip.

"Maria is glad you're able to come early. She has a room ready for you."

"I've never had my own room."

"It's about time that changed." He grinned at her.

They chatted about the weather, about Maria's health, about Dolores starting fourth grade in the fall. After about twenty minutes of driving out toward Diamond Head, Peter approached Maunaloa. "We have ten acres," he told Dolores, "and we supply milk for several local stores."

He pulled into a dirt lane that led to an attractive small house surrounded by a white picket fence. Cheery windows, open to the breeze, flanked the door. The roof peaked above the door and sloped sharply to the eaves. Beyond the house, Dolores could see buildings, the cow barn, and whatever else a dairy needed. Peter helped her out of the truck and grabbed her suitcase out of the back. "Let's go. Maria is eager to see you!"

Maria waited on the porch for Dolores and hugged her

close. "I'm so glad you're here! I've been waiting forever for this day!"

Dolores couldn't answer. Tears clogged her throat. Instead, she hugged Maria and then stepped back in horror. "I didn't hurt the baby, did I?"

"No, silly, my tummy protects it." She rubbed the small of her back.

Maria led Dolores into the house. The large front room boasted two comfortable couches, a coffee table, and a table with a radio on it. To the left was a large kitchen, but Dolores only glimpsed it before Maria dragged her down the hall to her new room. She stood back, excited to watch Dolores enter.

Dolores stepped into the room and froze. A wooden bed covered with a pretty quilt was pushed against the wall, with a low dresser across from it. Curtains billowed around an open window. A jar with fresh wildflowers sat on the dresser, and a round rag rug lay near the bed. Dolores took it all in. This whole space was hers alone. She turned to Maria with shining eyes. "Oh, it's beautiful!"

Maria clapped her hands. "I'm so glad you like it! Peter built the bed, and the dresser is an old one he refinished for you. I made the quilt and the rug. We want you to feel at home."

"This is much better than any real home I've ever had," Dolores said.

THE dairy reminded Dolores of her father, who'd worked as a dairyman on Kaua'i a thousand years earlier when she was a child. The soft lowing of the cows and the pungent odor of animals felt more like coming home than anything Dolores had yet experienced in Honolulu. Dolores loved the cows' big brown eyes and the sound of milk streams shooting into metal buckets. She remembered how her father used to let her and

Paul help—even though they must have slowed his work more than helped.

She sent Papa a letter with her new address and received one letter in response, with vague encouragement. Nothing since, but it didn't matter. At Maria's, even the work was fun since friendship and laughter lightened her heart every day. She remembered thinking about becoming a laundress and earning money for her own passage to California. Since then she'd learned to cook and sew. She could earn her way but was no longer sure she wanted to.

One Sunday, Maria and Dolores had just changed out of their church dresses and were about to begin preparations for supper. Happier than she had ever been at Noelani's, Dolores tied an apron around her own waist. Hard work alone had never brought her aloha. Love of family, working for family, did. She pretended to struggle with tying the sash of Maria's apron around her belly.

"There, I think I've got it secured," she told Maria. Maria turned to face her. Something in her friend's expression dimmed Dolores's joy. "Maria? What's wrong?"

"I've been thinking a lot. About the baby, of course, but also the dairy. Peter's working hard, but he's going to have to hire someone to manage the dairy while he's on duty at the fort. I know he doesn't want to."

Dolores waited. Nothing so far was news to her. She, too, thought it was too much for Peter to run the dairy in addition to playing saxophone in the regimental band at Fort Kamehameha.

"While I was downtown shopping last week I went by the Moana. The Hawaiian women there still need help making leis."

"Oh, Maria, don't be silly! You can't sit out there and make leis in your condition. Or with a baby. Peter will never approve."

"You're right. I can't. He won't. But I have an idea. When school starts, I'll drive you in the morning. I can stop by the

Moana and pick up fresh flowers. I'll make the leis at home in the kitchen and deliver them to the ladies at the Moana when I pick you up after school."

"But how will you convince Peter to let you drive me?"

"You two worry too much. This baby's not due until the end of the year. I can make this work well into fall. The extra income will be nice. Don't tell Peter."

Dolores wasn't convinced. Families didn't secretly take on jobs. Families should be open and honest with each other. It was part of the love, part of aloha. "I won't tell," she said.

PETER hovered over Maria. He had followed the Olympic Games in Paris that summer very closely. Maria caught Dolores up with the news. "Warren Kealoha took a gold medal in the hundred-meter backstroke, and the Kahanamoku brothers both medaled in the hundred-meter freestyle. Duke took silver and Sam got the bronze."

"That's great," Dolores said. "Way to represent Hawai'i!" She turned back to the tiny shirt she was hemming.

Maria had her own pile of tiny baby clothes to sew, and they chatted as they stitched. Peter had painted a small room in green and built a solid wooden crib. The crib and wooden rocking chair they'd painted white, along with a dresser that could be used as a changing table. Dolores used every minute of the days as she prepared for Maria's baby and worried about making leis in the kitchen.

Peter loved to share news of the outside world with them. The dredging of the Ala Wai Canal fascinated him. It would run parallel to Waikiki and drain the wetlands between downtown and Diamond Head. "It will extend the usable beach area of Waikiki. They'll build more hotels and tourists will flock to Hawai'i," he told them.

"And this is a good thing?" Dolores asked. She thought of Maria making leis with the Hawaiian women at the Moana Hotel.

"Can't stop progress," he said with a grin.

"Speaking of progress," Maria said, "I'll drive Dolores to school. That will free you to spend more time in the morning at the dairy before going to the fort."

"Oh, no," Peter began.

"Think about it," Maria interrupted. "I'm not a fragile orchid. I can drive back and forth to Honolulu without hurting the baby."

"You're the strongest woman I know." Peter's eyes filled with love.

Dolores felt sick at the deception. Later she asked Maria, "Why don't you tell Peter what you plan to do?"

"No, he likes to be in charge. The man of the house, you know? He wants to support his family. I don't want him killing himself when I can help."

Dolores nodded. Peter did look more tired these days.

ON the first day of school, Dolores climbed into the truck and waved back at Peter, who had to clean the barn before a buddy picked him up for work. Peter leaned on his hay rake and watched them with a stern face.

"Bye, hon!" Maria called. "Have a great day!"

"You send someone for me if there's a problem," he warned.

"Yes, yes, I'll be fine." With a big smile and a jaunty wave, she pulled out of the yard.

"Do the ladies know you're coming today?" Dolores asked.

"It's all set up."

The worry didn't leave Dolores as she reentered the routine of school. Fourth grade didn't look like it would be any different from third, except the math would be harder. After school, Maria was waiting in the truck. Dolores climbed in, taking a deep breath. "Oh, it smells wonderful in here." She turned to look at the boxes of purple and white orchid leis in the back. "How did it go?"

"I'm a little rusty, but my fingers remembered how to thread them onto the needle." She grinned at Dolores, obviously thrilled with her success.

They drove to the Moana. Dolores helped carry the boxes to the stand where the Hawaiian women sold leis, flower hairpieces, and shell necklaces. They greeted Maria warmly. Dolores returned to the truck while they completed their business. All the way home, Maria chattered happily as Dolores imagined scenes where Peter discovered them buried in orchids.

FALL in Honolulu often slipped by without notice. The sun still shone, the trade winds still blew, and there were no pretty fall leaves. Dolores marked the season watching Maria's belly increase. Peter pretended to fear his wife would explode like the volcano, but every day he laid a gentle hand on her belly. When he finally felt a kick, his face glowed with joy. Peter hired a foreman to oversee the day-to-day dairy business. Maria, of course, kept making leis.

"Has Peter asked you about the extra money?" Dolores asked one day on the way to school.

"I'm lucky he doesn't know how much things cost. He thinks I'm being frugal." Maria grinned.

Dolores looked at the belly that already barely fit behind the steering wheel. "It won't work for much longer. Then what will you do?"

"I'll figure something out. Maybe we can find a secret place for you to make leis."

She sounded like she was only half-teasing. Dolores imagined sneaking piles of orchids into some secret shed on the property. "I'll do anything to help. Familia es todo."

Maria darted a quizzical glance at her. "Spanish?"

"Something my father always used to say." As they neared the school, Dolores said, "I'm doing better in fourth grade. Rose and Kimiko sit with me at recess again."

"Do you girls jump rope or something?"

"No, Maria! We are much too old for that." She grinned. "We talk about boys."

"Boys!" Maria pretended outrage. "No boys for you! Not for lots and lots of years!"

She pulled up in front of the school. "Look," Dolores said, "There's Rose with Johnny. Isn't he cute?" She leaped out and shut the truck door before Maria could answer.

Walking up the yard to join Rose, Dolores scanned the groups of students for Makaha and Polunu. They weren't there. Again. They skipped school more often now, and when they attended, they ignored her as they had when she'd lived with them. Leia must have started school, too, but Dolores never saw her.

MARIA always picked Dolores up promptly after school. Today while Maria took her leis to the stand, Dolores got out of the truck and walked along Kalakaua Avenue parallel to Waikiki Beach. A group of boys were playing in the surf. They yelled and shoved each other. She squinted to see if she recognized any of them.

"They're out of control, aren't they?"

Dolores whirled to see a well-dressed boy, a few years

older than she. His round eyeglasses made him look even older, as did the hat he wore at a jaunty angle. "I'm sorry," she stammered. "Do I know you?"

He laughed. "Nope, I'm Manolo—one of them—one of the Medeiros boys." He leaned toward her and put a hand up to the side of his mouth. "Don't tell anyone."

She nodded. "Okay." More secrets. The lei money secret weighed on her more every day. She watched the boy step into the sand and walk toward the group. They accosted him with a flood of Portuguese.

"Dolores!" called Maria.

She waved and walked back up the street to the truck.

"Who was that?" Maria asked.

Dolores shrugged. "Just a boy."

"What's wrong?" Maria asked, peering at her.

"I'm uncomfortable lying to Peter, Maria."

"A lie is when you make up a story that isn't true. You haven't done that. We're just keeping a secret, like when you buy someone a present and don't tell them what's in it."

"Peter's present is the extra money?"

"Exactly!"

When they arrived home, Dolores scooted out her door to hurry around and help Maria get out of the truck. They went inside, and Maria hid the day's lei money in an empty can deep in the pantry. Dinner was well underway by the time Peter got home. He came in the kitchen door, and kissed Maria first, then leaned over Dolores at the kitchen table. She was working on her homework.

"Are you getting all of that done?"

His concern warmed her. No one ever cared about her schooling. "I wouldn't dream of not completing it." She looked at him out of the corner of her eye.

Peter laughed. "You'd better do it all, young lady. How is your math going?"

Dolores wrinkled her nose. "I'll never work in an office or anything."

Peter turned back to Maria. "Palolo Hill is being sold," he said.

Dolores pushed her book away. Anything interested her more than math.

"They're converting one hundred seventy acres of pineapple plantation to residential," he continued.

"That's a lot of houses," Maria said.

"How big is one hundred seventy acres?" Dolores asked. Peter pushed the math book back toward her. She sighed and picked up her pencil.

THE Christmas season and the baby's arrival approached, the latter as eagerly anticipated as the festival of our Lord Jesus's birth. Dolores hung garlands decorated with foil stars on top of all the windows.

"Let me help you with that," Maria said.

"Absolutely not," Dolores insisted. "You sit down and string the garland for the tree."

"Yes, ma'am," Maria said, pretending to be meek.

Peter brought in a tiny cedar tree and set it next to the radio in the front room. He fetched a box from the hall closet. "Come help with the ornaments, Dolores."

Maria strung a garland with red lehua flowers and white orchids while Peter put some of his mother's Polish ornaments on the sturdier branches.

"These are beautiful, Peter," Dolores handed him the glass ornaments carefully.

"Someday they will belong to this one," Maria said as she stroked her stomach.

Peter went back to the closet for more ornaments. "Maria! Where's the tinsel?" he called.

"In the kitchen cabinet! I couldn't reach to put it up in the closet."

They heard Peter walk into the kitchen and go through cabinets. Dolores raised her eyes at Maria. Maria looked nervous but didn't say anything. Noise from the other room ceased. They held their breath.

"Maria, where'd this money come from?" Peter came in with the can of lei money.

"It was a surprise for you, Peter." Maria didn't even look nervous.

Dolores twisted a bit of garland in her hand. She didn't look at either of her friends. She couldn't keep the secret any longer. Peter deserved to know the truth. "She earned it making leis for the Moana ladies." There. She'd said it. Maria looked disappointed. Peter looked shocked.

"How long have you kept this from me?" he asked.

"I've been making a few leis a day since school started. I never let it get in the way of my other responsibilities."

"Do you think I can't provide for my family?"

Dolores wanted to tell him that Maria just wanted to help. She wanted to tell Maria that keeping secrets from family wasn't the way to go. She kept quiet, afraid to leave the room and afraid to say anything.

"Of course not," Maria said. "But expenses have been increasing and I wanted to help."

"Are you going to drag our baby out to sell leis?"

Dolores couldn't help herself. "She doesn't sell them, Peter. She just picks up the materials, makes them at home, and delivers the leis when she picks me up."

"So you've known all along? And not said anything?"

Dolores squirmed under his glare.

"Peter, stop it. No one deceived you," Maria said.

"Then why not tell me?"

"You worry too much."

The baby kicked and Maria's hand went to her stomach. Peter rushed over to feel the baby's foot move across her tummy. He smiled, but when he looked up something shadowed his eyes.

❦

ALL three of them waited, and not for Christmas. One evening in early December, Maria couldn't contain her discomfort anymore. "I think it's time," she said.

Peter ran for her bag and forgot where she'd put it. Dolores located the bag and the keys to the truck. They shoved her into the truck in such an unladylike manner they all laughed. Maria clutched her belly with one hand and the dashboard with the other as Peter drove to Kapiʻolani Maternity Home on Beretania Street.

"The most modern facility in the islands," he'd told them a few months earlier.

"Our son will be born there," Maria had promised him.

A nurse hustled Maria into a wheelchair. Peter and Dolores rushed alongside until the doctor banished them to the waiting room. Windows flanked one wall, open to the breeze. Peter paced, locked in his own thoughts. Dolores watched the sun set over Beretania Street. She dozed fitfully until the sky lightened. With aching back and neck, she joined Peter in pacing the floor. They stopped to listen when Maria's cries intensified and resumed pacing when the cries subsided.

Just as the sun rose over Diamond Head, their son, Henry Gabler, arrived. Maria, exhausted from a night spent in labor, nonetheless was beaming. From the moment Peter laid eyes on his son, he was smitten. He barely remembered to ask after Maria.

"*Ho'omaika 'i 'ana,*" Dolores told them over and over. "Congratulations."

The little family, herself included, came home from the Kapi'olani Maternity Home to a welcoming environment. When he wasn't playing in the army band, Peter worked outside from sunup until sundown on the dairy and with the cows. Dolores kept a garden near the kitchen. Maria focused on the baby.

"How do you suppose this diaper works?" Maria asked Dolores, only half in jest.

"Didn't he come with an owner's manual like the appliances?" Dolores teased.

Maria laid Henry on the bed and struggled to undo the safety pins on the cloth diaper. "They showed me how in the home," she said. "But he didn't wiggle this much for them." Henry kicked his feet.

Dolores held her nose. "So much for that pleasant baby scent."

Maria pulled the diaper off. As soon as the air touched him, Henry peed a stream of urine straight into the air. "Aaah!" Maria exclaimed, throwing the clean diaper over her son.

Doubled over with laughter, Dolores wiped her eyes. Maria glowered at her and picked up the wet diaper. "You take this one," she told Dolores.

"He peed on the clean one, too, right?" Dolores asked.

Maria groaned. "We'll never keep up with clean diapers! Grab his feet and lift him a bit." Dolores did. Leaving the diaper that covered Henry, Maria slid another clean one under him.

"Ready?" Dolores nodded. "Okay, take it away." Dolores snatched the soiled diaper, and Maria hurried to bring the ends of the new diaper up between Henry's legs.

"We did it!" Dolores said.

Maria fussed with the safety pins. Henry kicked, and a pin stuck him. He howled, and Maria's eyes went wide. "Oh, no!"

Dolores peered at the baby's skin. "It's just a poke. He's fine, aren't you, baby?" Her high, light tone captured Henry's attention. Maria pinned the diaper and slid on plastic pants to cover it.

"I'm worn out," she told Dolores.

"I'll get his bottle," Dolores said. She went into the kitchen and warmed a bottle of formula made from evaporated milk while Maria moved into the front room with Henry. Dolores watched as Maria fed her son.

Sometimes Dolores bathed Henry, but the bulk of the baby work was Maria's. That left the house to Dolores. She made it her personal mission to keep the house clean. She always swept out the back door to keep all their misfortunes behind them. Dolores kept every superstition she could since she didn't dare offend any deity. God had his place in more than one culture, after all.

Peter gave direction to the dairy foreman and went to work at the fort. When he arrived home, he immediately sought Henry. "Where's my boy?" he called from the front door.

Dolores, finishing dinner preparation in the kitchen, smiled. "Having his diaper changed," she called back.

Peter headed to the baby's bedroom. Dolores could hear laughter and the voices adults use with small babies they adore. Then silence. She stopped stirring the sauce and listened.

"You know I didn't mean that." Maria's raised voice sounded defensive.

"Well, you've lied to me before." Peter stalked down the hallway. He looked into the kitchen at Dolores, a storm on his face. "Anything you need to tell me? Any other secrets I should know?"

Dolores shook her head in consternation. Peter went out-side. Through the window, she could see him walking to the barn. She turned off the sauce and untied her apron. "Maria?" she called as she headed for the back of the house.

Maria sat in the rocking chair in Henry's room, the baby in her arms. She looked up at Dolores with a stricken look. "Will he ever forgive me?"

"What now?" Dolores leaned over to hug Maria. It wasn't the first time in the last few months that the lei incident had reared its ugly head.

"He doubts everything I say. He doesn't trust me." Maria took a deep breath. "I may as well be cheating on him the way he's treating me."

"Cheating?" The idea shocked Dolores. "Of course, he doesn't think that. You never lied to him. You just didn't tell him. When he asked, you told him the truth."

Maria smiled as her words to Dolores echoed back at her. "I know, I know. It doesn't seem to matter. And to make mat-ters worse, the money is spent."

"Let me go finish dinner. You sit and rock Henry for a while. That helps." Dolores walked straight through the kitchen and outside. Peter leaned against the plank wall of the barn.

"She send you out here?" he asked.

"She's too upset. What are you thinking? This is your first Christmas with your son. It should be joyous. You love Maria and she loves you. Everything she's done has been to make your life together better."

"Every time I see the baby in a new outfit I wonder if she's bought it with that money, if I couldn't provide it for my son."

"Now you're being silly. You can love her without loving everything she does."

Peter's mouth turned up. "Sounds like something Maria would say."

FOR the first time since she'd come to Honolulu, gifts lay under the Christmas tree for Dolores. By Christmas Eve, the joy of the season had overcome all their hurt feelings. Dolores shopped along Fort Street. She planned carefully to make her small allowance stretch to three gifts, buying Maria a pretty scarf and Peter a small box of his favorite Whitman chocolates. She found a darling outfit for Henry and couldn't wait for Maria to open it. Maria and Peter bought Dolores a lovely green dress and fashionable cloche hat—something a young lady would wear, not a child. Dolores felt very grown up when she wore it to Christmas Mass. Maria and Peter enjoyed their gifts, too, and laughed as Henry fussed in the starchy new outfit.

After the excitement of Christmas morning presents, Mass, and breakfast, Dolores took Henry from an exhausted Maria. "Familia es todo," Dolores told her. "'ohana is for everyone."

Maria said, "Keep aloha in your heart, Dolores." She directed her words to Dolores, but her eyes were on Peter.

NINE

Papa 1927

The first week of sixth grade passed with a yawn. While at school, Dolores was anxious to return home where Maria needed her. Henry was almost three, his baby brother Alfred a year and a half, and baby number three would join them in January. Maria needed her. No one at Waikiki Elementary School did. Besides, taking her to school was out of the way for Peter, who already had enough to do with the army band and the dairy.

Dolores hated the rides with Peter because Maria had not stopped making leis when Henry was born. Lokelani, a woman who made leis outside the Moana, arranged for her grandson Kimo to deliver flowers to Maria after Peter had left for the base every day. At the end of the day, Kimo picked up the finished leis and paid Maria for them. Dolores feared discovery every day, either by something she let slip, by Peter coming home early, or by Kimo being late.

One day she let herself in the front door as Maria called, "Mail for you on the sideboard!"

Mail? She picked up the envelope. From California. She tapped it absently on the sideboard as she looked around the kitchen. Maria always kept flowers on the table to explain the floral scent that permeated the house. Dolores peered at the floor and sink. No flower bits. Good. "Are you feeling

better, Maria?" This pregnancy had been harder on her sister.
Maria grimaced and rubbed her lower back. "Still sick
every morning and aching all day. Don't worry about me.
Open your letter."

Dolores tore it open.

Dear Dolores,

*I still love California and have a good job here, but I find
that my home is not complete. Paul and I rattle around a
house we rent in Sunnyvale. He's fourteen now, strong for
his age. I'm sure you wouldn't even recognize him. I know
you have built a new life there in Hawai'i, but would you
consider joining us in California so the family can be
whole again? Please write soon so I know your heart.*

Love,
Papa

Incredulous, Dolores read the letter again. It had taken
four years for him to call her to California. The first year after he left, she didn't think she would live until this letter, but
for a long while now she hadn't even thought of California.
Could she tell him no? The idea of refusing sickened her
stomach. They were her father and brother. She loved them.
She barely remembered them.

Dolores stuffed the letter into the pocket of her dress.
"Henry's up. I'll get him." Dolores escaped into the boys'
bedroom.

At dinner, Peter asked, "I hear you got a letter from California. Everything all right?"

Dolores nodded. "Papa and Paul are fine." She took another bite of *paella*, wondering if Papa cooked Spanish food.
Did Paul help in the house? Maybe they wanted her to come
so they wouldn't have to do the chores. Dolores sighed.

"Big sigh," Peter observed, "for nothing wrong." His eyes met Maria's across the table.

Dolores set her fork on the table. "Papa asked me to think about going to live with them in California." She wiped the milk mustache off Henry's face so she wouldn't have to look at them.

Maria sucked in her breath. Peter glanced at her but nodded. "I figured he would eventually."

"What will you say?" Maria put in.

"He left me." Dolores was proud of how even her tone sounded. "I lived on Kaua'i, then with Noelani, now here. I don't know why I would want to start over again for a fourth time."

Maria began to breathe again.

"It's your decision, of course," Peter said. "We love you, though, and would hate to see you go so far away."

Inspiration struck. "If I go to California, I probably won't have to attend school. Maybe I could quit after this year if I stayed?"

Maria smiled. "We could work something out, I'm sure."

"No," Peter said. "Quitting school is not something you trade such a life-changing event for. This decision must be made independently of such promises, Dolores, and only by you."

Abashed, Dolores hung her head. "I'm sorry, Peter." She almost called him Papa.

After dinner, Dolores went to her room to write the letter.

Dear Papa,

Life is very busy here right now. Maria has two small sons and another child on the way. Henry will be three soon. He is walking now and will soon be into all sorts of mischief. Albert is crawling and pulling himself up on things. He needs constant supervision. They're good boys, but they are boys. Maria needs my help around the house.

Peter relies on me to keep her company when she wants another woman to talk to. He's away from the house a lot, either at the base or in the dairy. I know he doesn't worry when I'm there to watch the family.

I'm not sure now is the best time to move to California.

Dolores

Dolores reread it and wondered if her father would care about the baby details. Would he even remember what it was like when she and Paul were little? No matter. Dolores sealed it and tucked it inside her math book to mail the next day. She ignored the guilt that haunted her false words. Why couldn't she say plainly that she wanted to stay?

"Dolores?" Maria poked her head into the room. "I've been thinking." She crossed to sit on the bed next to Dolores's chair. "Your Papa lost his wife and job, and then moved to a whole new world. It was hard for him, too, not just for you. He's your family. Maybe you should go to California."

Dolores stared in shock. Was Maria sending her away? "He's not family." Hearing her own words, Dolores stopped. After a minute, she said, "He and Paul are my family by blood. Families are about more than blood though. You and Peter and the boys are family by heart."

"But your father and brother could be that sort of family, too. You deserve to have your own family instead of sharing mine."

"I guess." Dolores thought about how Peter struggled to make the dairy profitable. Maybe they would be glad to see her go, glad to save money. Maybe Maria could stop lying to Peter about the lei money. Maybe they could use her room for the baby.

The next morning, in the truck on the way to school, Peter broached the subject. "You're awfully quiet. Thinking about California?"

"About family."

"I'm a father now, and I can tell you a father wants his children nearby. Circumstances made that impossible for your father, but now he wants to make it right. I can respect that."

Dolores heard between his words. *Your father can support you better than I can.* Why couldn't they come out and say so? Were they deciding she wasn't part of their family after all?

In math class, the letter to her father fell out of her math book. She picked it up, remembering the confident words within. She tucked it back in the book.

After school, she was quiet in the truck.

"Dolores? Did something happen at school? Or are you still thinking about your father?" Peter asked. Dolores didn't respond.

At home, Peter told her he would be in the barn. She nodded and went into the house.

Maria yelled from the bedroom, "Welcome home! Did you have a nice day?" Again, Dolores didn't respond. She set her books on the kitchen table. Before she could decide what to do or say, a knock sounded on the front door. Dolores answered it.

Papa stood there.

He wasn't as tall as Dolores remembered, but maybe she had grown. Papa wore better clothes than he ever could have afforded in Hawai'i, and a crisp new fedora sat on his head. He looked nervous. She stared, frozen in place, for a long minute. Then she smiled as the social graces Maria had taught her kicked in. "Papa! What a nice surprise! Come in, please." Dolores stepped back and motioned him in. "Maria, look who's here!"

Maria came out of the bedroom with Alfred on one hip, Henry clinging to her other hand. She looked quizzically at Dolores.

"Maria, this is my father, Paul James." Dolores remembered when he was Pablo Jaime, one of many dairymen in Kaua'i. Now he looked successful.

"Oh, such a pleasure to meet you!" She released Henry's hand to reach out to Dolores's father, who took it. "E komo mai, Mr. James, welcome to our home."

Henry scrambled for Dolores and buried his face in her skirt. "This is Henry, Papa. Maria is holding Alfred."

"Beautiful boys," Papa said.

Maria smiled.

"Come sit, Papa. The voyage was surely a long one. Would you like something to drink? Tea? Guava or pineapple juice?"

"You've grown up so much, my little Dolores. It's good to see you again." His eyes raked her head to toe. He took off his hat and held it in both hands.

Uncomfortable, Dolores led him inside and invited him to sit on the couch. He sat on the edge, as he had the day he'd left her at Noelani's.

"Tea?" she asked again.

"Pineapple juice," he said. "Thank you."

Dolores scurried to the kitchen to pour the drink, hearing Maria ask Papa about his voyage to the islands. Dolores got glasses out of the cupboard and clutched one for a moment. Papa was here. After four years, Papa was here. Had he come to take her away? She would have raced out the door with him only two years earlier at Noelani's. Now she had a family. Now she didn't want to go. Her selfishness brought a tear to her eye. Maybe it was better for Peter and Maria if she went with Papa.

Dolores opened the fridge and retrieved the pitcher of pineapple juice. Henry had helped her make it fresh yesterday. He'd gotten more on himself than in the container. She smiled at the memory of the little boy's joy as she filled three glasses, and half a one for Henry, and returned to the front room.

Papa still sat on the edge of the couch, holding his fedora in both hands. Maria sat in her usual chair, a pleasant expression on her face. Dolores handed the drink to her father, and he lifted a hand from his hat to take it. "Mahalo," he said with a tight smile. "That's right, isn't it? It's been awhile."

"That's right, Papa." Dolores thought she recognized the sparkle in his eye. His brown hair held flashes of auburn that echoed her own curls. She tucked one behind her ear. She handed a drink to Maria and set Henry's on the low table in front of the couch. He sat on the floor to drink it, staring at the stranger.

Dolores sat in a chair opposite her father. The ceiling fan hummed as it stirred the air. "Is it this hot in California?" she asked, trying to make conversation with this stranger.

"It can be, but it's not as humid." He sipped his juice.

The air thickened around her and threatened to cut off her air. This small talk was beastly. Dolores just wanted to scream at him, demand to talk about his reason for coming.

"So I didn't wait for your letter before I sailed," he began, as if reading her mind. "You did get mine?"

She nodded.

"Dolores is a great help to us," Maria said. "She's a member of our family. You know what, though? Let me take the boys and let you two talk." Without looking at Dolores, Maria scooped up Alfred and shooed Henry along in front of her, leaving his juice on the table.

"Mahalo, Maria," he said. Dolores thought he was forcing the Hawaiian. It wasn't his culture anymore. "You look good, Dolores, so grown up. Paul and I will have to fight off the boys."

Dolores frowned. "Are you moving back to Honolulu?" At least he could *ask* if she wanted to come. She deserved that.

"I'm sorry. I suppose I jumped the gun. Would you consider coming back with me to California?"

And there it was. The summons she had burned for, prayed for. She remembered the dairy on Kauaʻi and how happy they'd been, the warm smell of the cows, their soft lowing. Wait. Was that Papa's dairy or Peter's? Suddenly, she was unsure of how happy they'd been on Kauaʻi. Papa had grown older, as had Paul. As had she. It would never be like it had been. "Papa, I like it here. Maria needs me, and they treat me well. We are such close friends; I'd hate to lose her. Wait until you meet Peter. You'll see how nice they are and how much they love me." It all came out in a rush. The only thing left inside her was tears, but Dolores choked those back.

He sat and contemplated his pineapple juice before looking up at her. "So no? Just for now, or forever?"

Dolores's heart twisted at the sadness on his face. When Mama was alive, he was always smiling. Those days were gone, but she was tempted to go with him and try to capture that carefree spirit. She was eleven years old and thinking of the good old days of her childhood. That's what living with Noelani had done to her. And this man had left her there. Happy memories faded as images of laundry piles surfaced. Going with him to California could not have been worse than the hard work and lack of appreciation at Noelani's.

Then she remembered the lei money that Maria so desperately needed. Maria may need help around the house, but she needed money to feed and clothe her sons, too. It would be worse when the new baby came in January. "Papa, I'm not sure. I want to stay, but it may not be all right with Peter. How's Paul?" she asked, desperate to talk about something else.

"Your brother's a hard worker. He's doing just fine." Papa turned toward the door. "Thank you for seeing me, Dolores, and thanks for the juice."

"What?" Shocked, Dolores took the glass and stared. "You're leaving already? Surely you can stay for dinner and meet Peter."

"Regretfully not. I have a room at the Moana. The *Maui* sails in the morning for the mainland. If you want to come home with me, come to the hotel in the morning."

He put his hat on and tipped it toward her in a gentlemanly gesture. Then he was out the door and down the walk in long strides. Dolores stared after him. He hadn't even kissed her good-bye. She shut the door and leaned against it, weak.

Maria came out. She'd heard the door, no doubt. "Is he staying for dinner?"

"He's gone."

"Gone?"

"He asked me to go with him, like right this minute."

"You said no?"

"He sails in the morning. He has a ticket for me."

"You said yes?"

Dolores hesitated. "I didn't say anything."

Maria's eyes welled up, and she folded Dolores in her arms. "I love you so much, sister mine. I will let you go, but I want you to stay."

IN the early morning, before the sun peeked over Diamond Head, Dolores was up and dressed. She paced the kitchen, picking up her books determined to go to school, then putting them down and picking up the suitcase she'd packed last night. She heard Peter get up and slip out the front door to his early morning chores. He never used the front door. He intended to avoid her.

Leaving without saying good-bye to her friends was cowardly. She must be strong and go so they could succeed. If she lingered to say good-bye, she wouldn't leave. She picked up her suitcase and left the house before she could debate herself any further.

She caught an early streetcar to Waikiki. The dark of night lessened. By the time she stood outside the Moana, the morning sun had fired the scattered clouds with orange. A group of silhouetted boys stood in the sand next to their surfboards. Curious, Dolores set her suitcase down and walked onto the sand. The boys already headed toward the water. One noticed her and waved. It was the boy with glasses she'd seen before—Manolo Medeiros.

"Aloha!" he called.

She walked over to him. "Aloha! Out early, aren't you?"

"Nope. By the time you finish breakfast this beach is crawling with tourists. Locals surf at dawn. What's your name? You know mine."

"Dolores." She smiled and turned her attention to the glory of the sunrise. Nothing was more magnificent than Diamond Head silhouetted against brilliant orange. "Have you ever wondered why the word aloha is for coming and going both?"

"Not at all. Aloha begins with love." He tapped his bare chest. "Love yourself first." He waved his arm across his chest, indicating the sand, ocean, sky, and mountain. "Love the land." He turned to grin at her. "Love the people."

She could see spots of dried salt spray on his glasses as the orange sky faded to blue. "So aloha is love."

"Aloha is the joyous sharing of life's energy." He gave her one more big smile and then rushed to join his friends among the waves.

The joyous sharing of life's energy. Her most joyous moments all included Peter and Maria and the boys. She wasn't sure she could be joyous in California with strangers who called her family. She would work hard to make Peter and Maria's lives easier. Decision made, she whispered, "Safe voyage, Papa," and turned away from the Moana to catch a streetcar home.

❀

WHEN January of 1927 arrived, Dolores's twelfth birthday went unnoticed in the flurry of activity that heralded the arrival of Maria and Peter's third son. They named him John and cooed over his dimples.

"Another boy?" Dolores teased.

"Why do I need a daughter?" she asked with a genuine smile. "I have you, Dolores. I can't believe you almost left us because you thought the money mattered."

Dolores laughed and hugged her tight. "I'm twelve now, and I know better."

She knew better about families, too. They were a happy, loving family, the three adults and three children, but Maria still made leis behind Peter's back. Dolores thought he must know, but he said nothing. His misplaced need to provide the only income forced Maria to lie to him. While not ideal, the situation had become normal enough that Dolores no longer worried about revealing Maria's secret.

When the new baby arrived home, it became Dolores's job to chase Henry, the best job she'd ever had.

When June arrived, Dolores planned to be obstinate. "Maria needs me," she told Peter. "A sixth-grade education is enough for a future farmer's wife. I'm not going back to school in the fall. After all, I don't plan to be a secretary at one of those fancy downtown offices. I'm happy on the farm."

"And we're happy to have you," Peter said.

"It will be nice to have you around during the day," Maria said.

It surprised Dolores how easy the decision had been for them. Her future, whatever it held, was now her own. No teacher would control her days. Free to dream, she imagined working in her own kitchen, waiting for her own husband to come in after a hard day in the fields. Happy children surrounded her in these visions. It wasn't until much later that she realized they weren't her own dreams. She had just inserted herself into Maria's family.

In June, a week after Dolores's last school year ever let out, a letter arrived for her from California. What could Papa want now?

But the letter was from Paul.

Dear Dolores,

Or should I say sister? I'm sure you are quite grown up, but I only remember the seven-year-old brat we left at Noelani's.

Dolores bristled, but read on.

I'm sorry, that's not what I meant to write. It's just that this is so difficult. You see, Papa passed away last week.

The room spun and Dolores sank into a chair. Papa passed away? It had been six months since she'd seen him. Six months and no letters. Her heart wrenched, and she forced her eyes back to Paul's letter.

He'd been fine, I thought, but I found him one morning when I was about to leave for work, and I hadn't heard him up and about yet. He wasn't sick, Dolores. The

*landlady thinks he took his own life. I can't think that. I
had to give the landlady notice. I'll be out at the end of the
month. I'll be a ward of the state since I have no
appreciable income. They've found a family in Fremont I
can live with until I turn eighteen. I suppose I can handle
anything for four years.*

The letter stopped; then it continued in a deeper color
ink, like it had been written at a different time.

*I know Papa loved you, Dolores, and I love you, too. I look
forward to the day we can be reunited, but unfortunately it
is not going to be soon. I would love to have your support
here with me, but I'm also glad you didn't come with
Papa. You would also be a ward of the state then, and we
would probably be separated anyway. Stay in Hawai'i,
little sister, and be happy. I will write.*

Love,
Paul

Scenarios raced through Dolores's head of jumping on a
ship and racing to her brother's aid. She'd bring him back to
Honolulu where he could help Peter with the cows. Or they
could find their own tiny place in California and she'd take in
laundry to make ends meet. But all her dreams fled. There
was no money for passage, hers or Paul's. For now, they must
remain separated by the Pacific Ocean.

Maria came to see why she was so quiet. "Dolores? Are
you all right?"

Dolores handed her the letter as her eyes filled. She
started to cry before Maria finished reading.

"Oh, sweetheart, I'm so sorry." Maria hugged her as Dolores cried into her shoulder.

Maria probably believed them to be tears of grief. Dolores knew they were tears of guilt, and maybe fear. Going to live with her father had been her life's goal. Even when she chose Maria, the California option had always been there. Dolores felt like life had ripped her security blanket away. Shocked that she felt that way, she gasped and dried her tears. She was happy with Maria and Peter. She didn't need a back-up plan.

❦ TEN

Family Days 1930

When Dolores turned fifteen, she marveled at the number. Most days she felt much older. Maria acted younger than her twenty-six years, so they were the best of friends. With three active boys under six, their days were never quiet. The best part of Dolores's day was when she took Henry to school. Peter bought a used car and taught her to drive his truck. She jolted along the road to Waikiki Elementary, which was actually the closest public school. The next closest was Waimanalo on the other side of the Koʻolau Range. She'd rather skirt Diamond Head toward Waikiki than go around Koko Head, the headland for the Koʻolau. Besides, the twenty minutes she spent on the road led to wonderful conversations with the little boy.

"Did you know that where we live was a favorite of Pele?" he asked one day after Dolores picked him up.

"Are you learning the *moʻolelo*?" she said, focusing on the road.

He nodded. "Yes, the Hawaiian stories. Pele visited Maunalua. It was a good fishing area because so many water spirits lived nearby."

Dolores took her eyes off the road long enough to admire the thin blond hair that fell across his face. He looked like

Peter in miniature, whereas Alfred and John both had brown hair and dark eyes like Maria. "You study hard in school. I know your mother wants you to be an important man with an office someday."

Henry scowled. "What would I do in an office?"

"Darned if I know," Dolores told him with a laugh. "But you'll make good money at it and be able to support a big family."

"Yuk."

She knew he was thinking of girls and hid her smile. She felt so old at fifteen and wondered how long Henry would remain innocent. Dolores vowed to make it as long as possible.

It had only been three years since she left school, but it hadn't been long enough for her to miss her classes. She kept a smile for Henry, but inside was glad every day to drive away from the school.

At home, Kimo's truck was in front of the house. Dolores waved to him as he came out of the house with empty arms. "Aloha, Kimo! How's your grandmother?" Maria's old lei-making friend had been feeling ill, and arthritis hampered her ability to use her hands.

"Aloha, Dolores! *Tutu* is all right. She's angry because we've been trying to convince her to quit at the hotel."

Dolores nodded. "She has her own flower stand now, though, a place out of the sun where she can sit comfortably."

"Comfort is relative. She's getting too old for this. I told Maria I'm going to slow Tutu down, bring fewer flowers. That will mean fewer leis, a faster sellout. Tutu can get home sooner."

That would mean less money for Maria, too. "You take good care of her, Kimo. She's lucky to have you."

Kimo shrugged and climbed into his truck. The bumper bounced off the roadway as he drove away, scraping and clattering as it had done for years. Dolores turned toward the house.

Alfred and John were playing in the yard. Four-year-old Alfred attracted dirt like a full-grown field hand. He had only to step one foot in the yard and dust covered him. Now it looked as though he was trying to initiate John into the wonders of mud. Dolores parked the truck and rushed forward as John put a handful of dirt in his mouth.

"No, John! That's not for eating! Alfred, you should know better than to let him do that!"

"But I eat it, Dolores," The little boy said, looking up at her with Maria's large solemn dark eyes. Telltale mud streaks covered his lips and chin. "Mud no ka 'oi."

"It's the best? Oh, dear." Dolores took each of them by the hand and nodded to Henry. "Let's go inside and help your mama, all right?"

Maria was in the kitchen arranging orchids for assembling into leis. Dolores held up the hands of the dirty boys. "Which do you prefer? Leis or bath?" she asked.

"They've only been out there for a few minutes!" Maria protested, scrunching her nose. "I'll take leis. They smell better."

That meant bath was Dolores's job. They had running water in the kitchen, but despite lavish promises from Hawai'i's new Board of Supply, the water wasn't always reliable. Dolores preferred the old hand pump in the kitchen that drew water up from an ancient artesian well. It built her arm muscles to fill a pot which she then put on the stove to heat. She filled the tub with a good mix of hot and cold water and stripped the boys of dirt-encrusted clothes.

"You two hop into the tub and let's get you clean."

"I don't need to be clean to eat," Alfred said, but he looked at the water and leaned over to dip a finger in. "Water *no ka 'oi.*"

Dolores smiled. With Alfred everything was no ka 'oi—
the best. Luckily, all the boys loved the water. They preferred
the beach to the bathtub, but any water would do. They went
into the tub without a fuss and splashed enough to assist with
rinsing. By the time Alfred and John were clean, water had
soaked the bathroom walls and the bodice of Dolores's dress.

Dolores dressed the boys and shooed them off to the
kitchen. She stretched sore shoulders and used a third clean
towel to mop up the water on walls and floor.

In her own room, Dolores changed into a dry dress and
thought how different her life would be if she'd learned to
sweep or cook by age seven. She never would have met Maria.
Today she'd be somewhere in California, working hard with a
foster family that wasn't hers. Dolores froze. Working hard
with a family that wasn't hers. She loved Maria and Peter and
their boys, but more and more she dreamed of her own family.

In the kitchen, Maria had two finished leis. Up to her
elbows in purple orchids, she strung each flower, careful not
to bruise the petals. Alfred and John occupied themselves in
the corner with crayons and paper. She could see that the paper had started on the table. Some crayons were still there.
The boys had moved to the floor, as they often did, for more
room to spread out. Vividly colored animals and fish covered
the paper. A green whale flew over a pink palm tree on one.
Dolores marveled at the scope of their imagination.

"I talked to Kimo out front," she said to her friend as she
picked up a lei needle and a piece of string.

Maria nodded. "He told you, then?"

"Won't be long before he cuts his grandmother off and
makes her retire."

"She deserves it. I feel selfish for wanting to make her
continue. I've thought about how I could run the flower
stand, or how I could have you do it. But Kimo has a cousin
who's going to step in. A cousin with a large family to make

leis." Maria set down the lei she was working on. Her shoulders slumped.

"Hey now, the lei money has been a big help, but it won't make or break you."

ON Saturday they loaded boys, food, and beach paraphernalia in the truck. After Peter made a secure nest of towels for the boys in the truck bed, he, Maria, and Dolores squeezed into the front like they always did. The road to Hanauma Bay had improved over the years, but that was good and bad. While it was easier to get to the beach, it now attracted more tourists. Peter found a place to park, and they unloaded everything, giving a stack of towels to Henry so he could say he helped.

Before long, the three boys were playing at the water's edge with Dolores, Maria, and Peter watching. Dolores admired the boys, so close in age. Shouts came from down the beach. Dolores shaded her eyes from the sun with her hand. The Medeiros boys were frolicking in the surf. They splashed each other and laughed. On the beach, a girl about Maria's age was shouting and gesturing at them. A huge floppy straw hat protected her head and face from the sun. She wore blue-and-white-striped beach pajamas, the height of fashion this spring. Dolores admired the soft fabric that flowed around her legs in billowy pants. In back, the top of the one-piece outfit crisscrossed with straps. A matching blue-and-white-striped band decorated the hat.

"Those are the Medeiros boys. A large Portuguese family from the Punch Bowl area of Honolulu. Lots of wild boys." Peter clearly disapproved.

Dolores scanned the group, looking for Manolo.

Maria laid a hand on his arm. "They're fun," she said.

"Always surfing and playing pranks. There's room for that in life."

"Hmph," Peter grunted.

Dolores watched them and smiled. One thing was sure—these boys loved to tease each other. They had worked their way down the beach and now stood between Dolores and the water where the boys were playing. "I'll get the boys," she said.

"Go ahead," Maria told her. "Have some fun."

"Watch yourself," Peter warned. "Don't go far."

Dolores walked over to where the girl in the floppy hat stood, the hems of her pajama outfit licked by seawater. She smiled shyly.

"Aloha," she said. "I'm Dolores."

"Aloha." She smiled. "I'm Ruth, *irmā*, sister, to the barbarian horde." Her hand indicated the boys in the water.

One of the young men stepped forward. It was Manolo. His black hair was thin on top, slicked back by the water, but when he smiled, his face lit up like the sun parting a cloud. Dolores's heart fluttered in response. Round wire-rimmed glasses, spattered with salt spray, sat on his nose. They made him look smarter, somehow. He wore black, tight-fitting swim trunks and a brown scapular on a cord around his neck. She knew some Catholics wore them to ensure the Virgin Mary's protection despite sinful living.

"Aloha, Dolores," he said with a grin.

"Aloha," she said.

Others echoed his aloha. They shook Dolores's hand and threw their names at her. Some spoke to each other in Portuguese, and Dolores felt they must be discussing her. It made her uncomfortable yet relieved her of the duty of conversation for the moment. Dolores knew far more Hawaiian than Portuguese. She watched Henry, Alfred, and John, but her eyes fastened on Manolo as he and his brothers raced into the surf, hurdled the breaking waves, and dove into the swell beyond. Manolo ducked into the surf with his glasses still on. When he emerged, water droplets sparkled like diamonds all over his body. Dolores couldn't take her eyes off him, and her stomach quivered so much her breath grew shallow.

"Let me get the little ones out of there before they're swamped," she told Ruth. Before she could move, though, Maria had already corralled her boys and set them to making sandcastles with a small pail.

A young man detached himself from the group of Medeiros boys and joined Ruth and Dolores on the beach. He grinned at Dolores with eyes full of devilment. "Want a drink?"

She smiled in spite of herself. This would be Alfred in ten years or so. "A drink?" she asked him. He was a couple of years younger than she, too young to be offering her alcohol, and besides, Prohibition made it unlikely he would flaunt an offer of liquor. "What do you have?"

"Guava juice." He reached out to shake her hand. "I'm Alberto. Manolo is my uncle."

"Nice to meet you, Alberto. Manolo must have much older brothers or sisters to have a nephew your age."

"Alberto's mother is my much older sister," Ruth confirmed.

Alberto ran back up the beach to their spot and returned with a guava juice. Dolores accepted the sweet pink drink as another boy came up, almost a duplicate of Alberto—short and sun-browned with curly dark hair—but without the devil in his eyes. "This is my *Tito* João." Alberto laughed. "Watch out for him!"

She gave up trying to figure out this convoluted family. "Aloha, João."

"Don't let Alberto here fool you. He's the troublemaker," João told her.

"Whacha sayin', you codfish eater?" Alberto pretended to be angry.

Dolores cringed at the epithet, but João laughed. "Get away, Alberto! Go bother someone who can't resist your charms."

Alberto laughed and joined Manolo in the surf.

"I won't apologize for him," João said. "He's just a baby— eight years younger than me."

"How old are you?" Dolores asked.

"Nineteen," he said with a grin, then dashed off to leap in the surf.

That made Alberto eleven. Looking over the crowd, Dolores realized that for once her fifteen years put her in the middle of the group.

"It seems Maria has retrieved her boys," she told Ruth. "Nice meeting you. Say good-bye to Manolo for me?"

"To Manolo?" Ruth's eyes lit with speculation.

"And João, of course, and Alberto." Dolores blushed and hurried away. For the first time, her mind was full of a handsome boy. It both exhilarated and embarrassed her.

"Meet anyone nice?" Maria asked, trying to feed a banana to Alfred.

Dolores took the banana from her and broke off a piece for Alfred. "Ruth Medeiros and her brothers." She made a face at Peter. "They're nice."

Peter smiled but shook his head as if he didn't understand. "They're wild and irresponsible."

"I'm glad you had fun," Maria said. "You should do it more often."

"I'd like that," Dolores said. Images danced through her head of Manolo in the surf. He played and laughed without a care in the world. Dolores had never been carefree. Even now, her responsibility to Maria and Peter kept her busy. Her days had settled into a routine of laundry and the care of her friend's children. She'd chosen that life, Dolores reminded herself. But in reality, hadn't she just traded hard work for Noelani for hard work for Maria? When would she ever have the satisfaction of hard work for herself, her own family, her own home? She turned away from the frolicking Medeiros boys to concentrate on sandcastles and on little boys she loved but who were not hers.

On the way home that afternoon, the boys all fell asleep in the bed of the truck. Dolores sat by the passenger window. She stared out into the dusk and imagined meeting her new friends again, even though the only face she could remember clearly was Manolo's. Maria and Peter talked next to her.

Something in Maria's tone caught Dolores's ear. "Oh, ku'uipo, it *will* be all right. It *will*."

She often called him sweetheart, but her tone was full of angst. Dolores listened harder.

"Another baby is wonderful," he said. "I love you and all my children. It's just the dairy . . . I don't know . . ." His voice trailed off.

Another baby? Why hadn't Maria told her?

It was quiet for a moment as Maria laid her head against his shoulder. Uncomfortable, Dolores wondered if they had meant for her to overhear. She was right there—not a good way to keep a secret.

"I know you're worried," Peter told his wife. He'd taken one hand off the steering wheel and put his arm around her. "I am, too. But this is our child. We will love and care for it like we do all the others."

So the dairy wasn't doing well, and Maria was pregnant. She was no doubt afraid they would lose the dairy. Together with the demise of her lei business, this must have Maria tied up in knots. The rest of the ride passed in silence, each of them busy with their own thoughts of the future.

✿ ELEVEN

Manolo 1930

*A*t church the next day, Maria sat between Peter and Dolores in their usual pew. The boys were arranged between the three adults. As they settled in, Dolores laid a hand on Maria's arm. "I will pray for you," she said. She tried to give the words a weight of hidden meaning. Maria had not yet told Dolores of her pregnancy. To Dolores's shock, tears filled Maria's eyes.

"Oh, Dolores, I'm so sorry."

Dolores waited.

"The bills are piling up, and the heifer is sick, and the boys are into everything. And I'm pregnant." Her tone went dead with the last two words.

Maria loved babies. She loved to welcome people of all ages into her home for a visit or to stay. This mood was unlike her. "Oh, that's wonderful! Isn't it?"

"I suppose."

They had kept their voices low, but now Peter leaned forward. "Are you talking about the baby? Isn't it wonderful, Dolores?" He mustered an excited tone, but his eyes remained worried.

At the front of the church, the priest intoned Mass at the altar. In their pew, the tension was thick. "I don't think either of you believe it's wonderful. What's wrong?" Dolores whispered.

The tears that Maria had been holding back fell unchecked down her face.

"Mama, why you crying?" John asked.

"Shush, love," Dolores put her arm around him. "Mama's fine. She's just a little sad, but your papa and I will make her better."

John turned his attention back to the words of the Mass. He tried to join in like Dolores had done at his age.

"I need to spend more time at the fort over the next few weeks, and then the band goes to California for a week of performances," Peter said, smiling at John.

"I'll look after Maria and the boys. Don't worry," Dolores said, but she sensed there was more.

"I don't know how I'll keep the dairy. I've been talking to Hind about buying it outright."

"*Aina Haina*? Buying it?" Peter's willingness to sell surprised her. The dairy had been a dream he and Maria shared. Selling it to Mr. Hind was even more of a surprise. He'd named his ranch Aina Haina, which meant Hind's Land, and he'd gobbled up smaller dairies from Diamond Head to Koko Head. Some predicted he would own all the land *maunalua*, between the two mountains. "Where would you live?"

Maria was quicker to answer. "Tell him not to do it. He loves that dairy."

"I love you and the boys more," Peter said firmly. "It's my responsibility to make sure you're fed and healthy. The army is much more stable than the dairy business right now. There's no competition in the army and plenty of army housing near Ewa Beach."

All around them, clothing rustled as parishioners stood. Conversation broke out, and Mass was over. Dolores told her friends, "You're both being silly. The future's never guaranteed. You do your best, and you do it together. We're a team who share the responsibility of the family and farm, all three of us. We do what we must and greet our newest family member with the warmest aloha when he or she arrives. That's our job."

Maria wiped her tears and nodded. "She's right. We'll be fine, Peter."

"We're agreed then." He smiled at Dolores over her head and mouthed, "Mahalo."

That wasn't the end of the discussion though. As the weeks rolled by, Maria's pregnancy gave her more and more trouble. Besides the physical sickness, the cloud of worry that had settled over the dairy caused her to tire faster. Sometimes she clutched her stomach as if labor had already begun early. Dolores told Kimo to stop bringing orchids and quietly assumed more and more of the boys' care and the household duties. It was a testimony to Maria's physical limitations that she let Dolores do it with no protest.

Dolores made her some tea and rounded up the boys. "Let's go to the beach, darlings, and leave Mama to rest, shall we?"

They clamored around her, but Maria had already fallen asleep, her tea untouched beside her. Dolores left her a note saying they'd be back in a few hours and slipped out as quietly as she could with three raucous boys.

The truck knew the way to Hanauma Bay. Dolores didn't get to take the boys to the beach alone often, but she loved it. She pretended they were a family, her family, and her heart sang. As she parked at Hanauma, she scanned the beach for the Medeiros boys, for Manolo. When she saw him laughing at a girl she didn't know, Dolores drew in a large mouthful of air and looked away. She unpacked the truck and settled the boys in the wet sand just above the surf line. Alfred filled a tin cup with sand and upended it to make a hill. Henry, of course, roared and stomped it down. John giggled. With them occupied, she dared to look up the beach. She saw Manolo walking toward her, and her face flamed. She looked back at the boys, but he'd seen her looking.

"Dolores!" He ran the last few yards and dove to his knees next to the boys. It was like he never left the beach. Her heart hammered against her ribs.

"Who are you?" Henry asked.

"I'm Manolo Medeiros. And you?"

"Henry Gabler."

Dolores hid a smile at Henry's attempt to act grown up. "And this is Alfred and John."

"Yours?" Manolo asked.

She laughed, letting the tension ring out of her body. "They're Maria and Peter's. I'm sort of a sister to them."

"Sort of a sister?" Now he laughed. "Sounds as crazy as my family. Did you just get here? Want to walk along the beach?"

"I can't." She waved toward the children.

"Oh, I can fix that." He whistled and waved. "Helen! Come here!"

The slender girl he'd been talking to came toward them, a storm on her face.

"You didn't have to call her like a dog," Dolores protested.

He grinned. "She's my irmã. She expects it."

"Beast," Dolores teased.

"Helen Medeiros Rodrigues, this is Dolores."

"Hi, Dolores." Helen smiled at her. Dolores examined her, trying not to be obvious. She was much older than her brother, and older than their sister Ruth who'd been at the beach last time. She flushed when Helen nodded, seeing her inspection. "I'm seven years older than my brother. He's the baby."

Manolo pouted. "Helen, can you play with these three fine boys so I can walk down the beach with Dolores?"

"Are you sure, Dolores?" she asked. "He's incorrigible." She glowered at her brother and beamed at the boys. "Of course, I'll watch them. You go have fun."

"I should. . . ." Dolores protested, but Helen would have none of it.

"Go." She waved them off.

"Watch Henry," Dolores said to Alfred.

The boy turned shining eyes on his big brother. "Henry no ka 'oi."

Manolo jumped to his feet, offering Dolores his hand to pull her up. She took it. He was so carefree, such a beach bum. And he was strong. "You know," he began, "my nephew Alberto was taken with you the other day. You were all he could talk about on the way home." He grinned. "He's Helen's son."

"Really?" Dolores wondered what he had said about her. "He seemed like a nice boy."

"Ha! He'll hate being called a boy. He's eleven, but in his head, he's eighteen and surfing Waikiki every day."

"Do you surf?"

"All the Medeiros boys surf." He puffed his chest out.

"Why are you at Hanauma then? No surf here."

"Hanauma is all about beauty."

He was right. The curved beach with its white sand set against the blue ocean always took her breath away. On one side, Koko Head loomed, and on the other, Diamond Head. It was a beautiful place, but Dolores blushed when she realized he was looking at her, not the beach. When she didn't answer, he changed the subject.

"Where's Maria today?"

"She's not feeling well." Something in her tone must have alerted him.

"And it's more than physical? I understand. There's a lot of emotion and hurt feelings at my house. I'm the youngest of five children. We all live near each other up in Punch Bowl. To make matters worse, my oldest brother and sisters have children my age—like Alberto. My mother's house is always chaos with people coming in and going out, but my mother rules it with an iron hand. Volatile lot, us Portugees." He grinned.

Imagining all those people as part of a loving family floored Dolores. "How wonderful, though, to have so much family! I can't imagine. It's only ever been my brother and Papa with me, and then they left." She grew quiet, but he said nothing so she told him about Mama dying, and Noelani, and Maria, and even Peter's dairy woes.

He nodded. "One good thing about a large family is that no matter who you're mad at, there's always someone else to talk to."

Dolores smiled because he'd seen her heart. She'd never had a confidante at all until she met Maria, and she could hardly confide worries about her to her face!

They walked back along the beach to where Helen was playing in the sand with the boys. When Manolo took her hand, Dolores allowed it.

She thanked Helen for babysitting. Helen raised an eyebrow at their linked hands. Dolores grinned, knowing Manolo would be in for some teasing. He'd be good-natured about it since his sister had made it possible for them to be alone. They walked back up the beach to where their friends, maybe family, were. He turned back to wave at Dolores once.

Dolores hummed as she packed their beach things into the truck and tried her best to brush sand off the boys. It covered John from head to toe. He must have rolled in it. Alfred wasn't much better, and his mouth was ringed with sand. Had he tried eating it?

"Sand no ka 'oi," he mumbled.

Henry had waded into the water up to his knees. Wet

sand was harder to brush off than dry. When they were as clean as Dolores could make them, they headed home. Dolores hummed all the way.

Maria seemed quite restored when they returned. She even took the boys to bathe off the rest of the sand.

Dolores followed to help. "The Medeiros boys were at the beach."

"Is that so?" Maria said.

Dolores frowned and focused on rinsing Henry's legs. Did Maria disapprove? "Manolo's sister watched the boys while we went for a walk. I hope that was all right."

Maria leaned back and looked at her friend. "I know I said you should have fun. I still think so. Peter is right when he says the Medeiros boys are wild, though. They may seem like fun and all, but it's no good getting serious about them."

"Who's getting serious?" Dolores protested, but her heart flipped over.

"Get on out of here," Maria said. "I can finish, and you've had a long day in the sun."

Dolores dried off her arms and walked into the kitchen for a cold drink. Peter sat at the table, his head in his hands, hair tousled like he'd been there a while. Piles of papers covered the table.

"Peter? Everything all right?" She poured them both a glass of pineapple juice and joined him at the table.

"Mahalo." He took a sip but didn't answer for a long moment. Then he sighed. "No, everything's not all right." He indicated the tallest stack of paper. "These are bills." He indicated another stack, much shorter than the first. "These are milk orders. A few small dairies over by Waimanalo are working together as one business and cutting prices to get more orders."

"Meadow Gold? But they've been doing that for years."

He nodded. "I know, but their new ice cream venture is

very profitable. Customers are beginning to trust them as being more stable than us little independent guys."

"Oh, yes, their ice cream is wonderful!"

Peter scowled at her.

"Sorry, Peter, but you can't deny it's tasty."

He laughed. "Yes, it is. We can enjoy it while we can still afford it." That thought sobered them both.

"Are you thinking of selling?" Dolores asked him.

He held up a lone piece of paper. "This is the bill of sale. Hind has offered me a good price. I only have to figure out how to tell Maria that we're moving to the base."

"The base?" Dolores wondered how far that was from Hanauma Bay, or from Waikiki where the Medeiros boys surfed. Before she could ask, a pale Maria stood in the doorway.

"The base?"

Peter jumped up. "Oh, kuʻuipo, I didn't mean for you to hear that . . . not now anyway . . . not like that. I was going to tell you when I got back from California."

Maria stroked her stomach. "But you don't mind discussing it with Dolores?"

Peter's stricken face pushed Dolores into action. She went to Maria and put her arm around her friend. "Don't you know that you're his number one worry?" Dolores indicated the table piled with papers. "Among a lot of worries. Please don't be mad at him. You need to get through this together. I'll be there for you wherever you go."

Maria hesitated, and her husband took her hands in his. Dolores backed away.

"I'm sorry. I didn't want to worry you." His apology was elegant in its simplicity. Maria loved him. He didn't need to plead with her or give excuses.

She wasn't ready to let it go yet. "I birthed three sons for you and keep the house." She glanced at Dolores. "With Dolores's help. We have a happy home and a good marriage. What were you afraid of? Why not tell me outright that it had gotten this bad?"

He ran a hand through his hair and answered. "I didn't want to admit it to myself."

"Oh, Peter. The baby isn't due until February. You'll be with the band in California for two weeks. When you get back, there's plenty of time to make a decision. Don't do anything yet." Her eyes pleaded with him, but her words were gentle.

"Hind wants an answer soon."

"Too bad," she insisted. "This is a huge decision and we need to consider all options. Can your foreman run the dairy by himself?"

Peter nodded. Dolores enjoyed seeing Maria so much in control. He would have no choice but to go along with her. She would not accept any less.

"Yes," Peter affirmed. "He can do it. I'll only have you to worry about while I'm gone."

"And that's my department," Dolores said. "I'll take care of Maria and the boys."

"Mahalo, Dolores, for all you do," he said.

Dolores couldn't tell if Maria had thrown herself into his arms or if he'd swept her into a hug. At any rate, in front of her stood a couple in love facing a tough place in their marriage together. Dolores thought of Manolo and for the first time felt something was lacking in her life. She went to find the boys and finish making dinner.

Much later, after the boys were in bed and the goodnight stories read, the three adults settled in the front room. Peter turned on the radio for the local news. A familiar name grabbed Dolores's attention.

"Three local teens robbed a liquor store near Punch Bowl this afternoon. Police identified the suspects as Jacinto Nunes, Felix Garza, and Roberto Medeiros."

The story went on, but Peter's voice drowned it out. "See? Medeiros. They're trouble, Dolores."

"I don't know a Roberto. Could be a different family."

"They're all related and all trouble. Watch yourself."

Dolores didn't argue. Peter had made up his mind about Manolo's family from rumor rather than personal knowledge. Maria said nothing, lost in her own worries.

TWO days later, Peter left the island with the regimental band. It was the first time he and Maria had been separated since their marriage, but it occurred much as any other ordinary moment would. He kissed his wife and sons good-bye like he would on any normal morning and gave Dolores a hug. "I'm leaving her in your hands, Dolores," he whispered. She nodded. Before he left, the boys demanded promises of presents from California.

"Let's pray for a safe trip," Dolores suggested.

Maria followed her into the front room, where they knelt before the crucifix on the wall and said a private prayer for Peter's safe return. Thus fortified, Maria went to start laundry. Dolores kept the boys occupied and out of her hair.

Over the next few weeks, Dolores spent a lot of time at Hanauma Bay with Maria and the boys, with the boys alone, or on her own. Manolo was there almost every day. She learned he was an office boy for a Honolulu firm, an intelligent man, seventeen years old. He was fun and friendly, and he made her heart beat faster than doing an entire day of laundry at Noelani's. When Dolores was with him, she felt cherished—pretty and important and fun. She could forget the responsibility of Maria and the boys for an hour or two and just be a fifteen-year-old girl at the beach with her boyfriend, for that's what Manolo had become. Manolo was fun. Dolores couldn't see what Peter thought of as the wild-ness of the Medeiros boys, unless Peter was being stuffy and thinking surfing and drinking created wild men.

The first time Manolo picked Dolores up at the house to go to a movie, she was surprised. She'd never seen him in street clothes before and smiled to see his glasses free of salt spray. He wore pressed tan slacks and a white shirt with the cuffs folded back. The ribbon of his scapular peeked through at the open neck. He took her hand as they walked out of the house.

Maria called, "Have fun and don't be late!" from the kitchen.

"I thought we'd go to Fort Street and get an ice cream soda," Manolo said as they walked to the streetcar stop.

Dolores smiled. "That sounds wonderful."

They chatted like old friends while they rode the streetcar into downtown Honolulu. Dolores wasn't the least bit ner-vous, even though it was her first official date.

"I want to take you for dinner, but I can't afford it yet," Manolo said, his tone full of apology.

"It's not the price of the meal, it's the company. Do you know I was with Maria and Peter for my first trip to Benson-Smith?"

"This trip will be even more memorable," he promised.

Their conversation bounced from topic to topic. When they reached the Fort Street stop, they walked into the store and took a place at the soda fountain. It was noisy and crowded, so she didn't hear what Manolo said after he or-dered. "What? Can you say that again?"

"I got a raise!" Now he was almost shouting.

"A raise? That's wonderful! I'm so proud of you!" And she was. It was difficult to find jobs after the stock market crash the year before, even in Honolulu. To hold one and manage a raise meant something.

"It's a good job with regular hours and regular pay." He twirled his spoon in his hand. "Dolores?"

"Yes?"

"What do you think about getting married? Us, I mean." Over the initial hurdle, his words rushed forth in a torrent. "We could live in one of my mother's houses up in Punch Bowl for a while."

The edges of her vision fuzzed until the only thing in the world was the man who sat before her. "We don't know each other, Manolo."

"I love you."

"I love you too." He kissed her, then leaned back and looked at her expectantly.

"I won't marry you until I have your family sorted out!" she teased.

He laughed. "I don't know how long that will take. I won't wait forever!" They lingered as the ice cream melted, planned their future, and even named unborn children.

Still glowing when she returned home, Dolores roused Maria, who dozed by the radio. "We're getting married," she told her friend.

"Married?" Maria frowned. "So soon? You don't know him, Dolores."

Her euphoric cloud burst like a balloon. "I love him."

Maria laid a hand on Dolores's arm. "Maybe you do. I'm just saying you have to think before getting married. The Medeiros boys are wild. Great fun, yes, but not great husbands."

Stung, Dolores snapped, "How do *you* know?"

Maria patted her friend's arm. "They're not the only big family in Honolulu, or even at our church, yet I've heard a lot about them. Three boys in that family."

"And two sisters. That just proves his mother is a saint. Besides, five isn't that big for a Portuguese family." At least that's what Manolo had told her.

"They all drink, Dolores. A lot. And motorcycles and late nights . . . I just don't want to see you hurt."

Dolores covered Maria's hand with her own. "I appreciate it, Maria, I do. But this is a chance to find my own aloha instead of sharing yours."

PART TWO

1931-1942

TWELVE

Punch Bowl 1931

olores crossed the street and let herself in through the screened kitchen door. She kicked off her shoes to honor her mother-in-law's claim that wearing shoes in the house brought the devil inside. Odd belief for a staunch Catholic, but no stranger than the dozens of Hawaiian superstitions Dolores was already familiar with. For good measure, she crossed herself as she closed the screen door behind her.

Grandma Jessie peeled potatoes at the sink. Dolores watched, fascinated by how fast her mother-in-law peeled them in a single long piece. Wisps escaped the older woman's tightly wrapped bun where hints of gray tinted her dark hair. Her apron, always present, covered her dress. Grandma Jessie without her apron was like Duke Kahanamoku without his surfboard. Dolores set her basket of vegetables on the counter and leaned over to kiss her mother-in-law's cheek, inhaling deeply. "Smells 'ono in here."

Grandma Jessie smiled and waved the words away. "Ah, just the stew."

Stew was what she called whatever was in the massive pot on the stove. It might be soup, sauce, or stew depending on what she added to it. The entire family—five grown children, their spouses, and several of their children—came home every day for lunch, and preparing enough food meant a large pot.

Manolo's sisters, Ruth and Helen, bustled around the kitchen, too. Ruth grinned at Dolores. "About time you got here! The work's almost done!"

"Oh, good, but I'm sure Helen did it all."

Ruth wrinkled her nose, and Dolores grinned.

Helen was fifteen years older than Dolores and the oldest of Grandma Jessie's five living children. Her dark hair was wrapped and pinned like her mother's. Helen was overly proud of her three children and her privileged position residing with Grandma Jessie in the main house. Ruth's teasing, though, confirmed Dolores's place in the family. It felt good. Dolores peeled and chopped the carrots and turnips she'd brought and put them in the pot. She reverently picked up Grandma Jessie's battered silver ladle to stir. "Are you still sick in the mornings?" she asked Ruth.

Ruth's hand went to her belly. "Not for a couple of days now. You?"

Dolores shook her head, her own hand covering the tiny new person inside her. Married only a few months now, she and Manolo were expecting their first child the following summer. Ruth's baby, her third, would be born first. "Just a bit. Not too bad."

It had felt odd not to have Paul at her wedding, but he couldn't make the trip. Manolo's family inundated her, but it wasn't the same. During the wedding, a wave of strong floral scent surrounded her, a sign that departed family members were visiting, so Mama and Papa had been there. Peter and Maria came, of course. Peter managed the boys while Maria stood by Dolores at the altar as her matron of honor. Maria had wanted her to invite Noelani, but Dolores balked. Memories of the big Hawaiian woman still brought back her fear of reprisal and failure.

She felt an arm come around her waist. Just before a kiss touched her neck, she smelled Manolo's cologne and smiled.

"Talking about babies again? Why don't you take a load off your feet?" He led Dolores to the kitchen table, sat down in a chair, and pulled her onto his lap. Helen looked disapproving. Ruth laughed.

Dolores waved the ladle at him. "So glad you're here for lunch, *querido*. But someone has to stir." She pushed her husband away and resumed her place at the stove.

Manolo's older brother swept through the kitchen door with a dramatic flair and a dimpled smile.

"I could have brought home a whole pig for you today, Grandma Jessie," João said.

"A whole pig?"

João nodded. "I ran into a Hawaiian woman just outside our construction site. She liked my blue eyes and offered me the pig if I would make a blue-eyed Hawaiian baby with her."

Manolo laughed. "A whole pig just for that?"

Grandma Jessie added her peeled potatoes to the pot and turned to her boys. "Who wouldn't want such a handsome young man?"

They all laughed. Most of the Medeiros family laughed easily, but João found joy in everything around him. Please, Lord, Dolores thought, let my baby have that easy humor.

"I couldn't take her up on it," João said, "because I didn't have a ti leaf with me." His eyes sparkled.

Grandma Jessie said, "Oh, good thinking. You should never carry pork without a ti leaf. It angers Pele."

Dolores turned to Manolo. "Angers Pele? Never heard that one."

Manolo said, "The goddess Pele and demigod Kamapua argued and agreed to split up. He's a half man, half pig, so pork makes Pele angry if you bring it to her side of the island. Ti leaves protect you."

João got two Primos out of the icebox. He handed one of the beers to his brother and joined him at the table.

"ʻ*Okole maluna*," Manolo said.

"Bottoms up!" João echoed, taking a long drink.

Manolo's oldest brother, Frank, came in from the harbor where he worked as a longshoreman. He wore his favorite chambray shirt, softened from decades of washing. In his large roughened hands, he held a large box of Oreo cookies. Dolores hid a smile. As usual, the box was already open and half empty. Frank always brought his mother half a box of cookies. The other half went to his mother-in-law. Dolores had heard Alberto say, "Why not bring them all to your mama?"

Frank had replied, "Just covering all my bases."

Now Frank kissed his mother on the cheek and set the cookies on the counter. He, too, got a Primo and took his place at the table.

Frank was the quiet brother. From him, Baby Medeiros would learn how to listen to others and think before speaking. Dolores wanted her child to be happy, to be folded into this loving family, and to give back. Frank would show the little one how to have patience.

Helen looked at Dolores then back to her mother. "Shouldn't someone fetch *Vovô*?" She was never rude, just distant, maybe because her son, Alberto, was twelve. At sixteen, Dolores was his aunt. This must make Helen feel old.

Dolores wiped her hands on a kitchen towel. She knew bringing the old man to lunch was her job. Ignoring Helen's pointed glare, she walked toward the back bedroom. "Lunch time, Vovô."

"*Obrigado*, dear," he said, thanking her in Portuguese.

Dolores never knew if Grandma Jessie's father realized who she was. He was smart though. As the family grew and the generations blurred in his mind, he called all the women "dear" and all the men "son."

Dolores settled Vovô in his chair as Alberto's father, Antonio, came in. He went first to give his wife, Helen, a kiss. He told his mother-in-law, "I have a friend who can repair the roof on the back lanaʻi."

"Mahalo," Grandma Jessie said, still focused on getting the meal ready.

Antonio worked in the office at Lewars & Cooke lumberyard, and his round wire-rimmed glasses and thinning hair gave him a scholarly air. He knew a lot of Japanese construction workers who did side jobs for him. He joined the men at the table, and Helen brought him a beer.

Antonio and Manolo were the smart Medieros men. They made the most money and could offer the baby good business advice. Dolores pictured Tito Antonio admonishing a child to study hard, and Papa Manolo checking over homework. She'd only completed sixth grade, but she wanted her child to be well educated.

Dolores, Ruth, and Helen helped Grandma Jessie put steaming bowls of food on the table. João reached for a bowl of vegetables and knocked over the saltshaker. Grandma Jessie snatched a bit of the spilled salt and threw it over her left shoulder. "Into the face of the Devil," she muttered.

Dolores smiled. More than anything, she wanted her child to grow up with Grandma Jessie's sense of balance. The older woman prayed to the Christian God but followed superstition, too. She reminded Dolores of Noelani. Both women led large, diverse families, and neither put up with nonsense. They followed traditions they felt deeply, traditions Dolores knew would ground her child in the little one's heritage.

Ruth's husband rarely came to lunch, and her children were at school. Frank and João's wives and their children were missing, and Dolores didn't know where Alberto was, either. Still, it was a noble representation of family. It felt like Dolores's family, too, unlike Noelani's gatherings. If Dolores were to show up tomorrow with ten strangers, Grandma Jessie would throw a few more potatoes in the stew and welcome them inside with a smile.

Dolores looked around the table. These people would be the most important influences on her baby's life. They would be family. It was what she'd always wanted for herself, and what she wanted for her children. Peter had been wrong. There was nothing wild, and therefore unacceptable, about the Medeiros family. They were a large loving family who liked to have fun.

In contrast, Noelani's family, also large, had no fun. Noelani found aloha in hard work, but Grandma Jessie found it in family. Dolores preferred the Medeiros way.

The doorbell rang while they were eating, and as Dolores looked around, her confusion echoed in the other faces. No one ever rang the bell.

Frank, the oldest son present, put his napkin on the table and went to investigate. The rest of the family heard a low conversation at the front door. None of them spoke, but none of them admitted to listening, either. Frank returned with resignation painted on his face, his nephew Alberto following. "The police picked up Alberto and Noa again."

Alberto grinned. "Noa's faddah get us out."

Conversation started at once, some about Alberto's wildness and his association with Noa, the lawyer's son. It was business as usual for the Medeiros family, but it was something Dolores still had to get used to.

Grandma Jessie waved her ladle at her grandson. "Why you always raise hell? Your uncles are a bad influence on you. Those boys of mine!" She shook her head.

"Ah, Grandma," Alberto protested. "Me and Noa celebrate, ya? He goin' to school on the mainland."

"What about you? What you gonna do?" Grandma Jessie's dark brown eyes bored holes in Alberto. "If you not in school, you should be working."

"Time was," Vovô put in, "that family looked after family. Someone here must have something the young 'un can do." His lined face and stooped shoulders showed his age, but his eyes were clear and his tone firm.

"I can keep him busy for a while." João pointed a finger at Alberto. "You better keep your nose clean when you're working with me."

"I help, Tito," Alberto told him.

Antonio looked at his son dubiously, but everyone else seemed to think it was a great idea. Dolores remembered how eager she'd been to leave school at twelve. She also knew Alberto preferred surfing to working. He often skipped school to surf Waikiki, climb the palm trees for coconuts so he could drink the juice, and buy *pipikaula*, a kind of Hawaiian beef jerky, in paper cones from vendors on the beach. He was the epitome of carefree youth. Dolores was only four years older, but some days it felt like a hundred. She didn't know what a carefree day was, and she wasn't likely to find out with a baby on the way. Dolores didn't want to trade places with Alberto, but sometimes she envied him.

João nodded at him. "Change your clothes. We're due on the job in half an hour."

Alberto sauntered from the room, taking his time. Dolores hid her smile.

A few weeks later, her first Christmas season as a Medeiros arrived in a swirl of love and bustle. Manolo's brothers knew how to celebrate the birth of the Lord, and the beer flowed. Prohibition was still the law, though, and Dolores asked Manolo, "Where does the drink come from?" She didn't want the family to think she was a prude, but she remembered Maria warning her about the Medeiros boys and their drinking.

Manolo laughed. "It's available if you know where to go."

It made her uneasy, but Dolores liked seeing him have fun with his brothers. They sang "Silent Night" in Hawaiian, trading volume for hitting the correct notes. Dolores winced and anticipated hearing it sung well at church on Sunday.

Dolores and Manolo's sisters added festivity to Grandma Jessie's house. Ruth held one end of a decorated garland that Helen climbed on a chair to hang. Dolores held the other end of the garland. She put one hand on the chair back near her, preparing to climb up to hang it.

"What are you doing?" Helen's tone was sharp. "No pregnant sister-in-law of mine is going to climb on a chair!"

"All right, thank you." Dolores smiled instead of letting her anger rise at Helen's tone.

Soon Grandma Jessie's house smelled of jasmine and plumeria. The women decorated a small pine tree with coconut frond ornaments, red angels made from kukui nuts, and Santas in red canoes. Grandma Jessie always insisted on a traditional pine tree from the mainland rather than the local cedars. It was her Christmas indulgence. They hung a string of new electric lights on the tree, and everyone exclaimed how pretty they were. Dolores was a traditional soul, though, so she put candles on the tiny cedar tree in her own house.

"Electric is the new rage," Helen said.

"Let her have her own ideas," Ruth said to Dolores.

"Ruth, you still use candles," Dolores said. She could tolerate doing tasks like decorating with Helen, but she preferred Ruth's company. She was tiny and vivacious. Like her nephew Alberto, Ruth sparkled. Her eyes and hands always smiled with her face.

"Of course, I do." Ruth lifted her nose into the air and flashed a wave of disdainful dismissal. "No newfangled decorations in my house." Helen harrumphed and turned back to the garland. "Can't afford them anyway," Ruth whispered to

Dolores. They giggled until they drew matching glares from the older sister.

Ruth had two small children under two years old, and it delighted Dolores to help her with them. Ruth didn't put much stock in what was proper and often wore her dark hair loose like a girl, even though she was twenty years old. She reminded Dolores of Maria. Best of all, though, she and Dolores were so happy to share their pregnancies with each other that they were often giddy, much to Helen's dismay.

Dolores left her sisters-in-law at Grandma Jessie's and returned home. She and Manolo had moved in to one of four small houses owned by his mother in the Portuguese section of Honolulu called Punch Bowl. Dolores couldn't decide whether her favorite thing about the house was the multitude of family that surrounded them or the sweeping view down the hill to Honolulu Harbor far below.

As she crossed the street, the mailman waved. "Letter for you, Mrs. Medeiros!"

"Thank you, and Merry Christmas, Kai." Dolores took the envelope. It was a rare letter from her brother, Paul, on the mainland. He was eighteen, Manolo's age. How odd that the two men had never met. Even though he was far away, Dolores thought of her brother making his way alone in California and prayed for him. She let herself into the house and tore open his letter.

Dear Dolores,

Merry Christmas! Or do you prefer Mele Kalikimaka now? Did I spell that right? I am still living in Fremont with the Dominguez family, but I am sharing this Christmas with a special girl. I'd love you to meet Sofia. You'd get on well, I'm sure.

Dolores's eyebrows rose. He hadn't spoken to her since she was seven. Hopefully, her adult self would like Sofia, too!

We are ready for the holiday. All the stockings are hung by the chimney with care, as the poem says. A fire is blazing in the fireplace—you can't imagine how comforting and romantic that is. I think of you walking the beach at Waikiki for Christmas, and it seems a lifetime ago since I was there. Have a very happy Christmas, dear sister, and think of me often.

Love,
Paul James

Dolores held the letter in her hand as if absorbing the essence of her brother as she looked out the window that faced *ewa*, seaward past downtown Honolulu. The lush green of the hillside, the deep blue of the harbor, the vibrant color of the city—these were real to her. Paul's California seemed strange, as did he.

Dolores remembered quiet Christmases on Kaua'i with Papa and Paul. At Noelani's, Christmas had been a brief bright spot in the drudgery of daily chores. Maria and Peter's house filled with noise and love at Christmas. Watching their boys' faces glow with excitement always made Dolores happy. This was her first Christmas as a married woman. Next year she'd be a mother! Would she be a mother like Noelani, who worked her children hard? Or a loving mother like Maria? She'd have to make sure the baby found its way in a large family. Dolores shook her head. As welcoming as Manolo's family had been, the family still felt new. Only a long shared history would take that away. Baby Medeiros would no doubt feel an integral part of this family before Dolores did.

She tucked the letter into the pocket of her dress and tied

on an apron to begin dinner. Before she could reach the kitchen, the front door opened. It was Manolo. He hung his hat on the rack by the door.

"Manolo, you're home early."

"Home for good. They let me go."

"Oh, Manolo!" Was that alcohol she smelled on his breath? Anxiety nibbled at her smile.

"Just before Christmas, too. What a bunch of Scrooges." He sounded relaxed rather than upset. He waved a hand in the air. "It's no problem. I have brothers with connections all over Honolulu."

She nodded. He was the smartest of his siblings. Dolores hoped he was right about connections. They'd need the money with Christmas and the baby coming.

Later she called Maria to offer holiday greetings. In her friend's warm wishes, Dolores longed to find reassurance. "Mele Kalikimaka, Maria!"

"*Feliz Navidad,* Dolores!"

"Are you ready for Christmas?"

"It's a little different at the base," Maria said. "The military surroundings don't really scream holiday, you know? I mean, it's decorated and all, but it's not home. How's the horde at your place? You and Ruth feeling all right?"

"We feel great. It's crazy around here, full of love and drama. That's family, I guess."

As she always had, Maria zeroed in on the word that had taken the exuberance out of Dolores's voice. "Drama?"

"Manolo lost his job."

"Oh, *querida,* I'm so sorry. Must be awful with the holidays so close and the baby coming."

It was, but Dolores felt the need to make it seem fine. "A large family always helps, right? We'll be fine. So will you. How's Peter?"

But she couldn't distract Maria. "There's always a lot of

drinking around the holidays. Combined with losing his job, this might be too much for Manolo."

"Maria, Manolo doesn't drink any more than his brothers. He's not a drunk."

Maria diplomatically answered the previous question. "Peter works hard and enjoys his boys. We miss you, but we're glad you have your own family now."

"Mahalo, Maria. Give all your boys a kiss for me."

They rang off, but Dolores kept her hand on the phone for another long minute, as if trying to prolong the connection to what was familiar and safe.

✣ THIRTEEN

Carmen 1932

Manolo took Dolores to dinner in January, when she turned seventeen, to celebrate his new job. Alberto's father, Antonio, had helped Manolo land a position as a power plant engineer at Hawaiian Electric. They went to the Alexander Young hotel. The restaurant inside was fancy with its white tablecloths and linen napkins, but then the hotel was one of Hawai'i's most luxurious. Honolulu's high society gathered here in the Rose Garden, but not during a tropical storm that drenched Honolulu with warm rain. The wind roared through the palm trees as loud as the crashing surf.

Dolores held her skirt to her knees with one hand, and with the other tried to keep her cloche hat from sailing down Bishop Street. Thank God she could wear this hat pulled down over her forehead since her *lauhala* straw hat would be halfway to Diamond Head by now. Inside the restaurant, she excused herself to the ladies' room. She removed the hat and repinned her damp brown curls. Before replacing the hat, Dolores shook off the raindrops. She brushed her dress with her hand and turned sideways to inspect her baby bump. Elegant again, she joined Manolo at the table.

"I'll be chief engineer soon," he said. He looked very handsome in his new suit. His smile revealed how happy he was.

"I'm proud of you," she told him.

Manolo poured them each a glass of mango juice from the pitcher on the table. At least Prohibition prevented him from ordering alcohol. Dolores was sure they'd have a nice dinner. She spread the napkin across her lap then rested a hand on her stomach with a smile.

"How are you feeling?" he asked, nodding to her stomach.

"I'm not sick anymore. I can hardly wait to feel the baby move! Ruth says I'll feel it around four months."

"Her baby is due next month," Manolo observed. "She's huge!"

"That's no way to talk about your sister!" Dolores scolded him.

They laughed and held hands. Dolores felt a part of the aloha surrounding her.

RUTH'S baby girl arrived in February, and the Medeiros family embraced her. Dolores noted the absence of Ruth's Chinese husband, Charles Chong. They had three children now, but he never seemed to be at the Medeiros house. Ruth made vague excuses for him, and Dolores let her.

Grandma Jessie's next-door neighbor, Yoshiko, came over one afternoon when the women were in the kitchen, but the men had returned to work. She brought her son, Hiro, a good friend of Alberto's.

"My mother would like to present Mrs. Chong with a baby gift," Hiro said formally, bowing to Ruth.

"Oh, my," Ruth said.

Yoshiko bowed and spoke in Japanese. Hiro translated. "She says three is the number for birth." He offered a plate with both hands. "Three kinds of sushi. You have *hosomaki*, *nigiri*, and *inari*."

Ruth took the plate. "Mahalo, Yoshiko-san," she said, bowing back to the neighbor.

Dolores peeked at the gift. Yoshiko had arranged the sushi on a white plate covered with Japanese characters in red. Dolores recognized her favorite sushi, the inari.

"Sushi rice and fried bean curd," Grandma Jessie said, pointing to the inari. "What are the others?"

"The hosomaki has tuna and rice wrapped in *nori*—seaweed," Hiro said. He conversed with his mother. "The nigiri has egg and eel on rice. And wasabi."

"Tell her it looks 'ono, Hiro," Dolores said.

"Delicious," Grandma Jessie agreed.

AS the months passed, Dolores went about the duties of a first-time mother-to-be. She cleaned the house, sewed tiny clothes, and gathered other baby things. She'd helped Maria do all these things during her pregnancies, but she discovered doing them for her own child meant more.

Since the dinner in January, Manolo had been home on time and sober every night. Dolores hummed as she made dinner. Manolo sat at the table, reading the *Honolulu Advertiser*. Dolores knew he wanted to talk about something serious when he folded his paper and laid it down. "Queen's Hospital is the place to go for the birth. It's nearby and modern."

"We'll see," Dolores said, trying to stay neutral. She kept her eyes on the pot, where she shredded with a fork the kālua pork that had simmered all day. "Ruth had her baby at home."

"It was her third," Manolo reminded her. "The first is harder."

"Maria had her boys at Kapi'olani Maternity Home. It's nice." Dolores explored the subject cautiously. His suggestion surprised her. None of his family had been born in the hospital. Hospitals were huge and impersonal and colorless, so unlike Hawai'i and its people that she knew she was right to be wary.

Every evening Manolo came home from work and Dolores bustled around the kitchen, telling him about her baby preparations. She knew he couldn't be as interested as she was, but part of her expected him to at least try. And if she kept talking, he couldn't discuss a hospital birth. More often as the days passed, though, his pointed suggestions about the hospital accompanied their dinner. Sometimes Dolores stood at the stove serving up his meal, sometimes she sat at the table. He fixed his eyes on her, and Dolores knew he was about to begin again. Over codfish fritters, paella, or Portuguese sausage Dolores heard the same words. They always struck fear into her heart. Babies should be born at home. If this baby wasn't born at home, it would never feel a part of the family Dolores had worked so hard for.

By May, a month before the baby was due, Manolo was mentioning Queen's Hospital at every mealtime, and they had their first real fight. They'd argued about many things, but this time Dolores cried, so that made it a fight.

Manolo sat at the table with his hands folded in front of him. Dolores got off her feet for a moment and sat next to him. Relief swept up her calves into her back.

"Queen's is where the modern woman gives birth," Manolo said.

Dolores groaned. "Modern woman? Will you buy me a new General Electric Hotpoint range? Or a super-powered Frigidaire?" He tightened his lips. Dolores asked, "Why is this hospital birth so important to you? None of your brothers or sisters were born there, and most of their children weren't, either. Your family is built on a tradition of home births. Having everyone there when a child is born is a family tradition."

"I want the best for you, Dolores," he said.

Dolores rose and turned away. She went toward the stove where Portuguese sausage were sizzling in a cast iron pan. Pao duce, the sweet bread, baked in the oven. The familiar scents calmed her for a moment. "I prefer to have the baby at home," she said, as firmly as she could manage. Her hand betrayed her. It shook as she turned the sausages.

"I know the hospital's a new idea for you, but it's the way it's done now."

"Manolo, I don't want to go to the hospital." Dolores's hands twisted in her apron. She wished she could explain her nervousness at the new idea of a hospital birth. Dolores wanted to be around women who had birthed before. Grandma Jessie, and Ruth, and even Helen would guide her and love her. No stranger at the hospital could do that.

"Are you afraid?" Like a tiger shark spotting a tiny reef fish, he moved in for the kill. "Don't be a child, Dolores. You will have my baby in the hospital."

"No." Dolores wished the word carried more conviction.

"Do you have a reason? Are you opposed to other helpful agencies like police and firemen? Or does your silly arbitrary denial apply only to hospitals?"

Dolores didn't answer him because she didn't want to give him the satisfaction of seeing her cry. She pretended to be fascinated by the sausage as it got too brown in its pan. If she took it out, she had nothing to focus on but Manolo's face. She left it to burn.

"Well? Can't come up with a valid reason? I'm an engineer now, Dolores. Hawaiian Electric pays me well, and I must keep up appearances. No modern wife gives birth at home. You realize many babies die in home births, right? The hospital has all the modern equipment. It's safer. Everyone I know at work says the hospital is the way to go now. We will not continue this line of conversation."

He had always listened to her, heard what she had to say. Now he was more concerned with what his colleagues thought than how she felt. Her tears spilled over. Dolores wiped them with her hand, but she still held a sausage on the fork, and grease splattered on her arm. At least it gave her a reason to cry, but they both knew she cried harder than a little grease justified.

They ate in silence. Again.

A few days later, she took the streetcar to Maria's house. The three older boys were at school, so they had a nice lunch with only little John toddling around.

"He moves fast," Dolores said. "Did Henry go that fast? I don't remember."

Maria laughed. "They're all fast. Just you wait!"

"Manolo wants me to have the baby in the hospital."

"It sounds like you don't want that."

"Everyone I know has their babies at home or at the Kapiʻolani Center. The hospital is so impersonal. I'm afraid, Maria, and I don't know why."

"Anything new is scary. Manolo shouldn't push you on the first one. Keep aloha in your heart, and I'll pray for you."

The juxtaposition of beliefs made Dolores smile. "Toss in a quick sacrifice to the goddess Haumea and we're covered." They laughed until Dolores's apprehension faded.

The next day Dolores walked up the street to Ruth's. Her baby was now three months old, a precious little angel. Rosa cooed and giggled, kicking her feet in joy. She brought back Dolores's own joyful anticipation.

"Rosa is growing so fast," Ruth said. "If you have a girl, I can give you some baby clothes."

"Obrigada, Irmã," Dolores thanked her with a smile.

Ruth's baby dresses were beautifully crafted. She would not hesitate to put her daughter, if she had one, in them.

"I'd give you William's clothes, but he wears them out faster than he grows." She gave Dolores a wry grin.

"He's a boy. That's what they do," Dolores said, thinking of Maria's four. William was not even two. Ruth hadn't begun to see how a boy could wear out clothes!

Manolo continued to jab at Dolores with hospital talk. Every morning he asked, "Should I call Queen's today?"

Every morning she answered, "No, not today." It wasn't even about her nerves anymore, nor about tradition. Dolores had to do what she believed to be the best for her child.

On June first, Dolores awoke feeling restless. Pains stabbed her harder than any she had yet experienced. When Manolo asked his routine question, Dolores's answer was sharper than usual. He looked at her curiously, mumbled something about work, and hurried out the door. Dolores struggled to her feet and rubbed her belly as she talked to the baby, "Are you coming today, little one? Could you manage it before Papa comes home tonight?"

The pains were coming too close together for her to walk to Ruth's. Dolores picked up the telephone receiver, but it was dead. Hawaiian Bell was a joke. Grandma Jessie refused to install a phone. She called it a decoration on the wall. It was out of service so much she wasn't wrong, though Manolo insisted on having one.

Dolores threw on yesterday's dress and made her way across Magellan Street. Grandma Jessie wouldn't give her any nonsense about a hospital, and she certainly knew what to do. Dolores entered the kitchen door, and Grandma Jessie looked up from the stove. "The baby. . . ." It was all Dolores needed.

"Alberto! Run for Manolo! The baby's coming," she ordered.

Dolores put a hand on her arm. "No, please, not yet."

She looked into Dolores's pleading eyes. "Never mind, Alberto! Go for Ruth instead."

Dolores closed her eyes in relief.

"Helen! Give me a hand!" Grandma Jessie called.

Manolo's sister helped Dolores into the front bedroom and Grandma Jessie spread every towel she owned under her. For the next few hours Dolores endured the pain only because of the encouraging faces of Grandma Jessie, Ruth, and Helen. In her head she kept telling the baby to hurry although it was too late for Manolo to insist on the hospital.

Finally, the baby heard her exhortations and made its way into the birth canal. Dolores's hair hung limp on the back of her sweaty neck, but she pushed. Then in a rush of pain and sweat, it was done. The scream of a newborn split the air.

"What a pretty angel!" Grandma Jessie cooed.

Angel must mean a girl, Dolores told herself. Her eyes closed with mental and physical exhaustion, even though she was triumphant that she had successfully managed a home birth. She'd been right. Having Grandma Jessie here, and Ruth, and Helen, was what she'd needed. Dolores winced as Grandma Jessie pressed on her abdomen to expel the afterbirth. Exhausted and sticky with sweat, she reached for her baby. Ruth put the blanket-wrapped bundle in Dolores's arms.

"What will you name her?" Ruth asked.

"Carmen Dolores Mederios," Dolores said. She didn't mention she and Manolo had discussed only boys' names.

"Carmen it is."

"She's beautiful, Dolores," Helen said.

Ruth went on to tell Dolores all about how healthy the baby looked, but it was Carmen's clear blue eyes and round bald head that fascinated Dolores.

Grandma Jessie sent Alberto to fetch Manolo. She and Ruth helped Dolores across the street. Grandma Jessie sponged her face, brushed her hair, and helped her into a clean nightgown and into her own bed. Ruth put little Carmen in the embroidered newborn dress Rosa had worn twice. When Manolo came in, his girls were calm and clean and full of smiles. Manolo took the baby from Dolores and cradled her in his arms as if she were more precious than gold. Dolores smiled. They were family.

He said nothing about Queen's Hospital.

The entire Medeiros family squeezed into the house to welcome little Carmen with coos and kisses. Manolo's brothers brought bottles of liquor to toast the new arrival, and their wives brought pretty baby dresses and ribbons and bows. Dolores frowned when Manolo put away the bottles without offering them to everyone. It seemed in bad taste. She pulled him aside.

"You can open at least one of the bottles, Manolo. Your brothers want to toast you."

"You wanted me to open them? I thought you were the temperance prude."

His words stung her. She'd imbibed beer and wine with him many times. "How dare you put that on me? I know your family drinks at every occasion." Besides, if his brothers helped him drink it, Manolo wouldn't drink so much. But he had gone into the kitchen and didn't hear her.

Two men who rented out one of Grandma Jessie's houses came to the door. Manolo went over to speak with them. Dolores watched from the couch where Ruth had laid Rosa next to Carmen on a blanket. The men at the door spoke in low tones, behavior that seemed at odds with the celebratory mood of the baby welcome. Manolo accepted two large earthenware jugs from them.

"Bootleggers," Ruth said in a low voice. "They pay off the Medeiros men with liquor to not say anything to the police."

Dolores nodded, her stomach in knots. This arrangement was too easy for her husband. Manolo added the jugs to his rapidly filling liquor cabinet.

FOURTEEN

Manolo 1932

Over the next few months, wisps of blond hair appeared on her daughter's head. Dolores would let them grow. To cut a baby's hair before the first birthday invited spirits to touch the hair. No spirits would harm this child. Carmen would be fair like Dolores's unknown ancestors from northern Spain. She would have to keep the baby covered so the Hawaiian sun didn't burn her delicate skin. Daily life returned to normal for everyone except Dolores. She had an angel in the house to feed and cuddle, to dress and rock to sleep.

One morning, when Carmen was six months old, Dolores woke up late. She stretched and looked at the clock. Carmen should have cried to be fed. Concern flooded Dolores as she threw on a bathrobe. Maybe Carmen had died in her sleep. Maybe she was old enough now to sleep later. Her heart and mind raced as Dolores hurried to the baby's crib. Carmen was sleeping peacefully on her side, pudgy little arms and rosy cheeks so sweet. Dolores reached in to wake her. She was surprised when Carmen didn't open her eyes. She picked her up, jostled her, and lightly tapped her cheeks. The baby's skin was on fire. Dolores couldn't wake her.

Dolores tore through the house with her baby in her arms. To her surprise, Manolo was asleep on the couch in the living room. Dolores screamed his name, but her nightmare continued. She couldn't wake him either. Then she took in his rumpled white shirt, his tie askew, and his sour breath. In disgust, she left him to sleep it off. Once again, her greatest help was across the street.

Grandma Jessie was in the kitchen, her strong hands kneading bread dough. When she saw Dolores's face, she wiped her hands on her apron and took the baby.

"I can't wake her! She's got a fever! Oh, I can't wake her!" Dolores sobbed through her words.

"Pull yourself together. She'll need you." Her mother-in-law tried everything Dolores had to wake Carmen. "She's unconscious. Get Alberto."

Dolores raced down the hallway, her bare feet like thunder on the hardwood floor, her bathrobe swirling like a cape. Alberto was just coming out of his bedroom when she got there. His eyes widened. No doubt Dolores looked like the goddess Pele swooping down the fiery volcano. She pulled him back with her to the kitchen, gasping out explanations. He was awake and running before she finished. Grandma Jessie bundled the baby against the December morning. Helen rushed out of the pantry to see what was wrong. She noted Dolores's bathrobe and wrapped her in a floor-length raincoat. It was Honolulu-chilly, meaning just under seventy degrees. Dolores wrapped Helen's coat tighter around her and got into Alberto's car. Grandma Jessie slipped into the back seat. They sped toward Queen's Hospital with the sick baby.

It wasn't a long drive, but time seemed to stretch. The light posts were gaily decorated for Christmas, hung with garlands and topped with stars. In the front window of houses they passed, Christmas trees awaited Santa in his red canoe. A few houses had trees lit with electric lights. Someone had even strung garlands on a palm tree in their yard. Dolores's fear for Carmen was so great she could not at that moment embrace the season. She muttered prayers blessing God and pleading with him as her fear threatened to choke her.

At the hospital, doctors and nurses bustled around, taking over her baby's life. As the adrenalin wore off, Dolores started to shake. Grandma Jessie put an arm around Dolores and guided her to a chair. Dolores leaned against her mother-in-law's shoulder and hid her face, trying to block out all fear.

Alberto paced the room. "You want I call Manolo at work? Go get him?"

Grandma Jessie responded, "Mahalo, Alberto."

"Wait." Dolores sat up. "He's not at work."

Alberto frowned. "Why he no bring you?"

Dolores realized she was sitting there in her nightgown and a borrowed coat, her hair a mess. She never left the house in such a state. She remembered how Manolo had looked, sprawled on the couch. The similarities were striking. "He's drunk. Passed out."

Alberto swore and kicked a chair. Grandma Jessie chastised him. "He need to get control. Too often he. . . ." He trailed off as he caught sight of her face.

Today was about Carmen, not Manolo. If she'd been wrapped up in her baby while her husband nurtured a drinking problem, who could fault her? Dolores knew she didn't want to discuss it. Not here. Not now.

"Sit down, Alberto," Grandma Jessie said.

"No, I be back later." The grim set of his mouth told them he would get Manolo. Dolores didn't have the energy to care.

Then the doctor came. "Mrs. Medeiros?" Grandma Jessie rose to stand beside her. They clutched one another for support. "I'm afraid your baby . . . Carmen . . . is very sick. She has a high fever and pneumonia. She probably won't live out the day. I'm so sorry."

The doctor's words swirled around Dolores's head. They sank in until her heart froze in her throat. She couldn't breathe. The doctor led them into the room. They'd put Carmen in a basket-like box with a clear plastic covering and too many tubes for such a tiny person. She lay still. Dolores could see her but couldn't hold her, couldn't talk to her. All she could do was cry, but that she refused to do. Plus Dolores must remain strong for Carmen. She was Carmen's link to family, to aloha. She must be strong.

A priest entered. Grateful for the doctor's instinct, Dolores crossed herself.

"Is she a baptized Catholic?" the priest asked.

Dolores nodded her head. "Why would God take my family, Father?"

"It's unusual to perform Last Rites on a baby," the priest began.

Dolores's mouth went dry at the words. "Please," she begged him.

He removed the stole from around his neck, murmured a Latin prayer, kissed it, and replaced it. He raised both hands toward heaven. *"Per istam sanctan unctionem et suam piissimam misericordiam, indulgeat tibi Dominus quidquid per visum, audtiotum, odorátum, gustum et locutiónem, tactum, gressum deliquisti."*

The Latin surrounded Dolores, the comfort of her religion, the only constant comfort in her life. She drew strength from the words. She didn't know their exact English meaning but knew they focused God's love on her daughter.

The doctor raised the oxygen tent, and the priest pulled a vial of holy water out of a hidden pocket in his robe. Dolores realized he must be asked to do emergency sacraments often at Queen's. She blinked quickly to keep her eyes clear of tears as he made the cross on her baby's forehead. Grandma Jessie and Dolores made their own sign of the cross as the priest traced the cross on Carmen's hot forehead.

The priest took his leave with Grandma Jessie's thanks. Dolores remembered Carmen's baptism, at just a few weeks old, as a joyous occasion celebrating a new soul pledged to God. Now, just six short months later, her father wasn't even here for her Last Rites.

Dolores stared at Carmen as the doctor replaced the oxygen tent. A tear slid down her cheek, and she accepted defeat. As she cried, someone handed her a handkerchief.

Manolo put his arm around her. Dolores hadn't even noticed his arrival. She didn't know whether to lean in or pull away. "Better now?" he asked.

"Are *you*?" Her words came out more sharply than she intended, but she didn't apologize. "You missed her Last Rites."

The doctor looked at Manolo, his eyebrows raised. "I'm the baby's father," Manolo said.

Grandma Jessie said, "Let's go sit down and let the doctors work."

They returned to the waiting room where Alberto was pacing. Manolo joined his nephew while his mother clutched his wife's hand. Dolores felt love and support from her mother-in-law. Alberto's pacing showed his concern and support. Manolo was neutral. He was here because the family expected him to be. If Alberto hadn't fetched him, would Manolo have come? He would have awakened to an empty house and gone to his mother's. Grandma Jessie was always in her kitchen. Would Manolo have worried? Helen would have told him where they were. Would Manolo have felt fear? Guilt? Dolores didn't know. She realized she didn't know her husband well at all. Maria had been right. They'd married too soon. She didn't know how he felt, and she wanted the support of the women in his family, not him. Dolores began to cry. Grandma Jessie patted her hand.

An overwhelming sense of illness and death drenched these walls. Above her, below her, on all sides, hundreds of sick and dying people were suffering. A thousand white-clad professionals zipped in and out with contraptions and medicine and forced good cheer. Carmen was at peace with God, and that eased Dolores's fears. Without God, how could anyone have hope? Dolores forced her attention to the doctor who had followed them from Carmen's room.

"Pneumonia is serious for such little lungs. We'll put her on pure oxygen, start antibiotics." The doctor's voice was solemn. It contained no hope. Dolores sank into a chair Manolo brought over to her.

"Where could she get pneumonia?" Manolo asked.

The doctor shrugged. "Almost anywhere. It's the season."

Dolores thought about the huge family—Manolo's siblings, their spouses and children, the older generation—and countless friends and neighbors, all kissing and holding the baby. If pneumonia was anywhere in Hawaiʻi, it could have found its way to their baby.

"I'm sorry, Mrs. Medeiros," the doctor said as he left them.

The nurse brought a glass of water and knelt beside Dolores with soothing words and a soft rub on her arm. What ancient medical genius taught that a glass of water cures all ills?

Grandma Jessie squeezed Dolores's hands, as if to imbue the new mother with her strength. Grandma Jessie clutched a rabbit's foot in her other hand, her superstitions always prevalent. Family arrived. Helen. Manolo's brothers and their wives. Manolo filled them in on Carmen's condition, and they took over a waiting room near the baby's room. Their presence supported Dolores with the unspoken strength of faith and family.

"Babies aren't as fragile as you think," Grandma Jessie told Dolores. "They make it through very serious illnesses. We'll all pray to Jesus for a miracle to help our little Carmen fight." She took a rosary out of her purse and wrapped it in their clasped hands. She made the sign of the cross and said, "*Em Nome do Pai e do Filho e do Espírito Santo*. Amen."

Her prayers were always in Portuguese. Dolores echoed her in English, "In the name of the Father, the Son, and the Holy Spirit. Amen."

Ruth arrived and brought Dolores a dress and shoes. She changed in the bathroom, at least looking better once she put on some lipstick and combed her hair. They sat in silence as the day wore on. The hospital showed no indication of the passing hours. Nighttime looked the same as daytime. Family came and went. Manolo's brothers stayed briefly, their wives longer. The children were in school. Alberto stayed, hovering around the periphery, lending support without requiring interaction. He took Manolo to get lunch and brought Dolores coffee and pastry when she declined to join them.

A day, a week, a month later—Dolores was sure it wasn't as long as it felt—the doctor stood before them. Dolores rose on trembling legs. He scanned the faces of those who were here—Grandma Jessie, Manolo, Alberto—and spoke to Dolores. "She's fighting and holding her own."

She was very, very sick, but she was alive. Dolores felt a slight relief at that.

"Come on, Vovô, I drive you home," Alberto said. He offered Grandma Jessie his hand.

Manolo looked at Dolores. "Are you staying?" At her nod, he said, "I'll be back later."

They left Dolores alone with her God and her sick little girl. She went into the baby's room and sat in the chair where she could see Carmen's tiny body. All night she stared at her baby's chest, watching it rise and fall in time with the machine. Once or twice she looked out the window where the palm trees swayed in a moonlit sky. Then her gaze returned to the crib, where the only family in the world that was truly hers struggled for life.

In the wee hours of the morning, Alberto returned, but Manolo did not. Alberto ran a hand through his dark hair and sat beside her without a word. It was a time of night where words were unnecessary. His presence comforted her, and Dolores didn't have to tell him so.

Natural light from the window faded with dusk and brightened with dawn, and still Manolo had not returned. A breeze waved the flowers of a bird of paradise plant outside the window. Birds hidden in its foliage twittered. Even lit with glorious dawn, the view couldn't hold Dolores's interest as much as the beeps and blinks of Carmen's machines. Early in the morning, Alberto left, squeezing her hand on his way out and saying, "Manolo is all right. He's book smart like my father. He'll do well in business. His common sense is lacking, but he'll provide for you and the babe."

Dolores nodded, pleased that he cared. "I know. Mahalo."

She was too worried to be angry with Manolo over his absence. They didn't both need to be there for Carmen, but part of her wished he would be there for her. It was another hour before he arrived with coffee and fresh malasadas from his mother. "Dolores, you must eat. When Carmen comes home, she'll need you to be strong."

Dolores took a bite of the sugary fried dough and a sip of the coffee. "Mahalo," she told him. He was dressed in his usual white shirt and tie, looking neat. She was a mess.

He looked at the clock on the wall. "I have to go to work. I can't sit here and watch her die."

"She won't die." Dolores's conviction gave the words strength. "I'll stay with her. There's no reason for us both to be here. I'll send someone if there's any change."

He nodded, kissed her and held her tight for a moment, then left.

When the doctor arrived, he greeted her solemnly. "Mrs. Medeiros."

Dolores nodded. "Doctor, how is she?"

He checked the machine, opened the oxygen tent, and

listened with his stethoscope to Carmen's tiny heart. Showing no reaction, he closed the tent back up and turned to Dolores.

She gripped the arms of the chair, her stomach roiling. She forced herself to breathe, in and out, in and out, to the rhythm of the machine.

He looked up from his charts. "She's going to live."

Dolores was numb with relief. The doctor smiled and left the room.

I T took a week for the doctors to declare Carmen out of danger and discharge her.

Dolores called Manolo at work. "She's coming home today!" Triumphant happiness surged through her.

"That's wonderful. But I can't get away right now. There's an urgent problem I need to deal with." He sounded distracted.

"I understand." Dolores felt her joy dissipate as she hung up the phone and turned back to the crib. Carmen was awake but sleepy. Dolores stroked her pale cheek. Then she picked up the phone again.

Alberto didn't ask questions about Manolo. "Lemme grab car keys. I be right der."

Grateful beyond words, Dolores beamed. "Mahalo, nephew." He laughed. Technically, he was her nephew since his mother was Manolo's oldest sister, but he was only four years younger.

Dolores dressed Carmen in one of her prettiest dresses. She held the baby tightly as tears filled her eyes. She trembled, overcome with emotion.

Alberto stroked the baby's cheek. Getting close to her face, he said, "Enough a dis drama, Carmen. We go home, ya?"

It was a brilliant day of tropical sunshine and clear blue sky. The trade winds ruffled the palm fronds high above them.

Alberto took a detour and drove them down Fort Street. Dolores's eyes opened wide in awe. Someone had strung Christmas garlands across the street as usual, but this year they were illuminated. Wreaths adorned lampposts and shop doors.

"It's beautiful," she told him.

"We come back at night. Carmen will like the lights."

He turned for home, and contentment eased the tension that had been Dolores's companion for the past week.

CHRISTMAS spirit infused them all with goodwill. No one argued or complained. With Carmen home and healthy, an already joyful season became even more so. Ruth and Dolores gave their children presents on Christmas Eve at Dolores's house.

"What is it, Winona?" Ruth encouraged her oldest, three-year-old Winona, to open the present.

The girl tore the wrappings. "A doll!" She picked the doll up, and its eyes opened. She experimented and put it down again. The eyes closed. "Like a real baby."

Ruth had saved her money for months to buy the doll, and she'd made extra outfits for it herself.

William looked at his present skeptically. "Dolly?" It was a different sized box, long and thin, but at two he couldn't make that connection.

"Open it, honey," Ruth said. "I know boys don't play with dolls."

He tore the paper open and jumped up. "A horse!" The stick horse had a painted head on one end and wheels on the other. William threw a leg over it and galloped around the house.

"Oh, goodie," Dolores said, "we'll have to put away anything he can crash into."

Ruth laughed, and Dolores joined in.

Rosa and Carmen were too young to open their own presents, so they let Winona help. Ruth and Dolores had made each other's baby a new dress. "When did you make this?" they asked at the same time.

The crash of the front door startled them. "Mele Kaliki-maka!" Manolo shouted as he came into the room on unsteady legs, supported by Alberto.

"Merry Christmas, Alberto. How was the office party, Manolo?" Dolores said. She felt Ruth's eyes but refused to look at her.

"I'm so tired. Going to bed." Manolo stumbled down the hallway.

Dolores didn't move to help him. "Mele Kalikimaka, ladies," Alberto said. "I see you tomorrow fo' dinner." He turned to go.

"Alberto," Dolores said. He waited. "Mahalo."

He waved her off and left. The door closed behind him.

"Love is a strange thing," Ruth said. "You fall in love with the nice things they do and ignore the bad."

"It's easier to look past some things when they are loving," Dolores said.

"How long can a woman be expected to look past, though?" Ruth asked.

"As long as she must," Dolores said. "A marriage is not always a beach being kissed by the sea."

Ruth smiled. "Alberto says that."

They were quiet for a moment. The absence of their husbands loomed between them. Every now and then, Ruth's brothers teased her about her invisible husband. Dolores wondered what it was like for Ruth when he came home. At least Manolo was there. When he wasn't drunk, he was a good father.

"He loves me," Dolores told her sister-in-law. "And he loves Carmen. That's enough."

FIFTEEN

New Year 1933

*P*utting away the holiday decorations was always bitter-sweet. It marked the end to a time of happiness, good food, and family celebration, but it was nice to get the house back to normal. Manolo wanted to hold on to the festive spirit. "Don't put the garlands away yet," he said.

"When the decorations begin to gather dust, they come down. I won't dust holiday decorations."

He sighed but didn't get up to help her.

"Can you get me the ladder?" she asked.

"Really, Dolores? Do you know how hard I work all day? Then I come home, and you expect me to work even more. When I'm home, work is pau. All done."

She stared at him. "Keeping a house and child is hardly a picnic in the park."

He laughed. "Yeah, that's what all homemakers say. Tell you what. You come to work with me for a day and see how hard a man works."

Dolores's hands whitened as she gripped the garland. "That's a mean thing to say."

Something in her tone must have alerted him. He looked at her face and said, "Oh, come on. I'm teasing. Of course, you work hard. And I love you for it."

But he didn't get the ladder. She didn't either. She left a lonely bit of gold garland over the door for three more days before she couldn't stand it anymore. Dolores waited until Manolo was at work and dragged the ladder in from the carport. She climbed up, removed the garland, and returned the ladder. Furious indignation gave her strength. Manolo came home from work early and never noticed the missing garland. He left before dinner though. "Off to do some business over dinner. Don't wait up for me."

Dolores wondered what business he could conduct over dinner besides drinking. When the doorbell rang scant moments later, she ripped the door open ready to confront him about his absences, his drinking, and his lack of respect.

Ruth stood on the step with her eyes red with tears. Rosa was in her arms, and the other two children stood close to her. "Oh, Dolores, I don't know what to do!" she said. She sobbed as she told Dolores that Charles had left her. "He's sold the house and all our furniture!"

"You'll move in here with us." 'ohana was everything. "There are rooms downstairs you can use. We'll fix it up nice, you and I. Come on. Let's get some cookies for the little ones."

Dolores was glad. Ruth was better off without Charles. He hadn't been around much anyway. At least when he wasn't around, he couldn't hit Ruth or be drunk in front of her.

Downstairs, in the basement, the house had three small rooms that had been storage for the family since before Manolo and Dolores moved in. Dolores fetched blankets to make beds for Winona and William. "Rosa can share Carmen's crib," Dolores said.

They went upstairs and gathered the children for dinner. Dolores gave Ruth the portion Manolo would have eaten. For the older children, she sliced mango and banana and cut pieces of haupia, the coconut pudding they all loved.

After they ate and read stories to the children, Dolores and Ruth managed to get all the children to sleep. Dolores made a pot of Kona coffee and sat in the kitchen with Ruth. They drank coffee and ate haupia, and Ruth never asked where Manolo was.

Over the next few days, Alberto and João cleared the basement. Dolores hadn't even realized it had a small bathroom. She didn't ask where all the dusty boxes ended up. Grandma Jessie opened her closets in the main house. "I never throw away anything," she told Dolores. "You never know when you'll need it."

They found furniture Ruth could use. Alberto retrieved the kids' things, Ruth's clothes, and her sewing machine from Charles before the sale of the house went through. He set the machine up in her small bedroom. She could sew for clients there and still watch the children playing on the rug.

"At yo' service, Aunties." His irrepressible grin made them both swat him and laugh.

"He makes me feel so old!" Dolores told Ruth.

"Next year you bot' get canes for Christmas, ya?" Alberto said.

"Better be careful, Alberto," Ruth warned. "We can use canes for more than walking." She pantomimed whacking her nephew on the head.

He raised his arms in self-defense. "*Lōlō* wahine! Save me, Dolores!"

"You're on your own, buddy." Dolores laughed.

Ruth laughed, too, and went to fix the kids a snack.

"Seriously, Alberto, why do you spent so much time taking care of your aunties?" Dolores asked.

"You and Ruth are family, ya?" he said. "I help when husbands no can do." He looked as if he would say more, but then decided not to.

Dolores smiled. "Mahalo." All she could do was thank

him. She wasn't prepared to get into a conversation about the difference between the absent husbands.

Manolo shook his head in disbelief when he came home to find his sister and her children living with them.

"It is your mother's house," Dolores pointed out. "It doesn't belong to us. Ruth has as much right to be here as we do."

"My buddies will get a kick out of me keeping two women," Manolo said with a leer. "Not so crazy about all her kids."

Dolores clamped her lips to prevent angry words from escaping. Manolo left without eating dinner and didn't come home until after she was in bed.

With four children under four at home, life was hectic but full of fun. They praised the Lord when all four napped at the same time. Manolo spent most nights out with friends. Ruth's presence seemed to give him permission to stay away, and Dolores didn't mind.

One day Ruth and Dolores sat on the couch and talked, holding Rosa and Carmen. The babies were sleepy, having just woken from their naps. Ruth wore a pendant on a long chain, something sparkly that caught the light. Rosa cooed and reached for it, kicking her legs. Ruth laughed and lifted the pendant over the baby's face. She waved it back and forth. Rosa followed it with her eyes. Dolores held Carmen up to see the sparkly thing but got no reaction.

Ruth frowned. "Here," she said. She took off the pendant and handed it to Dolores. "Let her see it up close."

Dolores took it and held it above her baby. She twisted it to catch the light. From Ruth's lap, Rosa reached for it. Carmen did not react. "What's wrong with her?" Dolores asked. She refused to panic yet.

"She's younger. Maybe she's not ready to track things with her eyes yet." Ruth's words were soothing, but her tone was anxious.

Later, alone with her daughter in her room, Dolores waved her hand in front of Carmen's face. Nothing. She pretended to strike her, bringing her hand as close to her nose as she dared. Carmen didn't even flinch. Dolores held her up close to her own face. She blew against her stomach to make a sound. Carmen laughed but didn't look at her mother's face. Dolores moved Carmen around to look directly at her. Dolores covered Carmen's face to play hide and seek. They'd played it before, and the baby always laughed. Now she fussed and reached out to her mother. In the wrong direction. Was it possible she couldn't see?

The baby glowed with health. Carmen had put on weight and grown out of her clothes. She turned toward the radio and listened. She babbled and had developed noises that showed clear disapproval or delight. But she didn't react to her mother's face, or to toys held above her, unless they made noise.

"Manolo, we need to take Carmen to the doctor," Dolores told him after dinner that night. He'd come home late from work, but not so late that he was drunk. His hair and tie were a little rumpled, so Dolores estimated a drink or two, that's all. He'd been drinking less since Hawaiian Electric had promoted him to chief engineer. As his responsibilities increased, he worked harder. He looked tired.

"Doctor? Why?" He looked at Carmen in her highchair. She babbled away to herself and made drool bubbles.

Dolores picked up the cold washcloth on Carmen's tray and held it to the baby's gums to give Carmen some relief from painful new teeth. "I'm worried about her sight," she told her husband.

"Why?" he repeated.

Dolores dangled the washcloth in front of the baby's face. She didn't react. Dolores touched her with it, and she reached for it. "I don't think she can see it."

He came around the table to them, took his keys out of his pocket and waved them in front of Carmen. She looked his way. "She can see these."

Did he really believe that? "She can *hear* them, Manolo."

He looked at Carmen. His face glowed with love. "She's fine. You worry too much."

"I don't think so," she insisted. Too late Dolores realized he'd had more to drink than she thought. She didn't know when and where. There was much about his life she didn't know. Dolores shook her head. "I didn't see it until now."

"Didn't see it? Are you trying to make a joke? Push me into thinking my daughter can't see?" His roar made his face redden and his eyes flame.

"Of course not." The fury on his face scared her.

"Why would you make up something like this?" He shouted now. Then he leaned in so close she could feel his spittle on her face. "Is the family's attention moving on to someone else? You like the attention a sick baby gives you?"

"What? No!" Dolores backed away.

He stepped forward and stood with his legs spread, hands on hips, shoulders back. He was the most aggressive she'd ever seen him. Carmen, still in the highchair, whimpered.

Manolo's anger erupted. He raised his hand to Dolores, across his chest so he could backhand her face. The force of the blow snapped her head back. The shock of it took her breath away. "I don't know why I ever married you!"

He stormed out of the room, and Dolores heard him rummage in the cabinet where he hid his bottles. Then the front door slammed behind him. Carmen cried, no doubt frightened by her father's loud anger. Dolores sank to the floor, her back against the wall. She hugged her knees and let herself cry. She had never been hit before. Not by Papa, not by Noelani or Kanoa, and not by Maria or Peter. It was a bruise to her soul as well as her face.

The door slammed behind Manolo, and the noise brought Ruth upstairs from her rooms in the basement. Dolores, on the floor, cried and stared at the baby in her highchair. Carmen cried, too. Ruth dropped to her knees and held Dolores. "Are you all right?" Then she noticed Dolores's reddened cheek and sucked in her breath. "Did Manolo do that? Oh, Dolores, I'm so sorry."

Dolores drew comfort from her sister-in-law's arms. She didn't need to talk about her husband. They cried together there on the floor. When Dolores could stand, she pulled Ruth up with her. Ruth picked up Carmen. She bounced the baby on her hip until she quieted.

Dolores got a cold washcloth for her face.

"I hope it doesn't bruise too badly," Ruth said.

"Ruth, what do I say to him? What do I do?" Dolores was lost. It seemed everything she held dear was built on clouds.

Ruth said, "It's like Grandma Jessie says—'ohana is everything and everyone is 'ohana. Nobody is perfect in the family, but we are all here to help each other through it. I'll help you, Dolores."

Dolores nodded. "And I'll help you, Ruth."

The next day Dolores powdered her face heavily. She dressed Carmen in a baby blue dress that had grown a little tight. She filled Grandma Jessie's plate with homemade sugar cookies since her mother-in-law would be the first to tell Dolores that returning a plate empty brought bad luck.

Dolores crossed the street to help with lunch as she did every day and looked for Manolo's car. She was relieved to see her husband wasn't there and relieved when Ruth and Helen took Carmen to play with Rosa. When his mother asked, Dolores told her she didn't know where Manolo was. She glanced at the right side of Dolores's face, and Dolores held her breath. She frowned but looked away. Dolores resumed breathing. Alberto sat on Dolores's right side and peered at her cheek. Dolores ignored him. He frowned, but she talked to Ruth across the table.

Much later, Alberto volunteered to walk her home. "Oh, mahalo," Dolores told him, "but I can cross the street on my own."

He snatched one of Dolores's cookies off the plate and joined her anyway. Grandma Jessie's door was barely closed behind them when he asked, "How you get dat bruise?"

"Bruise?"

"Dolores, no play dumb wit' me. Someone slap yo' face, hard. You try cover it, ya?"

She didn't want to tell him Manolo had done it. She didn't know what he'd do. Better to change the subject. "I'm worried about Carmen. I don't think she can see well."

They had arrived at her front door. "You take her to doc?" He opened the door and motioned for her to precede him.

"Not yet. I just noticed it yesterday."

"Get yo' purse. We take her now." He hadn't even closed the front door. "On the way you talk story about yo' face."

Dolores lifted her chin and said, "Manolo did it."

"Lōlō kanapapiki," he swore. She knew lōlō meant crazy. She knew kanapapiki was nothing she wanted her daughter to hear. Alberto curled his hand into a fist. Dolores could see the muscles tense in his arm. "I get some ice, ya?" he said.

It was too late for ice to curtail the swelling, but Dolores let him go. When he returned with a dish towel full of ice and placed it gently on her face while holding her daughter, she was so grateful for his kindness she almost cried. "Mahalo," she said. "He didn't mean—"

Alberto cut her off, his face hard with anger. "I sorry, Dolores, but it not orait."

"It's all right, Alberto. He'll be sorry when he comes back. He loves Carmen. It will be all right." Dolores used to know he loved her, too, but now she wasn't sure.

"You sho you no trying to catch fish in the air?"

She didn't answer.

"Come on, let's get our girl to the doc."

Without an appointment, they had to wait to see the doctor. Alberto entertained Carmen with his keys. Dolores didn't tell him that reminded her of Manolo the night before, trying to test the baby's vision.

Both Alberto and Dolores stood close by while the doctor examined Carmen. "She's eight months old?"

"Yes, Doctor," Carmen said.

"And she had pneumonia, I recall."

"Yes."

"That may have had some effect. They give seriously ill infants strong medication. Or the oxygen they gave her could have been too pure. There's a possibility it won't get any worse as she grows, but there's also a possibility she may be totally blind as an adult."

Alberto put his arm around Carmen. "She a beautiful angel," he said.

"Thank you, Doctor," Dolores said. She picked up Carmen and squared her shoulders. "Carmen won't be treated any differently than the others. My daughter won't be a burden."

The doctor nodded as he left the room.

In the car, before Alberto could say anything, Carmen said, "Don't tell Manolo unless he asks."

"You t'ink he no ask? Or you afraid o' him?"

Dolores didn't answer. She'd never been afraid before, but being hit was new. She wasn't sure how she'd feel when she saw Manolo again. "I don't even know where he is."

"I know a couple his buddies at a bar in Chinatown. I find him if yo' need him, ya?"

She shook her head.

They finished the drive in silence. At home, Alberto helped her change Carmen into a nightgown and put her down in the crib. Dolores stood and stroked the baby's back, her thoughts full of love and support no matter what Carmen could see. Alberto watched her from the doorway. When she came out and closed the baby's door behind her, he pointed toward Grandma Jessie's house and said, "I right dere. Any time, day o' night you come get me if you need me, ya?"

"I will." The intensity of his eyes and the tension in his muscles made her feel supported rather than afraid. How much would the rest of the family support her? How could they refuse Manolo when he needed so much help? Help she didn't know how to give. She could only hope that the family would help them both.

SIXTEEN

Balancing Act 1939

In January, people reflected on the past year and made resolutions for the new one. Dolores's birthday fell on the fifteenth. It was usually a private affair, tucked into the recuperation time after the Christmas season. The decorations, the shopping, the food, the parties were all over, and normal daily life returned.

This year, as Dolores turned twenty-three and reflected on the holiday season of 1938, she was content. Carmen would turn seven in June. Her younger sister, Betty, would be two years old next month. Manolo doted on the girls and would do anything for them. This included a promise not to drink so much. Each holiday Dolores monitored his drinking with anxious trepidation, especially at Christmas and New Year's. Every holiday, though, he stopped after one drink. Carmen and Betty loved their daddy, and Dolores did, too. Manolo still got angry over what seemed to be little things. Dolores had learned to defuse his anger, and they'd developed a fragile peace once Manolo stopped blaming her for Carmen's eyesight problems.

Dolores chased her daydreams out of her head and focused on dressing. Manolo was taking all his girls out to dinner to celebrate her twenty-third birthday. Dolores fastened the buttons of her newest dress and preened in front of the mirror. The skirt was longer than her older dresses, quite in fashion. The fabric was silky-swirly, a favorite of Carmen's, and the waist sat snugly against her, a little higher than her natural waist. It was blue, like the tropical sky, and scatter-printed with white plumeria. Dolores liked the way the skirt felt as it moved against her rayon stockings.

"You look beautiful," Manolo said as he came into the room behind her.

Dolores turned to greet him with a wide, open smile. "Mahalo, kuʻuipo." He kissed her, and she stepped back to admire him. He wore his usual white shirt with a gray striped tie. Dolores had bought him one in bold geometric colors, but he refused to wear it. His jacket was also gray but fit him like it was made for him. He was as handsome as the day she'd first seen him at Hanauma Bay eight years earlier. "You look wonderful, too, Manolo."

Carmen and Betty sat on the sofa just like little ladies. Their blond hair was curled and tied with ribbon, and their dresses were clean and pressed.

Betty kicked her feet and scowled at the shoes. "Mama, no shoes."

"Ladies must wear shoes in a restaurant, darling. Your sister doesn't mind shoes, do you Carmen?"

Carmen's blue eyes danced, and her mouth twisted up in the devilish grin Dolores always saw in the Medeiros boys. She held up her hand to forestall her oldest daughter's words. "Never mind! We are all wearing shoes!"

The girls laughed as they rushed into their mother's arms to hug her. Manolo brought the car around, and the three of them joined him. They were off to a nice dinner, something they enjoyed doing but just couldn't afford as much as they'd like to. Dolores supposed that made it special for all of them. Imagine being so wealthy you could take your family to dinner often enough to tire of it.

Manolo drove them to the Royal Hawaiian Hotel. Betty loved the pink hotel and described its color and flowers to her sister. "Walls pink, Carmen, and flowers pink and all pink."

Carmen could see shadows, but discerning pink was beyond her. The doctors now said that her vision would deteriorate as she got older, but Dolores refused to let it affect how she raised Carmen. Carmen would learn and play and do chores just like her younger sister, probably more since she was the oldest.

The Royal Hawaiian was a special treat. The restaurant menus had covers that were color etchings of paintings by John Kelly. Dolores loved his work since it depicted Hawaiian people. Her favorite was *Lei Makers on Greensward,* which reminded her of Maria and the Hawaiian women who made leis at the Moana Hotel. Whenever they came to the Royal Hawaiian, Dolores hoped to get a menu with a copy of that painting.

They sat in the dining room like they did it every day. The room glittered with beautiful people. Dolores imagined they were actresses and actors, wealthy families on holiday from the mainland.

Manolo ordered for all of them. The soup came in a giant tureen embellished with tiny pink painted roses and gold trim. Dolores heard Betty mutter, "Pink roses, pink."

"Betty, you're a good sister to describe everything to Carmen," Manolo said.

Dolores looked at him, always suspicious when he spoke of Carmen's lack of sight. They'd never discussed it at length. She'd told him about the doctor visit soon after it happened. For the ensuing five and a half years, it seemed Manolo weighed everything Carmen did or said. He loved his daughter very much, so Dolores said nothing.

The waiter brought rolls, served on a platter that matched the tureen. Dolores traced the gold rim. "Isn't it beautiful? I love this."

"Put it in your purse," Manolo suggested.

Dolores couldn't tell if he was joking. She eyed her lauhala purse. It was big enough. "No, I can't," she protested. The platter was so pretty. The girls were too young to understand. It was her birthday after all. Dolores giggled as she divided the rolls among their four plates and opened her lauhala purse wide. She slipped the platter inside and stuffed it so that the woven straw sides of her purse bulged. Betty's eyes grew wide, and Manolo slapped both hands across his mouth to keep from laughing. Dolores, too, held in her laughter with difficulty when the waiter came to the table. He did a double take when he saw the rolls on their plate but no platter. He asked no questions though.

Manolo's eyes sparkled. "What a terrible role model you are," he teased.

"I see what I want and go after it," Dolores said trying to put a positive spin on it. "I'll tell everyone it's a birthday gift." The girls talked to each other and ignored their parents.

Betty described, in her limited vocabulary, the entire restaurant and its patrons to Carmen. Manolo ordered a glass of wine instead of a bottle. Dolores had pink lemonade and ordered the same for the girls.

"`Okole maluna," Manolo said. "To my beautiful ladies!"

They all had a wonderful meal, full of laughter, and returned home full and happy. Dolores washed her beautiful platter and set it in a place of honor on a shelf in the kitchen.

The next day the entire house shook so hard that the platter fell off its shelf and shattered. Dolores scooped Betty up in her arms and pulled Carmen after her as she rushed outside. All along the street, people were doing the same. By the time Dolores's mind registered that it was an earthquake, it was over. Carmen and Betty seemed unfazed. They ran inside and resumed playing with their dolls. Dolores walked from room to room. Pictures hung askew on the wall, and things on top of dressers had moved. Some had fallen, but nothing had broken except the platter. When Manolo came home, Dolores was sitting in the kitchen, beginning to feel safe in her home.

"Everyone all right?" he asked.

Dolores nodded. Surely, he knew she would have called if something was wrong. "Just my platter broke."

"God must be angry with you for stealing it."

"He and I are even now, though, right?" Dolores asked, only half in jest. She tried to glue the broken pieces together, but the platter was never the same. Still, she couldn't bear to throw it away and stashed it in the cupboard behind her mixing bowls.

The next day's *Honolulu Bulletin* reported a Richter scale rating of 6.8. Maui had sustained the most damage with landslides and burst water pipes. On Lanaʻi, great cracks appeared in the ground. Honolulu and the rest of Oʻahu had seen only slight damage. Underneath its tropical beauty, Hawaiʻi was restless and destructive.

They still spent a lot of time at Grandma Jessie's. After Ruth got her four children off to school, she and Dolores packed up Carmen and Betty and went to the elder Medeiros house. It was always busy there, as they made a big lunch for everyone and cleaned the house. Rosa, Carmen, and Betty played in the yard while one of the women watched them from the kitchen window. Dolores washed her hands and peeled carrots. Ruth and Helen chopped potatoes.

Before long, Rosa ran into the house. "Rosa, what's wrong?" Ruth asked.

"It's Carmen!" She turned and rushed back toward the yard.

Dolores ran after her and pictured horrible things that could have happened. Ruth followed her. Carmen sat on the lawn, hale and hearty. Her face was oddly scrunched. Betty sat nearby, crying.

"She pushed a whole button up her nose," Rosa said, her voice full of awe. "But now she can't get it out."

"Can't get it out?" Dolores tilted her daughter's face upward and tried to look in her nose. She saw a missing button on Carmen's dress and assumed that was the one in her nose. "Carmen, what have you done?"

"I have a button in my nose." She pointed to her right nostril, her index finger inside her nose to the first knuckle.

"Yes, darling, I know." She imagined the button traveling up into Carmen's head and lodging in her brain. She scooped Carmen up and dashed back in the house.

"Grandma Jessie! I'm taking Carmen to the doctor!" Dolores looked at her daughter's grass-stained dress. Her feet were brown with dirt. Her face was a mess with snot dripping down her muddy face. Dolores couldn't take her anywhere looking like this. She told Ruth, "Call Manolo! Tell him to meet me at home! And watch Betty!"

Dolores dragged poor Carmen after her and was out of breath when she got to the kitchen. There, Dolores stripped off the child's clothes and gave her a fast but effective sponge bath. Then she dressed Carmen in a clean dress. Manolo rushed through the door just as Dolores was brushing their daughter's hair.

"What happened? Ruth just said doctor."

"Your daughter has pushed a button up her nose. It's too far up. I can't even see it. Come on, we have to go." Dolores tugged at his arm and smelled whisky on his breath.

"And you're giving her a bath?" His voice rose. "Give her to me!"

Dolores thought this was an overreaction since he had to give Carmen back to her when they got in the car. She hesitated and wondered how much he'd had to drink. It didn't matter. They needed to take Carmen. In scant moments, they were on their way. Dolores didn't wait for Manolo to open the car door but rushed right out when they arrived. Holding Carmen tightly by the hand, she told the receptionist why she needed to see the doctor.

It didn't take long for the doctor to extract the button. His patient, peaceful demeanor was a balm to Dolores's galloping heart. Manolo paced the narrow room with his arms folded across his chest.

"Promise not to put anything else in your nose?" The doctor said.

"I promise, Doctor," the sweet angel said.

"We'll watch her more closely, Doctor," Manolo promised. He patted Carmen on the shoulder and gave her a loving smile. When he turned to Dolores, though, his face was grim.

They thanked the doctor and headed for home. Ruth had picked up her children from school, and they waited on the step with Betty, full of questions.

"Did they let you keep the button?"

"What made you think to do that?"

"How did they get it out?"

Rosa just took Carmen by the hand and led her across the yard. "You be quiet," she told her siblings. "Carmen's having a bad day."

In the privacy of their bedroom, Dolores heaved a great sigh and turned to Manolo so they could laugh together about the day now that it was over. His face, though, darkened like a tropical storm. Dolores had smelled the alcohol. She knew he'd been drinking. She thought of running, of locking herself in the bathroom, of screaming. More importantly, she must protect the girls. A strange calm settled over her.

The blows rained on her chest and shoulders like God's vengeance. One particularly vicious one to Dolores's stomach doubled her over, and that stopped him. She straightened slowly. She watched the fire ebb from his face and waited for his fists to unclench. Dolores pulled her shoulders back and lifted her chin. She tried to put as much disgust in her face as possible. She clenched her hands into her skirt to keep them from trembling.

"I'll be downtown," he said. And just like that, he was gone.

Dolores's entire upper torso ached. It was difficult to breathe. Manolo had avoided her face this time. No marks would show. Dolores sank into a chair, overwhelmed, all pleasantries erased by Manolo's hate-twisted face. Love and hate were related, people said. No one ever said how fast a person could switch from one to the other. No one ever talked about how a family dealt with this.

The entire incident had happened quickly. Ruth was just coming inside with the children. "Where'd Manolo go? Doesn't he want dinner?"

Dolores shrugged, then gasped. Ruth's eyes narrowed. "Winona, will you take William and the girls to wash up for dinner?" Her eyes never left Dolores's as the children left. "He hit you." It wasn't a question.

Dolores sat on the bed. "I'm so afraid he'll start on the girls that I'm making myself sick." She rubbed her stomach, which had been upset all day.

"Oh, honey." Ruth sat next to her, went to hug her but stopped when Dolores flinched. She left the room, and Dolores could hear her talking to the children and getting into the icebox. Ruth returned with ice wrapped in a kitchen towel. "Where?"

Dolores took the ice and placed it on her chest.

"You should leave him," Ruth said. "You deserve better."

Leave him? That meant leaving Grandma Jessie and Ruth. She would truly be on her own. It also meant sinning against her church, which had joined Manolo and her for life. "I can't," she said.

"It's not so bad living as a single mom," Ruth said. "Family supports you."

"But it's your family, Ruth. How could Grandma Jessie take my side over her own son? How does that fit into family? I promised myself to Manolo in the church before God. I need to make this work. It's best for my family."

"But what about you?"

Manolo stayed away. Dolores didn't know, nor did she care, where he was sleeping. When she groaned as she got in and out of bed, she didn't have to stifle it. Dolores found four bottles of bootleg whisky in his cabinet hiding place and poured all of them down the sink. Her physical hurts were not important. They would heal. Her daughters were the most important. They must be whole. The first night of Manolo's absence, Carmen asked about her father at bedtime.

"He's working late, darling. He'll come in to kiss you when he gets home."

"Does it count if I'm not awake?"

"Of course, it does. Go to sleep." Dolores kissed her on her nose. "Here's one to hold you until Daddy comes." Dolores gave another from her. With her sister settled, Betty, too, was content.

On the second night of Manolo's absence, the girls were cross. Dolores's body ached and her stomach still hadn't settled. She was as irritable as her daughters. The front door opened, and Alberto called, "Anyone home?" He came in and found them in the girls' bedroom. "What's that, Carmen? You have a poopie doll?" He pointed at the toy in Carmen's arms.

The girls squealed in delight. "Not a poopie doll, Uncle Alberto. A Kewpie doll!" Carmen said.

"Yo' sure? Look like a poopie doll ta me." Alberto feigned total ignorance, and the six-year-old loved it.

"They're having some trouble falling asleep," Dolores told him. "Can you tell them a story?"

And he did. He told the girls a story about *menehune*, "The Three Menehune of Ainahou," and they listened with sleepy smiles. Alberto's full attention was on them until he reached the end. His eyes met Dolores's when he said, "The moral of the story is, no matter how hard yo' life is, there is always someone ta help you make t'ings better."

The girls snuggled into their pillows with smiles. Alberto quietly shut their bedroom door as he joined Dolores. They walked out to sit on the lanaʻi. The sun was just past the most glorious part of the sunset, but the palm trees still held golden glints of daylight. The mountain loomed purple above them.

"It's a beautiful evening," Dolores said.

Alberto looked at her. "Sometimes another person's fishing spot look better dan yours, and yo' lose sight of the important t'ings, ya? The ocean be beautiful ever' where, despite what lurks in the depths."

Dolores nodded. Life didn't seem beautiful at the moment.

Later that night, Dolores struggled to her knees at her own bedside to thank God for her little blond angels, and for Alberto and Ruth and the rest of the family. She asked Him to give her strength, but she didn't need to ask for the help of the menehune. She had Alberto.

When Manolo returned, three days later, he walked in as if nothing had happened, hung his hat on the rack, sat down in his big chair, and opened the *Honolulu Bulletin* to hide his face. Dolores said nothing as she set another plate for dinner. The girls ran to greet him, and he asked Carmen about her day. "Did you play with Rosa today?"

A silent emotional conversation swirled in the air between the adults. *What happened to your promise not to drink?*

"Yes, Papa," she replied.

"Did you see any of your uncles?" *Does the family know about my binge?*

"The girls went through Grandma Jessie's closets today," Dolores told him. "Carmen felt the fabrics and Rosa described the patterns." *I told no one. What would I say?*

"Then Rosa and I listened to Bing Crosby on the radio and whistled. I'm better than her." Carmen smiled her pride.

"I'm sure you are, darling. Did you watch out for your little sister?" *Your mother can't seem to take care of both of you.*

"The entire family watches the children. Alberto came by with his motorcycle, so both your brothers showed up." *Everyone else in the family was there.*

The conversation, spoken and imagined, lapsed. Dolores served dinner silently. She let the girls chatter to their father. She picked at some rice and pork but didn't have much of an appetite.

At bedtime, Dolores went into their bedroom alone and locked the door. She stood with her back against it and listened as Manolo tried the handle then made himself comfortable on the couch. She tossed all night. In the morning, she felt so nauseous she suspected she was coming down with the flu.

The illness persisted, worse in the mornings. At first Dolores passed it off to the high stress of her marriage, but eventually, to her horror, she realized she was pregnant. She spent the day in tears, alone in her bedroom. She could hear Ruth talking to the children during the day but felt so far removed from reality she couldn't stir herself to join them.

When dusk darkened the room, Ruth came to find her. "Dolores? No dinner tonight?" Then she saw the red swollen eyes and sodden handkerchief. "What did he do to you now?"

"It's not like that." Dolores's mouth twisted. "Well, he did it, but I'm not injured. I'm pregnant."

"Oh, Dolores." She sank to the bed and clasped Dolores's hands in both of hers. "You must do something now. You can't let him hit you."

"You think I let him before?"

"No, no, that's not what I mean." She got up and began to pace. "You can move in with Grandma Jessie."

"I took vows in church," Dolores reminded her. "I won't forsake them."

"Then Alberto can sleep on the couch."

"Oh, yes," I scoffed. "Manolo will be all right with coming home to find another man sleeping here."

"I don't know the answer, Dolores, but there must be one. You don't have to do this alone."

"I know that."

With Ruth's help, Dolores stood up, washed her face, and made pulled pork sandwiches for dinner.

Manolo arrived home and raised an eyebrow at the sandwiches. They ate in silence until Dolores worked up some courage. "Manolo, I have some news." She could not work enthusiasm into her voice. He must have thought she was dying. She took a breath. "I'm pregnant." She waited for the world to fall in.

"That's wonderful, Dolores! No wonder you've been a little testy all week." He pulled a flask from his coat pocket and drank in celebration. He offered her a slug, but she declined. A three-day binge followed. Dolores wished he'd go away again instead of reeling home drunk. The girls disliked spending all evening in their room, but she wouldn't let them near Manolo when he was drunk. Alberto appeared on her front room couch. He left only when Dolores did.

SEVENTEEN

World's Fair 1939

*F*amily surrounded her. Dolores didn't know what Ruth and Alberto had told them, but they rarely left her alone with Manolo. Her morning sickness went away, and her belly grew quickly.

"Your body remembers what it's like to be pregnant," Ruth told her. "The first time, you don't start a baby bump until you're four months along. By the third time, you start showing almost before you know you're pregnant!"

Dolores rubbed her belly. "I'm only a month or so in, but it looks like four months!"

Ruth laughed and took Betty by the hand. "Come on, Carmen," she said, "let's go see what Rosa is doing." She led the two girls outside to join the other children, who were playing with Helen in Grandma Jessie's yard.

The men were not yet home for lunch. Vovô snoozed on the couch. Grandma Jessie held her chopping knife. She turned to Dolores and said, "Aloha means taking others' pain as your own."

Dolores nodded, unsure where this was going. Was she talking about Manolo? Or about Dolores? "Maria used to tell me you could love someone without loving everything they do."

"No family is perfect," Grandma Jessie continued. "Lord knows I'm not saying what my son does is right, but we are all here to help you."

"I know that," Dolores assured her. "Manolo loves me; he loves his girls. They need him." When Grandma Jessie's gaze lingered, Dolores said, "I won't leave him. I can't. God created marriage to be permanent, and I know what's best for my family."

Grandma Jessie nodded, satisfied. "You're a good Catholic, Dolores."

Not for the first time, Dolores wondered about Grandma Jessie's own marriage. Her husband had left her with five small children. They had never divorced. Dolores didn't even know if he was still alive. He was gone, though, while Manolo kept coming back to inflict new pain. It didn't matter in the eyes of the Church. Dolores was married.

After Alberto got a job as a shipfitter at Pearl Harbor, he was gone most of the day. He worked on various ships in the harbor. Dolores was glad he was settling down. Ruth stayed close to home. She sold her hand-sewn clothes door to door to make a little money, but when Manolo was due home, Ruth was always there. Dolores could find no words to thank her, and she knew they were unnecessary.

About a block away from them on Beretania was a school that offered classes for children with sight problems. Dolores enrolled Carmen there in the fall. She expected backlash from Manolo, but he never said a word. So she walked Carmen to school every morning and listened to her chatter happily on the way home every afternoon. Betty toddled all over the house. Her chubby cheeks invited pinching. For all intents and purposes her husband had left them, but they were not alone. The Medeiros family had embraced them.

Manolo startled Dolores by appearing for dinner after Betty's birthday in February. His animated face showed how eager he was to see her. "I have a surprise for you," he said, barely waiting until he finished eating. Alberto and Ruth took the plates into the kitchen, and Dolores sent the girls to play.

Her stomach lurched, and then she flushed with guilt. A surprise was usually good. She gave him a thin smile. "What is it?"

He waved two tickets in the air, triumphant. "We're going to the World's Fair!"

"In San Francisco?" Dolores had never been to the mainland. She was excited to see the fair. And maybe they could see Paul and Sofia. But alone with Manolo? She calculated: six days there, six back, and how long at the fair? She wondered why he wanted to do this at all. "How can we afford it?"

He laid the tickets next to his plate and took her hand. "Please be excited about this, Dolores. A guy at work got the admission tickets from a customer. We can afford the passage—I got a raise last month, remember?" His thumb stroked her palm. "I know it's been hard for you lately." He looked at the table, at their hands, out the window. Everywhere but at his wife.

"Carmen needs shoes. Betty should have a new dress." Dolores could only think of expenses.

His eyes found hers. "It will be romantic."

Dolores saw the handsome young man she had fallen in love with at Hanauma Bay. She remembered him as he came out of the surf and shook water out of his dark curls. She remembered when his smile lit his eyes like Alberto's always did.

Manolo lost his temper when something happened with the girls that he could blame on Dolores. She assumed they'd leave them at home with Ruth. On a cruise, there would be no reason for him to get angry even if he drank. This would be their chance to reconnect, to fall in love again. The smile she gave him felt more genuine. "It sounds like fun."

On March 12, they boarded the *Matsonia*, one of Matson

Lines' finest ships. Every color was vivid, from the green rim of Punch Bowl on the hill above the city to the sapphire ocean below. On the pier, brass instruments flashed in the sun as the Marine Band in their white uniforms played "Aloha ʻOe," Queen Liliʻuokalani's beautiful song of farewell. Hawaiian girls danced the hula nearby, their hair twisted with white pīkake flowers that gave sweetness to the air. Family and friends waved good-byes, their clothing adding dots of color to the scene.

Green palm trees swayed behind the Royal Hawaiian Hotel, also known as the Pink Lady. Waikiki's pale cream sand stretched toward Diamond Head, majestic as always above Honolulu. On the white ship, fragrant leis, orange and purple and yellow and pink, covered Manolo. Dolores inhaled deeply. The leis that should be around her neck hung from Ruth's arm. "I want to wear them, Ruth."

"No, no. It's bad luck to wear them if you're pregnant!"

Dolores crossed herself and said, "In the name of the Father, the Son, and the Holy Spirit. There. I've cancelled out the Hawaiian superstition with the Catholic!" She laughed and slipped the flowers off Ruth's arm. The fragrant cloud settled around her neck, and she crossed herself again just to be sure.

"It seems every flower in Hawaiʻi has given its life to send you off in style," Ruth said. The bell clanged, signaling visitors to depart. Ruth gave Dolores a kiss and scurried down the gangplank.

Dolores turned to wave toward Pearl Harbor, out of sight beyond Hickam Field, in farewell to Alberto, who couldn't get away from his new job to see them off. She imagined seeing past Hickam Field, its gray runways, planes, barracks, Quonset huts, and jeeps, to Pearl Harbor with its American Navy ships.

The smokestacks with the big blue M belched dark clouds. The ship churned the water as it pulled away from the dock. Honolulu faded until she couldn't make out the Pink Lady. All eyes fastened on Diamond Head, the last view of home. In keeping with tradition, they threw a lei overboard as they passed the extinct volcano, a promise they would return to the islands. They watched until Diamond Head faded to purple distance and blended into the ocean.

The steward put the luggage in their cabin, which was spacious and well-appointed.

"I read that this ship was retrofitted only two years ago," Manolo said.

"It feels brand new," she said.

"Well worth the money they spent," he agreed. "Of course, the fares increased, too. You're worth it though."

They held hands like newlyweds and made their way to the main lounge. They would spend a lot of the next six days here as they read and talk to other passengers and to each other. The walls were all in beige tones, with bay windows on both sides. A central dome in the ceiling gave added height. The furniture and carpeting was very elegant, mostly chairs and couches placed around tables. It looked very inviting.

That night for dinner, they walked into the main restaurant as if they'd done it a thousand times. The center of the room soared upward for two decks, with a light fixture and grand dome in the center. Dark wooden chairs complemented the black-and-gray marble floor. Silver, fine porcelain, and crystal glasses gleamed on the tables.

"I feel as though I'm dining with ali'i," Dolores whispered to Manolo.

"No royalty could be as beautiful as you," he replied.

Dolores refused to ruin the moment by pointing out how trite he sounded. Instead, she smiled as they sat and picked up the menu. "I'm going to pick something I've never had before," Dolores said. "And can we have the Strawberry Charlotte for dessert? I promise to save room for it. My stomach is growing anyway, so I might as well enjoy the fancy desserts!"

"Sounds delicious." Manolo ordered a porterhouse steak. The steward brought a bottle of wine Manolo had preordered.

Dolores twisted the napkin in her lap. She reached out the other hand and laid it on his arm.

"I'm perfectly capable of having wine with dinner," Manolo said. His eyes bored into her.

"I'm sorry," she said. "I just don't want to ruin all this." She waved her hand to indicate the opulent room.

"You'll only ruin it if you have morning sickness or go into labor." The words stung. His tone, though, teased her.

She smiled. "No chance of that, I promise. I'll stick with iced tea though."

He raised a glass of wine to toast her. She clinked her tea glass against his and added a silent prayer. *God grant this trip is successful. I must repair my marriage.*

On their first full day at sea, Dolores commandeered a deck chair and lay watching the ocean. She tied a scarf over her hair so the sea wind wouldn't ruin it. The sun felt marvelous on her face and the bit of her legs that showed below her dress. Manolo joined her after a deck tennis game with some of the men he'd met the night before at the bon voyage party.

"This is lovely," she said, basking in the sun.

"Think of it as our honeymoon." He leaned over her and kissed her forehead. A whiff of whiskey tickled her nose. Her joy plummeted like a stone in the sea. She tried to tell herself it was possible the scent remained from a spill on his shirt from the island. Her mind was smarter though. It kept giving her images of a furious Manolo tossing her overboard. He whistled as he left her to shower. Once again, the surrounding luxury masked dark depths.

That night, after another wonderful meal in the main restaurant, Dolores put a hand on her belly. "I'm so full that our baby has no room in there."

Manolo's eyes darkened, his hand tightening on his glass of wine. "You shouldn't be discussing such things in public."

"It's just the two of us." Her stomach fluttered, and it wasn't the baby or the meal.

She saw his face run through a myriad of emotions as changeable as the ocean's colors on a stormy day. What emotion would it land on? With great effort, he smiled.

She relaxed a bit. "So shuffleboard tomorrow?" she asked. He agreed. Crisis averted.

The next day Dolores and Manolo played a languid game of shuffleboard with a couple on their way home to San Francisco after a honeymoon in Honolulu. Their arms reached around each other as if they couldn't live apart. They smiled at Dolores and Manolo, but the smiles they had for each other were brighter. Dolores focused on Manolo and sent him the brightest smile she could manage. She lightly touched his arm as often as she could, trying to infuse tenderness into her touch. He didn't respond.

"Oh, wonderful game," Dolores said, wiping her forehead with a handkerchief. "Next time we must play to twenty instead of seventy-five though!"

The couple laughed politely. Remembering Manolo's words of the night before, Dolores said nothing about her pregnancy and let them believe she was out of shape or lazy.

"Let's get a champagne cocktail and sit on the deck," Manolo said.

"We can sit without the champagne," she said.

"As you wish, ku'uipo." He ordered iced tea for both of them. He clicked her glass, gazed deep into her eyes, and said, "ʻOkole maluna."

She toasted him and drank the wonderfully cold tea. "Manolo, did you notice how affectionate they were?"

"Our opponents? They're newlyweds."

"Aren't we trying to recapture some of that?"

"Is that why you were pawing me? We have a baby on the way. We don't have to be so publicly devoted."

"Is that what you believe?"

"You relax. I'm going to play tennis with the guys." He walked away without kissing her good-bye or looking back. When he returned for dinner, his breath smelled of alcohol. Apparently, there'd been drinks after tennis. If there had been any tennis at all.

She wanted to rediscover the magic they'd had when they first married. That, for her, had been the purpose of this trip. So what should she do now? If she argued with Manolo about his drinking, it would ruin the trip. If she said nothing and he drank every day, it would ruin the trip. How could she win? After circular wrangling for several minutes, she shook her head. Ridiculous. She had to speak up.

"Manolo, no wine with dinner tonight." She didn't ask. She didn't plead.

He stared at her. "Feeling unwell, are you?"

"No, I'm fine. You look rocky though. Tennis must have taken more out of you than you realize." Without pausing, she looked up at the waiter. "No wine, tonight, please. Just tea." When he nodded and took the bottle away, she felt a burst of pride in herself. She met Manolo's eyes and didn't look away. "Join me for iced tea?"

He nodded. "Pregnancy must be making you cranky." When she took a breath to retort, he held up his hands to protest. "No, I'm sorry. Don't want to poke the shark. Let's have a nice dinner." He reached across the table to take her hand. "So what do you think Carmen did today?"

Dolores smiled, always ready to discuss their daughter. "She would love running her fingers over all the lush fabrics on this ship." Manolo laughed and all tension dissipated.

After dinner, they walked the deck in the moonlight. Dolores sighed, full of good food and good feelings. As they prepared for bed in their stateroom, Manolo said, "Tomorrow is a big day. Tennis tournament. Want to come watch?"

"Oh, I'd love to, but it's so bright and hot on the courts. You can tell me all about it at lunch."

"You and Baby relax." He kissed her goodnight.

Dolores thought back over the evening and smiled. She needed to speak up for herself more often. It worked.

The next day, Manolo was up and gone before she awoke. At luncheon, she sat alone at the table until the staff told her, with many apologies, that they had to close the dining room to prepare for dinner. Dolores hid tears of humiliation, anger, and frustration until she got back to her room. Then she cried and punched her pillow until exhaustion overtook her.

"Dolores?" His soft voice and touch on her shoulder woke her. The dusk-darkened room disoriented her at first. "Did you sleep all day, kuʻuipo? It's time for dinner."

She stretched and sat up. "Dinner already? Where were you?"

"Our team won the tournament! We played hard, and it took longer than I thought it would. Big celebration tonight! All the guys are joining us for dinner."

She got up and hurried to the closet. Slipping into her dinner dress, she said, "How nice. Congratulations." She hoped it came across less sarcastic than it sounded to her. "A little lipstick and powder, and I'm ready to go."

They walked hand in hand to the restaurant, where Manolo called greetings as he guided her to a table full of couples. He introduced Dolores to all the men, and they introduced their wives. The men then took over the conversation as they discussed every play of each tennis game. They emptied two bottles of wine at the table and ordered four bottles of whisky. Dolores sat between Manolo and a large man called Stu. She could not carry on a separate conversation with any of the women. Manolo entertained them all.

"Your husband has a mean backhand," Stu said to her at one point.

Dolores just nodded and smiled, but thought to herself, *if you only knew.*

That wasn't the only night they sat with the tennis group, and it wasn't the only night Manolo fell asleep on their bed, drunk and fully clothed.

The six-day passage was full of time suspended from reality, as she was sure the shipping line intended. Manolo tested Dolores's nerves at least once a day by drinking. It was much less than he drank at home. She convinced herself he was trying. Even so, the cuddling newlyweds reminded her what she didn't have, and the brash tennis group, whisky glasses in hand, reminded her what she had.

On the last day, with their bags packed and ready for the steward to take away, they stood on the deck as they passed under the Golden Gate Bridge. Dolores had read about it and seen pictures, but the reality struck her speechless. The massive steel and thousands of gigantic rivets screamed heft, but the airiness of the cables was delicate. "I can see why San Franciscans want the world to see this," she said.

"The Bay Bridge is new, too, but not as grand." Manolo wore sunglasses to hide bloodshot eyes. He saw her shiver and asked, "Would you like your sweater?"

Forewarned by other travelers, they carried light outerwear with them. San Francisco in March was much colder than Honolulu in December! Dolores took the offer of warmth and snuggled into it, not wanting to miss a minute of the docking.

With the suspended reality of the trip behind them, it wasn't long before Manolo's temper reappeared. He snapped at the steward as they disembarked and snarled at the delay as lines formed. "You'd think they would know how to do this more efficiently! If my office staff worked this slowly, I'd have them all fired!"

Dolores ignored him, scanning faces for Paul and Sofia. At last, she saw her brother waving, and they made their way to him.

"Welcome to California!" Paul said, greeting his sister with a warm hug.

"It's cold here," Dolores teased him. "Where's Sofia?"

"She's waiting at home. Shall we collect your bags?"

Manolo nodded. "If we can make it through this blasted crowd."

Despite Manolo's grouchiness, they retrieved their luggage and piled into Paul's car for the drive to his home in Sunnyvale, about an hour south. Paul and Manolo made small talk about the voyage, and Dolores put in a few things about their daughters and the family. She was surprised, when they reached her brother's house, that Sofia did not come out to greet them. Manolo and Dolores would be staying with them for seven weeks. Dolores would have welcomed them to her home. She followed Paul and Manolo up the walk but hesitated on the porch, blanching when she saw the address. How could she have forgotten his house number was 449? In Hawai'i, the numbers four and nine were unlucky. She hoped the address wouldn't affect their enjoyment of the trip.

Paul let them in the house, and there she was. Sofia sat in a large armchair, wearing black, her dark hair twisted into a tight bun. She held a rosary that was yellowed with age.

"Dolores, this is my wife, Sofia. Sofia has just found out she's pregnant," Paul told them proudly. "Sofia, this is my sister Dolores." He waved at Manolo. "And her husband, Manolo."

Sofia smiled. "Sorry I couldn't come greet you at the pier."

"Mahalo for having us in your home," Dolores told her. She was confused why a newly pregnant woman couldn't come to the pier. After all, she'd come all the way from Honolulu. Paul's Sofia was an odd one.

Sofia looked at Paul, who said, "She's thanking you." Sofia nodded.

Paul and Manolo took their bags into the bedroom Manolo and Dolores would use, and Manolo returned with two wrapped packages he handed to Dolores. "These are for you, to thank you for your hospitality," she said, giving one to Paul and one to Sofia.

Paul opened his first. "A real aloha shirt! Thank you." He held it up for Sofia to see.

Sofia frowned.

Palm trees covered the blue shirt, and hula girls danced across it. Dolores knew that in Honolulu it was a nice shirt, but somehow in California it was too bright.

Sofia opened her gift. "Oh. Thank you," she said in a flat tone when she saw the shell earrings and necklace. The shells were arranged and painted to look like roses. Sofia pushed the box to the back of the chair-side table and picked up her rosary.

"If you have a girl, I'll send a little hula skirt for her from Honolulu. She can be the smallest hula dancer in California," Dolores told Paul.

Paul laughed. "She'll be cute anyway."

Sofia's smile was so fleeting Dolores almost questioned that she'd seen it at all. "I appreciate your intention," Sofia said, "but my daughter will not grow up to embrace the exotic sensuality of the Hawaiians."

Exotic sensuality? Dolores just barely refrained from laughing out loud. Behind her, Manolo chuckled. As days went on, though, Dolores realized many Californians saw Hawai'i that way. Between the radio program *Hawai'i Calls* and the Hollywood movies, Dolores didn't recognize the place of her birth. It gave her something to laugh about with Manolo.

Paul owned a movie theater in Sunnyvale but gave his manager the running of it, so he could come with them to the fair and sightseeing. Sofia was reluctant to leave the house. Dolores didn't know if she was afraid something would happen to the baby or if she was just afraid to go out. Dolores wouldn't let it mar her visit even though Sofia seemed to expect her to spend more time sitting at home.

Manolo and Dolores attended the World's Fair every day. They'd read all about it before they left Honolulu and were eager to see it all. They knew the fair was to celebrate the new Golden Gate and Bay Bridges, but also to showcase all the nations of the Pacific. Dolores much preferred the nickname "Pageant of the Pacific" to "World's Fair." It sounded so much more romantic! Treasure Island, the site of the fair, was a man-made island. The Pacific Ocean surrounded it, and there were even palm trees! The gigantic white statue of Pacifica was the first jaw-dropping sight they encountered, but then they saw the Tower of the Sun, over four times taller!

The buildings housed wonder after wonder. They walked across a model relief map of the western United States, watched demonstrations of television and the electric eye, and explored pavilions from forty foreign countries. Some critics said the World's Fair pandered to women with all the innovations for the future that involved housework. Dolores's eyes went wide when she saw Bakelite toaster handles, automated cow-milkers, and air-conditioned coaches. She would never be able to afford any of these things, but she scribed every idea into her brain so she could share it with Grandma Jessie and Helen, who would wave it off as foolish, and with Ruth, who would share her longing.

"When we return to Honolulu, we'll buy our own house and furnish it with all of these," Manolo told her.

Dolores played the game, too. "An all-electric kitchen will save me ten thousand steps a year."

"Really?"

"According to General Electric."

"Well then, you shall have it all!" He swept his arm wide to encompass all of GE's Town of Tomorrow.

The best part of the fair, though, was outdoors. Flowers and fountains covered the grounds, surrounding buildings painted in soft colors. Light played over pools and lagoons, and nighttime was magic. That was when it took no imagination at all to picture Treasure Island as a city of light floating on San Francisco Bay.

Every night they returned to Paul's house tired and full of wonder like small children at a parade. Sofia prepared dinner for them and shot them sour looks, especially if Paul had been with them. Dolores was glad Sofia didn't come. She acquainted herself with her adult brother in a way she couldn't in Honolulu surrounded by Hawaiian family. A couple of times, Dolores saw him frown at something Manolo said to her and give her a quizzical look. Dolores wasn't close enough to her brother yet to confide the status of their marriage to him. She was determined to enjoy this vacation, to build a bridge between herself and Manolo, to heal her family for the future. In that light, she bought a lucky jade plant for Sofia, hoping to dispel the bad luck of the house number.

"Why do you think I need your Chinese luck?" Sofia asked.

"Everyone can use a bit of luck," Dolores told her. She forced a cheerful smile.

Manolo played like a boy at the Gayway, a forty-acre fun zone with a cyclone coaster, rocket ship, giant crane, and other thrill rides and shows.

"Come on, ku'uipo," he said. "One ride on the roller coaster won't hurt the baby."

Dolores shook her head, laughed, and said, "Oh, no, we don't want our little one to be born a daredevil!"

Dolores treasured her first pair of nylon stockings, introduced at the fair. She saw many women wearing them and exchanged secret smiles with them since they were so fashionable. Dolores bought a purse-sized sewing kit for Sofia from the J. P. Coats exhibit, but her sister-in-law turned up her nose at it.

"What's wrong with her?" Dolores asked her brother later in the kitchen. "She hates the gifts I give her. What have I done?"

"It's not you," Paul said. "Sofia comes from a conservative religious family. She thinks you're wild." He rubbed his neck and laughed, awkward and self-conscious.

"Wild?" The notion made Dolores laugh, but it also confused her. "Why did you marry such a shriveled up old soul?"

Before Paul could answer, a noise at the doorway made Dolores turn. Sofia stood there, face frozen in fury.

"*O meu Deos*," Dolores said. "Sofia, I'm—"

"Do not take the Lord's name in vain while you are a guest in my home. I have tried to be civil, but you heathens are more than any God-fearing Catholic can be expected to bear!" She left the room with her back ramrod straight.

"Heathens? She knows we're Catholic, too, right?"

"She does," Paul said. "I'm sorry, Sis. She really is a good wife, and she'll be a good mother. She's a fine God-fearing woman."

"That's funny. I've never found a need to be afraid of God." Dolores rejoined Manolo in the front room. She and Sofia would never be friends.

Inevitably, Dolores and Manolo's step out of reality came to a close. On April 6, they kissed Paul good-bye and wished Sofia well with the baby.

"Write and tell me all about him or her," Dolores urged her.

"Of course," she said with a cold little smile. She didn't return the request.

Paul drove them to the pier where the *Lurline* waited to return them to Honolulu. This time they traveled in cabin class. It was still a wonderful world, only a step down from the *Matsonia* and the World's Fair. This was the ship that Amelia Earhart had taken with her plane when she came to Honolulu four years before for her record-breaking flight to Oakland.

Manolo laughed when Dolores told him this. "We definitely focus too much now on records and wonder," he said.

"How could it be any different after what we've seen?" she asked.

His eyes laughed as they hadn't in Honolulu for a long time. The wonder that surrounded the World's Fair cocooned them, together and alone, as they shared favorite memories from the last two months. This time there were no tennis buddies. They spent the days and nights together. Laughter and smiles, and his arm around her shoulders, created warmth more suited to a honeymoon than a vacation.

But vacations, like honeymoons, never kept the magic alive once reality returned. After dinner on the last night of the voyage, many of the passengers went on deck to see if they could spot the far-off lights of Honolulu. Manolo and Dolores remained at the table, their plates already cleared. The soft music of dinner service gave way to the clanking of dishes from the kitchen. Manolo nursed a glass of wine. Dolores thought it was his fifth. His smiling conversation had turned to a sullen quiet she hadn't seen in months. She'd put off the important discussion of his drinking, but if they didn't discuss it before they docked, they never would. "Manolo," she began. He looked up. "This has been a wonderful trip."

Something in her tone alerted him. He downed the rest of his wine and signaled the waiter to bring another. "Yes, it has," he said.

A chill touched his eyes. Dolores shivered. This was a bad time. She leapt forward anyway. "You haven't lost your temper once since we got to California, and Sofia sure tried her best to make you." She hoped her attempt at levity would lighten the mood. It didn't.

"And?" His voice was sharp now. The waiter poured his wine, and Manolo took the bottle.

Dolores winced. "Maybe the drinking doesn't help," she offered.

"Help what?"

"Come on, you know what I'm trying to say." Exasperated, she just said it. "This trip was wonderful, but it's over. How can we keep this happiness when we return home? Is it the children that set you off? Or me? I never know. I do know the drinking makes it worse."

"You don't know anything."

"You've only had one or two glasses of wine each night. I may not know much, but I know you only hit me when you've been drinking too much." There. It was said. She didn't know whether she should be defiant or sweet and pleading. The latter had never been her style.

He stopped in the middle of raising his wine glass to his lips and set it back on the table so hard red droplets splashed onto the white tablecloth. "You know I'm sorry about that, Dolores. I don't mean to hurt you."

"Please stop drinking, Manolo. Or at least drink less." Dolores clasped her hands together in her lap.

"All the Medeiros boys are drinkers," he said in a voice that almost sounded proud. "Mama always says, 'Those boys of mine!' when we drink and raise hell. But she loves us."

"I've also seen her slap João's face and tell him the whole town knows about him and his drinking, and why does he want to drink that stuff. She never drinks, or smokes, either."

"My mother, the paragon of virtue."

"No one's asking you to be a paragon. Just try a little harder to drink less."

"Sure, Dolores, all right." He smiled, but she felt like he agreed just to stop the conversation.

Dolores stood and put her napkin on the table where it stayed in a twisted rope. "I need to finish packing before the steward comes for the bags. Are you done?"

He waved her on. "I'll come up in a little while."

Dolores walked away from the table. She paused in the doorway to look back. The dining room was empty except for her husband at their table. The dim lighting, at first romantic, was now just sad. She watched Manolo empty the wine glass and pour another.

By the time she reached their cabin, she could no longer wipe away her tears before more fell.

❦ EIGHTEEN

Honolulu 1939-1940

A week after their return from the World's Fair, after they'd shared stories, distributed souvenirs, and life returned to normal, Dolores woke with a stomachache. She moaned as she got out of bed and doubled over. Struggling to stand, she took a deep breath. Manolo was in the shower. He had to go to work, and she had to fix breakfast. She wrapped herself in her robe and carefully walked into the kitchen. Alberto, his hair tousled from sleeping on the couch, already had the coffee on.

"Good morning," he said. His smile lit the room, bringing an answering smile from Dolores. He poured her a cup of coffee. When he set it in front of her, his hand brushed hers. He let it linger there. His touch made her entire arm tingle. She wanted to pull away. No, she wanted to clasp his hand. She settled for not pulling her hand away.

"Mahalo," she told him. The laughter in his eyes changed to something deeper.

Manolo rushed in. "I'll get coffee at work. Running late." He pulled up short when he saw Dolores spill her coffee as she yanked her hand away from Alberto's. He frowned.

"Happy to pour some to take wit' ya," Alberto said smoothly.

"I don't need you to do that," Manolo snapped.

Another cramp caused Dolores to moan again.

"You aurite?" Alberto asked.

"Go back to bed and rest," Manolo told her. "I'm off." He turned his head toward her and kissed toward her face before rushing out the door.

Dolores sank into a kitchen chair, clutching her stomach.

"You aurite?" Alberto repeated. "You look pale."

"My stomach hurts."

"Stomach mean baby. Dis normal?"

"I didn't have pain like this with either of the girls."

Ruth came upstairs, preceded by her children who swept in like whirlwinds. In the ensuing commotion, Ruth gave all three pao duce they could nibble on the way to school. Meanwhile, Carmen and Betty came out of their bedroom. Alberto handed each of them a roll. The oldest of Ruth's children, Winona, marshaled William and Rosa out the door with shouted good-byes.

Dolores sat at the table and watched the normal chaos. She tried to breathe deeply instead of gasping with pain. Ruth peered at her and frowned.

"She say stomach hurts," Alberto said. He used a napkin to wipe up the spilled coffee.

"How bad?" Ruth asked.

"Bad," Dolores admitted.

"I take Carmen ta school," Alberto said. "You take Betty ta Grandma Jessie's, ya? Then take Dolores to the doctor." He peered at Dolores's pale face. "Or ta Queen's."

"Definitely Queen's. You're three months along, right?" Ruth asked.

Dolores nodded. "Almost three months."

Ruth took Dolores's coffee cup and bustled her into the bedroom. "Let's get you dressed." Dolores wasn't able to help much as Ruth slipped off the robe. "Dolores? You're bleeding."

She yanked a dress over Dolores's head, slipped shoes on her feet, and brushed her hair. "We'd better hurry."

The pain was so bad now that Dolores couldn't protest. Betty's eyes were wide as Ruth rushed her across the street. "Is Mama sick?"

"She'll be fine, sweetheart. You help Grandma Jessie, and we'll be back real soon."

The house was silent for a minute or two, silent except for Dolores's ragged breaths. Ruth rushed back in and helped Dolores to the car. "I'm worried, Dolores. We're going straight to the hospital. No arguments."

Dolores didn't object.

At Queen's, the nurse helped Dolores into a wheelchair. "She's three months pregnant and having stomach pain," Ruth told her. "She's bleeding."

The nurse whisked Dolores away. Chaos of another sort ensued. Instead of the normal morning routine, it was the organized confusion of doctors, nurses, beeping machines, orderlies, tests taken, and over it all the pain that threatened to take her baby. Dolores concentrated on breathing to control pain and panic.

"Where's my sister-in-law?" Dolores panted between words.

"She's waiting outside," the doctor said. "As soon as I finish the pelvic exam, she can come in. Let's check on baby, all right?"

Dolores nodded. The next wave of cramps brought beads of sweat to her forehead. She concentrated on the doctor's actions and clamped her teeth.

"There, Mrs. Medeiros. All done. I'll bring your sister-in-law in." Dolores just nodded.

Ruth entered. Alberto followed her. They took up positions on either side of Dolores's bed. Alberto took her hand and wouldn't let go. His touch warmed her through.

"The doctor said he'd be in to talk to you," Ruth said. Her smile seemed strained, her eyes worried.

"We here now, ya?" Alberto said.

The doctor returned with a nurse. He nodded at Ruth. Facing Alberto, he asked, "Are you the husband?"

Dolores wanted him to say yes, but Alberto said, "Nephew."

"I would like to speak to Mrs. Medeiros alone, then. Wait outside, please."

Alberto's hand tightened on Dolores's. "We not going nowhere," he said.

"Please let them stay," Dolores asked.

The doctor nodded. "You've lost the baby, but I think you suspected that."

Dolores nodded. Tears trickled down the sides of her face and puddled in her ears. Ruth and Alberto both squeezed her hands. She wasn't alone.

"I noticed something else," the doctor continued. "You have quite a few old bruises on your torso."

"Dose injuries make her lose the baby, Doc?" Alberto said.

"No," the doctor said. "I'm wondering about the pattern though. Some were fresher than others. Not from a single fall. Either you are very clumsy, Mrs. Medeiros, or someone is hurting you." He hesitated and looked at Ruth and Alberto. "Is the husband here?"

"He is at work," Dolores said. "Ruth will call him now that I'm all right. I am all right, Doctor?" A sob swallowed the last few words.

"Yes, you'll be fine," the doctor said. "The nurse will help you get settled in your room. I'll be by later."

He left the room. The nurse patted Dolores's leg. "I'm so sorry for your loss, Mrs. Medeiros. Do you have other children?"

"Two daughters." Dolores told her all about Carmen and Betty, their ages, Carmen's blindness and her school.

The nurse chattered away. She asked questions and exclaimed over Dolores's answers as she drew a curtain around the bed. The curtain excluded Alberto and Ruth with no apology. "Keep telling me about your precious girls," the nurse said. "I'm going to give you a little sponge bath before moving you to your room." She wiped Dolores from the waist down and draped her with a clean blanket. An orderly arrived with a gurney and helped the nurse transport Dolores to a new room. Alberto followed. Ruth slipped away to call Manolo.

Settled in a bright room with palm trees outside the window, Dolores assimilated what had happened. She cried in Alberto's arms and held Ruth's hand.

A loud voice in the hallway roused her. "What have you done to my wife?"

Alberto's lips tightened. Ruth wiped the tears off Dolores's face with a handkerchief. Manolo stormed into the room. "What's happened? What's going on?"

"I told you on the phone. She lost the baby," Ruth said.

"Whose fault is this?" He turned to Alberto. "What are you doing here?"

Dolores recognized the level of belligerence that accompanied several drinks after leaving work early. She lifted her chin and stared at Manolo. "Ruth and Alberto brought me. They've been a tremendous comfort."

"Get your own wife," Manolo snarled.

"Auntie need help. I there." Alberto used a calm tone that nonetheless accused Manolo.

"Our baby is gone, Manolo." Dolores ignored the tears staining her cheeks. She took a deep breath. "Our baby is dead. Alberto didn't do it."

Before Manolo could respond, the doctor entered the room. "Is this your husband, Mrs. Medeiros?" he asked. Dolores nodded. "You must lower your voice, sir, you are disturbing the other patients." The doctor stepped in front of Manolo. He stood between Manolo and Dolores's bed. "And you are disturbing my patient. Mrs. Medeiros, do you want him to leave?"

"Please," Dolores said.

Two orderlies appeared behind Manolo. They ignored his protests and helped him out of the room. Dolores could hear Manolo's anger increase as his distance did.

The doctor turned to her. "Is he the cause of those bruises?"

"He's my husband, Doctor, the father of my daughters. We are family." Dolores kept her voice strong and looked the doctor in the eye. "He loves us, and we love him."

"She has a lot of family support," Ruth said.

"We got dis, ya?" Alberto echoed.

The doctor nodded. "If you ever need it, the hospital can provide help beyond healing bruises."

Dolores nodded, and the doctor left. "I should have let Manolo stay," she said.

"No, he was too disruptive," Ruth protested.

"He not in a mood ta help right now," Alberto said.

"Thank you so much for being here," Dolores said. She addressed both of them, but her eyes clung to Alberto's.

DOLORES returned home sore in body, heart, and mind. Ruth and Alberto stayed close. Manolo didn't. Ruth told the girls that their mother was sad, and they covered Dolores with hugs and kisses. They hadn't yet begun to be excited about a baby, so Dolores didn't tell them of its loss. Ruth and Alberto did their best to help her keep her mind off the tragedy.

A letter arrived from Paul. He was still effusive over their visit to the World's Fair.

Attendance at the fair has fallen off, but I remember what we saw there. Do you remember the miniature gold mine?

Their trip to California seemed a lifetime ago. Dolores took a deep breath and focused on Paul's words instead of the memory of laughter.

But the World's Fair has been eclipsed in our household. Sofia gave birth to a lovely daughter on April 27. We named her Dolores. She is a delight! I hope you can visit soon to see your namesake. I'll even put her in that little hula skirt you promised.

Her jaw opened wide. They'd named the baby after her? Clearly that was Paul's idea. Dolores tried to picture Paul telling his wife to put the baby in a hula skirt. How was it possible that sour old Sofia had a new baby and she did not? What was God thinking?

"That be a letter from the mainland?" Alberto came in the front door. He was there in time to greet Manolo if he came home from work.

Dolores nodded. "Their baby was born. A girl. They named her Dolores."

He sat next to her on the couch and pulled her close. "I so sorry, querida."

His concern and the endearment flooded her with emotion. Alberto always knew how she felt.

"Let's take the girls to Pearl ta watch the ships. Or we go to the airport and see airplanes," he suggested.

"They'd love the airplanes," Dolores said.

"Airplanes it is. We pick up Carmen at the school and go from dere, ya?" He called to Betty, who played in her room, and grabbed his car keys.

"Let me brush my hair and get my purse." Dolores smiled at him. The smile chipped away at the block of grief inside her.

Both girls were excited to be on another adventure with their cousin Alberto. Betty loved the mighty roar of the Pan American Airways' big clippers that brought the mail from the mainland so much faster than ships. Carmen clamped her hands over her ears and scrunched up her face.

"You do dat, Carmen?" Alberto asked her. "Fly in an airplane over the ocean?"

"A ship is much safer," Dolores said.

"I do it!" Betty announced. She ran with her arms outstretched to each side and roared.

"You don't have to *be* the plane," Carmen chastised her in a superior tone. "You just have to ride in it."

Betty ignored her. Running was her lifeblood, and she took to it like the awa fish to water.

"They're for dreamers," Dolores said, her eyes on the sky. "The airplane will take you wherever your dreams want to go."

"Den we go together, ya?" Alberto said. They looked into the sky together. "We take the girls to Pearl when the fleet arrives," he said before she could respond.

On the day that the US fleet arrived at Pearl Harbor, however, Alberto was at work. Dolores took the girls to watch the 130 ships slowly move into the harbor. Carmen had trouble seeing the gray ships against the sea, and the ponderous movement of the big ships bored Betty. Dolores found the show of military might troubling, a reminder of conflicts far away in other countries.

The nagging feeling that might become fear worsened when the entire territory practiced a blackout drill. It seemed an omen of unpleasantness to come. Ruth and Dolores tried to make it fun for the younger children by making a tent with blankets over chairs. Ruth's older children rolled their eyes.

"The war is far, far away," Dolores told the girls. Rosa and Carmen nodded but looked confused. Betty just stared. "Italy and Germany are fighting Britain in Europe, way on the other side of the mainland, across another ocean." They had no concept of the distance. Neither did Dolores, really, but the words settled them all.

The next day, to banish all fears, Alberto took them all to Kapi'olani Park to see the first crane hatched in captivity at the zoo. It seemed appropriate since the new mayor was named Mr. Crane. Rosa and Carmen brought paper cranes they'd folded in school using origami. Carmen's looked better, Dolores noticed proudly. Her fingers felt details her eyes couldn't see.

Rosa locked elbows with Carmen. Heads together, the sighted girl described the crane and its enclosure to her blind cousin as she always had. Dolores wasn't sure Carmen could imagine the colors, but she loved that Rosa took the time to describe it all. Hours later, Carmen talked about the crane using Rosa's words as if she'd seen it.

In the evening, after dinner, they all loved to listen to musicals on the radio. Carmen memorized all the words and sang along. She begged for a record player, but they just couldn't afford it. Manolo dropped by often enough to keep the bills paid. His family would never let them wallow in need, but a record player was a luxury. Dolores had no money for luxuries.

"Mama, all my friends at school have them," her eldest daughter said. She sat on a chair and swung her feet.

They were at Grandma Jessie's, where they were preparing lunch for the hungry family as usual. Ruth, Helen, and Dolores washed and peeled vegetables, and Grandma Jessie stirred the pot as she had every day for decades. There was a sense of security in the tradition.

"I'm sorry, Carmen, but I cannot afford it. You know this," Dolores said.

"What's the problem?" Antonio, Alberto's father, came into the kitchen. Alberto's family still lived with Grandma Jessie. Antonio worked in an office as Manolo did, but he didn't drink. Carmen was a favorite of his.

"I want a record player, Tito," Carmen said.

"A record player sounds like just the right thing for a girl who loves music like you do." He grinned at her and tousled her hair. She beamed at him.

"I can't afford to get her one," Dolores said.

He looked from Dolores to her daughter. "Don't you worry," he said.

The next day, Antonio brought a record player to their house, along with three records. Carmen was ecstatic. She and Rosa immediately set it up. "Look, Carmen," Rosa said, "Tommy Dorsey! He's wonderful!"

"Frank Sinatra sings with his band now, doesn't he?" Dolores asked Antonio.

"You girls are more up on the latest music than I am," he protested, but his eyes sparkled as much as the girls'.

Dolores knew he didn't want or need her thanks. He was part of the family network. It was all about hard work, love and support—the aloha spirit. Familia es todo, and everyone is 'ohana.

❧ NINETEEN

Alberto 1941

Dolores turned twenty-six years old in January of 1941. Twenty-six. It seemed such a big number. She'd been married now for ten years and didn't see her husband ten days out of a month. Alberto stayed so often that Manolo didn't dare come by drunk. Apparently, he was drunk a lot. On a positive note, he hadn't beaten her recently.

One day Dolores was helping Grandma Jessie clean her house. Helen and Ruth were in the kitchen. Antonio wasn't home from work yet, and the family lunch crowd had dispersed. Alberto rushed into the house like he was being chased by Pele herself. He slammed the door behind him and collapsed into a seat at the kitchen table, panting.

"Alberto? Now what?" Grandma Jessie asked, one hand on a hip and a frown on her face.

"My car need gas. I don' got no money so Noa and I siphon some off a car parked on the next street, ya?"

"And where is Noa?" Helen asked. Her motherly frustration with Alberto's antics sharpened her tone.

Alberto waved a hand. "His faddah get him out."

"They arrested him?" Dolores said in horror.

"A'ole pilikia," Alberto insisted. "Not a problem."

Grandma Jessie waved her ladle at him. "Talking to you is like water through a sieve."

206 { LINDA ULLESEIT

They went back to cleaning the kitchen. Dolores shot a glance at Alberto now and then, but he seemed content to sit at the kitchen table and watch them. Carmen served him a late lunch with a smile of adoration. She turned nine in June. Dolores remembered how significant nine had been to her, how she had felt useful and hoped it would impress Papa. Carmen was capable around the house. She helped cook and clean along with her cousins. The family followed Dolores's lead, and no one coddled Carmen. Well no one except Vovô, now in his eighties, but what else was a great-grandfather for?

"Noa won't say you helped him." It wasn't a question. Dolores knew it was a fact.

Alberto flashed his angelic smile, the one that went with the wicked gleam in his eye. "We bruddahs," he said with a shrug.

"When did Noa get back from the mainland?" Ruth asked. She put a glass of guava-pineapple juice in front of him.

"Ah, Auntie, you really want ta know if he finish school, ya?" Alberto leaned forward, elbows on the table to build suspense.

Dolores smiled. Alberto's pranks were legendary. No one wanted to encourage him, but none of them could stop asking about them. Dolores remembered when Alberto and Noa climbed up the statue of King Kamehameha that stood outside the *Ali'iōlani Hale*, the Iolani Palace. It had once been home to Hawai'i's kings, but now housed the territorial government. The bronze statue was a noble one, all tall and regal, the king's hand outstretched. Alberto and Noa, under cover of darkness, had put a roll of toilet paper in the king's hand. Great hilarity had ensued on the part of young people, and embarrassment on the part of officials. Dolores hid her laughs behind her hand when Alberto related these adventures. A married woman with two children required decorum, but she enjoyed a good joke.

"Noa, he miss me so much," Alberto continued. Carmen laughed and leaned against him. His tanned, muscled arm reached out to encircle her. "And we had a hole, ya? In our gang? Only Noa an' his Harley could fill it." He picked up a fork and feigned innocence as he ate.

Grandma Jessie shook her head, but Dolores saw a flash of the smile she tried to hide. "Those boys of mine," she murmured.

Those words came out of her mouth often. Alberto, as part of the next generation, continued his uncles' tradition. He rode all over Honolulu with his motorcycle gang but never got into any serious legal trouble. He heard everything that went on in Honolulu.

The war news reached them like fairy tales from another place and time. It seemed unreal, far away, but Alberto and his cousins dug an air raid shelter in the space between Grandma Jessie's houses. Ruth and Dolores covered it with a vegetable garden and hoped they never had to use it. "Crazy nephews," they scolded the boys.

Dolores and her girls loved to window shop at the Fort Street Mall. Alberto sometimes walked with them. Bob Hope's "Thanks for the Memory" wafted out of a store, and Alberto sang along with Carmen. Dolores laughed when Alberto pointed to absurd outfits for the girls. One window showed a young girl in a wool sweater and cashmere scarf with hat and gloves. "That's the same outfit they put out every winter," Dolores told Alberto. "They can't sell many of those in Honolulu!"

The girls adored Alberto and joined in his game. "Look, Cousin Alberto! See the pretty bottles."

"Chantilly is in a round bottle with sun's rays," Betty told Carmen.

"Do they have Blue Grass?" she asked.

"Horsey!" Betty confirmed, spotting the oval bottle with

the blue horse head. The girls each had their favorites, having sampled them often. How nice it would be to have money to spend on perfume for small girls.

They looked in the window of the jewelry store but didn't go inside. The diamonds glittering in the window took Dolores's breath away.

"You don' need sparklies, Dolores," Alberto told her. "You sparkle enough by yo'self, like the sun on the sea, ya?"

"Oh, Alberto," was all she could say when he complimented her like this. It made her uncomfortable because she responded to it like a wilting flower drinks in water. She responded to it, yet she was a married woman.

Later that day, after dinner and baths and bedtime, Dolores sat on the back lanaʻi with Alberto and pretended he belonged there. The palm trees rustled in the trade winds, which smelled of saltwater, plumeria flowers, and the neighbor's adobo chicken dinner. Tonight, her nephew-friend was serious, which was unusual for him.

"Today remind me of seeing the spinner dolphins off my surfboard, ya?" he said, eyes on her.

Dolores remembered how awed Alberto had been by the dolphins. She looked up to the height of Punch Bowl. In the other direction, Honolulu stretched down to the sea. Downtown's usual lights were dark, and the buildings' windows covered with blackout curtains. Further out, Pearl Harbor let dusk turn to dark illuminated only by the setting sun. She turned to Alberto. "Me, too."

His eyes captured hers. For a long minute, Dolores was lost there. Then he closed them and moved in to kiss her. He'd never done this before. It felt so right in her heart, so wrong in her head. Dolores kissed him back, harder than she intended. When they pulled apart, she was shaking.

"I not sorry," he said, his tone almost belligerent.

"Me either," she said. "But you'd better go."

He nodded. Dolores stared up at Punch Bowl as the last bits of sunset lit the mountain. Alberto rose and left the lanaʻi. He picked his way through the yard. She heard a chair creak as he sat on Grandma Jessie's lanaʻi. He would watch from there tonight. Dolores sat on the lanaʻi until well after full dark, tears wet on her face. She couldn't afford pleasure for herself, and that made her sad. Feeling sorry for herself, though, was something she'd given up long ago. Dolores angrily wiped away the tears. Despite her rational mind, she had enjoyed Alberto's kiss, and she was afraid that if she went inside it would turn cold on her lips.

LATER that year, Boy Scouts in Honolulu had a drive to collect metal. School children throughout the city helped.

"Do you have any tin cans, Tito?" Carmen said over and over to her uncles. "It's for a good cause."

"That it is," João told her. "I'll ask the guys at work for their cans."

Carmen beamed. She continued to pester her uncles until Dolores imagined them deconstructing every machine in the neighborhood to get her some of the precious metal.

One evening they were just sitting down to dinner when Manolo came home. He tossed his hat on the rack by the door and sat at the table like he did it every night instead of once every couple of weeks.

"Welcome home, Papa!" Carmen said. "Did you bring any cans home for me?" Her hopeful smile warmed Dolores's heart.

"Carmen, stop." His sharp words killed his daughter's smile. "You shouldn't pester me right when I get home from work. Hasn't your mother taught you that? Eat your dinner and we'll speak later."

Dolores put her hand on Carmen's shoulder. Both girls kept their eyes on their plates as they ate rice and teriyaki chicken and sliced mangoes. No one talked or laughed about their day, so the girls finished quickly.

"May we be excused, Mama?" Carmen asked. Her mouth was full of her last bit of rice, swallowed only after she finished her request.

"Do you have any schoolwork?" Manolo asked.

"I finished it right after school, Papa."

"Then you may be excused," Manolo decreed.

Carmen looked to her mother for confirmation. "You may go," Dolores said.

Manolo set his knife and fork on the table. When the girls disappeared into their bedroom, he got up and went to the refrigerator. "Dolores, where's my beer?"

"I poured it out."

He glared at her and went to his liquor cabinet. "Poured this out, too?"

"Yes."

"You realize I can get whatever I want to drink?"

"Of course, I do. But I won't have it in my house. You drink whatever you want wherever you want. Come home after the girls are in bed or come home sober. You're not always pleasant when you're sober, but you frighten them when you're drunk."

"Is this what you tell them? That their father is frightening?"

"I don't have to tell them. You show them."

"When have I ever hurt those girls?"

"When you hurt me, you hurt them."

"So you cry to them? To those babies? Or do you pour it all out to Ruth while they are in the room?" His tone dripped with sarcasm.

"Carmen is nine. She's very perceptive, and she's not stupid."

"She's nine? That makes Betty what? Six?"

"Five."

"Why doesn't she go to school, then?"

"I thought it best to keep her home with me another year."

"And why was that your decision?"

"You weren't here."

He'd come back to the table during their clipped exchange and stood next to the table. She stood up to face him.

"Did Alberto advise you?" he snarled.

"I spoke to Alberto about it. I also talked to Ruth and Grandma Jessie. They all agreed." Dolores rapidly ran through possible directions for this conversation. He could fixate on why Betty wasn't ready, and maybe accuse Dolores of babying her. He could fixate on Ruth and Grandma Jessie making decisions for his daughter. Or he could fixate on Alberto, and she didn't want to discuss that with him.

"Alberto is here too often. The neighbors probably think you are having an affair."

Dolores took a deep breath. "Alberto is family, just like Ruth and Helen, just like your brothers. Families are there for support."

"And poor Dolores needs support because her husband is never home?"

"Goodnight, Manolo." She walked out of the kitchen, the dirty dinner dishes left in the sink. In the girls' room, she read a bedtime story and cuddled. Their love was a warm blanket over raw emotions. Carmen promised to turn off the lights and go to bed at eight thirty sharp. Dolores kissed them goodnight and went into her room. Manolo had moved into the front room and sat in front of the radio. Dolores said nothing as she went into their bedroom and locked the door behind her.

❋

IN November, Alberto's friend Hiro, who lived next door, roared up to Grandma Jessie's on his Harley. They sat in the kitchen to talk as Dolores stirred the day's stew. Hiro said he had enlisted in the army and was off to the language school at the San Francisco Presidio. Alberto teased him about learning Japanese.

"A third of Hawai'i's population is Japanese," Hiro said, "and seventy-five percent of them are *nisei*, born here. Like me, they know more English and Hawaiian than Japanese."

"Maybe yo' heritage make it easier ta learn," Alberto said.

Hiro laughed. "Can I leave my bike with you, Alberto?"

"'Ae, of course. Park it in back. Mālama pono, Hiro. Be safe."

"Mahalo, friend." Hiro waved and was gone, one more Honolulu boy lured to war.

"It's coming, isn't it?" Dolores asked.

"Nah, not ta paradise," Alberto assured her with a cocky smile.

Grandma Jessie came in from the garden, and Alberto slipped out the door. She washed and peeled carrots, talking to Dolores as she did so. "You spending a lot of time with my grandson, Dolores. He's a nice boy, but don't let him turn your head."

Dolores stirred the pot silently, wondering how much to say.

"I know your marriage isn't perfect. Not many are." She looked up and pointed the peeler at Dolores. "You take control. Make the best of what God has dealt you. Never put a rotten potato in the pot."

"Yes, ma'am." It was the automatic response, but there was nothing more to say. Grandma Jessie sided with the church. Manolo it was, for rich or poor, good times and bad times, 'til death did them part. Dolores allowed herself a sigh.

Later that night, just at dusk, Alberto and Dolores walked around the block. It was more balmy than humid, the air scented with Grandma Jessie's gardenias, but at least she was getting used to the lack of light from windows covered with blackout curtains. Despite Alberto's offhand reassurances, Dolores felt uneasy about the future.

He took her hand as they walked, and pleasant warmth suffused her. "Dolores, what yo' gonna do about Manolo?"

"Do?" she asked.

"He not good ta you, and he ignores the girls. He never will leave you. . . ." His voice trailed off. "Make your canoe go back, ya? No keep heading into the storm."

"So I should leave him? Are you joking? How can I leave my husband yet continue to live in the bosom of his family? Your grandmother is quite clear on the matter. My place is with my husband. I won't deprive my girls of this family because my husband is a jerk."

"I marry you if you be divorced."

"Marry me?" Dolores's head spun. "The Catholic Church won't allow a divorced woman to marry in the church. I can't divorce him. I can't marry you. It's more than that, though. I chose him to be the father of my children, the head of my family. Making that choice work is up to me."

"No matter. I here." Alberto squeezed her hand. "Keep yo' chin up, especially when yo' drowning, ya?"

Dolores was glad for his presence, for his support, but she worried that she was being selfish. She couldn't keep Alberto near her when some woman out there could make him a fine wife, give him sons and daughters with those devilish eyes and rakish grin. She turned to face him. "Alberto. . . ."

He misread her and pulled her into a kiss more passionate than the last. Every nerve ending in her body sang. She couldn't push him away. She would be selfish in this one thing.

He kissed her once more, on the tip of her nose, and waited for her to go inside. Dolores closed the door behind her and leaned against it, listening to him walk away. The girls cuddled on the couch listening to the radio.

"Mama, is it bedtime?" Betty rubbed her eyes.

"Yes, darling, time for bed." Dolores tucked Alberto's kisses away into a secret part of her brain. She took Betty's hand and led her to the bedroom. Both of her daughters, in their pretty pink nightgowns, were angels. They knelt beside their beds and said the Lord's Prayer together. Carmen added, "And bless my mama, papa, and sister."

As she did every night, Dolores added a silent prayer of her own. *Watch over my littlest angel, Lord, that you have taken into your kingdom.*

Dolores tucked Carmen and Betty into bed, kissed them goodnight, and headed for her own bed. With the government-sanctioned blackout, she had no light to read or sew. Early bedtime had become the norm. She slipped between cool sheets, and they felt good on sun-warmed skin. Now that she was alone, her traitorous thoughts focused on Alberto. She saw the devil in him, and the angel, and loved them both.

Dolores heard the front door open, then close sharply. Her heart quickened in fear as she turned on her side to face the wall. Manolo stumbled into the bedroom and tossed his hat onto the dresser before falling on top of the covers. He smelled of cheap beer. Dolores kept her eyes closed and focused on even breaths. Her hands clutched the pillow. When he began to snore, she relaxed, but Alberto's kisses were gone.

Grandma Jessie's pack of wild boys, sons and grandsons, had a lot of spirit and raised some hell, but they were family men. This sprawling Portuguese 'ohana belonged to Dolores now, and to her girls. Most of them would understand if she took up with Alberto—she knew for sure Ruth would—but others expected her to support Manolo as they did. If she divorced Manolo, she divorced his family. She couldn't do that to her girls. It was their family, too. Dolores didn't know how to live without this family's support anymore. Manolo was a man engulfed by his demons. She didn't know how to help him, but a divorce would finish them both.

TWENTY

Pearl Harbor 1941

Early on Sunday, December 7, 1941, Dolores was struggling to get the girls dressed for church. Mass was at eight thirty, and their feet were still bare, their hair uncombed. Manolo slumped on the couch. From the dark circles under his reddened eyes, Dolores assumed he was nursing a hangover. She encouraged the girls to join her in loud singing of Christmas carols, hiding a perverse smile as he winced. Then he sat up like a dog who'd perked its ears at an intruder and ran to the window.

Dolores heard the planes a second later. Through the window, she and Manolo watched as they came in low over Punch Bowl like a flock of dark birds, and the circular red sun painted on the wings chilled her blood.

Thunderous explosions assaulted their ears and shook the house. Betty began to cry. Manolo rushed out the front door. Dolores was close behind but shouted at the girls to stay inside. From their lanaʻi, they looked over a scene of horror. Devastating fireballs shot up hundreds of feet in the air. Dark billows of smoke boiled from a handful of places across Honolulu. The ocean was burning. Dolores's stomach roiled like the smoke that devoured Pearl Harbor.

"Manolo, Alberto is working this morning! He's down there!"

More planes flew over, and Manolo pushed her inside. "Get the girls!"

Dolores grabbed Carmen's hand and Carmen took Betty's. They rushed down the steps from the lanaʻi. Carmen turned her face to the sky, then the sea. Even with her poor sight, she could see the fires of hell that dotted the heart of Honolulu on the hillside below them. The vegetable garden sat serene and undisturbed. Dolores saw Antonio lead his mother-in-law out of the house. "Is Vovô coming?" she called.

"Helen has him," Antonio said. "Come on, Grandma Jessie. You can get down these steps. We'll be safe in the shelter." He kept up a string of comforting words until he had settled both of the elder family members on a hard bench. Grandma Jessie moved closer to her father for support.

"What's that now?" Vovô said, dazed and querulous. "Too many people and not enough room." He wriggled his shoulders until Grandma Jessie gave him a little more space.

Dolores had never seen Grandma Jessie so out of her element. She was still wearing her apron and had her silver spoon in hand, but down here there was no stew to stir. She sat with her eyes down, shoulders hunched. Manolo sat beside her and brought his clasped hands to his head. Dolores wondered if that helped the splitting headache of his hangover. It was too bad they didn't have a raucous alarm to set off.

Behind them, a wall of shelves held staples like cereal, sugar, and coffee. The highest shelves held light cotton blankets. Another bench faced the first, set against floor-to-ceiling shelves of canned food. Dolores remembered filling those shelves with Ruth, joking about making sure they had a can opener. Now Ruth huddled on the bench, trying to enfold all her children in her arms. Winona and William usually resisted such demonstrations of motherly affection, but the attack had scared them. Dolores sat next to Ruth, keeping her daughters close.

Helen clutched the radio as if it were a lifeline. Antonio held her tightly. The KGMB radio announcer said, "This is no maneuver. Japanese forces are attacking the island. This is the real McCoy!" Explosions and sirens assaulted them from the radio and from above. The ground around them rumbled, but the shelter stayed safe.

"Look, girls," Dolores said. "We're having an adventure." She had to stay calm even though inside she was terrified for them all, and for Alberto down in the middle of everything. She tried to picture the chaos at Pearl Harbor, the smoke and fire and confusion. It was beyond imagination. Silently she said a prayer for Alberto's safety.

"An adventure instead of church?" Carmen asked.

"Shall we have some cereal?" Ruth said. Dolores recognized her own calm mother voice, the one that hid the panic within. Ruth went to the table at the back of the shelter where two kerosene lamps were burning. She filled old white porcelain enamel bowls with Wheaties and put a spoon in each bowl. In another bowl she mixed powdered milk with water from a jug.

Antonio took his bowl and forced a smile. "Yumm. Very 'ono," he said.

The children ranged in age from Betty at five to Winona at thirteen. They sat on the floor and used their bench as a table. Dolores took her bowl but couldn't eat. She noticed Helen and Ruth didn't even take cereal. At least she and Ruth had their children here. "I'm sure Alberto will be fine," she told Helen. Helen's tight smile said she appreciated the sentiment, but no one knew who would survive.

The radio called all navy and civilian workers to Pearl Harbor and reported the roadway clogged with cars. A bomb had fallen on King and McCully, setting fire to a grocery store. Another fell near Washington Place, the governor's residence.

"Please, God, let Alberto be all right," Dolores chanted over and over. She didn't care who heard. "Please, God, spare my daughters."

"*Em nome do Pai e do Filho e do Espírito Santo. Amen.*" Grandma Jessie prayed in Portuguese.

Dolores gathered the cereal bowls, with various amounts of leftovers, and put them on the table. She sat down again, and Betty climbed into her lap. Manolo leaned against the closed shelter door.

About ten o'clock, Governor Poindexter came on the radio and declared a state of emergency. He asked Honolulu residents to stay indoors and remain calm.

When the attack was over, though, the family tentatively left the shelter, reborn into hell as they came above ground. Grandma Jessie clutched Antonio's arm. She cried and crossed herself. For once the stalwart matriarch was not in control. Relief washed over Dolores when she saw all four houses standing undamaged. "Look, it's all right," Dolores murmured. She patted Grandma Jessie's arm, "it's all right."

But all reassurances faded as they looked out over their city. Dolores still couldn't see Pearl Harbor for the smoke. Maria and Peter were down there, too, in their tiny base house near Fort Kamehameha. Dolores tried to imagine Peter manning the anti-aircraft guns at the fort, but she could only see him with his saxophone, or laughing in his yard with his boys.

All seven adults and five children gathered in Grandma Jessie's kitchen. Grandma Jessie turned on the stove and stirred the stew pot with a shaking hand. Winona and William took the younger children into the front room. Dolores could hear them telling stories of Pele and her anger as they tried to reassure themselves as well as the younger ones.

That afternoon, President Roosevelt declared martial law on US soil for the first time since the Civil War. Still in shock, Ruth, Helen, and Dolores sat at the kitchen table and stared at the radio. Manolo comforted his mother, and Antonio took Vovô to his favorite recliner before returning to the kitchen.

They listened for every scrap of news on the radio. Wounded residents found their way to Queen Emma Hospital. One Japanese plane had been shot down at Fort Kamehameha, and Dolores silently cheered for Peter. Someone found a large bomb fragment on Queen Street and took it to city hall. Frantic residents deluged telephone lines. Radio announcers asked them not to use the phone if they could help it. The military governor called the Territorial Guard to action, which was ironic since they were mostly Japanese-American.

"But what about civilians at Pearl Harbor?" Dolores said.

"People are dying all over the city, Dolores." Manolo's tone sharpened. "Alberto will get word to us."

The day passed slowly. Time dragged with deep worry and debilitating fear. With every announcement, Dolores imagined Alberto and Peter in the rubble, injured or dead. Around dinner time, called that even though no one felt like eating, a boy ran up to the house. Dust coated his clothes and face.

"Mrs. Rodrigues!" he called.

Helen stepped forward and said, "Yes?"

He handed her a dirty scrap of paper and ran off down the hill. The family crowded around her. "It's a note from Alberto," she told them and read it aloud.

Mama—

I am in the fires of Hell, but not hurt. Tell you all about it when I can get away—so many to save—don't worry.

All my love,
Alberto

Cheers broke out among the men. They slapped each other on the back, congratulations spilling forth as though someone had become a father. Dolores sank into a chair, weak with relief. Manolo looked at her curiously, but she didn't care. Alberto was safe. She could handle anything now.

Dolores couldn't understand how the hours continued to pass. In times of crisis, families bonded together. Manolo's brother João arrived with his wife and two children. Frank, the oldest brother, brought his wife, too. Ruth urged Grandma Jessie to prepare food, to keep her busy and pretend life was normal. When it was ready, no one could eat. Dolores helped her mother-in-law in the kitchen because it was better than pacing and waiting. The sun set, but the sky remained vivid and orange as the oil on the sea burned. Manolo and his brothers drank beer out in the carport.

The next day they hovered around the radio as President Roosevelt spoke. "Yesterday, December seventh, 1941—a date that will live in infamy—the United States of America was suddenly and deliberately attacked by naval and air forces of the Empire of Japan."

To hear it spoken so plainly chilled Dolores inside. Finally, the president said, "I ask Congress to declare that since the dastardly and unprovoked attack by Japan on Sunday, December seventh, 1941, a state of war has existed between the United States and the Japanese Empire."

Her ears roared with the white noise of shock. She had known it was coming, had to come, must come, but it was done. America was at war.

Dolores ventured outside. The neighbors did the same. They paused in the street, afraid to congregate in the open but longing for human interaction. They shared stories that began with, "Did you hear. . . ?" In this way they heard about planes that knocked each other out of the sky, battleships sunk in the harbor, steamship offices bombarded by people who begged to get off the island. Dark smoke hung in the air, stark against the blue Hawaiian sky. For the first time in Dolores's life, the air didn't smell of flowers.

Yoshiko's oldest son came over to share a copy of *Hawai'i Hochi*, the Japanese newspaper. "It urges loyalty to the United States," he told them.

Carmen asked, "Why wouldn't they be loyal to the United States?"

"Of course, they will, sweetheart," Dolores assured her. "It's just that this attack will make people suspicious of all Japanese."

Carmen shook her head. "That's crazy."

The adults settled back in front of the radio. They didn't want to hear more horror, but they could not turn away. They learned that Queen's Hospital had run out of anesthesia, treating burns. Hospital gowns had been torn up for bandages. Over one thousand civilians gave blood—people from all walks of life, all ethnicities. Honolulu checked its blackout curtains, painted car headlights black, grieved its losses, and hunkered down to protect its island.

After dark that day, Alberto returned home, his feet leaden with exhaustion, his face haunted. Dolores wanted to hold him and never let him leave her sight, but she left that action to his mother and grandmother. Grandma Jessie insisted he wash up and eat before he talked story. They waited, nervous to hear what he had to say. Helen put a bowl of stew in front of her son, and they all settled around, to hear him and support him.

"I be changin' clothes when the bombing began," Alberto said. "Strafing bullets come right through the roof, corrugated, ya?"

Alberto's speech always had even more pidgin when he was nervous or upset. Dolores began to reach for his hand, then pulled back.

"I mo' scared," he continued. His uncles nodded, making affirming noises. "I want hide, but Julio DeCastro, ya? The caulker?" His uncles nodded again. "He round us up an' send us out der. I tear scaffolding off ships and tro it in the water, and dodge strafing bullets by duckin' 'round turrets on the ships, ya?" He paused, and the family relived his horror in silence. "They try get the ships underway, but. . . ." his voice trailed off. He took a breath. "Afterward a weird silence hang in the air, no planes an' no explosions, ya? The wounded they start crying, and the *tap tap tapping* of sailors trapped in capsized ships. I help on *Oklahoma* all day today wit' a blowtorch, ya? We got the first group, six men, I t'ink, out 'bout eight o'clock. Every coupla hours, few more men. Dis afternoon they let most of us go." His eyes looked out toward the harbor. "Some wait still, see if mo' survivors found. I had ta come home, ya?" He put his head in his hands.

The family showered him with gratitude and encouragement, and then left him to rest. The benefit of Alberto's level of exhaustion was that he could sleep, something the rest of them could not.

But humans are resilient. The city resounded with shock and grief, but it went on. The Red Cross held classes on surgical dressing. Gas rationing, ten gallons a month, went into effect. Christmas lights were torn down or left off throughout the city. Residents might be resilient, but they were afraid.

A rumpled letter arrived from Paul. Guilt stabbed Dolores. It had never occurred to her to call him. Well, she'd been busy surviving an attack.

Dear Dolores,

I hope this letter finds you whole. The attack on Pearl Harbor shocked the nation, and now we are at war. I hope you are weathering it well.

He was so impersonal. She marveled at his disconnection. He knew the family. He knew Alberto worked at Pearl Harbor and the family all lived scattered throughout Honolulu. Yet he didn't ask about any of them.

You must be scared. I hear many people are leaving the island. If you want to do so, you, Manolo, and the girls are welcome to stay with us until you can get on your feet.

Aloha,
Paul

Stay with him? And Sofia and baby Dolores? Dolores felt relief and trepidation at the same time. It was nice to have somewhere to go, but even more frightening to think of going. The idea remained in her head though. Every time Manolo didn't come home, she thought about what it might be like in California. When fear overcame her, Dolores thought of California as a refuge, but Ruth wouldn't be there. Nor would Grandma Jessie. Could she lose her extended family to save her girls? Honolulu no longer felt safe.

They had reason to be afraid. On December 15, a Japanese submarine shelled Kahului Harbor on Maui. Dolores held her girls tight and prayed. She put rabbit's feet in their pockets and followed all Grandma Jessie's other superstitions for luck. She gave them each a birthstone necklace to wear and made them wear their clothes inside out. Carmen balked but decided she didn't care since the military governor had cancelled school. Dolores prayed their good luck would not run out.

Alberto tramped back and forth to work in silence. He worked hard and came home exhausted. Dolores told him he couldn't repair every ship in the harbor by himself, but her words fell on deaf ears. Manolo went out to gather news, but she was not interested in the news he found at the places he frequented. Good thing, since he came home drunk or not at all.

Christmas arrived just three weeks after the attack. By then, law required all islanders over six years old be fingerprinted for ID cards. Dolores looked at precious Betty, five years old and still with chubby baby cheeks, and wondered how anyone could suspect her of anything. The military declared Christmas Day a workday, and no one complained. Dolores vowed to make this a normal holiday for her girls. Rumors said crates of bikes and wagons and dolls were sitting on the docks in San Francisco, pushed aside by war supplies headed to the islands. That meant nothing to Dolores since she couldn't afford those things. She altered two of Rosa's dresses for Carmen and Betty. At Kress, she bought them each a small toy. Remembering her first caramel candy, Dolores stopped in at Benson-Smith to buy candies for the girls. All over Fort Street people fought over food and sundries that were fast disappearing from store shelves. The scarcity of sweets in Benson-Smith's display case was another blatant reminder war had arrived.

This year Dolores wanted to keep her small family close. She began cooking dinner after breakfast, and soon she could smell the kālua pork all over the house. They decorated their tree together. Carmen, as the oldest, put the most precious glass ornaments on the top branches. Dolores helped Betty hang wooden ornaments on the lower branches. As they stepped back to admire it, Manolo came home with a crash of the door and thump of boots. His too-loud voice made Dolores wince.

"Ah, here are my beautiful girls! Stopped for an eggnog with some buddies on the way home. Just one, no need to run to Alberto and complain now." His voice was jovial, as if he were relating events from his day. "Mele Kalikimaka, my darlings."

"Mele Kalikimaka, Papa!" they chorused, and ran to him for a hug.

Dolores took time to force a smile on her face. He noticed. He focused on the girls, but his brow turned up at her, and his mouth down. He looked around the decorated room and smelled the pork cooking. "Aren't we going to Mother's?"

"I told you I wanted to have a holiday with just us this year. We're over there every day. Just the four of us tonight." Dolores smiled and headed to the kitchen to serve the meal. Her heart hammered and her hands shook.

"You never told me that! The family is always together on Christmas Day!" He didn't bother to follow her into the kitchen but just raised his voice.

Dolores reflected on how foolish it had been to have dinner here alone. At the time, she'd had no guarantee her husband would join them. She had wanted to try it out, see what life with just herself and the girls would be like. Dolores sliced the pork and piled it on a platter. With the platter in one hand and a bowl of poke in the other, she sailed into the dining room as if hers was the happiest of families on the happiest of days. Dolores never could fool him.

He greeted her just inside the door and slapped the platter out of her hands. It crashed to the floor. "You can't cook kālua pig in an oven," he snarled. "It needs to be done underground in an imu."

Dolores set the poke on the table and picked pieces of pork off her dress. The girls examined the wrapped presents left for them by *Kanakaloka*, the Hawaiian Santa, that he'd brought after his canoe arrived at Waikiki. They hadn't heard the crash of the platter. Maybe they were used to it. Dolores narrowed her eyes and glared at him. "Dinner will be delayed. I need to heat some leftovers."

"I'm going to my mother's." Manolo slammed the door behind him and staggered across the street.

With the world full of horror near and far, it was ever more important to preserve the spirit of Christmas. Dolores returned to the kitchen for leftover Portuguese sausage and pao duce. She even brought the haupia, coconut milk dessert. Dessert for dinner improved anyone's day. The three of them sang Christmas songs and ate all the dessert. Then it was time to see what Kanakaloka had brought them. Dolores sat on the couch watching her girls laugh and tear open packages.

"Carmen, your new dress is a pretty blue," Betty told her. Dolores smiled at the way Betty took Rosa's job when her cousin wasn't there.

"Look what I've found!" Carmen called. She held out the caramel candy for her sister.

The candy stopped their chatter, and they crawled up on the couch. Carmen and Betty flanked their mother. Full of sweets, their cheeks rosy red, they laid their sticky hands on Dolores and fell asleep. She cuddled them protectively. Dolores had no idea what the future held. She couldn't even see past tomorrow.

The illumination in the room changed as the sun turned orange and set. She should get up and draw the blackout curtains, douse the candles on the tree, but she couldn't bear to dislodge the girls. Half dreaming, she thought about the families she had known.

Her parents and brother she remembered fondly through the fog of time. The pain of their leaving didn't ache as much as it had when she was seven. Dolores knew her mama had loved her like she loved her own little girls. Papa had always said, "Familia es todo."

Kanoa and Noelani's children were grown and gone. All they had was each other and the endless work. They raised their children strong, all of them, strong enough to fly away and be on their own. Dolores wondered if they always knew that meant they'd be alone. No wonder Noelani had said, "Everyone is ʻohana."

Peter and Maria were like one person, but Dolores had never felt left out. They added her to their love as they added their four boys. Peter planned to retire from the army as soon as he could. It seemed he had a new appreciation for family in the wake of so much loss. Maria kept aloha in her heart.

Grandma Jessie was fifty-eight years old. Single-handedly, she'd managed a clan of five children, their spouses, and grandchildren. Her capacity for love was endless. More than anyone, she had taught Dolores that family just *is*. You didn't choose it or grow it. Most of the time you just dealt with it. The challenge lay in doing it with love, with patience and aloha, learning to love a person without loving everything they did.

Finally, Dolores's little circle, here in her arms. Manolo came and went like the trade winds. She didn't include him in her thoughts of family. More and more he lived outside family altogether. Alberto didn't fit in this circle either. He was family, a good friend, but not part of Dolores's circle. Her responsibility was here in her arms. It was her job to guarantee the safety of these girls, to teach them to find the aloha spirit for themselves.

❦ TWENTY-ONE

Honolulu 1942

When the Japanese captured Manila just after the new year, Dolores thought of the mothers in the Philippines who tried to protect their children, and she held her own girls tight as she prayed the enemy wouldn't come back to O'ahu. The law said they had to be home by six in the evening and couldn't leave before six in the morning. Lights had to be out during that time. Although fear thickened in her throat and curdled her stomach, Dolores locked it inside to avoid scaring the girls. Mothers throughout time had done so, and mothers throughout the world did so now as war spread.

Martial law kept Honolulu safe, but it also brought Manolo home early. She held her breath when the door opened each night and he staggered through.

"Dolores!" he called.

She could tell from his tone whether he was staggering from drink or exhaustion.

"Welcome home." She always greeted him with a smile. Sometimes, though, she'd shoo the girls off to wash up before dinner.

Just after her birthday, the announcer said members of the Hawai'i Territorial Guard were being released.

"Released?" Dolores asked her husband. "They were just formed after the attack. Why disband now?"

A short laugh punctuated his sarcasm. "They aren't disbanding, just letting the nisei guards go."

She ignored his tone. "These are educated men, ROTC from the University of Hawai'i."

"I know." Now he sounded sad. "But their parents were born in Japan. All three of Hiro's older brothers are in the Guard."

"What will they do now?" Yoshiko was already missing Hiro, at the language school in San Francisco. Now her other three sons would be released from a position of honor in the Territorial Guard.

Manolo shook his head. "Some people want to send all the Japanese to the mainland."

"All of them?" One third of the island was Japanese. Her mind struggled to imagine Honolulu without its Japanese residents.

Later that week, Governor Emmons formed a labor battalion of all nisei soldiers, volunteers who would aid the military effort however they could. It seemed an acceptable compromise, and Manolo reported that Hiro's brothers all joined.

"But it's a volunteer battalion, right?" Dolores asked, frowning.

"It's a way they can save face and help with the war effort."

Manolo seemed convinced, but she felt sorry for Yoshiko and her family.

EVEN in late February, the sun was still up at six in the evening. When Manolo barely made it through the door by curfew, she frowned at him. "Where have you been? Ruth took the girls over to Grandma Jessie's already." Actually, she'd sent them early, knowing what he was like when he was home late.

"Aw, Dolores, I just had a few drinks with the guys after work." He slumped on the couch and turned on the radio. War, war, and more war blared through its speakers.

"Do we have to listen to that now? Grandma Jessie is expecting us for dinner."

Manolo took off his hat and tossed it on the coffee table. He leaned his head back against the couch, looked at the ceiling, and didn't say anything.

Dolores went into the kitchen. She could make sandwiches for dinner if she must. She rummaged for bread, cheese, meat, and mayonnaise.

"I thought you said my mother was expecting us."

She jumped, not having heard him approach. "She is. Are you ready to go?"

"Not with you in that apron." His tone and gesture held a great deal of anger.

"I can take it off." She hurried to do so and grabbed her purse. "See? I'm ready."

He picked up his hat and opened the door. He waved her ahead with a curt nod. She forced herself to smile. Then, when he was behind her and she couldn't see his face, he suggested a picnic at Kapiʻolani Park.

"Let's make it special for the girls," he said.

She turned to him in consternation and searched his face for a trap. His eyes were clear, and they sparkled like they had when they first married. Dolores's heart fluttered free of its anxious cage. She needed to believe the simplicity of his words instead of looking for underlying emotion. "Wonderful idea. I'll make a chocolate cake."

The next day she used some of their sugar to make a tiny cake. Dolores had no idea when sugar would be available again in the store, but this was an important occasion. She put it on a tin plate and covered it with waxed paper. After wrapping it all in white butcher paper, Dolores was confident it would arrive intact at the park. Manolo made a mountain of sandwiches from sliced ham in the refrigerator. Dolores made bread and butter sandwiches for the girls. She filled a thermos with coffee for herself and Manolo and another one of lemonade for the girls. A basket of mangoes completed their lunch.

She slipped into the car next to her husband, and her daughters scrambled into the back seat. Before they said anything, Manolo told them, "Guess what? We're going to the park for a picnic!"

They bounced on the seat. "Picnic!"

They found a perfect spot in the shade of a banyan tree that must have been there when King Kalakaua created the park over seventy years earlier. The Hawaiian sun shone high in the sky, but a refreshing, almost-March breeze blew off the sea. Betty grabbed Carmen's hand, and they ran across the grass toward the sandy beach. Clear blue ocean waves crashed, and Carmen screamed with delight. Dolores spread an old blanket on the ground and laid out the lunch. Manolo started with the cake. She playfully chastised him, but the day was too beautiful to be angry. Or fearful. Diamond Head watched over them as it always had. Nowhere could she see bombs or Japanese planes. As long as they sat facing the ocean, they couldn't see the barbed wire installed on the beach by the US military after the Pearl Harbor attack. The tension inside her eased.

"We should make a habit of doing this more," Manolo said as he watched Dolores with a smile.

"It's good for the girls," she said, and turned to the ocean. "Look at Carmen splashing her sister."

"They're good girls."

It was the best compliment in a long time.

They returned home happy, sandy, and tired. Dolores helped the girls into bed and returned to the living room. Manolo sat beside the radio with an open bottle of Primo beer.

"Where did you get that?"

He looked at her and took a long sip. "Governor repealed the law against liquor sales yesterday. We have to ration it though, we can only buy a case a week."

She shook her head. "A case a week." The law hadn't slowed Manolo down. He always found plenty to drink, as did his friends. She turned away and picked up her mending to do in the bedroom. She'd pour out his beer tomorrow morning before he got up.

Danger didn't only exist in the skies over Pearl Harbor. It lived much closer to home, in her own house. Manolo would sit on the couch and drink beer until he fell asleep or until something on the radio sent him into a rage. She was a fool to believe he would keep the family safe, and she was even more a fool to believe she could do it alone.

ON another day, they drove up to Pali Lookout, atop the Koolau Range. Dolores stood at the edge and looked out over the windward coast of Oʻahu as if she were a chieftain of old, watching for approaching enemies. The wind pushed against her as if trying to keep her from falling.

"In the old days enemies would come by canoe," Manolo said, echoing her thoughts.

Carmen stood well back, holding her sister's hand. "Mama?"

"She's right at the edge, Carmen," Betty said.

"Mama, please come away," Carmen begged.

Neither of them liked the winds that howled and pushed against them. Manolo laughed at the wind, and the sound echoed over the canyon. Dolores remembered that laugh from the days of surfing at Hanauma Bay before they married. It brought back memories of a reckless young couple without a care in the world. Before marriage and children. Before the war. Before drinking.

"This would have been a good place to see the Japanese coming," Manolo said, looking out over Kaneohe Bay past Coconut Island.

"Wouldn't seeing them on their way be as frightening as seeing the actual attack?"

"No, the attack was worse. Our view from Punch Bowl was the best on island," he said, tone dry. He looked away from the view to his wife, he said, "You were worried for Alberto that day."

"We all were."

He looked at her thoughtfully and started to say something, but Carmen's scream whipped their heads around and flung unsaid words out over the cliff. Betty had worked her hand out of Carmen's grip and was walking toward the cliff edge. "Mama!" Carmen screamed again, her face tortured as her sightless eyes searched for her sister.

Manolo leaped for his youngest, and Dolores hastened to hold their eldest. "Hush, darling, Betty's fine. Papa has her."

Sobs wracked the girl. "I'm a bad big sister. I should have had her."

"You did have hold of her, Carmen. She was determined to pull free. You did nothing wrong."

Dolores looked up at Manolo, still holding Betty in his arms, for verification. He disappointed her.

"I told you she's too young for that responsibility." A scowl marred his face.

"She's very responsible," Dolores protested.

"Get in the car." He wouldn't hear it. He didn't hear anything he didn't want to.

On the way home, Dolores played the incident over and over in her head. She would have been able to get to Betty if Manolo hadn't been there. And she wouldn't have humiliated Carmen in the process.

AFTER dinner in the evenings, the adults sat around the radio. Dolores mended socks and tears in clothing while she heard about the Women's Air Raid Defense operating radar stations all over Oʻahu. They had new stations on Kauaʻi, atop Mt. Haleakala on Maui, and on the Big Island.

Other bits of life were changing, too. Meat and fish were shipped to soldiers, so Grandma Jessie's stewpot became vegetables only. She tried to make it thick and hearty. Manolo's brothers complained over lunch at Grandma Jessie's big kitchen table, but never about the meal.

"The governor forbids withdrawing more than two hundred dollars a month from our bank accounts." João said.

They talked politics and war. Dolores sent her girls outside to play with Rosa and her brothers. She couldn't keep them innocent forever, but she wouldn't encourage their education about the worst parts of life.

"When have you ever had two hundred dollars?" Frank scoffed. He rarely joined the family for lunch. Frank pointed his fork at his brother. "Bad enough we had to replace our currency with the 'Hawaiian series' money that's stamped 'Hawaiʻi.' They say if the Japs take a pile of US currency in a raid, they won't be able to use it."

"Stop it now," Manolo told them, his dark eyes serious. He turned to Antonio, Alberto's father. "You have a lot of Japanese friends in construction, right?"

Antonio nodded.

"They join up with Emmon's battalion?"

"Most of them. Toro Ishikawa's family volunteered for relocation." Dolores gave him a puzzled look. "About forty Japanese families, exchanged for Americans living in Japan. They're all volunteers, but it smacks of prisoner treatment."

"They will live in Japan?" Ruth asked.

Antonio said, "Toro's parents have family in Tokyo. They'll be fine. Toro will miss Hawai'i though. He grew up here."

They considered this in silence. Dolores had met Toro Ishikawa a couple of times, a quick nod in passing, but it still seemed like a friend was being mistreated. No matter how afraid she became, she couldn't reconcile Japanese bomber pilots with Japanese neighbors.

Rosa, Carmen, and Betty rushed into the kitchen. Their faces glowed with damp. "It's raining and sunny, Grandma," they said to Jessie. "Tell us the story again."

Dolores opened her mouth to tell them not to bother her, but Grandma Jessie wiped her hands on her apron and gathered the girls close. They sat together at the kitchen table. The men moved aside to make room. "Well, there was a time when the sun didn't shine in Hawai'i. Not at all."

The girls giggled. They loved this story and made her tell it every time it rained while the sun was out, which happened frequently in Honolulu. João and Manolo grinned. They loved it as much as the girls.

"The king of Tahiti took the Hawaiian sun, you see, and hid it in a cave on his island. He piled blocks of lava high to close up the entrance and ordered a bird to guard the cave. The people of Hawai'i suffered without the sun and prayed for relief. One of the gods went to Tahiti and strangled that bird in its sleep."

Her hands mimicked piling the blocks and strangling the bird. The little girls listened with rapt attention.

"The god removed the lava blocks and hurled the sun

high into the sky over Hawai'i." The girls cheered. Grandma Jessie continued, "No enemy of the sun can reach him now. Even the rain can't hide him for long. Remember, children, the sun conquers rain with liquid sunshine."

"Liquid sunshine!" Rosa hollered, dragging Carmen back into the yard. Betty galloped after them.

Dolores stepped up to the sink and looked out the window. "There they go, playing in the liquid sunshine."

Grandma Jessie laughed. "They'd never play in the rain if they were worried about getting wet. This way they can still have fun and the sun will dry them when the rain stops."

Dolores looked at this amazing woman, sixty years old but stronger than all of them. She kept the ugly parts of the world away from her door. Jessie took care of those closest to her, of family. Of her. She didn't need her long-absent husband to do it. Ruth had her mother's strength, too. She continued to make a loving life for herself and her children without her husband. They'd done it with unwavering family support. Manolo's family, not Dolores's.

TWENTY-TWO

San Francisco 1942

Over the next weeks, Governor Emmons thwarted the efforts of Navy Secretary Paul Knox, who wanted to remove all Japanese from Hawai'i because of the possibility of sabotage. Even so, the president's executive order sent almost a thousand Japanese Hawaiians to detention camps on the mainland. Sand Island, on Oahu, received more Japanese internees. When the authorities came for Yoshiko and her husband, Alberto went outside to protest.

"Her boys are in Emmon's labor battalion," he told the officers.

"We know that, sir. They've been picked up."

Yoshiko collapsed in tears. Grandma Jessie, who had followed Alberto into the yard, went to her neighbor's side to comfort her. Yoshiko's husband stared at the police in shock.

Honolulu's tension grew. Something had to break. Dolores must keep her girls safe. Bouts of panic fanned the fear inside her. More and more, she considered living and protecting her children without Manolo's family. In that scenario, friends became critical. Her best friend had always been Maria. After she married Manolo, Dolores had felt the need to make it work and show Maria she'd been wrong. When Maria's concerns proved valid, Dolores had been too embarrassed to call her. Using the attack as an excuse, she mustered her courage and called.

"Dolores! So wonderful to hear from you."

Dolores's anxiety melted away. "Are you all right? All of you?"

"None of us hurt," Maria said. "Just shaken up. It was a terrible thing."

"That it was." They were silent for a moment with memories too raw to share.

"Peter put our names on an evacuation list right away," Maria said. Her voice shook.

"Evacuation? Where will you go?"

"California. He'll join us when he can."

"But you don't know anyone in California. What will you do?"

Maria hesitated. "I don't know, Dolores. The army wants its dependents off the island."

"My brother is in California. He's asked me to come," Dolores said.

"Evacuation is a choice for you. Will you go?"

"I'm not sure. It's a big step. Send your address to Ruth when you settle in. Ruth can send it to me if I go to the mainland, too. We can stay in touch that way."

"Be safe, Dolores. Keep aloha in your heart."

"I will, and you do the same." Dolores hung up but kept her hand on the receiver for a long moment as if reluctant to break contact with Maria. Evacuations were a mess. The army, the navy, and the steamship company took names of women and children who wanted to evacuate. The army and navy wanted to force dependents to go, but many didn't want to leave. To make matters worse, Hawaiian residents stuck on the mainland were not allowed to come home.

Ruth said she would join the Women's Air Raid Defense and learn to man a radar station. She was glad she hadn't when, before dawn on March 5, Japanese planes approached Hawai'i once more. The Kaua'i Air Raid Defense station picked them up and sent out an alert. The family rushed for the shelter once more, instantly wide awake and fearing the worst. Sleepy children clung to them as they waited by the radio. Dolores focused on Carmen's head, heavy against her shoulder, and on Betty's legs as she kicked and squirmed to get off her mother's lap. Carmen was old enough to know what they were hiding from, and her face paled. Dolores squeezed her hand and held it tight. The moon was dark tonight, hidden by clouds, and a steady rain pattered on the shelter doors above their heads.

"Where's Manolo?" Ruth whispered, her lips in a tight line.

Dolores shook her head. She didn't know. William and Winona, both teenagers now, sat with ten-year-old Rosa between them. Ruth hovered over them.

The Japanese planes eluded Honolulu's radar. When bombs shook the earth, they didn't hit their shelter. The radio called the planes "flying boats" and claimed they couldn't see their target either. Two bombs hit at the harbor entrance, and a couple hit inland. No ships in the harbor were damaged.

No ships damaged, but her body could contain no more fear. On March 5, Dolores wrote to her brother.

Dear Paul,

It's been a hectic three months. I only want my daughters to be safe, and it seems they will not be so in Honolulu. I hope your invitation to California is still open as I plan to come as soon as I can.

Your sister,
Dolores

Ruth attempted to dissuade her. "You hardly know your brother. Family is here, Dolores. We look out for each other."

"Now, Ruth," Manolo said, "ship passages are hard to come by. If hunting for one keeps Dolores's fears tamped down, we should encourage her."

"That's not much support," Dolores said, stung.

"What if she finds spots on a ship?" Ruth asked.

"Then it will be a grand adventure," Manolo said with a grin. He was humoring her. Dolores ignored him.

"Some navy ships are taking passengers," Dolores said, determined to persist in her efforts.

"Yes, you go check that out," her husband said as he turned away. His distracted tone made it clear he thought she would reconsider.

Navy dependents had three different locations where they could put their names on a list for evacuation. Non-dependent civilians were told to register at the Honolulu Gas Company. After Dolores did that, she went to Castle & Cooke, another navy registration location, and registered there, too. She was told to be ready at a moment's notice. To protect the convoys, departure dates were not announced ahead of time. Dolores packed a suitcase for herself and one for the girls.

In May, Governor Emmons assembled the Hundredth Infantry Battalion from the island's Japanese men, which included Yoshiko's three sons. He sent them from Sand Island to the mainland for training. Their motto was "Remember Pearl Harbor." That was for the mainlanders. Islanders didn't need a motto for remembrance.

In Dolores's kitchen on a balmy spring night, Ruth and Dolores were sipping glasses of wine and talking quietly so as not to wake the sleeping children. The moon bathed the yard in silver and prompted spiritual conversation.

"Love is a crazy thing," Ruth began. "It begins with physical attraction. I mean, you have to think he's cute, right?"

Dolores laughed. "I first saw Manolo at Hanauma Bay. He was soaking wet and smiling. Salt spray covered his glasses."

"Ah, so he was in his element." Ruth smiled. "But you have to get to know a man to love him. You need matching dreams and desires."

"I don't know," Dolores protested. "Can't you support each other's dreams if they are different?"

"I don't know." Ruth contemplated the moon. "I've never had that experience."

Dolores considered Manolo. What were his dreams? At one time, he'd dreamed of being her husband and father of her children, the man of their house. And twelve years into their marriage they still lived in one of his mother's houses. Dolores dreamed of keeping her children safe. Manolo must agree even if he didn't discuss it with her. "So physical love and mental love. It seems there should be more."

Ruth waved at the moon-silvered yard. "A man I love must have the same spiritual beliefs. He has to believe in heaven, and God's love."

Dolores nodded. "So we've got it all figured out!"

"But our marriages were disasters."

Surprised, Dolores didn't respond right away. Charles had left Ruth although they never divorced.

"Come on, Dolores, we both know your marriage is no marriage."

Dolores sipped her wine.

"You picked the wrong Medeiros boy," Ruth said. "The best choice for you isn't a Medeiros at all, is it?"

"What do you mean?" She knew though. Alberto's mother may be a Medeiros, but he was a Rodrigues. "Ruth, we can't discuss this."

"Avoiding it won't make it go away," Ruth said.

Dolores didn't respond. Alberto didn't seem to have a darker side. Because she was married, she could never dis-cover the depth of her true feelings for Alberto. Or his for her.

Ruth's open conversation solidified Dolores's resolve to leave the island. She made the rounds of evacuation agencies, asking about her status. Dolores wasn't pregnant or infirm, and she didn't have a job critical to the war effort. She wasn't a tourist, nor did she have a large number of children. That put her at the bottom of the priority lists. Thousands were ahead of her.

At the beginning of June, the Japanese attacked Midway, and fresh panic broke out in Honolulu. Thousands more changed their mind and registered to evacuate. At last the phone call came. She was told, "Be at the dock by nine o'clock in the morning." Less than twelve hours' notice. Her first call was to Alberto. He left work immediately and came to her.

"We're leaving," she said. The words left a hollow place inside her. They seemed so final, so irrevocable.

"Oh, querida, yo' passage come! When?"

"Tomorrow morning. Alberto, I have to go, but I'm scared."

"Yo' scared ta stay and scared ta go, ya? I get it. Yo' a strong woman, Dolores. Yo' survive, and yo' do what's best fo' your girls. Men no being evacuated. Manolo follow yo' later?"

"I called you first. He doesn't know yet. He didn't think I could find three passages, so I don't think he's made any plans. Who knows when he'll be able to follow, anyway?"

"You go ta Paul?" Alberto knew all about her brother's offer.

"Living with Sofia can't be worse than living with Manolo." Her attempt at humor sounded flat, but Alberto laughed.

"Tito Mano has his demons, ya?" he said.

"I don't want to talk about him," Dolores said. "I will miss you, Alberto."

"Querida, the sun desert the island when ya go. You be my heart. No forget dat. Never."

Alberto took her in his arms and held her close. Electricity tingled along her body. She pulled away and looked into his eyes until his lips brushed hers. Then she closed her eyes and surrendered to the feelings she'd denied so long.

ON June 22, 1942, Dolores and her daughters prepared to board the *USS Republic*. It was a navy troop transport ship, not a passenger liner, but it was going to San Francisco with families who wanted out of Hawai'i. Carmen gripped Betty's hand, and Dolores had Carmen's. Summer breezes played with their skirts and twisted the girls' dresses around their legs. Manolo drove his wife to the dock.

"This is foolish, Dolores," he said yet again.

"Too many people want to leave Honolulu," she said. "I can't risk losing this opportunity."

"When will you be home?"

She couldn't have this conversation. Alberto's farewell the night before still sang in her heart. "The convoy will crisscross the ocean. It'll take longer than the usual six days. I should be home in ten days or so."

His jaw set as he understood. "Sofia will make you miserable. Paul's place is not your home."

"There is no reason for me to come back to Honolulu."

"I don't know how long it will take to sell all our belongings and join you," he said. Men were not yet being allowed on evacuation ships. He was just laying groundwork for later excuses.

"Take your time. We'll be fine." Dolores turned away. "Come on girls. How exciting this will be!" She carried her suitcase and held Carmen's hand. Carmen had the girls' suitcase. At six, Betty was responsible enough to follow her mother. At least Dolores hoped so. She was anxious to leave.

In California, her family would be safe. In California, she would be safe.

Dolores didn't look back as they walked up the gangplank. Below them, the lower decks received cargo. An armed soldier led chained men on board. Prisoners? Dolores frowned.

On deck, one sailor stepped forward. He found them two beds together in a cabin intended for two that now held eight bunk beds.

"I want to sleep on the top," Betty announced.

"You and Carmen will share the top bunk. I'll sleep on the bottom." The cheerful tone Dolores tried to set dissipated as she shoved their two suitcases under the bottom bunk. She understood now why that was all they could bring. Taking the folded blankets stacked on the bed, she made up the two bunks so others would know those were taken. She was doing this. She was setting off on a voyage all alone. She longed for Alberto with a physical pain that caused her to gasp. She forced a smile on her face and took her daughters by the hand. "Come on girls, let's go explore."

"Mama, I'm dizzy," Carmen complained.

"Dizzy?" Was it the ship's gentle rocking? Without sight, Carmen's equilibrium couldn't adjust. "You can lie down once we are underway."

Carmen put on a braver smile than her mother's.

"Here, Carmen, this helps." Betty handed her sister the rabbit's foot Dolores had given her.

Dolores smiled.

Carmen pulled her own rabbit's foot out of her pocket and gave Betty's back. "Grandma Jessie said to hold them tight when we were scared, and they will bring us luck."

"Rabbit's feet are very good luck." Dolores took Carmen's empty hand and walked up to the deck. She looked back and smiled encouragement at Betty.

The ship was utilitarian gray and full of uniformed

sailors. Three years earlier Dolores had set sail with Manolo for the World's Fair. She remembered the color and joy and elegance of that departure, making this one seem even grayer. Dolores was more disturbed than she cared to admit that she had no lei to toss toward Diamond Head.

She stood at the railing and watched the islands fade into the distance, wondering if leaving Hawai'i meant leaving aloha behind. She'd miss Grandma Jessie's calm strength and Ruth's unwavering support. Maria had been her rock for as long as she could remember, always as close as the phone. These women had shared so much, taught her so much. Dolores's thoughts drifted to Noelani, who had loved her in her own way. Guilt stabbed Dolores. She'd been awful to Noelani. As long as she could, she put off thinking about Manolo and Alberto. They would both follow her in spirit, one restraining her with fear and one encouraging her with love. If only the right one would follow her in person to California.

Dolores's first duty was to get both of her girls into life vests. The sailor who brought them called them Mae West vests, but blushed and stammered when Dolores asked why. Later, seeing one inflated across the chest, she understood and laughed. Dolores struggled with getting the rubberized vest over each girl's head and fastening the strap around them. She took Carmen's hand and showed her the knotted cords that would inflate the vest when pulled. Even uninflated, the vests were bulky. At night, Dolores used extra blankets to secure the girls in the bunk because the vest made rolling out of bed easy.

Every morning at five o'clock, they got up and participated in a lifeboat drill. The captain required they sleep in their day clothes and vests, so dressing wasn't an issue. They learned where their lifeboat was and how to launch it. Dolores wasn't sure if the knowledge relieved her or made her more fearful.

The *Republic* zigzagged across the Pacific in a convoy of seven ships that were transporting men and supplies and God knew what else. When the ship conducted gunnery practice, the light fixtures fell out of the ceiling in their cabin. If they stayed on deck, the boom of the guns frightened the girls. The guns added to the constant fear of being torpedoed.

The captain noticed them during the first morning drill. "Who have we here?" he asked, looking at Carmen. His tone told Dolores he was a father with a daughter about Carmen's age.

"I'm Carmen," she told him.

"Carmen? What a pretty name. Would you like to walk around the ship with me?" his eyes found Dolores.

"Mama?" Carmen asked.

"Go with the captain, sweetheart," Dolores said. She placed Carmen's hand in his. At the very least, if Carmen was friends with the captain, they wouldn't try to separate her from her mother.

They walked away. The man looked down at the little girl, and she looked up toward his face. Dolores noticed that he encouraged Carmen to hold on to the railing to steady herself and hoped this would alleviate her dizziness. She waited by the railing, surrounded by blue-gray sea and blue-gray sky, and held the hand of her younger daughter. She peered into the distance, locating the convoy ships, all painted wartime gray.

"Mama, look!" Carmen returned with a smile and a doll. "It's Charlie McCarthy, Mama! The captain says I can keep it."

"She says she just turned ten years old," he said. "My daughter is about her age. She left this doll on board, but she'll be happy for Carmen to have it."

Dolores smiled and thanked him. Carmen's birthday hadn't been much of an affair this year, with their preparations to sail. Dolores had spent most of the day in line to register for evacuation. Carmen showed her doll to her sister. She promised to share if Betty took care of it.

The three of them stood at the railing. Dolores was the only one tall enough to see over the railing. The hull created a solid wall between the deck and the railing, with frequent spaces for chains and drainage that opened to the sea far below. She positioned her body between the closest hole and her girls.

"Come back here!" A mother's shout rang out, angry and afraid.

Dolores turned to see a little boy racing across the deck toward them. The ship rolled, and he lost his balance. He slid on his side, out of control, the boy's gleeful grin slipped to fear. He headed for the hole just beside Dolores. There was no time to think or plan or consider the consequences of her actions. She threw herself toward the boy and grasped his ankle. His forward progress halted, and he broke into lusty wailing. His mother covered him with kisses. "Oh, thank you! You are an angel," she told Dolores.

"Mothers must stick together," Dolores said.

She nodded and clutched her son. Their eyes spoke of maternal fear and strength, but neither of them found more words. The boy's mother nodded and turned away.

Not every day was so rewarding. Despite zigzagging and the convoy's protection, one day the alarm klaxons ripped through the ship like bombs over Pearl Harbor. Sailors rushed for battle stations, and confined civilians to their bunks. Dolores huddled on their bottom bunk with arms clasped around her daughters, her heart hammering so hard she couldn't utter reassurances. The all-clear sounded. A sailor came to tell them the danger was over. "What was it?" she asked him.

"Torpedo, ma'am, from a submarine." He grinned. "They missed."

They missed. But next time they might not. Her fear for their safety, never far from the surface, welled up again. The family spent that afternoon on Dolores's bunk, telling stories. Dolores loved the tale of the ancient chief Maui and how he created the Hawaiian islands. The familiar story provided a distraction for all three of them.

One day the ship's engines ground into reverse, churning the ocean and slowing the great ship. Rumor flew through the civilian passengers.

"A prisoner has escaped! He's gone overboard!"

The only safe place was their bunk. Once again Dolores held her daughters close and told Hawaiian stories.

The ship's engines once again moved the ship forward, but Dolores waited. The mother of the boy she'd saved came to find them.

"A prisoner went overboard," she told Dolores, "but they recovered him right away. He said the water was too cold!" They laughed together in giddy relief.

The air, too, was cold. Wind slashed their faces and left salt spray on their skin. As they neared San Francisco, the family spent most of their time huddled in their bunks. As a result, they were cross with each other.

"Stop it!" Carmen snapped at her sister. "Mama, she's pulling on my doll."

"Her precious doll," Betty sniped.

"Betty," Dolores said, "you're six years old. Be nice to your sister."

Betty climbed to the top bunk to sulk.

It took eleven days to zigzag across the ocean, almost double the voyage of the *Matsonia* a year earlier. A great energy pulsed through the passengers as the ship crossed under the Golden Gate Bridge. Relief and hope surged in every heart. Dolores hurried the girls up to the deck for their first sight of the bridge and its marvelous city.

"I'm cold, Mama," Betty complained. Carmen put her arm around her sister, but she, too, was shivering.

Fog rolled across the orange towers of the bridge and hid the tops. The cold gray obscured San Francisco, too. Ship, sky, water, and city were all gray. Dolores refused to let hope wither.

By the time the ship docked and they disembarked, the girls' cheeks and noses were red with cold. They each gripped a rabbit's foot but kept their hands in their pockets. Ladies from the Red Cross had been first on board and given each of them a coat. Warmth from both the coat and the ladies' smiles enveloped Dolores. One step at a time. Dolores must focus on this minute and the next. She snuggled into the wool and picked up their suitcases as Carmen took her sister's hand. She hoped Paul's car had a heater.

PART THREE

1942-1950

❦ TWENTY-THREE

Sunnyvale 1942

$\mathcal{I}$n California, the air smelled of fruit ripening on trees instead of Honolulu's gardenias. Solitary and ramrod straight palm trees dotted the San Francisco Bay Area, with no trade winds to beguile them into swaying. Mountains ringed the Santa Clara Valley where Paul lived, but they were green and gold with oak trees and dried grass instead of overflowing with colorful tropical foliage. Mindful of her daughters watching from the back seat of Paul's Buick, Dolores enthused over their new circumstances, hoping the fervent words would win her own heart over, too. "Look, Betty! Did you see the pretty birdie? And a palm tree, just like Honolulu! Carmen, I wish you could see how tall the mountains are!"

"It's not like Honolulu at all, Mama." Betty shook a finger at her, mimicking Ruth correcting Rosa.

"The air smells funny." Carmen wrinkled her nose.

Dolores's best efforts exhausted her. "We must adjust to California, girls. Just think how proud Papa will be when he arrives to find us all settled in." Dolores's words sounded insincere even to her.

"California's not so bad," Paul said. "Look, girls, there's Moffett Field. See the big hangar?"

"Hanger?" Betty asked, frowning. "For clothes?"

"No, silly," Paul said. "The navy put a blimp in that big rounded building. It was called the *Macon*. The blimp crashed, but the hangar is still there. The army runs the base now, and the Ames Aeronautical Laboratory is there."

In Honolulu, the American Navy ships filled Pearl Harbor, and air force planes occupied Hickam Field. In California, no signs of war existed anywhere, even at Moffett Field. At home, she and the girls walked along Waikiki Beach with its barbed wire. Behind Paul's house, the water tower from Libby's cannery towered over the town. It was the largest cannery in the world, a testament to Sunnyvale like the ships and planes were to Honolulu.

Paul's house in Sunnyvale had small windows, closed against the summer heat instead of open to catch trade winds. He parked the car in a full garage instead of a carport. Lush green grass covered the yard, with bordering bushes trimmed to a respectable uniform round shape. Dolores searched in vain for a single flower. Beside the front steps, shoved behind a healthy bush, she saw the jade plant she'd brought to Sofia on her last visit. It had crisped to a brown hulk. Her sister-in-law had never watered it once.

The strangeness of the world around them didn't end with the landscape. Dolores and her daughters crossed the threshold of Paul's house and automatically slipped off their shoes.

"What are you doing?" Sofia was even sterner than Dolores recalled, her black hair twisted into a tight bun at the back of her head. Dolores wore her hair in stylish short curls like the movie stars.

"In California, we wear shoes in the house," Paul explained.

Carmen turned to her mother. "Isn't that bad luck, Mama?"

Dolores said, "That's only true in Honolulu, sweetheart.

This is your auntie's home so let's put our shoes back on." They did so, but Sofia still didn't smile. "Thank you, Sofia, for welcoming us into your home." Dolores thought she heard Paul stifle a snort of laughter at her jibe.

Sofia's dark Spanish eyes glowered. Compared to her, Dolores wasn't Spanish at all. Sofia went to church every day, so Dolores wasn't Catholic in her eyes, either. Dolores had traveled across the Pacific Ocean without her husband and didn't want to know what kind of wife Sofia thought she was.

Dolores's two-year-old niece hovered behind her mother's skirt. She was a miniature of her mother, dark hair tied back and dark dress. Dolores's heart skipped a beat at the anguish that swept over her. She remembered being pregnant during their visit to the World's Fair. She should have a little one this same age. Another daughter . . . or a son. She inhaled slowly and smiled. "Come out, little Dolores," Dolores implored. "Come meet your auntie."

"She doesn't like strangers," Sofia said.

"I'm not a stranger. She needs to learn that." Dolores understood there was more missing than flowers and sunsets. There was no aloha spirit in Paul's house. He was 'ohana in name only. Paul never had Maria to teach him to love family first, and Sofia never had Grandma Jessie to show her how to see the good in everyone.

Sofia glared at Dolores, no doubt for daring to tell her how to raise her little angel. Meanwhile, Dolores's girls laughed and played with the Charlie McCarthy doll given to Carmen by the captain on the ship. They tried to lure Dolores to them, but their cousin was too shy.

"She'll get used to all of you," Paul promised. Dolores wasn't sure if he meant his wife or his daughter. "When can we expect Manolo?"

"They're evacuating women and children first. He'll sell our furniture. It's impossible to ship it all here—we were lucky to get passage for the three of us. What news do you have of the war here?"

Paul glanced at his wife, who scowled. "No need to talk about the war right now. Let's get you all settled." He herded them into the back of the house where Dolores had a bedroom to herself. The girls would share with their little cousin.

"This will be nice, Paul. Thank you for taking us in. It can't be easy."

He looked a little sheepish. "She's a good wife, Dolores, a good mother. I know she's not what you're used to."

"I'll make it work, don't worry."

He returned to his wife and daughter, and Dolores opened the first of their two small suitcases. She clicked the latch and the contents sprung forth like a child's jack-in-the-box toy. With so little room to pack, it was amazing how much dirty laundry they'd accumulated in eleven days at sea. It smelled as if every sailor on board had sent his uniform home with the girls.

Leaving the girls playing in their room, Dolores went to find Sofia.

She was in the kitchen, putting a small chicken into the oven. Dolores missed Grandma Jessie's stew pot. "Sofia? May I use your washing machine? We have more dirty clothes than clean at the moment."

Sofia wiped her hands on a kitchen towel, managing without words to convey her complete and total disgust at Dolores's request. She pointed to a small service porch off the kitchen. "Do you need assistance with the machine?"

Her tone was so imperious that Dolores refused help. She'd figure it out. Once the load started, she was at a loss. She had no chores to do, and it felt odd. Reluctantly she returned to the kitchen.

"Laundry started," she said with a cheerful smile. "Can I help with dinner?"

Sofia put a small pot of potatoes on the stove and turned on the gas burner. "It's better if I do it myself."

"I'm thankful you and Paul let us come stay with you. I know it's more work, and I want to help you."

"You are a guest." She waved Dolores away.

Dolores had never sat idle while dinner was cooking. "I'm family."

Sofia didn't respond. It made no sense to stand and stare at her back, so Dolores went into the living room. Little Dolores sat on the floor with a rag doll, but she ran into the kitchen when she saw her aunt. "Please, Lord," Dolores muttered, making a sign of the cross, "give me the means to make this a short stay."

Later, standing on Paul's porch as daylight faded, Dolores turned to watch the sunset. In Hawai'i, spectacular shades of gold marked day to night, a healing balm to the spirit. Here the gray light extended the dusk so there was no clear beginning or end to the day. The houses across the street became silhouettes, charcoal against the ash of the sky. Very soon it was all dark. Another California day had slipped away without fanfare. In the distance, a dog howled. The sound sent a shiver up Dolores's spine as she wondered what death it foretold. Shaking superstition out of her head, she turned her back on the night and entered the house.

Nothing in her life had prepared Dolores to be a lady of leisure in someone else's home. She managed it for almost a week before she followed Paul out onto the porch as he left for work one morning. The sun topped the mountains, promising another ninety-five-degree day. Nights were thirty degrees cooler! In Honolulu, temperatures stayed between seventy-five and eighty-five degrees. While the morning was still cool here, sparrows chirped in the big olive tree that attempted to shade the house. "I can't live like this for much longer."

He frowned. "Is Sofia working you too hard?"

Dolores laughed aloud. "No, no, not at all. I've worked hard my whole life, Paul. Now I sit around and do nothing. Do you think I can get a job? Maybe rent a small place?"

Paul nodded. "Del Monte always needs women on the packing line. I'll inquire. And I can help you and the girls find a place to live."

Their eyes met. He must understand Dolores couldn't live in the same house with his wife. In fact, he probably got an earful from Sofia every night about Dolores.

"Have you thought about leaving her, Paul?" Dolores asked.

He looked at her sharply. "Never. Sofia is a good wife and a good mother even if she is prickly with others. Besides, marriage is a sacrament, a union blessed by God. I promised to remain married until death parts us."

"And you need to make it work. I understand, Paul, I do." Dolores didn't want to go into the details of her own marriage. It would sound like complaining. Paul understood that a promise to God was sacred.

T HE next day Paul loaded the girls and Dolores into the Buick. "Do you like movies, girls?" he said, looking over his shoulder into the back seat.

Carmen perked up like a puppy with a bone. "Movies? I love them!"

"Well, your Uncle Paul owns the movie theater. You can watch all the movies you want for free."

"Free? We watch for free?" Betty's mouth dropped open as she and Carmen bounced.

"Have you seen *Dumbo* yet?" he asked.

They'd all seen it in Honolulu, but not for free. The girls giggled.

"It'll be fun to go out as a family." Paul smiled at Dolores.

Evidently Sofia and little Dolores didn't go out much. Carmen obsessed over movies. She listened to every radio show that talked about actresses and movies, and she adored musical shows. At six, Betty mimicked her big sister.

At the theater, Paul nodded to the counter clerk who brought each girl a bag of popcorn. Carmen told Betty not to spill hers. The four of them watched the movie, but Dolores watched her girls, too. Despite leaving their cousins and friends, their home and toys, they were happy with each other. They were 'ohana. Dolores's job now was to teach them to spread that love. She vowed the aloha spirit of Hawai'i would live in her children no matter what happened to them here.

After the movie, Paul drove home past orchards and empty farms. "Where are the people?" Dolores asked.

"These were Japanese-American farms. The government took all the Japanese a few months ago, relocated them to Tule Lake."

"Relocated?" Dolores thought of Honolulu's Japanese-Americans sent to Sand Island. "Did they object?"

"Most went willingly, but they lost everything."

They rode in silence while Dolores remembered Yoshiko and her sons in Hawai'i.

"This area is beginning to have more than canneries," Paul told her. "A couple of high-technology companies have opened. Hewlett-Packard makes the oscillators that Disney used in the movie *Fantasia*."

"I love *Fantasia*!" Carmen said. "It has great music!"

"Too bad you can't see the pictures," Paul said. "We also have Varian Brothers. They make radar. The factories and canneries have drawn a large number of African-Americans from the South, and lots of women who work in the shipyards."

"Women in the workforce support their men at war," Dolores mused.

"Yes, and Del Monte is one plant that needs women now."

⚘

DEL Monte did indeed need women. The pickle plant was a world Dolores didn't know. The scent of vinegar and garlic permeated everything. She could feel it infusing her clothing. Dolores had never worked outside her home before, but the war made it common for women to do so. The packaging line in the pickle factory was all women. With their gloves, hairnets, and blue coats, they looked alike. Dolores stood out because she was unsure what to do.

"Over here." One woman motioned to her. "I'm Lucia. We stuff the cucumbers in the jars, si?"

"Si, Lucia, gracias. I'm Dolores."

"Hello, Dolores." She grinned. "You speak English?"

She spoke with a heavy accent—she said *hallo* and *Eeenglish*. But Honolulu was full of accents, so Dolores felt at home. "Yes, I speak English."

Dolores stepped up to the conveyor belt where endless rows of cucumbers marched their way. Before long, she fell into the rhythm although she was not as fast as Lucia. Yet.

"Your husband in the war?" Lucia asked.

"No, he stayed behind in Honolulu to sell our things. He will join us when he can."

"Us?"

"I have two daughters, ages ten and six."

"Two daughters! *Que fortunado*! I have only one son."

The woman on the other side of her spoke up. "Seven for me! And a worthless husband who sit at home and drink beer." She almost sounded proud. "Paloma."

"Hi, Paloma, I'm Dolores."

"Yes, Dolores from Honolulu with two girls." Her hands never missed a cucumber or a jar as the conveyor belt continued past them. "What you know about pickles?"

Dolores said, "They're crunchy?"

"Cleopatra ate pickle. She believed they made her beautiful and healthy."

"Don't encourage her," Lucia whispered. "She'll go on all day."

Dolores nodded and let Paloma's words fade to background noise as she concentrated on doing her job. After a couple of hours, a loud bell rang.

"Break time," Lucia announced, pulling Dolores away from Paloma. They walked down the line of women who stretched aching backs and feet. "Thought you might like to see where the jars go."

They watched an opaque green waterfall of pungent spicy vinegar fill the jars. Lucia waved on down the line. "The machine heats them so they have a longer shelf life. Then they're capped, sealed, labeled, boxed, and sent out to the world."

She led Dolores back to their spot on the line where other packers stood talking to each other. Breaks were too short to go anywhere and sit down. Dolores rubbed her own stiff back. Then the bell rang again, and the women stepped up to the conveyor belt. In a few seconds, the belt lurched forward with a grinding noise, and they resumed stuffing cucumbers into jars.

At lunch time they sat in the cafeteria. Dolores was amazed how soft her body had grown after just two weeks of shipboard living and doing nothing at Paul's house. It felt good to be working.

"So Honolulu?" Lucia began as they sat at a cafeteria table. "You were there for Pearl Harbor?"

Dolores nodded. Her brain flashed images of planes and fires and smoke covering the harbor. She could talk all day and never be able to convey the deep fear of that day. She hesitated.

Lucia patted her hand. "I understand. You don't want to talk about it."

Relieved, Dolores smiled and took a bite of the ham sandwich she'd brought to work.

"Family in Honolulu?"

This was easier. "Lots. More in-laws than coconut palms on Waikiki. My sister-in-law and her three kids lived with us. It was crazy, but I miss them."

Lucia nodded. "That's a full house. *Mi mama* lives with us in an apartment. She watches my son during the day."

"Apartment?" Dolores realized Lucia must be able to afford the apartment on her salary. She'd said nothing about a husband. "Any vacancy?"

Lucia smiled. "I think the unit upstairs is available. Mama would love to have little girls around!" She picked up her things and stood. "Back to work."

One shift lasted twelve hours. Dolores was exhausted but happy when Paul picked her up.

"How's my pickle packer?" he teased.

She regaled him with one of Paloma's stories. "Did you know Julius Caesar thought pickles made his army strong?"

He laughed. "No, but I know this area is the largest packing center in the world for canned and dried fruit."

"My story is more interesting."

They laughed until they reached his house. Paul opened the front door, but no one greeted them. Dolores was used to entering through a crowded, food-scented kitchen. Paul's house appeared abandoned. "No one home?"

Paul looked quizzical. "Of course, she's home. Sofia never goes anywhere."

If Sofia was home, then so were her girls. Why didn't they greet her at the door?

Sofia came out of the kitchen. Her apron showed evidence of meal preparation. Little Dolores, of course, was close behind her.

"Dolores, sweetheart, where are your cousins?" She hoped that addressing the child would annoy Sofia. It worked.

"I sent your band of ruffians to their room."

"What did they do?" Sofia had probably overreacted to an infringement her babies knew nothing about.

"They went *outside* to play in the yard."

"Oh, the horrors." Dolores's sarcasm was not lost on Paul.

"Sofia, did they ask first?"

She turned her attention to him as if Dolores weren't standing right there. "They never ask. They run and shout like hussies. All day they want to eat! Then they open the door and just go outside." Her frustration showed in her tone.

"They played outside all the time in Hawai'i," Dolores said.

"Not here. Not in my home. They need to learn to act like Americans."

"They *are* Americans," Dolores said.

"Hawai'i is not a state," Sofia said. "It is not America."

"It's an American territory," Dolores said.

"Paul, please." Sofia sank into a chair with her hand on her forehead and her daughter at her side. Paul scurried to get a rag with cool water. "I can't take any more of this," Sofia muttered as he wiped her face.

Dolores clamped her lips tight together to avoid saying anything she'd regret. In the bedroom, her daughters sat on the bed. Betty held *The Little Engine That Could* on her lap. She turned a page, described a picture, and Carmen told the story. Carmen's short hair was parted on the side, caught back on the other side with a hair clip. Betty's parted in the middle and curled under her chin. They both wore clean play dresses. Dolores's heart burst with love.

"Mama!" Betty was first off the bed and into her mother's arms.

"Auntie Sofia won't let us out," Carmen said.

"Mama, is it evil to play outside in California? Auntie Sofia said so." Betty's forehead wrinkled in confusion.

"There, there, darlings," Dolores crooned. "Mama's home

now. We won't be staying here for long. Remember, Papa is coming soon. Maybe we can find a nice place to fix up to welcome him, all right?"

Paul came down the hall and stood in the doorway. "Any word from Manolo?" he asked.

Dolores shook her head as she came to the door. "You girls keep reading your book. Uncle Paul and I have to talk." She stepped into the hallway. "There's a small apartment near the cannery." She told him what Lucia had said.

He gave her a wan smile. "You can afford it if you're frugal. I'll help you stock the larder, and if you need anything before Manolo arrives, you come to me."

Dolores understood. He wanted to be her brother, but he wanted to stay married. Sometimes family was best if it wasn't all crammed together into a too-small space. That reminded her of Grandma Jessie, and family that sought each other out every day to have lunch, family that loved each other even when it was hard. She gave her brother a thin smile and went back to her daughters and their story.

❦ TWENTY-FOUR

Apartment 1942

The furnished apartment was not only small, it was dingy. Dirty yellow curtains sagged from a rod over the windows in the living room. Tucked in a corner of the hallway, a clunky black telephone sat on a small dusty table that held a phone book on a small shelf. The living room boasted both a tiny television and a radio, but the carpet puffed clouds of dirt when the girls ran across it.

"Girls, why don't you keep your shoes on until we've given this place a good cleaning?" she said.

"Of course, Mama!" Carmen and Betty returned to her and slipped their shoes back on.

"I brought you something," Paul said. He held out a jade plant. "You said it was good luck, right?"

Dolores felt tears welling. He'd remembered despite Sofia's obvious lack of care for the plant Dolores had given her. "Thank you, Paul."

"I also brought this. Want me to hang it for you?" He handed Dolores a simple crucifix.

"Oh, thank you! Now Hawai'i and Jesus will protect me."

Paul smiled. He hammered a nail above the door and hung the crucifix.

In Honolulu, Dolores would have sent the girls off with Ruth and buckled down with a bucket of suds to clean the place. Here no one but her watched the children. But that had been her choice, to leave the family and find a safe future for her girls. Even in her own mind, she'd never put into words whether she was fleeing the terror of Pearl Harbor or of her husband. Maria had told Dolores to keep aloha in her heart. Over the years, she'd learned that meant giving kindness and appreciation to everyone, even family members who were hard to love. She remembered an exuberant young Manolo who told her, "Aloha is the joyous sharing of life's energy." But to have aloha, you had to love yourself first. Both Maria and Manolo had told her that. Dolores hoped this time alone with her girls would allow her to learn how to do that.

The kitchen was a one-person affair, with no room for anyone to stand and talk, much less help with a meal. A Frigidaire refrigerator dominated one wall where it rumbled and groaned like an old grandmother. It worked, though, and Paul made good on his word, filling the refrigerator and pantry before he left. Her brother had bought a six pack of beer, telling her she could drink it if Manolo didn't arrive soon. Her face blanched, and she poured all six down the drain as soon as he left. She would never keep beer in her fridge just to have it. She certainly would never drink it. Nothing good came of drinking alone.

Paul also made sure she had her ration book ready to re-stock as needed. She would have to plan her use of sugar, coffee, meat, and cheese. Most strange was not having a garden. In Honolulu, fruit grew everywhere, and they planted vegetables. At least here Dolores could get fresh vegetables from the market. With none of her familiar brands and items in the house, though, she felt like she was cooking in someone else's kitchen.

Two bedrooms flanked one small bathroom. The girls would share one room. Dolores would have the other and share with Manolo when he arrived. She sent the girls to their bedroom to unpack their few possessions, took down all the curtains, and bundled them together. The apartment was brighter with the windows uncovered, but the view of railroad tracks and the run-down buildings that flanked them depressed her.

"Carmen!" she called.

"Yes, Mama?"

"I'm going down to the laundry room. I'll be right back. Stay with your sister."

"Yes, Mama!"

Dolores left the apartment and ran down the wooden steps that hugged the building's exterior wall. Necessity forced her to leave them alone, but she was reluctant to do so too long. The washer and dryer sat at the back of the empty garage. She put in the soap and a coin, started the machine, and ran back upstairs. After checking in with the girls, who were working on a Johnny Jeep coloring book Paul had bought for them, Dolores focused on her dirty apartment. Starting with the linoleum on the kitchen floor, she scrubbed until her shoulders ached and the floor gleamed. She eased her back by working on the counters next, wiping old grease from the Formica. The cabinets were solid wood, but the walls had tacky fake wood paneling. She'd have to clean them tomorrow.

"I'm going downstairs, Carmen!" Dolores called. She ran down to the laundry room. Her load wasn't quite done.

A small woman with a huge basket of laundry came into the garage. "Hello? Would you like help?" Dolores called and rushed to take the basket without waiting for an invitation. She set it on the top of the washing machine and turned.

The Hispanic woman before her was older than Dolores but not as old as Manolo's sister Helen. Her hair was graying, cut short, and she wore a dark old-fashioned dress. She was short and thick all over: legs, arms, belly, and neck. She smiled at Dolores. "Gracias, *mija*. This basket gets heavier every day. I seen you going by. You live in these apartments?"

"Upstairs," she said, pointing through the roof. "I'm Dolores."

"Ah, Dolores. I Consuela. Lucia my daughter. I live next door." She waved, indicating the door next to the stairway to the upstairs apartment.

"So nice to meet you, Consuela! Oh, I hope I don't bother you going up and down so fast," Dolores said.

"Sometimes nice to be hard of hearing." She grinned.

The washer finished, and Dolores hurried to remove her clothing and put it in the dryer. "This is so much easier than when I was a girl," she said with a smile.

"Oh, hush, mija, you barely more than a girl now."

"Let me tell you, Consuela. I've been doing laundry over twenty years."

"Easier now maybe, but still no fun." Consuela's face lit up as she laughed.

"No, you're right," Dolores said. "I need to get back upstairs. My girls are alone."

"Go, go!" She pushed Dolores out and started her own load.

Dolores hurried back upstairs. The girls didn't even look up.

"Use this blue one, Carmen," Betty told her sister. She held the book, gave her sister the crayon, and put Carmen's hand on the page to color the sky.

Dolores went into the kitchen. As she thought about what to cook for dinner, the windows started to rattle. She thought it was an earthquake and ran to protect her girls. "Stand in the doorway, Carmen!" She grabbed Betty by one arm. Crayons rolled across the floor and Betty started to cry. Breathless, Dolores clutched her girls as the floor and walls rumbled. Outside she heard a great roaring. Then a mournful steam whistle screamed. She laughed and ran to the window.

"A train, look!" she said. Sure enough, a train rumbled by

on the tracks across the street. Smoke and steam belched from it and seeped through the loose window frame. Now she understood why the curtains got so dirty.

That night, Dolores brushed Carmen's hair with a hundred long strokes as she did every day. Betty played with her dolls in the kitchen. Carmen began asking questions around stroke twenty-five.

"Mama, is Papa ever going to come live with us again?"

Sometimes her topics took Dolores by surprise, but she never let on. "Of course. He's still in Honolulu tying up loose ends."

"Tying up loose ends?"

"It means making an end to our life there, selling the house and car." And all the other things her hasty retreat had left behind. Dolores was sure Manolo would bring none of the girls' toys or her kitchen gadgets with him.

"Why is it taking him so long?"

"I don't know, sweetheart."

She thought for a moment. "He hasn't sent a letter, has he?"

"Ships between San Francisco and Honolulu are busy with war supplies. I'm sure he'll get here as soon as he can."

Carmen turned her head as if listening to the radio. Dolores could almost hear her ten-year-old brain at work. "I don't think you believe that at all," she said.

Dolores stifled a gasp. "What do you mean?"

"You told Uncle Paul you wanted a place for you to live with your girls. Then we got this apartment. There's no place here for Papa."

"He'll share a room with me, of course."

"When we lived in Honolulu, it was like Papa visited us. We saw Cousin Alberto and Grandma Jessie more than our own father."

Her tone was matter-of-fact. Dolores continued in the same vein. "Some days that was true."

"Here we don't have Cousin Alberto or Grandma Jessie."

Dolores longed for Alberto, too. She forced a smile to her face. "We have Uncle Paul."

"He takes us to the movies. But Auntie Sofia doesn't like me. Will Papa take me to the movies when he comes?"

"He'll take us all to the movies, sweetheart, and we'll buy a nice house where we can all live together."

"Will he be here before Christmas?"

"It's still summer. I'm sure he'll be here for Christmas. He'll probably be here for your first day of school in September."

"I met a boy that lives downstairs. He'll be in my class at school."

"Consuela's grandson?"

Carmen nodded. "His mother works at the pickle place like you do. Anyway, Pedro says there is no Santa Claus. He says his mommy and daddy leave the presents."

Dolores didn't know what to say. She'd worked hard to make Christmas and Santa special, hoping the girls would believe in magic as long as possible. Dolores brushed Carmen's hair and counted out loud, a ploy to avoid answering. "Eighty-two, eighty-three. . . ."

"It's okay, Mama. I won't tell Betty. And if Daddy's not here by Christmas, I'll help you make Christmas presents for her."

Dolores set down the hairbrush and took Carmen in her arms. As she readied her girls for bed, she thought about Carmen's words. Later, in the quiet apartment, she felt truly alone. She couldn't even call Ruth or Maria to talk about her day. Grandma Jessie wasn't just across the street. The wide net of uncles and aunts was too far away. And Alberto wasn't on her couch. She vowed to make a home for her little family on her own.

AT work, Dolores couldn't wait to see Lucia. "My daughter Carmen met your son," she said as she tied on her apron.

Lucia nodded. "Pedro said he'd met the new girl upstairs."

Dolores laughed. "Your mother seems very nice."

"She's a godsend. I never have to worry about Pedro while I'm at work."

The alarm klaxon sounded, and the conveyor belt moved. Both women stepped up to begin filling the day's jars.

"I worry about the girls when I'm here," Dolores said. "I don't like them alone all day until school starts. It will be Betty's first year." She smiled at Lucia. Two empty jars escaped past her.

"Why not have Mama watch them? I'm sure she'd love to play with little girls for a change."

A tremendous weight slid off Dolores's back. "Oh, what a good idea."

"I'll speak to her tonight, then come upstairs and meet your girls."

Dolores grinned. "Wonderful!"

ALL that summer, Dolores cleaned house at night while the girls slept. She ran to close the curtains when the approaching train whistled, trying to keep the soot out as best she could. Dolores struggled to balance household with workplace and keep everyone happy, healthy, and fed. Nowhere could she find time or energy to contemplate aloha.

Paul took them to see *Song of the Islands,* with Betty Grable and Hilo Hattie, at his theater in Sunnyvale. Dolores enjoyed watching the girls with their uncle. She wished her niece could join them, but that would mean Sofia would come, too, and that would ruin the entire outing. The girls sang the movie's silly songs for weeks, and it made Dolores miss her island home. This tiny apartment in Sunnyvale was not yet home although she tried her best to make it so.

In the meantime, she heard nothing from Manolo. It reminded her of the years she had worked for Noelani and heard nothing from her father. The only difference was that she had longed to hear from her father while she dreaded any message from Manolo. She also didn't hear from Ruth or Alberto. She imagined a chatty letter from Ruth that filled Dolores in on all the family gossip. In her heart, she imagined a letter from Alberto that told Dolores how much he missed her.

School started in September. To Dolores's dismay, she discovered Carmen's fifth grade and Betty's kindergarten would be at two different schools that started at different times in two different directions from home. After much consideration, she broached the subject to her girls at dinner one night.

"I have to work to pay the bills, girls. You know I can't stay home with you. Work starts long before you can be at school, and it's too far, too dangerous for you to walk. Carmen, I know you wanted to go to school with Pedro, but his school doesn't accept blind students. I think you both need to stay at home for now."

"Home?" Betty's face threatened to crumple. "No school at all?" She'd been looking forward to school.

"I'm sorry, darling. When your father comes, you can go to school."

"We understand, Mama," Carmen said. "We'll be good." Her tone was calm, but her face was tragic. Carmen was terrible at controlling her face, maybe because she couldn't see how emotions were reflected there.

"Consuela will look after you."

Consuela refused any payment, but Dolores promised to bake her cookies as often as her ration book allowed. Dolores's heart pained to see her girls having to spend so much time indoors. The neighborhood where they lived, though, was industrial. Too many big trucks and trains, too little grass for play.

Every night the girls greeted her with smiles and stories about their day as if it had been the best day ever. Dolores's heart swelled with pride and love as she took them in her arms. She worked hard to make a happy life for her little family. Sometimes she imagined Alberto coming home to her each day. She waited in vain for a letter from him, or from Ruth telling her about him.

❦ TWENTY-FIVE

Christmas 1942

In October, Dolores rushed downstairs to retrieve the laundry and arrived before the machine finished the load. She'd started dinner, and she didn't like to leave the girls when the oven was on. When she returned Carmen was sitting on the couch holding Betty tightly on her lap. Dolores recognized the tactic. Carmen had exhausted reason with her sister and resorted to physical restraint.

"Betty, have you been giving your sister a hard time?"

"I wanted to cook dinner," she said with a scowl.

"I'll take her, Carmen. Thank you for keeping her out of the kitchen." Carmen released her sister and escaped to the other room. "Come on, sweetheart, you can help with dinner."

Dolores took Betty's hand and they went into the tiny kitchen. Betty stood right behind Dolores as she opened the oven door and took out the pan with the chicken. Scents of garlic and onion and potato surrounded them. "Mmmm, smells good," Dolores said.

"Mmmm," Betty mimicked.

Dolores had been just a year older than this baby when Noelani put her in charge of laundry. She feared she'd coddled her youngest. "Come here, Betty. Let me show you how to cook this."

Dolores put the six-year-old's hand on the big wooden

spoon and folded her own hand over it. The two hands re-minded her of Grandma Jessie with her battered silver spoon. How many children and grandchildren had the older woman taught to cook? Slowly Dolores and her youngest daughter stirred the chicken broth in the pan and spooned it over the chicken. Together they scooped the onions out of the broth and put them in a bowl. "Good job! Can you go tell your sis-ter now that dinner is ready?"

Betty beamed at her mother and scampered off. Dolores put the chicken on the cutting board and sliced enough for dinner. Tomorrow she'd make soup from the carcass and left-over meat. She could stop at the corner market on the way home for carrots and celery. With careful planning, this bird could last more than a couple of days.

At dinner, the girls chattered about Halloween.

"I want to be a princess," Carmen declared, "with a pretty dress and a crown."

"I think we can manage that," Dolores told her. "And maybe we can make your good shoes fancy enough for a princess. How about you, Betty?"

"I want to be a witch!" She widened her eyes and showed her teeth and cackled.

"I can make you a witch's hat and cape. And you can use my kitchen broom," Dolores said.

After dinner they snuggled on the couch and listened to *Fibber McGee and Molly* on the radio. The girls laughed at everything that fell out of his closet. Sundays were their only days together, the only day Dolores wasn't working. Between church, laundry, and cleaning, Dolores made sure she saved time just for them. Sunday evening time was as sacred as church in the morning.

In the morning, Dolores let Betty sleep in but woke Car-men to let her know she was going to work. Carmen got up, her hair mussed and her eyes half open.

"I put out the Rice Krispies," Dolores told her. She knew Carmen could manage cereal for both of them. Dolores hated leaving them for six days of twelve-hour shifts and thanked God every day for Consuela. "Bye, darling." Dolores kissed Carmen on the top of her head.

As Dolores reached the bottom of the stairs, Consuela opened her door.

"*Buenos dias*, Dolores. Do you have time for coffee?"

"Oh, no, I don't, Consuela. I would love to, but I have to get to work."

"Lucia left twenty minutes ago. You go. I'll see to the girls."

"My brother, Paul, might come by today."

"Ah, yes," she nodded in recognition. "The tall one with the brown hair."

"Yes, that's him. I really must go. Thank you so much."

Dolores ran all the way to the bus stop so she didn't miss the bus she needed. At work she hummed, and the other girls teased her about having a boyfriend. None of them believed she had a husband. What would they say if they knew the man she wanted in her arms was not her husband?

That night Dolores fell asleep during a radio comedy. When she woke up, the room was dark, but the curtains were still open. The radio was playing war news. She shut it off. In the girls' room, Carmen and Betty were in their pajamas and saying their prayers. Dolores stood in the doorway and watched, her heart spilling over with aloha. She could do it. She could run her life without Manolo. Dolores could almost hear Alberto telling her to stay the course and weather the storm. Her heart flipped over at the image. She smiled and blew kisses to her girls.

When the girls were asleep, Dolores made soup from the chicken. After it had simmered for an hour, she put it in two bowls, one for their dinner tomorrow and one for Consuela. Finally, Dolores fell into bed like a stone.

The next day, she came home to two chattering girls. "Look, Mama," Betty said, pulling her by the hand. "Consuela brought cookies. Carmen said we couldn't have any without asking you."

"That was very grown up of Carmen," Dolores said. The cookies were homemade shortbread. Consuela had used her rationed butter and sugar to make them. Dolores ate one and gave each of the girls one to eat before dinner. They were wonderful.

Over the next few weeks, Dolores settled into a routine. Paul stopped by during the days she worked, just to check on the girls. Consuela kept them at her place for much of the day, and Carmen did a great job of entertaining her sister. Dolores was proud of how they all managed. In Honolulu, the girls had been too busy with cousins, with aunts and uncles coming and going, to miss their father. They noticed his absence more now. Dolores felt guilty that she continued to pray he'd stay in Hawai'i.

"Mama, when's Papa coming?" Betty asked her every night as Dolores tucked her in to bed after they said their prayers.

Dolores wanted to answer with a flip response like "When pigs fly," but she couldn't. "He'll be here soon, darling. He has to sell all our furniture. That might be hard during wartime when everyone is trying to sell stuff and come to California."

"Do you think he's all right, Mama? It's just that today is Friday the thirteenth, and I don't want bad luck to bother Papa when we aren't there."

Stunned for a moment, Dolores couldn't believe she'd forgotten the unlucky day. She'd never done that before. "Grandma Jessie gave him a rabbit's foot, too, right? Did you have yours today?"

"I made sure," Carmen said, pulling her own out from under her pillow.

Betty's little face twisted in concentration. "Do you think he remembers us?"

"Of course, he does. He misses us all very much, I'm sure." Dolores gave her a kiss on her forehead and the furrows of worry eased.

"Sleep now, sweetheart. Think of Papa in your dreams."

As Christmas approached, Dolores got creative with her budget. She wanted the girls to have a real California Christmas. They hadn't brought toys with them from Honolulu. They needed winter clothes, too. She bought a doll for her niece, a bottle of inexpensive perfume for Sofia, and a tie for Paul.

Using two weeks' worth of her sugar ration, Dolores made an eggless chocolate cake to bring to Paul's for Christmas dinner. Last year, she'd made a similar cake for their family picnic at Kapi'olani Park as Honolulu had been reeling from the attack on Pearl Harbor. She knew she could be just as content without Manolo this year but wasn't sure the girls would agree.

Paul had decked his house in electric Christmas lights that made Betty's eyes go wide with delight. Inside, a large fir tree stood in the front room. Gaily wrapped presents covered the red blanket underneath it. Old European glass ornaments that must have been in Sofia's family for generations hung from the tree's branches. Dolores had gone to Sears for ornaments to put on the tiny tree in her apartment. She was disappointed that the familiar shiny balls weren't shiny. A clerk explained that the factory couldn't get any silver to coat the inside of the glass globes. All metal was going to the war effort. Even the caps and hooks on the ornaments were made of cardboard.

"Mele Kalikimaka, Auntie Sofia," Betty called as she dragged Carmen to the tree. "Pretty, Carmen! The tree is so pretty!"

"What did she say?" Sofia asked coldly.

"Mele Kalikimaka is Hawaiian for Merry Christmas," Dolores said.

"In America we speak English," Sofia said.

Dolores clenched her teeth and smiled.

"It's Christmas, ladies," Paul said. "Would you like a martini, Dolores?"

"Thank you, Paul," Dolores said, resisting the urge to say mahalo.

"I may need more than one," Sofia said.

Dolores could almost hear the *hmph* at the end of her sentence. She ignored her sister-in-law and joined her daughters by the tree. Little Dolores hung back. She leaned against the couch instead of kneeling on the floor to inspect packages like her cousins. "Betty, why don't you show Dolores the present we brought for her?"

Betty spotted the package with its homemade bow and handed it to Dolores. The girl took it reluctantly, eyes on her mother.

"Put it under the tree, darling," Sofia said. "We'll open the presents after dinner."

Dinner was a surprise. Honolulu had never rationed food, just gasoline. The island hadn't needed it since so few supplies made their way to the islands. Besides, Hawai'i had an abundance of bananas, mangoes, papayas, and other fruit growing everywhere. In California, Dolores dealt with ration books, and learned to plan meals. Nonetheless, Sofia's meager Christmas dinner surprised her.

Dolores's chicken from the week before was almost bigger than the turkey. No more than two cobs of corn had contributed to the bowl of kernels. The gravy was thin. Conversely, a giant bowl of mashed potatoes dwarfed the other items. Dolores hoped her daughters wouldn't say anything rude. She let Paul serve the food and took his lead on portions. Little Dolores didn't eat as much as her cousins. Dolores thought rapidly. She might have to feed them more when they got home. What did she have in the cupboard?

"How's the movie theater business?" Dolores asked her brother as she cut her turkey.

"People still love going to the movies. One of the few pleasures during wartime. We show newsreels between features though. How about your work at the plant?"

"It's the same every day," Dolores said. "Not so bad once you get used to standing all day."

Sofia broke in. "As fascinating as this discussion is, can we focus on eating the Lord's bounty?"

Dolores stared. Sofia wanted them to eat Christmas dinner in silence? She tried to imagine Noelani's brood keeping silent for a whole meal and had to stifle a laugh. The Medeiros clan, too. They would have looked at her in shock had she suggested such a thing as a silent meal. Alberto's eyes would light up with the wicked twinkle that warned her he was about to tease her. But they weren't in Honolulu anymore.

Betty looked at her with big round eyes, and Dolores nodded. Both girls kept their eyes on their plates. Little Dolores did the same. Forks clinked against plates as they ate. Dolores had never realized they did that.

As the family finished eating, Dolores stood and gathered her plate and those of her children. She took them to the kitchen, rinsed them, and stacked them on the counter to wash later. Returning to the dining room, she asked, "Sofia, should I cut the cake now?"

Sofia gave her a look that indicated Dolores was in the wrong somehow. Dolores took a deep breath and reminded herself it was Christmas. Before she could respond, though, the doorbell rang. Sofia's frown deepened as Paul got up to see who it was.

"Mele Kalikimaka, Paul."

Dolores closed her eyes and took a deep breath as her heart stopped beating and her stomach flipped on its side.

The girls' eyes opened wide and they ran to the door.

"Papa, Papa!" Betty careened into him, hugging his legs.

Carmen stood by the table with Dolores, her face glowing and her arms stretched wide.

"Aloha, my darling!" Manolo said over and over.

He came into the dining room and smiled when he saw Dolores. He greeted her with a kiss. No alcohol on his breath. Dolores smiled. She looked past Manolo, hoping someone else had come, too, but her husband was alone.

"Merry Christmas, Manolo." Dolores hated that her voice sounded as cold and detached as Sofia's.

"Have you eaten?" Sofia asked. "There's food left."

"And a chocolate cake," Dolores added. She went to the kitchen and found plates and forks. She took her time cutting the cake she'd brought and listened with mixed feelings as Manolo talked to her brother about his voyage and job prospects.

Manolo was smart. He would get a job, and the money would help. But how long before he found new drinking buddies?

❦ TWENTY-SIX

California 1944

Manolo found a job and worked hard at Hendy's Ironworks in Sunnyvale. He dressed in a white shirt and tie, neat as a pin, even when he wasn't going to the office. Best of all, Manolo came home sober. He charmed Consuela, who made him something special to eat every couple of days. Dolores reduced her hours at work but refused to quit. She treasured Betty's beaming face as the girl entered her kindergarten class in January. Carmen smiled just as widely when Pedro's teacher made an exception and allowed Carmen to join her fourth graders.

In 1944, when Carmen finished sixth grade and Betty second, they bought a house in the last block of South 21st Street in San Jose. Manolo said nothing about their belongings in Hawai'i. Dolores chose to believe he'd sold everything and put the money toward the new house. It sat on the corner of South 21st and a narrow half-paved alley. The house had two bedrooms, a laundry room, and living room. Off the kitchen, was a bathroom with a big claw-footed tub. Dolores spent a morning walking through the house dreaming of the future and then buckled down to cleaning it top to bottom.

Carmen helped with the housework and her sister. Since

her sight was limited, she scrubbed the floor on her hands and knees, often in the dark.

"My little menehune," Dolores teased her oldest. "You clean in the dark when no one is watching."

"More like *The Elves and the Shoemaker*, Mama," Carmen said. "They cleaned overnight while the family slept. Besides, I'd rather be an elf."

"Either way, you will be a wonderful wife someday."

"Wife! I don't even have a boyfriend yet!"

"You'll have to find one who's not afraid of menehune."

"Mama!"

Dolores laughed, and Carmen's devilish smile rewarded her. It was a smile she'd seen often on Alberto but never on Manolo. Dolores remembered how Alberto would laugh at the girls' antics and encourage them to play hard. How he would enjoy seeing how they'd grown.

During this time in California, the war seemed far away. Dolores experienced rationing and empty store shelves and fear of Japanese bombs, but the only daily evidence of war was an occasional blimp leaving Moffett Field to patrol the coast. Blimps never got her heart racing like squads of fighter planes over Honolulu or barbed wire fences along Waikiki. On June 6, though, the radio and newspapers erupted with news of D-Day. It reminded Dolores of Pearl Harbor, far away yet ever present.

July proved to be a bearer of more bad news. Two ammunition ships exploded at Port Chicago, in Concord, only an hour north of them in California. Two-thirds of the men who died were Negroes. When fifty Negro survivors refused to return to work, they were court-martialed.

"Negroes and Chicanos don't get no respect," Lucia told Dolores at work. Her hands deftly swooped over the pickles. "Our men serve country, die for country, but our families live under suspicion and distrust."

"Japanese, too," Dolores said, "now that we are at war. It was different in Honolulu." Her hands were as quick as Lucia's as they worked.

"Different how? I would expect people there to hate the Japanese, too."

"Oh, there's plenty of fear. Honolulu has always had a wide diversity of races though. I speak bits of Hawaiian, Spanish, Portuguese, and pidgin. I know words in Japanese and Chinese, too. No race is a target until a disaster happens. After Pearl Harbor, everyone became afraid of the Japanese. But I was never afraid of my neighbor Yoshiko or her sons. After Port Chicago, people are afraid of blacks."

"And in LA, the zoot suiters are stirring up hatred for Chicanos."

"Stay above it all," Dolores advised. "Love everyone, even if it's hard. That's aloha."

"Crazy Hawaiian," Lucia teased.

The Port Chicago explosion was big news, but the personal bad news came later when Dolores returned home from work. It was that time of day when the girls were excited to share their day, but she was so tired she couldn't process what they were saying and think about fixing dinner at the same time. The phone rang, offering a brief respite from the whirl.

"Ruth! So good to hear from you!"

"I'm sorry, Dolores. It's not as good as you think." Ruth's voice choked with tears.

"What's wrong?"

"Grandma Jessie passed away yesterday."

"Oh!" Dolores sucked in air as her eyes widened in shock. She couldn't picture Grandma Jessie's kitchen without her. "Oh, no, Ruth, I'm so sorry."

"She was only sixty-one. She died at home with family."

"That's what she would have wanted." What would the family do without its matriarch? "May God bless her and welcome her to heaven." Dolores made the sign of the cross.

Ruth filled in the details of Grandma Jessie's passing, the service, and the family's reactions. "Antonio and Helen are getting some pushback from my brothers about the house. The Rodrigues family still lives there. Some of the family believe one of my brothers should have the house now."

"I don't understand. Helen's your sister. Why shouldn't her family live there?"

"João and Frank say the Rodrigues boys get everything. Alberto just laughs. He never takes anything seriously."

"Alberto can't possibly be getting any more now than he was before."

"People argue when someone they love dies. It's sad. This, too, will pass. Gotta go before I spend the family fortune on this call. Bye, Dolores."

"Mahalo, Ruth, for calling us." She hung up the phone and called the girls into the kitchen.

Carmen, at twelve, was tall and lanky like a colt. Her blue eyes sometimes slid to the side and revealed their lack of vision, but her hair was always brushed. Betty still had a round face and chubby cheeks, even at eight. She always had some sort of stray animal to care for. Today she held a frog. Normally Dolores would make her take it outside, but today the news wouldn't wait.

"Mama, are you crying?" Carmen asked.

"Yes, darling. Come here." Dolores enfolded both her girls in a big hug. "That was Auntie Ruth on the phone. She called to tell us Grandma Jessie died." Her voice cracked.

"She's not at home anymore?" Betty wanted to know.

"No," Carmen's voice was harsh with emotion. "We won't see her again. Ever."

"But I love her." Betty's round eyes filled with tears.

"We all do, darling, and we will forever," Dolores said, "but she's gone to be with God." She laid her cheek on Carmen's head and held them as the girls cried. She stifled her own tears to murmur soothing words to her girls.

That night dinner consisted of grilled cheese sandwiches and Campbell's tomato soup. Manolo raised an eyebrow when he came in from work, either at the food or his daughters' reddened eyes. He sat at the head of the table and Dolores served him his dinner and sat beside him.

"Manolo, Ruth called today."

"How nice. Did you two catch up?" he said.

"May we be excused?" Carmen asked. Dolores nodded, and the girls escaped to their bedroom.

"She called to tell us that your mother passed away," Dolores said when the girls had gone.

"What?" Shock transformed Manolo's face. He took off his glasses and laid them on the table. He put his head in his hands and asked, "What happened?"

"She died at home in her kitchen."

Manolo got up from the table, picked his glasses back up, and left the house. Dolores cleared away the dinner, listened to the girls' prayers and got them into bed. Finally, she went to bed herself.

Manolo came home the next morning with a case of Olympia beer, the first that he'd bought in California. That's when Dolores cried.

That day at work, she was tired and quiet.

"What's wrong?" Lucia asked.

Dolores searched for words to explain her fear of Manolo's return to drinking. Lucia had been delighted on Dolores's behalf when Manolo arrived from the islands. She knew none of his history. "My mother-in-law passed away."

"Oh, mija, *lo siento,* I'm sorry." Lucia patted Dolores's arm with a pickle-scented gloved hand. "Was she ill?"

"It was sudden."

Lucia nodded. "The worse for shock. Your husband, he will be fine. You need to be strong for him, si?"

Dolores nodded. Her thoughts hadn't been on being strong for Manolo but on how many beer bottles would be missing in the fridge tonight. If he started drinking again, if he spent nights away, she'd have to be closer to the girls during the day. It was all right to leave them home alone or with Consuela when they lived close to the plant in Sunnyvale, but San Jose was farther away. Long shifts at the pickle plant wouldn't do.

After work, she went to Paul's house, which she seldom did. Dolores rang the bell and held her breath. She didn't know what she'd do if he wasn't home. She was in no state to deal with Sofia. She exhaled in relief when her brother opened the door.

Paul stepped back and motioned her into the house. "Dolores! What a nice surprise. Sofia isn't here right now. She and little Dolores went to church."

Dolores appreciated Paul's reassurance as her forehead wrinkled. Had she forgotten a holy day? "Church?"

"They go a couple of days a week to pray."

Dolores felt impious as she imagined four-year-old Dolores praying on her knees. "Paul, are you still thinking about buying that restaurant in San Jose?"

"Yes, we signed that papers earlier this week. Ross's Steakhouse. It's on San Fernando Street behind St. Joseph's Church, between Market and First Streets."

"I know it. Carrie Allen Photography is on the same block, and Lean's Jewelry is on the corner."

Paul nodded and waited for her to continue.

"Will you need help? Can you pay a waitress?"

"Dolores, what's wrong?"

"I need to find a job closer to home."

He looked at her but decided not to question her. "Can you help in the kitchen, too?"

"How about potato salad and chili beans?"

"When can you start?"

Dolores quit Del Monte the next day and said good-bye to Lucia.

HER feet hurt after a twelve-hour shift at the cannery, but everything hurt after a day at the restaurant. She lifted bags of potatoes, stirred pots of beans, and raced back and forth to please customers. Muscles hurt where Dolores hadn't known she *had* muscles. She never complained, though. If she helped Paul make a success of the steakhouse, she would have a job close to home as long as she needed it.

Her second day at the restaurant was the first night Manolo didn't come home after work. Dolores wanted to worry that something had happened to him, but old habits die hard. She assumed he was drunk somewhere. Sure enough, he found his way home well after midnight and noisily collapsed on the couch in the living room.

Life returned to what had passed for normal in Honolulu. She knew how to handle the situation, and she was even more capable now. She'd lived as a single mother for seven months. Ruth had given her Maria Gabler's number, and one evening she called.

"You live in Mountain View!" Dolores exclaimed. "My brother is in Sunnyvale. We lived with him for a while after we arrived."

"So close! I'm sorry it took so long for the mail to connect us. How are the girls?"

"They're doing well. Your boys?"

"The same."

Dolores chafed at the polite necessities. "Is Peter still in Honolulu? What do you hear from him?"

"Still active duty. Martial law forbids casual travel, and the military censors all his letters and phone calls."

Dolores nodded. "I remember. When Yoshiko called her sons from Sand Island, they insisted she speak English."

"That's true everywhere, especially for Japanese."

"Everything all right with you?" Maria asked.

Dolores said, "Paul's restaurant is doing well. Betty tried to save a bird yesterday that flew into the window, and Carmen knows all the words to every song from *Oklahoma!*"

"And you?"

"I'm fine. I miss the family in Honolulu. It's so much quieter with only us."

"Manolo behaving himself?"

Maria had never approved of him. Dolores didn't feel like having an I-told-you-so conversation. "Pretty much. He has a good job."

They talked about the war, and more in depth about each of their six combined children. Somehow beneath the polite conversation, two good friends reconnected and vowed to stay in touch. Neither knew what the future held. Peter's tour of duty would end. Manolo would drink. And what would Dolores and Maria do?

"Keep aloha in your heart," Maria said before they rang off.

TWENTY-SEVEN

San Jose 1946

"Come on, Jack, where is he? You know I don't normally insist, but this is important."

"Ahh, Dolores, don't be like that. Manolo will be home soon, I'm sure." The man on the other end of the phone had a lazy voice with a placating tone.

She was not placated. "His sister is arriving today. He's supposed to pick her up in San Francisco."

"Oh, he's in the city, I'm sure." Jack's laugh told her Manolo was on a binge.

"Then I'm just surprised you're not," she said icily. She slammed the receiver into its cradle.

Manolo's drinking bouts had gotten more frequent and longer. Dolores wasn't even sure he was going to work every day. But she never complained. It wasn't often she called his buddies to find him because it was futile. They always covered for him.

"Girls! Put your shoes on!" Dolores called. "We're going to the city."

Carmen scrambled to get her sister ready while Dolores looked for the car keys. They weren't on the hook in the kitchen where they belonged, but the car was in the driveway. She searched the dresser top and the end table on Manolo's side of the bed. With a deep sigh, she brushed her hair out of her face and stood with a hand on her hip.

"Mama? Looking for these?" Carmen held out the keys.

"Carmen, where did you find them?"

"On the table in the family room."

"Oh, sweetheart, you find things better than anyone I know!" It was true. Where Dolores would scan a room with her eyes, Carmen had to feel her way around it. She looked for things methodically with her hands. Nothing hid from her for long.

Dolores hustled her daughters into the used Chrysler Manolo had bought for her when he arrived in California. The tank was only half full, so she stopped for gas at the Shell station. The attendant filled the tank, washed the windshield, and checked the oil and tires. A radio in the office played Perry Como's hit "Prisoner of Love," and Dolores sang along.

"Carmen? How much is dollar sign point two one?" Betty loved to test her older sister even though she knew Carmen was smart.

"That's twenty-one cents. Gas is twenty-one cents a gallon," Carmen said.

"Is that a lot?" Betty asked.

"It is if you don't have any money," Carmen said. Both of them laughed.

Dolores paid the attendant, and they got on the road. It was an hour's drive to San Francisco along Highway 101. They'd been there before, of course, but it wasn't an everyday occurrence. Dolores pulled out the folded road map that lived in the glove compartment. "Here, girls, look at this."

Betty unfolded the map and laid it across both laps. She peered at the map. "Paved roads are red. Here's 101." She looked at the passing street signs. "We'll pass Sunnyvale soon."

Dolores listened to her daughters discussing the names of towns and smiled. They were so wonderful together, such a blessing. And soon they would reunite with Auntie Ruth and their cousins. Right now, Ruth and the kids were on an airplane, approaching San Francisco. She could hardly wait to hear Ruth tell of their adventure. It was much faster to fly than sail, but it must be more terrifying, too.

Martial law in Hawai'i had ended six months earlier, in October. The 1946 passenger demand meant planes now flew out of John Rodgers Airport in Honolulu. The cruise ships were losing business. Dolores remembered watching planes land with Alberto and the girls. His teasing grin haunted her still. She missed him, but he'd sent no word. How could he? What would he say in a letter? Not what she wanted to hear.

Dolores parked the car at San Francisco Airport and hustled the girls into the terminal just as passengers left the Pacific Ocean Airlines plane. Rosa spotted them first and ran to Carmen. Her scream of delight warned Carmen of the greeting that almost knocked her off her feet. Winona and William sauntered over. They were teenagers now and had to be cool, but their eyes darted back and forth and ruined all efforts to appear disinterested. When she saw Ruth, Dolores felt tears welling. The two women clung together in a hug and sobbed out greetings.

"Mom, it's only been four years." Adults clearly embarrassed Winona.

Dolores pulled away from Ruth and wiped her eyes. "Longest four years of my life." They laughed.

Arm in arm, Dolores and Ruth walked through the airport and laughed like girls. In fact, Carmen and Rosa mimicked their hooked arms and laughed, too. Carmen took Betty's hand so she wouldn't feel left out. Ruth's older teens walked apart from them and pretended they didn't know the adults. Dolores stuffed the luggage into the trunk of the Chrysler while Ruth stuffed the teenagers in the back seat with Carmen and Rosa. Betty sat between the adults in the front.

"Where's Manolo?" Ruth asked, her voice over-innocent.

"He would have picked you all up, but he's not home."

"Don't tell me he had to work, Dolores."

"I won't. I don't know where he is. Some nights he doesn't come home." Dolores struggled to keep her tone even so she wouldn't alert the big ears in the back seat.

"Was it easier or harder to be here without him? Before he came over, I mean."

"In some ways it was harder, but in the ways that counted, it was easier. I mean, I was used to being without him, but I wasn't used to being without you and all the family." Dolores paused. "How is the family?"

"Alberto's fine," Ruth teased. She laughed when Dolores blushed. Good friend that she was, Ruth changed the subject.

The spirit of euphoria lasted all the way home. When they pulled onto 21st Street, though, it evaporated. Manolo's car sat across the small lawn in front of the house. Lips set in a line, Dolores turned into the alley and parked the car in the driveway.

"Should we wait?" Ruth asked.

"It won't matter," Dolores said.

Ruth allowed some distance before she followed Dolores. She kept the kids back, too. Manolo sat at the kitchen table, a beer in his hand. "Where you been?" he asked. Dolores noted his bleary eyes and let the belligerent tone wash over her.

"Picking up your sister at the airport."

As if on cue, Ruth and the kids came inside. "Aloha, Manolo," she said.

He got up and folded her in a bear hug. "Hi, Sis. Sorry I didn't make it to pick you up. Stuff came up. I'm a busy man, providing for my family, you know."

"I know," Ruth said. Her eyes raked her brother's rumpled clothes.

Dolores managed a smile. She was beyond being embarrassed by Manolo. "Come sit and we can catch up." She grabbed a plate of Oreo cookies off the kitchen counter and led Ruth into the front room. Ruth put her purse on the end table next to the couch. "Can't put a purse on the floor," she said, her voice breaking.

Dolores recognized one of Grandma Jessie's superstitions and completed it. "Bad financial luck." She wiped her own eyes.

Carmen dragged Rosa into her bedroom. Betty followed. The older teens went outside to sit on the porch. Manolo stayed in the kitchen with his beer. Ruth and Dolores sat on the couch. Ruth took an Oreo before Dolores set the plate on the coffee table. "It's so nice to have family here. It's what I've missed," Dolores said.

They talked about Grandma Jessie's passing, gossiped about Ruth's brothers and their misadventures, shared stories of their children's school efforts. They were still talking when Manolo poked his head in.

"Going for beer," he said.

"Manolo, is that necessary?" Dolores asked. "Dinner will be soon."

"Don't give me that. You haven't started dinner." Without waiting for a response, he left through the kitchen door. He slammed the screen behind him. Dolores sighed.

"He's worse," Ruth said.

Dolores nodded. "I hate to admit it, but when I was away from him for those months, I learned I can do this on my own."

"I've always known you could."

"But Catholics don't divorce." Life had been better without a husband. Divorce was different, though, than having a husband who would return any day. Neighbors, friends, the Catholic Church could all understand a husband being kept away by war. Being sent away was different.

"Catholics can separate."

"Oh, Ruth, how do I tell Manolo I want him to move out and not come back? He's gone more than he's here. When he is here, though, the girls love him, and he loves them. He's a good father when he remembers them. The most important thing is that families need to stick together. Families need to *be* together." Dolores believed that, but doubt stung her.

Ruth just looked at her sister-in-law for a long moment. "Is it a shock when he comes home?" she asked.

"Not quite. Almost."

Ruth shook her head. Dolores laughed and changed the subject. "Carmen turns fourteen in June."

"Rosa, my baby, is already fourteen. How is that possible?"

"Carmen will go to high school in the fall," Dolores said. "There's a school for the blind in Berkeley."

Ruth frowned. "You don't sound convinced."

"Manolo enrolled her. It's a boarding school."

"Boarding school? Oh, Dolores, that will be hard for you." Ruth placed a hand on Dolores's arm.

They hadn't discussed the boarding school. Manolo had made the decision. "It will be best for Carmen," he said. End of discussion.

The small house bustled with activity over the next two weeks. Eight people instead of the usual four came and went every day. Dolores loved having family nearby.

When Ruth and the kids left for home, the house was too quiet. The Medeiros family in Honolulu was large, and they only had one relative in California. All summer Manolo's brothers came to visit California, bringing their wives and children. Dolores wasn't alone with Manolo and the girls until September.

Dolores and Manolo drove Carmen to the school in Berkeley. It was a quiet ride. Dolores wished they'd brought Betty to chatter at Carmen and describe everything they were passing. Dolores would do it, but she didn't trust herself to keep from crying.

"You'll learn useful skills here," Manolo told his daughter. He glanced at her in the rear-view mirror. Carmen said nothing. "Things like piano tuning, broom making, and weaving cane chairs. That's in addition to music, swimming, and homemaking."

"She already has homemaking skills," Dolores said. Carmen said nothing.

Manolo pulled up in front of the Spanish mission style building. "We're here," he said cheerfully.

Dolores's tears welled, but she fought to smile. Taking Carmen's hand, she led her daughter inside. It was a simple matter to check her in, and then it was time to go. Carmen clung to her mother.

"Mama, don't leave me here. I want to be with family." Carmen's tears wet her mother's shoulders.

Dolores could no longer hold back. She sobbed and held her daughter. "I will miss you. Study hard." Behind her daughter's back she crossed her fingers.

"Stop bawling. Come on." Manolo pulled at Dolores. "Carmen, be a good girl. I know you'll do well." He turned and left his daughter crying as he dragged his wife to the car.

Dolores cried all the way home, pulling herself together only when they got off the freeway in San Jose. She didn't have long before Betty came home from school. She washed her face and put a cool cloth over her eyes. Manolo shook his head and walked out the door. Dolores tried to tell her younger daughter how lovely the school was, how excited Carmen had been, but Betty didn't believe her.

"Carmen likes us best," ten-year-old Betty said. "I already miss her."

"I miss her too," Dolores admitted.

They didn't hear from Carmen that night. The next day

classes started, and all day Dolores pictured Carmen and sent her loving prayers. After dinner, the phone rang.

"Mama, can I come home?" The rasp in Carmen's voice revealed she'd been crying.

Dolores swallowed hard but couldn't respond without tears in her own voice. "Oh, sweetheart, I miss you, but try, please? For your father?"

The next night, Carmen called again. Dolores made Manolo answer the phone. He didn't give her the phone at all, just slammed it in the receiver and stormed out the door. Dolores pursed her lips in anger. He never admitted he was wrong, but this time it affected their daughter. Every night, she cried with Carmen and handed the phone to Manolo. Every night he left the house with haunted eyes and a furious slam of the door.

"Manolo, she hates it there," Dolores said, after getting off the phone with her eldest daughter yet again. She wiped tears from her eyes. "How can she learn anything if she is upset all the time?"

"She's with other blind students, learning what blind students need to know."

"And how is that different from what Betty has to know? Carmen will have to cook and clean. She won't be making brooms! She'll be much happier at home here with her sister."

"Carmen doesn't have to be happy. She only has to learn."

Eventually Dolores, and his daughter's tearful pleas, wore him down. Manolo brought Carmen home. She'd been away almost four months, but made it back for Christmas, which delighted Dolores and Betty. Carmen promised to work hard at home. Manolo's action admitted he'd been wrong, but his words never did. Dolores's anger burned hotter. He was smart enough to sense that and spent more time away from home.

Dolores baked gingerbread cookies and decorated the house with pine boughs. She put electric lights on the tree and let the girls arrange the ornaments. Nat King Cole's "Christmas Song" played on the radio.

"Who's Jack Frost?" Betty asked. "Why does he want to bite me?"

Dolores laughed. Carmen answered, "It's a name for winter. Just saying it's cold out, silly."

"They should just say that," her sister said.

While Betty was at school the last day before Christmas vacation, Dolores and Carmen wrapped presents in gaily printed holiday paper. "I can wrap mine, Mama. I can't see it anyway," Carmen offered.

"No, you don't," Dolores playfully scolded. "I know you'll feel it, and then it won't be a surprise."

Her smile faded when she heard the kitchen door open and close. Manolo came into the bedroom. He stared at her with clear eyes. She met his eyes and stifled the urge to back against the wall. "Carmen, go in your room, please." He waited until Carmen left the room. "This isn't working," he said.

"Isn't working? What isn't working?"

He swung his arm, taking in the bed, presents, herself, the house. "None of it. I can't do it anymore."

Dolores thought it sounded like her line. "So why don't you move out?"

He nodded. "For the best, I guess. I can stay with a buddy in San Francisco. I'll come by to visit." He pulled a suitcase out of the closet and stuffed clothes into it.

Dolores sat where she was, stunned. Was she supposed to beg him to stay? Or wait until he left and dance around the house? Then realization dawned. "Did you lose another job?"

"We're still married," he told her with an arctic glare. "I expect you to remember that."

"Why do you care about that?" She couldn't remain silent any longer. "You haven't acted like a husband in months. Don't forget that you're a father, too. I expect you to remember that."

"Oh, cute."

"This is your failure, Manolo, not mine. You have a nice house, a loyal wife to keep it, and two beautiful daughters you don't even know."

"You can't say that. I love my girls."

"It's not the same to tell your buddies over a beer that you love your kids. You need to be here to know that Carmen is better off at home. I should never have let you send her to Berkeley." She waited for him to admit he'd made a mistake.

"You gave in too soon. She would have come to enjoy the school."

Exasperated, Dolores got up and went to the dresser. She opened the top drawer and scooped up his Jockey underwear and mismatched socks. On her way out the door, she threw the armload of skivvies into his suitcase.

In the kitchen, she seasoned a chicken and put it in the oven.

It was twenty minutes before Manolo appeared with two suitcases. "I'll be going then."

"Aloha. Stay in touch with the girls."

He nodded. She turned back to the sink to wash her hands. The kitchen window faced the alley. She watched her husband walk to a waiting car and get in. His buddy Jack was behind the wheel. They drove off, and her day became normal again—just her alone, waiting for the girls to come home from school.

"Keep aloha in your heart," she said out loud, not sure whether she meant it for herself or Manolo.

Gradually the tension eased from her shoulders. She leaned against the kitchen counter, weak with relief. Her marriage had failed, but it hadn't failed today. And what had changed, really? Manolo wouldn't be there for the girls, but he hadn't ever been. She was on her own, able to start over and make her own choices. All but one. Manolo would never divorce her. She wasn't free to marry Alberto.

TWENTY-EIGHT

Alberto 1947

Business was booming at Ross's Steakhouse. Dolores spent a lot of time in the kitchen stirring big pots of beans. It reminded her of Grandma Jessie's kitchen and feeding the Medeiros horde. On Dolores's recommendation, Paul hired Lucia to wait tables. Despite the drive from Sunnyvale, Lucia was delighted to work with Dolores again and to earn more money with tips.

One day Lucia buzzed into the kitchen, spouting rapid Spanish. When Dolores didn't look up from the pot of beans, Lucia stopped and asked, "*Que pasa?* Is something bothering you?"

Dolores looked up with a start. She gave her friend a wan smile. "Not as much as you. Have a rough customer?"

"Jerk didn't leave a tip. Riled my Chicana temper. At least there's a lull out there now. What's wrong with you, Dolores?"

"Got a phone call from Hawai'i last night. Manolo's sister is coming."

Lucia waved off the words. "More relatives? Hasn't all of Honolulu visited you by now?"

"Manolo has a large family." Dolores's attention wandered again, back to the phone call she'd received last night. Helen and Antonio were coming to visit, and they would bring their son, Alberto. Her skin tingled as she thought his name.

"You work in a restaurant during the day and a hotel at night," Lucia teased.

"At least the girls aren't surprised when their father comes and goes just like the rest of his family," Dolores said.

"Is he working now?"

Dolores nodded. "His third job since he left us six months ago."

"Have you told him his sister's coming?"

"His buddies lie about his whereabouts when I call. Carmen thinks that means he's hurt or dead, so I've stopped trying to call. Next time he stops by, I'll tell him."

"So the whole family is coming? Are they staying in California?" Lucia asked.

"Helen sold Grandma Jessie's house and split the money between her brothers. Maybe she was tired of hearing them complain that her kids get everything."

Lucia took three full plates in her arms and backed through the swinging kitchen door. She returned after she'd served the table. "So you have three adults coming for a long visit. Do you have room for them?"

"For a short visit we'd make do, but this is an open-ended one. Paul found them a house in Mountain View, near my friend Maria's house."

"My big family is all in Mexico," Lucia said. "I miss them, but I couldn't host them at my house either. Too much like work, all the cooking and serving food."

"That's my life," Dolores said with a smile.

After a long day, she returned home. She cleaned it every day, but for Alberto's visit she polished and re-polished it. He wouldn't notice, but it kept her mind from playing scenes of their reunion over and over.

Antonio rented a car and drove his family from the San

Francisco Airport to San Jose. Dolores met them on the porch. She smiled at Helen. Antonio swooped the girls into his arms. Alberto stood in front of Dolores, and she drank him in with her eyes from the rolled-up sleeves of his blue work shirt to the scuffed hems of his tan trousers.

"Dolores." His voice warmed her like caramel over ice cream.

"Alberto, welcome." She took his hands in hers. He held them tight. "Come inside." She looked at everyone and smiled. Alberto held on to one of her hands. The roughness of his calluses felt right.

Dolores freed herself from Alberto's grip and went to the kitchen. She brought out a tray of Ritz crackers and cheese she'd prepared before the family's arrival and put it on the coffee table.

Helen started to put her purse on the floor next to the couch but hesitated.

"No," Dolores said. "Let me take it."

"Not on the floor," Carmen said. "You'll run out of money."

"My mother used to say that," Helen said.

Dolores took the purse into her bedroom and put it on the bed. Returning to the kitchen, she fetched a pitcher of cold guava juice. "It's not as good as at home," Dolores apologized as she poured.

They chatted about family events and plans. Betty got bored and went to play in her room, but Carmen sat and listened. At fifteen, she was very interested in what the adults had to say.

Later, Dolores stepped outside for a moment of quiet as she often did when the house was full. Clouds drifted across the sky, just enough to ease the heat of the sun and cast shadows on the ground. Above the houses of the neighborhood, she could see palm trees and fir trees and fruit trees—evidence of San Jose's mixed heritage.

Alberto came to join her. "Nice home you made here, calm like deepest blue ocean of home, ya?"

"It works for us."

"The house Paul found is near places I can work. Tomorrow I apply to Vanderson. They need concrete finishers."

"Did your uncles teach you how to do that?"

He grinned. Her heart flipped at the familiar devil in his eyes. "I can get by 'til I learn, ya?"

Alberto always made her smile.

"You ever t'ink 'bout adding on to this place, Dolores?"

"Adding on? It would be nice to have another bedroom. We get a lot of visitors."

It wasn't long afterward that the sound of a hammer became the background noise of 1947, punctuated by the shrill whir of lumber being cut. Dolores hated the dust and dirt created by the construction, but Alberto arrived every day, and that thrilled her. He was busy, but she could make him a sandwich, and talk to him, and watch him when he wasn't looking.

Alberto had decided she needed more than another bedroom. Even though the addition would share a wall with her kitchen, it would also have its own door to the outside, its own bathroom, and a small kitchen. A complete apartment.

ONE day after work, Dolores walked down the alley to the door of the addition. She loved seeing the daily progress. She loved hearing Alberto tell her all about his day. The half-walled room smelled of fresh cut lumber and drywall. The apartment door was open. Manolo stood in the middle of the room. Alberto's eyes met hers over Manolo's shoulder.

Dolores plastered on her face the special fake smile she used for her husband. "Aloha, Manolo. Did you come to see what Alberto is working on?"

He turned and gave her a tight smile. His brown scapular peeked out from under his rumpled white shirt. She couldn't believe he still wore it. Did he still believe the Blessed Virgin would protect him if he wore it? No matter how much he lived like the devil?

She joined them in the room as Manolo turned back to Alberto and asked, "How long before you finish?"

Alberto didn't respond, and Dolores looked at him with raised eyebrows. "I got a job, ya?" Alberto said. "I'll come by on the weekend." His voice was distant and professional.

"It's coming along nicely," Manolo said. He looked from Dolores to Alberto and back and frowned. The three of them fidgeted in uncomfortable silence for a long moment. "I guess I'd better be going," Manolo said.

"Will you see Helen while she's here?" Dolores asked.

"Alberto gave me their address. I'll stop by tomorrow. Do you have any beer, Dolores?"

She hadn't expected anything else. Manolo followed her in the kitchen door and helped himself to a six pack of Alberto's Pabst Blue Ribbon. "Nice to see you, Dolores."

"Don't you want to see the girls?"

"Not now. I have to get to work."

"Where are you working?"

He waved a hand in the air. "Oh, here and there." He stepped forward as if to kiss her good-bye, but she pretended not to see him and turned to the sink to wash her hands. When she turned back, he was gone.

One day Dolores came home from the restaurant to silence. The day before, Alberto's father had passed away. Antonio's sudden heart attack took everyone by surprise. Helen was distraught. It was Alberto's duty to stay with his mother. Dolores took a tuna noodle casserole she'd made the night before out of the refrigerator and called to the girls, "Carmen! Betty! I'm home! Let's go to Auntie Helen's, shall we?"

"Will she be crying, Mama?" Betty wanted to know. At eleven, her entire world was sunny. She hated tears.

"I'm sure she will be. She's very sad. It's our job to make her feel better, all right?"

"Not by telling jokes, either," fifteen-year-old Carmen warned.

"You're right, Carmen," Dolores said, "jokes are not appropriate. Just be sweet and sit with her." She bustled the girls out the door and into the car. She gave the casserole to Carmen to hold.

Just as she pulled out of the driveway, a battered pre-war Chevrolet clattered to a stop in front of the house. Manolo stepped out of the passenger seat.

"Thanks, Jack," he said as he waved to the driver.

Manolo saw Dolores in the car and headed that way as Jack left. Dolores watched for staggering steps and didn't see any. She slid over to the passenger seat and let Manolo into the car.

"Were you going to leave without me?" Manolo asked.

Dolores looked at him. His voice seemed mild enough. "I wasn't sure you were joining us," she said.

"Daddy, did you know Uncle Antonio passed away?" Betty said in her most adult voice.

"Yes, sweetheart, but thank you for telling me."

"We're bringing dinner, so she doesn't have to cook," Carmen said.

"I'm sure she'll be happy to see all of us," Manolo said.

For the rest of the drive, Carmen and Betty regaled their father with tales about school and their friends.

"Carmen has a boyfriend!" Betty declared. She subsided into giggles.

"Oh, she does?" Dolores asked. She grinned at Carmen's scarlet face.

Delighted to be the source of gossip, Betty said, "He's the

older brother of one of my friends. He dropped off Sara the other day and stayed to flirt with Carmen."

Manolo frowned. "They were home alone?"

"I have to work, Manolo," Dolores reminded him. "Carmen is responsible. I'm sure this boy didn't even come into the house, right, Carmen?" Dolores said a silent prayer.

"No, Mama, of course not. We talked a few minutes on the porch, that's all," Carmen said.

Dolores smiled with relief and pride.

When they arrived at the house in Mountain View, Alberto let them in. The customary twinkle was absent from his eyes. Dolores took his hands in hers. "How's Helen holding up?"

"She's. . . ." He shrugged.

Dolores nodded. "I know." She took the casserole from Carmen and went to the kitchen. She didn't want to think about the way her heart raced when she touched him.

Alberto and Manolo took the girls in to see Helen. Dolores could hear her sister-in-law's ragged voice thanking them for coming. In Honolulu, there would have been three or four times as many family and friends. Dolores was glad Manolo had come for his sister.

After dinner, Dolores put the radio on. She didn't want to have to talk to Helen, which was difficult in the best of times. The girls sat on the floor near their aunt and listened to the radio. Dolores washed the dinner dishes and wiped them dry. Through the open kitchen window, she could hear Alberto and Manolo in conversation on the porch.

"She's my wife, you know," Manolo said.

"Just helpin' out family."

Dolores felt a stab of disappointment, but then chastised herself. Did she expect Alberto to declare his undying love to her husband?

"You should lose the pidgin now that you're in California.

It makes you sound ignorant." When Alberto didn't react, Manolo said, "Nice apartment you're building for her."

"She need the extra space, ya?" Both men's tones were carefully even.

"Maybe I'll move into that apartment," Manolo said.

"You her husband. You should be in her bed or nowhere," Alberto said, and his clipped words betrayed his rising anger.

Dolores grabbed two beers from the fridge and sailed out to the porch with a smile on her face. "Here you two are. I came to see if you needed another drink."

Manolo gave her a smile of possession. Dolores realized the show was for Alberto, not her. "Thank you, darling."

He'd never called her darling before. She handed him a beer and gave the other one to Alberto. She couldn't look at Alberto. It was too dangerous.

Alberto talked about Honolulu and the construction going on since the war. Dolores escaped back into the kitchen. She waited long enough for Manolo to finish the one beer and then rounded up the girls. They took their leave from Alberto and Helen. The drive home was quiet.

Dolores took the girls inside when they arrived home, but Manolo didn't come in.

"Manolo, I need the car for work. Can't Jack come and get you?"

"Do you think I live with Jack?"

"I have no idea where you live, but you can't take my car." She took the keys out of his hand. "I'll call you a cab." She let herself in and shut the door firmly.

Manolo waited on the porch for the cab.

PROGRESS on Dolores's apartment slowed. After they laid Antonio to rest, she busied herself with the restaurant and the girls and told herself she didn't notice when Alberto didn't come by. He was working long hours at Vanderson, and she missed him.

When he finished the apartment, Alberto came to Ross's Steakhouse to see Dolores. He sat in a booth and ate a big bowl of her beans. When she had a break, she joined him.

"I came to talk to you about my mother," he said.

The time working in San Jose had smoothed Alberto's speech. She missed his pidgin. "Is she all right?" Dolores frowned.

"She's fine. It's not that. She misses Papa, of course. She wants to go back to Honolulu."

Dolores held her breath. "And you?"

"Dolores, how often does Manolo come around?"

Irritated at the change of topic, Dolores snapped, "You know how much I see him."

Alberto nodded. "About once a week. He's not much help."

"You went with him a couple of times."

"I did. I met some of his friends and I know where they hang out in the city. If you need him, I can find him."

Dolores's irritation dissolved. "But you're leaving."

"No, I said my mother is leaving. I'm selling the house in Mountain View. Any idea where I might live?" His words were serious, but his eyes teased her.

"Oh, Alberto, are you planning to live in the apartment you're building?"

"If you'll have me."

Joy filled her. "Of course."

"It's settled then. I'll move my things in this weekend."

Her break over, Dolores went back to the kitchen with a wide smile on her face.

That weekend Alberto moved in. From the kitchen, Dolores could hear him moving around his room, and she smiled.

He spent a lot of time in her kitchen and reserved a spot in her fridge for a six pack of Pabst. She was so happy to have him nearby that she overlooked the beer. It wasn't like he had to replace it every day. He ate meals with Dolores and the girls and watched TV with them each night. She let herself believe he was the missing piece to her family.

Alberto 1950

"Happy New Year!" Alberto said as he clinked his bottle of beer against Dolores's glass of sparkling cider.

She looked at him with shining eyes. "Can you believe the forties are over? That the girls are both in high school?"

"Amazing that old folks like us can even stay up 'til midnight," Alberto teased. He tipped his beer up and drained the bottle. The TV rang with "Auld Lang Syne" and showed crowds of people in Times Square as they cheered the ball drop. Alberto got up from the couch, tossed the empty bottle in the trash, and got a fresh beer from the fridge. He returned and waved his bottle as if to brush away her words of the future. "It seems like yesterday when I first saw you on the beach at Hanauma Bay. You were the most beautiful girl there."

"I was fifteen!" Dolores protested. "You were only eleven. Just a kid." Her eyes twinkled as she teased him. He'd made her smile for almost half her life.

"Twenty years. I been waiting to make an honest woman outta you for twenty years."

And there it was: the sticking point in their relationship, the one subject they could not resolve. "Alberto—" she began.

"I know. You're married. You're Catholic."

He sounded resigned but determined. She knew how stubborn he was, like a shark chasing an awa fish. But she was stubborn, too, had learned it from him. "So are you. Catholics don't divorce, and Catholics can't marry divorced women."

"You are more important than my faith," he told her. His tone and eyes were serious, and that always made her uncomfortable.

"Who knows what 1950 will bring?" she said brightly.

His eyes narrowed as he finished his second beer. "Happy New Year." Alberto went into the kitchen and put another empty bottle on the counter. He helped himself to a third beer, and without saying any more, he disappeared through the connecting door to his apartment.

Dolores wiped counters that were already clean. They'd avoided a major confrontation over the future of their relationship for twenty years.

And where was Manolo this New Year's Eve? Her guilt didn't allow her to think of his life on the streets. Manolo spent his time in San Francisco, she knew that. He refused help and refused to come visit her now that the girls were nearly grown. Alberto brought him food and money, she knew that, too. Manolo was Alberto's uncle, after all. Helping his uncle had nothing to do with Dolores. She winced as that thought crossed her mind. Of course, it had everything to do with her.

Falling in love with Alberto hadn't been dramatic. It had been more like discovering a part of herself. And wasn't that aloha? Learning to love and respect all parts of yourself? At sixteen she hadn't known to listen to her heart. She'd married the older man, the smart one who could give her a family of her own. She hadn't ever seen a relationship like the one she and Manolo had, so how could she have known to be wary?

Noelani and Kanoa had worked together as if they were one person. Together, they supported their family with food and shelter. They had never been affectionate. She hadn't realized it, but they loved their large family. Noelani and Kanoa showed love by working hard and teaching their children to do the same. Because of Noelani, Dolores had taught her girls to cook and clean, and she'd never allowed Carmen to use her blindness as an excuse.

Maria and Peter were giddy lovers. Sometimes Dolores had felt like an interloper, but Maria and Peter taught her about showing affection to family. Because of Maria, Dolores had lavished her daughters with love, praise, and encouragement.

Grandma Jessie had been there to show Dolores that sometimes love was difficult. The entire Medeiros family had supported her in the early years of her marriage. Family stuck together. Family helped each other, no matter what. Because of Grandma Jessie, Dolores's support of Manolo didn't die when her love for him did. Because of Grandma Jessie, Alberto could live in Dolores's apartment addition here in San Jose and help her raise her children.

It was ironic that Manolo was the one who'd always said aloha was the joyous sharing of life's energy. He never seemed joyous anymore.

As a small child, she remembered going to Mass on Kaua'i with Papa and Paul. Like many natives, Noelani and Kanoa followed the old Hawaiian gods as well as the Christian one. Dolores learned to respect superstition as well as the Christian God. Her Catholic faith had only deepened since. She'd prayed for a husband and family. She'd prayed for Manolo's health, for Carmen to live, for the strength to carry on. God gave her strength to get through difficult days even now. Aloha encouraged you to follow your heart, but Catholicism forbade that heart to change its mind and grow. No divorce.

Dolores sighed, folded the dish towel, and hung it over the refrigerator handle. The new year would bring love and heartache. It always did. She turned off the lights in the kitchen, shut off the TV in the living room, and went to bed.

❧

ON January 15, Dolores turned thirty-five years old. After a late Mass, Carmen and Betty made lunch for their mother. Alberto supervised and made sure Dolores didn't lift a finger. After a leisurely meal, the girls went into the kitchen to clean up, and then they were off to their friends' houses for the afternoon. Silence descended over the house like a shroud.

Dolores picked up her juice glass. In the kitchen, she rinsed it in the sink. And noticed a row of empty beer bottles on the drainboard. She and the girls had sipped guava juice— not as good as in the islands but refreshing. She counted the bottles. No normal person would consume six beers in an afternoon. Alberto knew how she hated his drinking, yet he displayed the empties like trophies, taunting her. Dolores opened the refrigerator and found eight more bottles. She opened each one, poured it down the sink, and added the empties to the row already lined up on the dashboard. With each bottle, her fury mounted.

Alberto knew how helpless she felt, shackled to Manolo. Did he think she would take care of him when he was too drunk to know what was best? He knew how much she hated the years when the drink conquered her husband. She had quaked in terror and waited for the violence. Alberto knew, and he drank anyway. She'd known men who could drink reasonable amounts. Kanoa drank on Sundays at the family lūʻau, but working the cane fields exhausted him too much to drink during the week. Dolores wrinkled her brow, trying to remember if she'd ever seen Peter take a drink, even one. He hadn't been against drinking, but she'd never seen him drunk. Then Manolo and the wild Medeiros boys had come along. So fun, so carefree. Always drinking. Why had Manolo been the only one who couldn't control it? Why were his demons so much worse than his brothers'?

Alberto came into the kitchen. "Whatchu doing?"

She set the last empty bottle at the end of the row with a solid thump. "There will be no more drinking in my house."

"Aw, Dolores, it's jus' beer. Beer is the Medeiros boys' family drink." He laughed.

Dolores peered at him. He wasn't a violent drunk like Manolo. He was lucid. His cheeks were rosy, and he leaned as he stood, but his pidgin was back. "You're drunk." She infused as much scorn as she could into those words.

"Drunk in my own home. A nightmare, ya?" He waved his hand around in a circle to indicate she was crazy.

Dolores held it together until he rolled his eyes. "I won't tolerate a drunk living in my house. I tried that. Didn't work. You need to stop." Her tone rose with each word until it was out of her control.

"Your house? Stop?" his voice went low and cold. "I build most of dis house, an' I put blood, sweat, and *moolah* into it fo' years. I be entitled to a beer now and den."

"Entitled? Maybe that's the problem. You're too entitled. Too comfortable. Let me remind you we are *not* married. This is *not* your house. My house, my rules."

"Like I be one of yo' daughters, ya?" Alberto sneered.

For too many years she'd cowered under Manolo's wrath. Since then, her own wrath had come into its own. "You're their cousin!" she shouted at him, trying to put enough weight into the volume to hurt him. "You've played the role of stepfather their entire lives, but that was my choice, not yours!"

"Your choice? I coulda left any time I wanted! Then where you be?"

"Right here in *my* house with *my* girls and *no* beer in *my* fridge!" Her anger was too great for words. She picked up the nearest empty bottle and hurled it at his head. Alberto ducked, and the bottle crashed against the door frame. "Get out!" She threw another bottle. *Crash.*

"Hot Spanish blood!"

Crash.

"Woman, you pupule!"

Crash.

"Kanapapiki! Son of a bitch!"

Crash.

"I goin,' woman."

He slammed the kitchen door so hard that another bottle fell off the counter and broke. She heard his truck start. He gunned the engine and roared down the street.

Her anger drained and left her muscles shaky as if she hadn't eaten for days. Dolores dropped the bottle she was holding. Shards of brown glass littered the kitchen, crunching under her feet as she went to the closet for the broom. What had she done?

The tinkle of the broken glass was the only sound as she swept the floor. The rest of the house was silent. She loved that man. More than she'd ever loved Manolo. Why did he feel it was necessary to drink? Couldn't he respect her enough to stop? By the time she'd swept up every bit of glass, tears were running down her cheeks. Dolores took the bag of broken glass out to the trash can, took a deep breath, and wiped her face. She could rely on herself. She'd done so before. Life had just been more fun with Alberto.

Dolores boiled water in a battered kettle one of the girls had given her years earlier for a Christmas present. She made herself a cup of Lipton tea. She bobbed the Lipton tea bag in a cup and stirred in a scant spoonful of calming honey. Dolores took her tea into the silent living room and sank onto the couch. The phone rang.

Jarred out of her fragile reverie, Dolores got up to answer it. Standing in the kitchen next to the wall phone, she struggled to make sense of the stranger's voice on the line.

"Terrible accident . . . badly injured . . ."

"I'm sorry?"

"This is the home of Alberto Rodrigues?"

"Yes. . . "

"I'm so sorry. He's at O'Connor Hospital, ma'am. Critical condition. Are you his next of kin?"

"I . . . yes, I guess so . . ."

"Ma'am? You should come right away."

Dolores hung up the phone and grabbed her car keys off their peg. She raced out of the house. She left her calming tea to grow cold on the end table in the living room.

As she drove, she clutched the steering wheel and leaned forward as if that could make her go faster. Dolores tried to remember what the person on the phone had said. Car accident. Alberto badly hurt. That part she understood. She parked in the first place she could find and rushed into Emergency.

A calm, competent nurse sat behind the counter. She greeted Dolores with a serene smile. "How may I help you?"

"Alberto Rodrigues? I got a call?"

"Yes, I'll get the doctor." She disappeared into the bowels of the hospital but returned soon.

The doctor's blue scrubs were wrinkled, and he looked tired. He'd been here all day while she celebrated her thirty-fifth birthday with her family. "Mrs. Rodrigues?"

"Yes." No sense clarifying.

"Did they tell you what happened?"

"I . . . don't know."

"Come with me." The doctor led her through the Emergency Room doors. Machinery whirred and clicked. Serious-faced nurses and doctors and orderlies rushed about. The doctor led Dolores to a room, but stopped her before she went in. "Your husband was in a car accident. He was drunk and piled into a semi-truck. Never even hit the brakes."

Dolores's heart clenched to stone. She gasped for air. Drunk. Yes, he'd been drunk. And she'd angered him and chased him away.

"Mrs. Rodrigues, he's badly injured. The impact of the crash pushed his truck's engine well into the passenger compartment. The steering column crushed his chest. He's bleeding internally. Severed his liver, ruptured his spleen, and fractured a femur."

"Oh . . ."

"One ambulance driver assumed he was dead, but the other one gave him oxygen. That's what got him here, but—"

"Will he live?"

"We don't know yet."

"Can I see him?"

The doctor motioned to the open doorway. Dolores stepped inside. Stainless steel machines beeped and flashed. Four people hovered over the bed, a cloud of urgency surrounding them. A crucifix hung above the bed, and Dolores fastened her eyes on it as she pressed herself against the wall. She crossed herself. Between the doctors and nurses, she glimpsed white blankets, white bandages. Only Alberto's eyes were visible, and they were closed.

"Would you like a chair?"

Dolores turned. A nun indicated a chair near Alberto's head. "Thank you."

Immediate crisis averted; the tension leaked out of the room like water through a sieve.

"We're right outside if you need anything," the nun told Dolores. She left a rosary on the bedside table.

Dolores pushed the chair as close as possible and sat down, her eyes fastened on the man in the hospital bed.

Maybe it wasn't Alberto. Maybe they were wrong. She focused on the gnarled brown hand nearest her, a hand used to hard work. Dolores picked up the rosary and clutched it, cold beads warming in her hands. She crossed herself and whispered the Apostle's Creed. "I believe in God, the Father almighty, creator of heaven and earth. I believe in Jesus Christ, God's only Son, our Lord, who was conceived by the Holy Spirit, born of the Virgin Mary, suffered under Pontius Pilate, was crucified, died, and was buried; he descended to the dead. On the third day he rose again; he ascended into heaven, he is seated at the right hand of the Father, and he will come to judge the living and the dead. I believe in the Holy Spirit, the holy Catholic Church, the communion of saints, the forgiveness of sins, the resurrection of the body, and the life everlasting. Amen."

Dolores stopped before moving her fingers to the next bead and starting the Our Father. Her thoughts shifted to aloha, and in silence she prayed, "Aloha welcome; what I have I share with you. What I say comes from my heart. I am happy to serve with humility and meekness. Near or far, you are always in my heart. Aloha, my love."

Slowly, her brain started working again. He'd left her house . . . their house . . . drunk and angry. This would never have happened if she hadn't confronted him about his drinking. He would have passed out on the couch and all would be well. She shook her head to dispel the image. No, if it hadn't happened tonight, it would have happened tomorrow. Or next week. It wasn't like Alberto had just started drinking. He'd been drinking beer since his uncles had slipped it to him as a child.

She pictured Manolo's brothers, their wives and children. The sprawling Medeiros brood drank heavily, but they took care of each other. Here in San Jose, even among her daughters, she and Alberto only had each other. Only the two of them understood the aloha of the native Hawaiians deep in their soul. Dolores frowned. Maybe the fight was such a disturbance in their aloha spirit that he'd been injured. She could almost feel her Christian God flinch. In a Catholic hospital she should pray only to Him.

The noises in the hallway blurred. The voices and footsteps and rumbling gurneys became background noise to the rhythmic beeping that told her the man in the bed was still alive. Her heart knew it was Alberto. She reached out and laid her hand on his, careful not to disturb the intravenous lines. "You'd better not die on me, Alberto."

❦ THIRTY

1950

olores stared at the motionless body in the bed. She tried to visualize Alberto underneath the tubes and machines and bandages and splints. "Please, Lord, let him live," she whispered, crossing herself. "I don't care if he drinks. I want him to live. He can drink as much as he wants if he comes home." She rubbed her eyes so tears wouldn't fall.

"Can I get you anything?" The nun was back.

"Sister. . . ?"

"Sister Anne. And you are?"

"Dolores." She hesitated. "I'm not his wife. I'm . . ." She wanted to say she was the love of his life as he was of hers.

"You are here for him. That's what matters most. Those chairs can get really uncomfortable. Let me get you a pillow, and we'll say a rosary together."

Dolores nodded. Sister Anne went out to the nurse's station and returned with a pillow that she fluffed and put behind Dolores as if she were the patient. Then she leaned against Dolores and put an arm around her shoulders. With her other hand, she took the rosary from around her neck and began to pray, "I believe in God, the Father Almighty, Creator of heaven and earth; and in Jesus Christ, His only Son, our Lord . . ."

Comfort settled over Dolores. She joined in the prayer. By the time it was complete, she felt a great deal more in control.

"Is there anyone I can call, Dolores?"

"He's got all the help he needs, I think."

"For you, my child."

"Oh. Yes, could you call my daughters?" Dolores dug in her purse for the numbers of her daughter's friends and wrote them down for the nun.

How long would it be before Carmen and Betty arrived? Carmen would cry. Betty would be angry at Alberto for being so stupid as to drive drunk. Dolores let the whirring machines lull her into a moment-to-moment confirmation that Alberto was still alive.

Dolores heard her daughters in the hallway before she saw them. They came in arm in arm. Carmen reached out one hand toward her mother. "Mama?"

"I'm here, Carmen." Dolores reached for her daughter's hand. Squeezed together into one chair, the three of them tried to comfort each other.

"Why was he driving drunk?" Carmen asked. "He doesn't do that often, does he?"

Dolores heard the underlying fear of drinking that dominated her own life. Her daughters had been touched by their father's drinking, too. "He's a hard-headed man," she said. "No one can tell him anything."

The anger in her mother's words surprised Carmen. "Mama? Had you been fighting?"

Dolores flinched. Carmen knew her innermost feelings. "It's my fault," she whispered. "He was drunk on his own, but he never would have left the house if I hadn't made him mad."

"Oh, Mama, I'm sure he is to blame, too," Betty said.

Carmen's face twisted in shock and grief. She never could hide her emotions. Dolores suspected it was because she couldn't see how other people's faces gave away their inner thoughts.

Nurses came in to add medicines to IV drips, to inspect dressings. One of the nurses brought in a second chair, and Carmen and Betty huddled together in it. Dolores never left Alberto's side. If she left, he'd die.

The girls left to return home with the neighbor who'd brought them. They had homework to do, and they'd manage dinner. Their lives continued to be driven by normal daily tasks. Dolores's life had shattered. What would she do if Alberto died? The house would be so lonely. Alberto's apartment could be rented out. She'd have to put a lock on the door that connected it to her kitchen. She'd never needed that before. Her shoulders slumped, exhaustion taking its toll.

"Dolores? Have you had dinner?" Sister Anne was back, a cup of something in her hand that sent curls of steam into the air.

Dolores straightened her back and sat up. Stretching felt good. "No. No, I'm not hungry."

"You're not hungry because you haven't taken time to think about dinner." The nun's tone gently admonished her. "Try this broth. You can drink it like tea."

Dolores took the cup and held it in both hands. The warmth seeped into her, warming hands and arms and heart. She smiled. "Thank you, Sister." She sipped the broth.

Sister Anne sat in the chair vacated by the girls. She adjusted her habit around her legs and said, "So tell me about this man here." She gestured toward the bed.

Dolores's brain sorted through possible ways to begin. A nun represented the Church, represented God. She could never lie to God. "He's not my husband, but I love him more than my husband." Dolores's face crumpled. That was maybe too bald of a start, but Sister Anne just waited with no frown of judgment on her face. "I met him when I was sixteen," Dolores nodded toward the other bed. "Both of them, Alberto and my husband. They were part of a big Hawaiian family, a loving family like I'd never had. Lots of cousins and aunties and uncles . . . They were fun."

"You met them in Hawai'i?"

"Yes, Honolulu." Dolores thought of Kaua'i, her dead mother, her absentee father and brother. Her life had so much background. "I married Manolo, and we had two daughters. You saw them earlier, right?"

Sister Anne nodded. "Lovely young ladies. We said a prayer together in the waiting room before they left."

"Oh, how nice." Dolores smiled. "We all lived near each other in Honolulu—the whole family I mean. Alberto was there every day. And when my husband began to drink too much, Alberto was there. We came to California after Pearl Harbor, and Alberto followed. He helped me raise my daughters, helped me do everything. He's my life." She stared at the bed and tried to envision the vitality and humor of Alberto at his best.

The nun reached for Dolores's hand and clasped it in her own. "Marriage ties a man and a woman together for life, but it doesn't mean you can't love other men in your family. Alberto's a relation, right?"

"My nephew," Dolores said. "He hates me calling him that."

"God will reward you for staying by your nephew's bedside when the rest of his family is in Hawai'i."

Dolores nodded. The weight of notifying family members in the islands crashed over her. It would have to wait until tomorrow. Sister Anne began to pray. "Our Father, who art in heaven. . . ."

Dolores listened, in tune with both the prayer and the medical machines keeping Alberto alive.

DAY after day passed in a monotony of nurses and doctors with nothing positive to report. Carmen and Betty spent long hours after school at the hospital and even lured Dolores down to the cafeteria. She dozed in the chair next to Alberto's bed. She never slept deeply and never got enough rest. By the end of the first week, the nurses had stopped suggesting Dolores go home for a few hours each day. Except for the night nurse. Louise never had time to talk beyond the usual polite greetings, but she was efficient. She even brought a fresh pillow for Dolores each night. But on the seventh night, she crossed her arms and stood in front of Dolores.

"You can't stay here tonight."

"What do you mean?"

"This man will be here months, if he makes it through these first weeks. There is nothing you can do for him, but plenty you can do for yourself. Go home. Eat a good meal. Get a good night's sleep. Come back in the morning. The night shift is my job. I will call you if anything changes, good or bad."

"You could have been a nun," Dolores said, trying to smile.

"I work in a Catholic hospital." Louise smiled, but didn't move.

"I can't leave him," Dolores said, but she felt her protest weaken.

"Go." Louise pointed to the door.

Dolores nodded. Her presence here wasn't necessary to Alberto, only to her. She doubted that she could eat or even sleep but didn't want to argue with the nurse. She picked up her purse off the small shelf, blew Alberto a kiss, and left the room. All the way down the hallway to the elevator, tears trickled down her cheeks.

She returned in the morning, and Louise greeted her. "Good morning. Alberto had a good night. I'm going off shift in a while. I'll see you tonight just before you leave to touch base."

"Thank you, Louise, I needed that."

The nurse nodded and hurried off to her own bed.

When the doctor came in, he commented on how refreshed Dolores looked.

"Thank you, doctor. The evil night nurse kicked me out."

He grinned. "Louise? She's great that way."

Dolores's attention had already returned to Alberto. "When will he wake up?"

"We need to be patient. When his brain heals enough to allow it, he'll wake."

"He'll be able to talk?"

"We'll have to wait and see." The doctor reassured her with a smile and left the room.

Dolores swallowed the dread that threatened to overwhelm her. Would Alberto want her there? After all, she was the one who'd indirectly caused the accident. Of course, it wasn't her fault he'd drunk too much beer. It wasn't her fault he'd driven away from the house. But it was her fault he'd been angry. Drunk and angry, he'd made a bad decision. She'd had time to think about it. What would he think?

She took his hand in hers. She stroked his calluses from years of working construction. It was odd to have his hand warm but motionless in hers.

Just before noon, the day nurse came in. She bustled with efficiency and morning perkiness. "Time to go for the X-ray."

Dolores knew it made no sense to follow as the orderlies wheeled Alberto's bed out of the room. Her presence wouldn't change anything about the procedure or its outcome. She waited in Alberto's room, silent without the medical machinery. She must have dozed off because it seemed as if they were back in only a few minutes. The orderlies positioned the bed and reconnected the machines. Nurses chatted and the machines resumed their steady whir.

The doctor came in a few hours after everything returned to normal. "Looks good," he told Dolores with the nurse standing at his side. "It may take a while to see results," the doctor said, "and he may not want to wake up. Hearing your voice will help. Talk to him." He and the nurse left the room.

Dolores took Alberto's hand again. Feeling self-conscious, she spoke. "Hello, Alberto. Time to wake up, my darling." What should she say? It wasn't necessary to look at his closed eyes. He just had to hear her voice. She sat back in her chair, still clasping his hand, and let the past run pictures through her head.

"You've been a beach bum your entire life, Alberto, haven't you? I remember the first time I saw you at Hanauma Bay. You were such a part of the ocean, the waves, the sun, the sand. I was born in Hawai'i too, but I was never that much at home in the water. All the Medeiros boys were there, but you shone brighter than any of them. Yes, I know it was Manolo who attracted me first. He was older, more mature. You were so carefree. Maybe I was looking for a father and found Manolo. You were the bad boy on your motorcycle with your gang of friends."

Dolores paused to smile at the memory. "I guess I always had a thing for bad boys. Who knew? Yet you were the angel underneath, and Manolo the bad boy. I never could have lived through those years of my marriage without you. Have I ever told you how much I loved you even then? You were always there when I needed strength, my rock, my heart."

Her eyes lifted to the crucifix above the bed. "Our faith keeps us going in tough times. That's what God teaches us. It's true my faith gives me strength of mind, but your physical presence gives me daily strength. Manolo and I married in the Church. The Bible says God joined us together in marriage as one flesh and no man can separate us. God is faithful to us and desires us to be faithful to each other. I never knew it would be so hard, that I would be tested so."

Dolores drew a shaky breath. "The Hawaiians believe in the spirit of aloha, in mutual affection with no obligation asked. You have always loved me like that. With aloha, each person is important to every other person, and we all live together better than we can alone. Noelani and Maria taught me more than they know about love and marriage, but you, Alberto, taught me the most about aloha. With you, aloha always felt joyous. I know you love me without expectation, but I also know you want to marry me more than anything in the world." She paused. "Wake up, my love, and I will marry you. We will find a way. Just wake up and come back to me. I cannot live without you. I never want to live without you. Please, Alberto, come back to me. I love you. *Aloha au ia 'oe.*"

Her words faded to silence behind the ever-present mechanical noises of Alberto's life.

"Excuse me?"

Dolores startled at the words from the doorway. Turning quickly, she saw a police officer hesitating, an odd look on his face. "Mrs. Medeiros?"

"Yes?" He ran a hand over his close-cropped hair.

"Your daughters told me you would be here. I'm here to tell you we found Manolo Medeiros in San Francisco. Your husband?" She nodded. "Took us a while to identify him. I'm sorry to tell you he'd dead, ma'am."

Stunned into a vacuum of feelings, Dolores didn't know what to say. Euphoria and guilt warred inside her. She shook her head, not wanting to hope it was true and be denied. The officer nodded at her and left the room.

"Oh . . . Alberto . . ." Her voice sounded ragged. She stopped talking for fear of tears.

Ever so faintly, she felt his hand tighten around hers. She squeezed back, and his eyes opened. She watched recognition wash the fog away. His lips moved and she leaned forward to hear him say, "Aloha, my love."

GLOSSARY

WORD	PRONUNCIATION	LANGUAGE	ENGLISH
a hui kaua	ah HOO-ee KOW-ah	Hawaiian	until we meet again
'ae	ah-eh	Hawaiian	yes
ali'i	al-LEE-ee	Hawaiian	royalty
aloha	ah-LO-ha	Hawaiian	hello/good-bye
aloha au ia 'oe	ah-LO-ha oweea oh-eh	Hawaiian	I love you
aloha mai e	ah-LO-ha mai eh	Hawaiian	aloha to you— letter greeting
a'ole	ah-OH-lay	Hawaiian	no
awa	ah-wa	Hawaiian	monkfish
buenos dias	BWAY-nos DEE-uhs	Spanish	good morning
bumbye	bum bye	Pidgin	by and by
e komo mai	ee ko-mo mai	Spanish	welcome
ewa	EV-uh	Hawaiian	toward Ewa Beach
familia es todo	fa-MEEL-ee-uh es toe-doe	Spanish	family is everything
Feliz Navidad	fa-LEES nav-ee-DOD	Spanish	Merry Christmas
forno	FOR-no	Portuguese	beehive stone oven

WORD	PRONUNCIATION	LANGUAGE	ENGLISH
gracias	GRA-see-iss	Spanish	thank you
hana	HAH-nah	Hawaiian	work
hānai	Ha-NAI	Hawaiian	informally adopted
haole	HOW-lee	Hawaiian	white person
haupia	HOW-pee-ah	Hawaiian	coconut pudding
hiki nō	HEE-kee no	Hawaiian	okay
ho'omaika'i'ana	ho oh mak kai ee ana	Hawaiian	congratulations
hosomaki	ho so ma kee	Japanese	sushi roll
imu	EE-moo	Hawaiian	underground oven
inari	en-NAH-ree	Japanese	fried tofu pocket
irmā	Eer-ma	Portuguese	sister
kala	KA-la	Hawaiian	money
kālua	ka-LOO-ah	Hawaiian	to cook in an underground oven
kanaka	ka-NAH-ka	Hawaiian	Hawaiian person
Kanakaloka	Ka-NAH-ka-lo-ka	Hawaiian	Santa Claus
Kāne	KA-nay	Hawaiian	man; Hawaiian god
keiki	KAY-kee	Hawaiian	child

WORD	PRONUNCIATION	LANGUAGE	ENGLISH
kine	kine	Pidgin	kind, type
ku'uipo	KOO-oo-ee-po	Hawaiian	sweetheart
laiki	LAI-kee	Hawaiian	rice
lana'i	la-NIE	Hawaiian	porch
lauhala	LAU-ha-la	Hawaiian	woven straw
liliko'i	LEE-lee-koi	Hawaiian	passion fruit
lo siento	lo see-EN-toe	Spanish	I'm sorry
lōlō kanapapiki	lo-lo kah-nah-pa-PEE-kee	Hawaiian	stupid son of a bitch
lomi	LO-mee	Filipino	dish made with thick fresh noodles
lū'au	LOO-au	Hawaiian	party, feast
luna	LOO-nah	Portuguese	foreman
lychee	lee-CHEE	Chinese	small fleshy fruit
mahalo	ma-HA-lo	Hawaiian	thank you
maha'oi	ma-HA-oi	Hawaiian	rude
makai	ma-KAI	Hawaiian	toward the ocean
malahini	ma-lee-HEE-nee	Hawaiian	tourist
mālama pono	ma-LA-ma PO-no	Hawaiian	be careful
malasadas	ma-la-SA-das	Portuguese	donut

WORD	PRONUNCIATION	LANGUAGE	ENGLISH
malunggay	muh-LONG-gay	Tagalog	tree with flavorful and nutritious leaves
maunalua	MAU-na LOO a	Hawaiian	between two mountains
me ka aloha	may ka a-LOW-ha	Hawaiian	with love
mele kalikimaka	may-lay Ka-lee-kee-MA-ka	Hawaiian	Merry Christmas
menehune	may-nay-HOO-nay	Hawaiian	mythical Hawaiian little people
mi mama	mee ma-MAH	Spanish	my mother
mija	MEE-ha	Spanish	my daughter
mo betta'	mo BET-ah	Pidgin	better
mo'olelo	mo oh-LAY-lo	Hawaiian	Hawaiian stories
mu'umu'u	moo moo	Hawaiian	loose bright-colored dress
na haumana	nah how-MAHN-ah	Hawaiian	students
nigiri	ni-GEE-ree	Japanese	piece of fish on a rice ball
niña	NEEN-ya	Spanish	girl
nisei	nee-say	Japanese	born in America, parents born in Japan
no ka 'oi	no ka oi	Hawaiian	the best (follows a noun)

WORD	PRONUNCIATION	LANGUAGE	ENGLISH
nori	NOR-ee	Japanese	seaweed
obake	oh-BA-kay	Hawaiian	ghost
obrigado, obri-gada	oh-bree-GAH-doe, oh-bree-GAH-da	Portuguese	thank you
'ohana	oh-HAH-na	Hawaiian	family
'okole maluna	o-KO-lay ma-LOO-na	Hawaiian	bottoms up! (a toast)
ono	OH-no	Hawaiian	delicious
orait	or-ITE	Pidgin	all right
paella	pai-AY-ya	Spanish	dish of rice, chicken, seafood, etc. served in a large flat pan
pali	PAH-lee	Hawaiian	cliff
pao duce	pow DOO-say	Portuguese	sweet bread
pau	pow	Hawaiian	done, finished
pilikia	pee-lee-KEE-ah	Hawaiian	problem, trouble
pipikaula	pee-pee-KOW-lah	Hawaiian	beef jerky
poi	poi	Hawaiian	taro paste
poke	PO-kay	Hawaiian	diced raw fish
pōmaika'i	po-mai-KA-ee	Hawaiian	good luck
Portugee	POR-too-gee	Pidgin	Portuguese person

WORD	PRONUNCIATION	LANGUAGE	ENGLISH
pupule	poo-POO-lay	Hawaiian	crazy
pūpū	POO-poos	Hawaiian	appetizers, snacks
que fortunado	kay for-too-NAH-dah	Spanish	How lucky!
que pasa	kay PAH-sa	Spanish	What's up?
querida, querido	keer-EE-da, keer-EE-doh	Portuguese	sweetheart
saimin	sai-MIN	Chinese	Hawaiian ramen soup
si	see	Spanish	yes
tito	TEE-toe	Portuguese	uncle
ukulele	oo-kay-LAY-lay	Hawaiian	string instrument
vovô	VO-vo	Portuguese	grandfather
wahine	Wa-HEE-nay	Hawaiian	woman
wikiwiki	Wee-ke WEE-kee	Hawaiian	hurry up

✟ LATIN CATHOLIC PHRASES

Per istam sanctan unctionem et suam piissimam misericordiam, indulgeat tibi Dominus quidquid per visum, audtiotum, odorátum, gustum et locutiónem, tactum, gressum deliquisti.

Through this Holy Unction [oil], and through the great goodness of His mercy, may God pardon thee whatever sins thou hast committed by evil use of sight, hearing, smell, taste and speech, touch, ability to walk.

Em Nome do Pai e do Filho e do Espírito Santo

In the name of the Father, the Son, and the Holy Spirit. Amen.

AUTHOR'S NOTE & ACKNOWLEDGMENTS

The character of Dolores was inspired by my husband's grandmother. Despite a difficult childhood, she was one of the most wonderful women I've ever met. Everyone was welcome at her house, no matter the time of day or night, no matter how many friends they brought with them. Everyone was ohana. As a native Californian, I cannot presume to fully comprehend what a Hawaiian means when referring to the spirit of aloha. Although Grandma was born in Hawai'i, of Spanish descent, she was raised by native Hawaiians and lived in the islands into adulthood. On my many visits to Hawai'i, the local people have been welcoming, with positive attitudes and respect for all life. It's how Grandma lived her life every day, and I hope I've done justice to the notion of aloha.

The events of Dolores's life mirror Grandma's as much as I could research. I know her childhood was hard. I know her marriage was hard. The rest is fictionalized for the sake of the story. I began delving into her story to try to understand how someone could be strong enough to find her own role models and persevere. Thank you to my late mother-in-law and her sisters for their family stories. I hope I've done them justice.

During the five years I spent writing *The Aloha Spirit*, I earned a master's degree in fiction writing from Lindenwood University. Many of the chapters were workshopped during that program. Thank you especially to Dr. Wm. Anthony Connolly, who believed in this novel from the beginning.

Thank you, too, to the Northern California chapter of the Historical Novel Society, whose members critiqued much of the book. Special thanks to Melanie Spiller and Mark Dooley for their detailed editing.

Thank you to Brooke Warner, Lauren Wise, and the others at She Writes Press and Sparkpoint Studio for their work to bring this book to life.

Finally, thank you to my husband, sons, and daughter-in-law who provided encouragement when the words just weren't coming out right.

ABOUT THE AUTHOR

Photo credit: William E. Ulleseit

LINDA ULLESEIT, born and raised in Saratoga, California, has an MFA in writing from Lindenwood University. She is a member of the Hawaii Writers Guild, Marketing Chair for Women Writing the West, and a founding member of Paper Lantern Writers. Linda is the author of *Under the Almond Trees*, which was a semifinalist in the Faulkner-Wisdom Creative Writing Contest, and *The Aloha Spirit*, to be released in 2020. Linda believes in the unspoken power of women living ordinary lives. Her books are the stories of women in her family who were extraordinary but unsung. She recently retired from teaching elementary school and now enjoys writing full time as well as cooking, leatherworking, reading, gardening, spending time with her family, and taking long walks with her dogs. She currently lives in San Jose with her husband. They have two adult sons and two yellow Labradors.

For more about Linda and her books, visit:
ulleseit.com